By Aline Templeton

DI KELSO STRANG SERIES
Human Face
Carrion Comfort

DI MARJORY FLEMING SERIES
Evil for Evil
Bad Blood
The Third Sin

CARRION COMFORT

ALINE TEMPLETON

Allison & Busby Limited
11 Wardour Mews
London W1F 8AN
allisonandbusby.com

First published in Great Britain by Allison & Busby in 2018.
This paperback edition published by Allison & Busby in 2019.

A CIP catalogue record for this book is available from
the British Library.

10 9 8 7 6 5 4 3 2 1

ISBN 978-0-7490-2425-3

Typeset in 10.5/15.5 pt Sabon by
Allison & Busby Ltd

The paper used for this Allison & Busby publication
has been produced from trees that have been legally sourced
from well-managed and credibly certified forests.

Printed and bound by
CPI Group (UK) Ltd, Croydon, CR0 4YY

In fond memory of Fiona Robertson, who had an indomitable spirit

*Not, I'll not, carrion comfort, Despair, not feast on
thee,
Not untwist – slack they may be – these last strands
of man
In me or, most weary cry, I can no more.*

Gerard Manley Hopkins

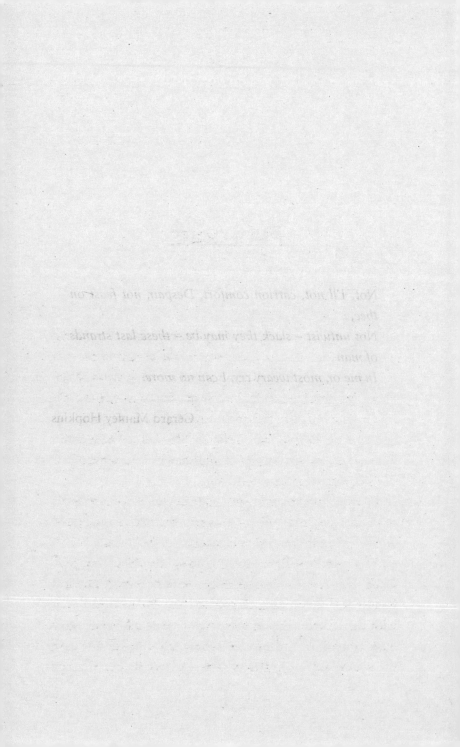

Not, I'll not, carrion comfort, Despair, not feast on thee;
Not untwist — slack they may be — these last strands of man
In me ór, most weary, cry I can no more. I can;

Gerard Manley Hopkins

PROLOGUE

In high summer on the bleak northern coast of Scotland where the land at last gives way to the hungry seas, it is never completely dark. The bogs and standing pools of the Flow Country shimmer in the pale but relentless sun and life is in a state of frenzy before the brief light season gives way again to the long winter darkness. There is a background hum of insects and on the heather moors bees labour in a dizzy ecstasy of scent and colour.

For days now the sun had shone in one of the rare spells of windless weather and as Gabrielle lay in bed the humid air seemed to lie like a thin blanket layer on her skin.

The merciless light, and her own troubled thoughts, made sleep impossible. She longed with an almost physical hunger for the blessing of soft, velvety darkness but even with the curtains drawn there was at best a lavender-grey dusk around midnight for an hour or two. At last she gave up, sliding off the mattress with a glance at her sleeping partner, and with infinite caution left the room. If David woke and saw her she knew he'd want to get up and make her a cup of tea, keep her company. He knew the small hours of the morning were a bad time for her.

In the kitchen she ran the tap cold then filled a glass with water, pressing it to her flushed cheek as she went through the silent house to stand at the great picture window in the sparsely furnished living room, looking out but barely seeing the bleak moor and the random patterning of pools and lochans, ink-black in the low light.

A movement caught her eye: a small owl, quartering the ground on its broad, rounded wings, noiseless as a moth, listening and watching for movement. Gabrielle shuddered, feeling in herself the shivering of a terrified vole, afraid to stay, afraid to run. As she watched, the bird swooped in an unhurried, elegant glide. She shut her eyes so that she wouldn't see the tiny limp body hanging from its talons as it rose from the kill.

When she opened them again, the bird had gone. But death was all about you in this place, brutal and alien as a lunar landscape. The killers were the kings here: the birds of prey, the foxes, the skuas, the ravens that did not always wait for life to be extinct before they went for the eyes. Even the marshland bred carnivorous sundews and butterworts and the bogs around even the tiniest dubh lochs were traps where animals could be drawn in to their death. Animals, and even—

But she knew she mustn't think about that now. That was a long time ago. And she'd promised David she wouldn't obsess over things that couldn't unhappen. She'd promised – but then words were easy.

Only words, though. Everything else had become hard and painful since her father died. Paddy had been her anchor; now she was adrift. Day by day, little by little, she was getting worse. It had been such small things at first, like believing she'd put her keys in her handbag when she hadn't. Everyone did that, didn't they? But then she had to make a list before she did anything – and still something would go wrong. She had even struggled to be sure what she'd dreamt and what was real – and the awful humiliation of confusing a dream with reality still made the sweat spring out on the back of her neck even as she thought about it.

Friends had made allowances for her, telling her about their own idiotic forgetfulness on occasion and she was grateful for their kindness, if not reassured. You didn't lose your mind all at once; it was small things that accumulated quite gently and slowly, like snowflakes falling, falling, until the day when the avalanche came crashing down and swept away the pretence that nothing was wrong.

After that, they blamed losing the baby for her distracted state. It was only natural, David told her soothingly, kind and loving even though it had been her fault and his baby too. But it was more than that. She had to face up to reality and recognise that she needed a complete break.

So, she'd come back to the very basic house that Paddy had refused to give up even when he hardly used it any more, as if she might find here something left of the love that had enfolded her like a security blanket. David had arranged everything, even to restructuring his job with an Aberdeen oil firm as a computer troubleshooter so he could work a lot from home while she took time off to recover.

She should have found peace up here where there were no demands on her and no stress, where it was so quiet. Deathly quiet. But she hadn't. Somehow, she'd managed to forget how toxic the atmosphere was in the village, where even after all these years no one had forgotten or forgiven anything.

Gabrielle took a deep breath, and another, and another, fighting down the sense of panic that never seemed very far away. She must go back to bed, take one of the pills that would give her a couple of hours' sleep before the dawn woke her again to another long day.

It was getting lighter already. As she turned from the window she heard the eerie, haunting whistle of the owl returning but she didn't look back.

CHAPTER ONE

He had been waiting in the yard, watching the farmhouse. The light in her bedroom had gone out, but he knew she wouldn't be asleep.

It had been later than usual before the lights in the downstairs room went off and there was still a light in her parents' bedroom. Kirstie wouldn't move until she was sure they were asleep, and it was another of these warm, light nights; even people as old as they were might feel the restlessness that seemed to possess everyone at this time of year.

Calum wedged his skinny, adolescent body into the angle of the barn where he would be invisible from the house. He seemed to stand here for longer and longer every night and it was driving him mad. He gave something between a sigh and a groan; enforced patience and rampant lust were a bad combination. It was like voluntarily entering a torture chamber every single night.

At last the bedroom light went off. This was almost the worst bit, waiting when he was sure they must be asleep, but she apparently wasn't yet convinced. Then at last he saw the back door open and her slim form slip out and run across the grass towards him.

He grabbed at her, but she fended him off. 'Not here! They might get up to open the window or something,' she hissed, darting ahead of him out of the garden and looking back teasingly over her shoulder as she ran along the stony track that led up the hill at the back of the village to a building right on the edge of the moor.

The old croft house, abandoned many years before, had always been an illicit playhouse for the local children; being forbidden to go there because of the dangers of broken glass and crumbling stonework had only made it more attractive. But there weren't so many kids here now and most of them spent their lives inside staring at a tablet anyway.

Now it was Calum and Kirstie's own secret place, out of the sight of prying eyes. At this time of year, you never knew when people might be about, and Kirstie was nervous. She had mega-strict parents and while it might not be true that her father would kill her if he found out what was going on, that was certainly what she always said.

Most of the roof was off, but there was still a sheet of corroded corrugated iron in place over one end of the main room, where you could get a little bit of shelter if the rain came on. The door had been roughly boarded up with a couple of planks nailed across it, but you only had to pull on it and it would swing back on its rusted hinges.

He caught up with Kirstie just as she reached it and

caught her in a rough embrace. The door was standing wide open tonight; they must have forgotten to shut it properly. Giggling, she responded as he walked her backwards through the doorway, still kissing her. Then he stopped abruptly and let her go.

There was a man asleep on the floor under the open sky, a man with dirty, smelly clothes, his face begrimed with dirt. And he was lying on their rug, the rug Calum had stolen from his mother's linen cupboard.

He swore. Kirstie looked over his shoulder, gave a little squeal of fright and pushed him back outside. 'It's a dosser! How'd he get there?'

'How the hell do I know? I'm going to find out—'

Furious with rage and frustration he turned back but she hung on his arm. 'No, no! We don't want to start anything. If he goes, "Who are you, then?" and begins maybe yelling and shouting, they might hear it down the house and my dad would come out. Just shut the door and let him be.'

Even as he shut it obediently, he knew with a terrible sense of inevitability what she was going to say next. She was saying it now.

'I'm away home, Cal. Even if he left, I'm just, like, revolted with that smell. It's gross. And he's likely got bugs.'

'We could go up on the moor,' he urged with some desperation. 'We're not needing shelter on a night like this.'

Kirstie looked at him blankly. 'On the *moor*? With not even a rug? Yeah, that'll be right! I'd get eaten alive, Cal. The midges are bad enough out here, anyway. Dad would go, "How come you've got all these midge bites when you've been in your bedroom all night, Kirstie?"'

He could recognise when he was beaten. 'Oh, all right, if you're going to be fussy,' he said sulkily. 'I don't suppose I can make you.' Before the words were out of his mouth he realised his mistake. 'Sorry, sorry, that came out wrong—'

But a mulish look had come over Kirstie's face. 'No, you can't, Calum Cameron. No means no, remember, and that's what I'm going to say right now. No. Got it?' She walked off back down the track without looking back, scrubbing her fingers through her dark curly hair as if the midges had got to her already.

He could feel them biting himself, clustering round him in an infuriating, inescapable cloud. Tormented, he flailed at them, then swearing in a fury of frustration he kicked the door of the croft house again and again, but there was no sound from inside. The dosser hadn't wakened – drunk, probably. And God knew how long he'd be planning to squat there.

Even if he managed to patch things up with Kirstie he still couldn't see her agreeing to go back in there, even if the man had gone tomorrow. She'd made her views clear about open-air sex too.

The bastard had only ruined his summer, that was all.

'What shift are you on today, Kirstie?' Fergus Mowat asked pointedly on Friday morning.

His daughter, looking bleary-eyed, was sitting at the table in the farmhouse kitchen, hunched over a mug of coffee. She eyed him resentfully. 'Well, like, early, obvs. Wouldn't be up at this time otherwise, would I?'

Fergus, who had risen as usual at six to get out round

the farm and was back for his mid-morning break, looked pointedly at the clock. 'It's five to ten now,' he said. 'You can't walk down to the cafe and be there by ten o'clock. You're going to be late.'

Kirstie said, 'So?' and gave him the dumb insolent look that would make the Archangel Gabriel himself long to slap that pert little face.

He could feel himself going red. 'Look, lassie. Your mother went to a lot of trouble to get you this job. It's not just yourself that you're letting down, it's your mum.'

His wife, Rhona, working at a battered desk in one corner of the room with a chequebook, an account book, a pile of bills and a frown, looked up. 'Don't worry, Fergie. If Morven's not happy she'll soon let her know. Kirstie, ask yourself, "Do I feel lucky?" I wouldn't choose to get the rough end of her tongue, myself.' She went back to her task with a sigh.

Kirstie gave her a darkling look but after a face-saving ten seconds slid off her chair. 'I was just going, anyway,' she said to no one in particular, grabbed her canvas satchel from the floor, slung it over her shoulder and left, not quite slamming the back door.

Fergus blew a 'Phou!' of frustration. 'How long till she leaves home?'

Rhona gave him a sideways look. 'You just make her worse,' she said calmly.

'Well, she started it,' he said, then had the grace to laugh. 'Oh, I know, I know. I don't suppose it does any good.' He carried his mug, along with Kirstie's, over to the sink and put it into the dishwasher. 'And why couldn't she have done that?'

Bent over her bills, with her lips moving, Rhona didn't reply but then he didn't expect her to. They both knew the answer – she was fifteen and a half, and she had made it into an art form.

'I'm away off up the hill. One of the hoggets up there was limping yesterday so I better take a wee look at her, see she's all right today. Back at half twelve.' Rhona grunted something that might have been a farewell as he left but he wasn't entirely sure that it wasn't a swear word addressed at the accounts.

It was another improbably beautiful day. What was it – almost a fortnight now without a drop of rain? Just every so often you got a spell like that, which was all very well but if it went on any longer he'd have to start shipping water out to the troughs.

He set off as he always did up the track that led past the abandoned croft house, gradually being weather-beaten to a ruin. He'd known the old couple who'd lived there; they'd had a few sheep on the little field near the house and there'd been a productive vegetable garden too, long overgrown. Fergus had bought the land from the family who'd inherited for grazing but the house itself was worthless. He often thought about them as he passed, struck by the melancholy thought that with the way farming was these days, one day his own much larger house and farm would lie abandoned to nature. Kirstie wasn't going to want his sort of life, that was for sure.

There were ravens circling around it, he noticed suddenly. Like any sheep farmer, he hated the birds, the ruthless killers who hung about at lambing time and homed in on the sheep, helpless in labour, and the weaker lambs. It added insult to injury when the bird protection lot claimed they only took carrion; he'd lost ten lambs this year in attacks that seemed positively sadistic, yet you left yourself open to prosecution if you defended your vulnerable sheep with a shotgun. Not that he didn't do it – sheep should have animal rights too.

Another raven arrived, and then he saw one dropping down inside. Had a sheep got in there, somehow? The walls of the house had been crumbling away for years so it wouldn't be surprising if an enterprising ewe, pursuing the sheep's favourite hobby of self-destruction, had wandered in and then been too dumb to find her way out again.

Surely, he'd have heard her complaining about the situation, though. They didn't normally suffer in silence, so it was probably some other carrion – a rabbit, a hare, maybe? He walked round the house, looking for a break in the wall but couldn't see one; the door was still barred. He shrugged, ready to walk on.

But something stopped him. There were too many ravens for small carrion; as he looked up, another arrived, and he could hear coarse cawing arguments going on from the other side of the wall. With growing concern, Fergus went to the door – the nails in the planks fixing it shut might be rusted enough to break if he pulled at it. To his surprise the door swung back easily under his hand and he stepped inside.

It was like a scene from a horror movie. There was a man lying on the floor and five of the great glossy-black birds were perched on his shoulder and around his head, so absorbed in their struggle as they tore at his exposed flesh that they didn't react to the door opening.

Hoarse with the horror of it he yelled and rushed at them, clapping his hands. They were huge, threatening, this close; they startled at the noise, turning to eye him, their scimitar beaks bloodstained, but with insolent slowness did not immediately relinquish their prey. He caught one of them a blow with the back of his hand and at last they flew off. As a wing brushed his face he felt pure panic in a Hitchcock moment; were they rising only to attack him from the air?

But they were flying off, though only to join the others circling watchfully. The moment Fergus left, they would be back. What was he to do?

Reluctantly, he looked at the body. He was sadly accustomed to the savagery of their attacks on his sheep and his lambs – the pecked-out eyes, the tongue torn from the socket, the intestines pulled out from the creature while it still lived – but he had to fight nausea as he looked at the mutilation of one of his own kind.

It was in their usual pattern, going first for the soft flesh of eyes and mouth. The clothes – jeans and a long-sleeved checked shirt – had protected him so far, though before long a questing beak would break through these too; just an unusual type of fleece.

Dear God, he hoped the man had been dead before they started. Surely, he must have been! Even ravens would have been wary of attacking a living man – and when Fergus thought about it, surely there would have been more blood. No, this was some down-and-out who'd been shacked up here and just died; probably a druggie.

He'd have to phone the police, but by the time someone in a central office somewhere had taken the call and passed it on to Thurso and they managed to get themselves out here, hours could have passed with Fergus stuck on guard, fending off a renewed attack. The birds wouldn't give up easily on such a promising meal.

He looked around. The man's clothes were filthy, damp and muddy, but he was lying on a surprisingly clean-looking tartan rug. If he pulled it out from under him he could cover him up with it and surely that would give him long enough to fetch a tarpaulin cover and weigh it down with stones.

Moving him would be a distasteful task. Shuddering, Fergus tugged at the rug and the body flopped over as if it were boneless – a while dead, then, and with the movement he caught the sickly smell of corruption. He shuddered, though in its way it was a relief to know the poor sod definitely hadn't been alive when the birds began their gruesome picnic. He didn't touch him afterwards, just left him in the position he'd fallen into, covered him up with the rug and hurried out to the barn.

When he came back, the ravens were still there; more, even, than there had been. Grabbing some stones from the garden first, he spread out the tarpaulin on top of the rug and weighed it down.

Then he went back to the house and before he even made the phone call came back with a shotgun. They could prosecute him if they liked. If he got a couple of the bastards, it would be worth it.

CHAPTER TWO

It had been a serious tactical error. In a bid to distance himself as much as possible from the guests arriving for his father's seventieth birthday drinks party, Kelso Strang had positioned himself in the farther corner of the sitting room but as it filled up and the sound of braying well-bred voices reached decibel levels to rival the parrot house in the zoo, he found himself trapped.

It all took him back to the cocktail parties of his army days. He had loathed them in the days when attending at the whim of the colonel was a professional duty; as a filial duty it was no better. Like the colonel, Major-General Sir Roderick Strang loved cocktail parties.

Mary Strang loved them too. Her face was bright with the joy of holding a party in her very own house after more than forty years of army billets and she was bustling about, greeting old friends and new neighbours and plying them with her very own cheese straws. Kelso might have pleaded a sudden emergency if it would only have annoyed his father – always so ready to take offence – but he couldn't bring himself to deny his mother her transparent pleasure in his presence.

Now, as he found himself pinned into the corner by a mustard-cords-wearing Perthshire neighbour who had nothing worth saying to say but was saying it at length anyway, he cursed his conscience.

'Do you shoot?' the man said at last.

As a one-time sniper in Afghanistan and former member of the Police Scotland Armed Response Unit, Kelso had a mad impulse to say, 'Only people,' but again his social conscience got the better of him. 'No. Do you?' he said instead.

The man looked at him as if he'd said, 'Do you speak English?' 'Well, yah. Not much point in living in Perthshire if you don't shoot.'

'Mmm.' Kelso couldn't think of anything to say to that, but the man was up for the small-talk challenge.

'Though there's fishing, of course. D'you fish?'

Kelso had to disappoint him again. 'No,' he said, then added in extenuation, 'I live in Edinburgh.'

'Weekends too? Can't think what you'd find to do at weekends, staying in the city.'

It was almost with relief that Kelso saw his father's rigidly upright figure spearheading its way towards him, as the crowd of guests parted like the Red Sea before Moses. The relief ebbed as he saw that he was leading across a tall girl with dark hair in the Kate Middleton style framing a long narrow face with large brown eyes.

'Someone I want you to meet, Kelso,' he said, ruthlessly interrupting the anecdote his neighbour had embarked on to illustrate how boring it had been last time he'd had to stay in Edinburgh. 'Rosie Metcalfe – you remember Major Metcalfe, of course?'

'Of course,' Kelso said politely, nodding to Rosie, who gave him a smile that exposed rather too many teeth with a flash of upper gum and unfortunately accentuated an already-strong resemblance to a horse. A thoroughbred, naturally.

'She's here on her own with her parents.' Smiling, he turned to Rosie and patted her arm. 'Can't have a pretty girl like you wasted on all these old buffers like me. And Kelso's on his own now too, since his wife died last year.'

He should be past caring about his father's tactlessness but Kelso's stomach knotted at the casual mention of Alexa, killed with their unborn baby in a car crash. Perhaps someday he would stop being haunted by grief and the irrational feeling of guilt at having signed the authorisation to switch off life support, but that day still seemed a long way off.

Sir Roderick turned to the other man. 'Now, Douglas, you come with me and leave these young people to get to know each other,' he said and swept him off.

There was a small, awkward silence. Then Rosie said, 'I'm very sorry about your wife.'

She seemed a nice girl. She was looking sweetly sympathetic and she had carefully not noticed the scar that ran down the right side of his face. Kelso gave a small grimace. 'So am I,' he said lightly. 'And I apologise for my father. He's had a subtlety bypass.'

Relieved, she smiled. 'Oh, I know! Aren't parents *ghastly*? My ma is just as bad. Are you on leave?'

Kelso frowned. 'On leave?'

She looked puzzled in her turn. 'Aren't you in the army? Your father—'

His lips tightened. 'I used to be, and he wishes I still was. I think he imagines if he states it often enough it'll come true.'

He could sense her discomfort. 'So – do you have another job?' she asked.

'I'm a policeman.'

Her eyes opened wide. 'A policeman? Really?'

She might as well have said, 'Good gracious, how awful!' It wasn't that he hadn't had this response before. Indeed, among his parents' friends it was the standard reaction, so it was probably unfair of him to say, 'Yes. Dreadfully déclassé, isn't it?' and he felt guilty when Rosie went red with embarrassment.

'Sorry,' she stumbled. 'I didn't mean—'

'No, of course you didn't. I'm sorry – that was rude of me. I'm a detective inspector.'

Her face brightened. 'That sounds very interesting. Do tell me about it.'

Training would out. Girls like Rosie, veterans of a hundred dinner parties, knew all the levers they were supposed to press to keep a conversation going. Veteran of a distressing number of army dinner parties himself, he felt the familiar wave of almost overpowering boredom sweep over him.

'Oh, you know,' he said. 'Lots of paperwork and stuff, like everything else.' A description of the last murder case he had been involved in wouldn't be exactly cocktail party conversation.

He was suddenly gripped around the legs and an accusing voice said, 'Unkie, I was looking for you. You were hiding.' His niece Betsy was scowling up at him, her big blue eyes full of reproach.

He laughed and bent to pick her up. 'Well, I've been here all the time. Maybe you were hiding from me.'

She shook her blonde curls violently. 'No, I wasn't.' Then she turned to study Rosie and, all woman even at three, gave her a suspicious look. 'This is *my* unkie,' she said firmly.

'It's her version of Uncle K,' he explained. 'This is the redoubtable Betsy.'

Rosie laughed. 'I can see that,' she was saying when Kelso's sister Finella came up, carrying a bottle of Prosecco. She held it out.

'Mum wants you to circulate with this. There are senior army officers dying of thirst out there. Sorry to drag him away, Rosie.'

Rosie said goodbye with a certain amount of relief, Kelso thought, as he went to do as he was told with the bottle in one hand and Betsy on his hip, casting a triumphant glance at her rival over his shoulder.

'You owe me one,' Finella said in his ear as they walked away. 'There was a look a desperation on both your faces.'

'Oh dear. Nice girl, but—'

'I know. Daughter of the Regiment. Not your type.'

He didn't have a 'type'. Alexa had been a one-off and there wasn't another. He let it pass. 'Do you think I can escape once I've gone round with this till it's empty? I don't want Ma to be upset.'

Betsy grabbed hold of his cheeks on either side and

turned his head towards her. 'I want you to come and see my drawing I did for you. Now!' She jiggled up and down.

Her mother gave a resigned sigh. 'You shouldn't pander to her. On the other hand, it would give you an excuse.'

Kelso grinned. 'Discipline's your job. OK, Betsy. You're a brat but I'll do anything to get out of here. It's bringing me out in a rash. I do sometimes wonder what Grandad would have made of all this.'

'Knees-up down the pub with his miner mates after the shift was more his style. Dad always says darkly that you're very like him. How are things going, anyway?'

'Fine. It's an interesting job. I've just got back from Ayrshire helping to mop up a crime syndicate – targeting farm machinery, would you believe.'

Finella nodded. Then she said, 'Are . . . are you around for a bit? I might pop in sometime.'

'Sure,' he said easily but, trained in observation, he looked at his sister more closely. She'd tried to make that sound offhand, but her body language was saying something different. She was looking tired too, he thought, though Betsy – tugging at his hair impatiently now – was enough to exhaust anyone. 'Are you—' he began, but before he could finish his sentence his mother appeared.

'Now, you two, we didn't arrange a party for you to stand talking to each other. Fin, Audrey Stephenson was hoping to have a chat – she's over there by the corner cabinet. Off you go!'

Rolling her eyes, Finella departed. Kelso said, 'I'm just going to do a round with the bottle and then Betsy's going to show me her drawing, aren't you, monster?'

Mary wasn't fooled. 'I expect you'll be taking off after that, won't you? Thanks for coming anyway, darling. It means a lot to Roddy.'

Kelso doubted that, but he didn't argue. As he finished his task and made his way to the door with Betsy crowing in delight, he saw that Roderick had noticed and his lips were tightened in exasperation.

PC Davidson, sent out from the Thurso Police Station to the Mowat farm on the edge of the village of Forsich, was very young, chubby-faced and pink-cheeked. Perhaps in a gesture towards gravitas he had grown a small moustache, but to Fergus Mowat's jaundiced eye it looked rather as if it had been stuck on for a fancy-dress party. Wet behind the ears, he concluded.

'You took your time. Did they tell you what the situation is?' he asked.

The man shook his head. 'Never do,' he said simply. 'Just, incident reported out here.'

'Ah,' Fergus said. 'Got a strong stomach, have you, laddie?'

'Course,' the constable said stoutly, but Fergus could see his Adam's apple moving up and down as he swallowed convulsively, and the pink tinge faded from his cheeks as he listened to the details. 'That's . . . that's horrible. Was he . . . was he properly dead?' he said at last.

'Oh aye, he was dead. Very dead, is my guess.'

'Right.' Davidson squared his shoulders. 'Better get it over with, then.' He followed Fergus up the track, casting nervous looks up at the sky on the way.

'It's all right – they've given up. Brought down a couple of the buggers and then the rest scarpered,' Fergus said, gesturing towards the sagging wire fence round the garden of the cottage where a couple of the black birds, like crumpled rags, hung upside down.

The sun was high in the sky now, baking down on the tarpaulin that had protected the corpse from the birds, but the flies were gathering and when the constable lifted it up the stench was indescribable. He dropped it back, choking, but Fergus, who was standing at a safer distance, gave him credit for managing not to throw up.

'Come down the house and we'll get the wife to make a cuppa,' he said, and Davidson nodded, not trusting himself to speak.

Rhona was nowhere to be seen. Fergus switched on the kettle, fetched the mugs and waved him to a seat at the kitchen table.

At last Davidson found his voice again. 'What happened to him?'

Fergus shrugged. 'Your guess is as good as mine. Dossing down there, maybe a drug overdose? Who knows. Could have been there quite a while.'

'I'd say.' Davidson got out his notebook. 'Better take down all the details. Full name?'

It took some time; the constable wasn't the speediest writer. But by the end Fergus was satisfied that he'd got down the main point – that the man had been lying as if he was asleep and had only tipped over onto his face as Fergus pulled the rug out from under him to be able to cover him up. 'Quite a smart-looking rug for a down-

and-out,' he added. 'Not that I suppose that matters.'

'No sign of foul play, though?'

'None at all. Unless you're talking about the birds.' Fergus gave a short laugh at the pun, though Davidson only looked bewildered.

'Right, right.' He tucked away his notebook and stood up. 'I'll request immediate assistance. They'll have to send someone along from CID.'

'Better make it fast,' Fergus said grimly. 'The smell of that'll have every fox in the area gathering and if they think I'm going to stand guard all night they've got another think coming.'

The head office of Curran Services was in a building overlooking the busy harbour in Aberdeen where trawlers and the great ferries for the Northern Isles and Scandinavia competed for harbour space with the PSVs – platform supply vessels – that provide logistic support to the oil rigs out in the North Sea. It was a lot quieter these days, with the downturn in oil prices, but Curran Services was well-enough established and shrewdly enough managed to have weathered the initial storm and had even taken over a couple of its less-well-managed rivals.

Ailie Johnston was short and stocky, with grey hair cut in a neat middle-aged bob; shrewd blue eyes, very bright behind sensible spectacles, were her only striking feature. She was frowning as she came into the boss's office.

The man who sat behind the huge solid teak desk that had been Pat Curran's up to four months ago looked up and noticed her expression.

'Got a problem, Ailie?' he said.

'It's just that Niall's still not in. I've tried phoning and leaving messages, but he's not replied. Should I maybe be getting someone to go round to his flat?'

Bruce Michie seemed irritated by the question. His small mouth tightened into a pout and he shrugged. 'If he's sulking because I gave him a right flea in his ear last week, it's his problem. It's Friday now – leave it over the weekend, Ailie, and if he doesn't turn up on Monday you can send someone round with his P45.'

The PA hesitated. 'That's all week no one's seen him. Should we not . . . ?'

Michie gave a short, sneering laugh. 'Are you feart he's perished all alone in his flat and any time now his cat'll get round to taking wee nibbles – supposing he's got one? For God's sake, he's a healthy loon. Probably went out on the randan at the weekend and now he's playing sick. Like I said, leave it till Monday.'

There was a flush of annoyance in his pudgy cheeks and Ailie subsided. Arguing with the boss was way above her pay grade. She turned to go, then paused. 'Any news of Gabrielle? You went up that way last weekend, didn't you?'

Michie didn't look pleased about that either, his stubby fingers drumming on the desk impatiently. 'Gabrielle? Didn't see her. It was just a fishing weekend. Last I heard she was still much the same. Just needing a good rest. Probably.'

'Right.' Ailie went out, her mind still on the woman who had briefly been her boss. It was a shame about Gabrielle Ross; she'd been determined to carry on Pat's business – not easy in the fevered financial climate at the moment.

He'd been a good boss and a smart businessman, though there were those who said if you went to sup with him you'd be wise to take a long spoon. His drainage business up in the Flow Country had gone bankrupt but he'd come out all right and then made his fortune with Curran Services. There were folks up in Caithness who'd spit on the ground if you said his name, though.

Right enough, not a lot of people were neutral when it came to Pat, but Ailie always spoke as she found, and she'd liked him. Larger than life, Pat had been – a big man in every way, a force of nature with the legendary charm of the Irish, and it seemed all wrong to see Michie with his pot belly and his bald head sitting in Pat's great leather swivel chair, his wee leggies almost too short to reach the ground – but fair away with himself even so.

Working for Pat had been like living with a north-east gale: exhilarating, as long as you could still stand up and it didn't actually blow the roof off. It hadn't seemed possible that he could go, just like that, at only fifty-four.

And Gabrielle, poor wee soul, had done her best to step into his size twelves, when she couldn't be more than twenty-four or five. She'd thought the world of her dad and he'd been grooming her to take over – just not for another ten years, supposing he could ever be persuaded to retire. She'd come in the day after the funeral, white as a sheet and with black circles round her eyes, but she'd still put Michie back in his place when he'd tried to sideline her.

Oh, she was her father's daughter all right – tough enough to do whatever had to be done and like him not prepared to suffer fools gladly, so she'd enemies as well as friends. But in the oil world you needed to be tough, especially if you were a woman, and Ailie admired that. She'd rather be working for her now than for the sleekit Michie – sly, slimy wee nyaff.

Latterly, though, Gabrielle just seemed to lose the place. She'd been utterly devastated by Pat's death and maybe she hadn't given herself enough time to grieve. There was a lot of talk about that fire, and then the tragedy of her losing the baby, but Ailie had seen the signs of problems even before that – always neurotically double-checking on everything, panicking that something vital would be missed. She hadn't been surprised when the breakdown came.

She could only hope that a rest would do the trick. But if Ailie had Gabrielle's income she'd have been thinking about relaxing by a pool with a sun umbrella and a glass of chilled Chardonnay somewhere warm, not Caithness. She'd only been up there a couple of times herself and it seemed gey bleak. Still, maybe she was wanting to be near her mum – though she'd never seen any signs of Gabrielle wanting that before.

Ailie sighed as she walked back to her office. She still was a wee thing worried about Niall too – funny that he hadn't answered her messages all week, but with Michie ready to take her head off if she brought it up again she'd better leave it till Monday.

CHAPTER THREE

Gabrielle came out of sleep reluctantly, her mouth thick from last night's sleeping pills. The familiar feelings – misery, fear – swept in like a tidal wave, worse than ever today. She gasped at the onslaught, but she had a choice – stop thinking, stop feeling. Just – exist. Breathe, in and out. No more than that. Think automaton.

She sat up, swinging her legs out of bed and standing up far too quickly so that light-headedness forced her back down again for a moment. But then she was up and in the shower, the force of water beating on her head drowning out everything else.

She spent as long there as she could, but when she came out and looked at the clock it had only taken ten minutes of the long day that lay ahead. Ten minutes – was that all? It had felt much longer. She towelled her long dark hair and left it to dry in its natural tousled state – no more hair straighteners for her, ever again, and she pushed the memory fiercely out of her mind as she struggled to drag her comb through it. It just looked a mess now; she'd really have to get it cut, she thought, as she dragged it back into a ponytail.

She'd have to get her own breakfast today. David had gone offshore for a couple of days dealing with a computer problem on one of the rigs, but when he was at home he always left out her breakfast before going to work – Dorset Cereals honey granola, a pot of natural yoghurt and the cafetière primed with coffee so she had only to pour in the boiling water, almost as if he didn't trust her to do it for herself. She'd got a bit tired of the honey flavour but he'd stockpiled several boxes in case she couldn't get her favourite out here in the sticks. Well, it had been her favourite, but it was like that old joke of Paddy's: 'Monday you like baked beans, Tuesday you like baked beans, Wednesday you like baked beans, Thursday you like baked beans – how come all of a sudden on Friday you *don't* like baked beans?'

It made her smile, then the tears came to her eyes. Oh Paddy, Paddy! She'd always thought of herself as so independent, tough – ruthless even, when necessary. But she'd been kidding herself. She'd been dependent on her father all along and when he died she'd fallen apart and could barely function. And David had been there, so calm, loving, utterly loyal, somehow holding the pieces together. He'd never reproached her; for that she owed him a debt she could never repay. It wasn't his fault that day-to-day his too obvious concern and protectiveness was driving her—she clamped her lips shut before she could say 'mad'.

She mustn't, even as a joke. The memory of early onset Alzheimer's claiming her gran was always in her mind;

she had watched with an aching heart as the clever, lively woman slipped with terrible inexorability into a demented twilight. *It ran in families, sometimes.*

She gave a little shudder. She felt as if her nerves were strung on a rack being pitilessly stretched tighter and tighter. One day they would snap, unless she did what David said to do: blank out the past and live only in the moment.

When she was working it had all been so different. The big diary open on her desk would be crammed with meetings, visits to suppliers, lunch dates with possible new clients. She'd lived on adrenaline, relishing every minute of it. Paddy used to laugh at her enthusiasm, telling her to pace herself a bit better, but she knew he was pleased.

She had met David, not in Aberdeen, oddly enough, but at a drinks party her mother had given when she was up here for a duty visit. His best friend had at that time been working on the decommissioning of the Dounreay nuclear plant and David was a regular weekend visitor. Their attraction had been immediate; he'd called her the following day and it had gone on from there.

Paddy had taken to him at once and given his blessing to the marriage. When they'd told him she was pregnant, he'd been moved to tears. Gabrielle had never been so happy.

The shattering suddenness of his coronary had destroyed her too. She hadn't quite realised it at the time, though, being too busy taking over the reins. Bruce Michie, the junior partner, was both vain and feeble, which was a bad combination; she wasn't going to let him sideline her and take control of Paddy's company. She thought she could cope. Oh, she had the will, all right, even now. It was her mind that was betraying her.

The trivial memory blanks like forgetting where she'd left her mobile became bigger mistakes, like finding her wallet in the freezer or the milk in the cupboard under the sink. She couldn't seem to get even simple arrangements, like appointments, clear in her head.

Her doctor had soothed her with talk of hormones and 'baby brain' combined with shock and grief. 'Take proper time off,' he said. 'No emails, no phone calls. You'll be fine.'

She had promised to keep her weekends work-free and on that Saturday morning she'd got up late, had a long, leisurely, self-indulgent pampering session and took time to choose what to wear for lunch with friends after David's golf foursome.

She'd joined him as he finished breakfast in the conservatory kitchen they had built onto their small terraced house. She looked at her watch.

'You should be getting ready to go,' she said, then realised he was hesitating about leaving her alone.

'Will you be all right? They won't mind, you know, if—'

'Don't be daft!' she said robustly, though it chilled her that he should be concerned. 'I'm fine. There's nothing wrong with me.'

'All right, then. If you're sure.' She had shooed him out to sort out his clubs and then waved him off from the doorstep.

He should have stayed. If he had, it wouldn't have happened. But she mustn't think about that.

It seemed to be hardest in the morning. She was so infinitely weary, so vulnerable to the confused, despairing, frantic thoughts that still kept piling in. It was like throwing her whole weight against a door while violent forces kept battering it and battering it. Someday, she knew, the hinges would give way and it would fall over and crush her.

The waiting room at the doctor's surgery in Forsich was busy this morning and at the reception desk Francesca Curran was out of temper, a not uncommon occurrence.

'No, Mrs Macintyre, the doctor can't fit you in today and there isn't a free appointment until next Thursday.'

Mrs Macintyre seemed inclined to argue and Francesca's lips tightened. 'No, I told you, Mrs Macintyre. There just are no spaces and it doesn't sound urgent—'

Mrs Macintyre wasn't impressed by that. Her tirade went on for some time and Francesca waited until it eventually ran down, tapping her fingers on the desk. 'If you've managed to convince yourself that you need immediate attention, I'm afraid you'll have to go to Accident and Emergency at Wick. Goodbye.'

She put the phone down and said tartly to her colleague, who was working at the computer, 'You can take the next call, Cathy. It'll probably be Mrs Macintyre arguing the toss and if I take it I'll be rude to her.'

Cathy made a non-committal sound that could have been either sympathy or a comment on the politeness, or otherwise, of the previous response. As the doctor's stepdaughter, Francesca could be as unhelpful as she liked without running the risk of being sacked. And now here was the other stepdaughter coming in from the door that led into the doctor's house, the one who was allegedly ill though no one talked about what was wrong with her.

Francesca greeted her sister without enthusiasm. 'Ah, the prodigal daughter!' She knew there was an edge to her voice; somehow it always crept in when she was confronted with her younger and prettier sister, who was skinny with thick wavy dark hair, where she herself was definitely bulky and had fine straight hair of a shade that Gabrielle had once maliciously described as 'animated mouse'. And now her sister was wealthier too, thanks to their father's gross favouritism – and that hurt, that really hurt, especially when she needed the money for a home of her own. At her age she shouldn't still have to be living with her mother and stepfather.

'Where were you this morning?'

Gabrielle looked at her coldly. 'Aren't you getting tired of that particular joke? And what do you mean, where was I? I was to meet Mum at eleven-thirty but she's not in the house.'

Francesca gave her a pitying look. 'According to her it was ten-thirty – she came in here at quarter to eleven and said she wasn't prepared to wait any longer. God, you're in a bad way, Gabby!'

She knew how her sister hated the name and she knew, too, that Gabrielle was making a big deal out of being stressed out, but it was an attention-seeking ploy, in her opinion. Admittedly losing the baby had been sad but this was all about Pat's death, really. Fran had lost her father too, but somehow only Gabrielle was entitled to make this sort of melodramatic fuss about it. The way she had poor David dancing attendance on her was positively disgusting too. All that was wrong with her was not having Dad around to tell her every five minutes that she was wonderful.

He'd never bothered telling Fran she was wonderful, had he? She'd hated him for that – at least, that was what she told herself; loving him when he made it so clear he was only interested in his other daughter was too painful. Of course, she hadn't sucked up to him like Gabrielle had. It had always set her teeth on edge when Gabrielle called him Paddy, her cutesy mixture of Pat and Daddy. What was wrong with Dad?

A flicker of reaction showed on Gabrielle's face, but she only said airily, 'Oh, Mum must have got it wrong. Can't think why she didn't phone me. I'll catch up with her later. Not to worry, *Fanny*.' She walked out.

'Fran' was fine, but Francesca hated Fanny just as much as Gabrielle hated Gabby, so now they were quits. Somehow their conversations always ended up back in the nursery. Every so often when she saw other sisters who were friends as well she felt a pang of wistfulness, but with Gabrielle it simply wasn't possible. Thanks to Pat Curran, their relationship had always been dysfunctional and now what she felt for her sister was something close to loathing.

How like Fran, trying to get her on the raw. Gabrielle hoped she'd managed not to show what a jolt it had given her, being told she'd got the time wrong. She had written it down carefully last night on her list to herself, but the arrangement had been made in the morning when she often felt a bit woozy, so she could have got it confused at the time – or else, as she had claimed, her mother could have got it wrong. She wouldn't put money on that, though.

Still, it was odd that Lilian hadn't called her; it would

only have taken Gabrielle ten minutes to drive in to Forsich. She fished in her bag, but even as she did so she remembered that she hadn't switched it on this morning. Her stomach lurched; something else she'd forgotten. But that was quite normal, she told herself firmly; everyone forgets to do that sometimes. Even so, her hands were shaking as she checked it.

Sure enough, there was a missed call and a couple of texts from a presumably irritable Lilian. She didn't want to read them, and she didn't want to respond to David's 'All right, love?' right now either. She switched it back off again and drove on to Thurso alone for her groceries, just to get out of Forsich. She spent as little time as she could in the place; even when you'd learnt long ago not to care what people thought, it wasn't pleasant to get hostile looks – and worse.

Fran's constant sniping didn't help. Admittedly, they'd never been close. Perhaps the small age gap had meant that Fran had resented her right from the start, for usurping her position as the baby. They'd bickered their way through childhood until, when she'd been fourteen and Fran sixteen, their parents had separated. Fran had chosen to stay here with their mother – and still lived at home – but Gabrielle had insisted on going to Aberdeen with vibrant, exciting Pat.

Oh, maybe he'd made it a wee bit more obvious than he should have that she was his favourite, but you couldn't blame him. Fran had been such an infuriating, whiny child, forever nursing a grievance, and it was no wonder he couldn't disguise his irritation with her. Jealousy had corroded the girls' relationship long, long before the business over Paddy's will. And then there was Gabrielle's sin in marrying David – unforgivable, apparently, despite 'I saw him first' not really applying to adult relationships. Fran seriously needed to grow up.

That childhood decision hadn't done anything for Gabrielle's relationship with her mother, either. She'd been labelled a traitor, even though it was Lilian who'd been unfaithful and broken up the marriage. Just when Pat's drainage business was collapsing, Lilian had embarked on an affair with the local doctor – the rat deserting the sinking ship, in her teenage daughter's eyes. She hated, she truly hated disloyalty and she'd never been able to forgive her mother for this betrayal at the time when her father needed all the support he could get. Malcolm Sinclair was good-looking, certainly, but prosy and pompous and Gabrielle was convinced it had a lot more to do with Lilian making sure of a comfortable lifestyle and status in local society than it had with any sort of illicit passion.

Whatever the locals might have said it hadn't been Pat's fault that environmental theory changed and the draining of bogland to plant trees stopped being the way to save the planet and became an ecological crime. He'd been a local hero before that for bringing work to the community, and if some of them had lost money by investing in the business, so had he. It was only because he'd had the guts and vision to pick himself up, work flat out to start another business and prosper that they hated him.

That, and Gary Gunn's death . . .

She refused to accept the burden of guilt for that; it was an accident, that was all. Death and sore loss were the story of her life just now and if she didn't shut her mind to all of it the darkness that lurked about her, so close now that she could almost see it out of the corner of her eye, would sweep in.

Thirteen was hideously young to die, though. She never failed to put flowers on his grave when she came up to Forsich.

'That all right for you, Mrs Sinclair?'

The hairdresser held up the big round mirror behind her. She was fussy and he was pretty sure she wouldn't be impressed by his handiwork. She only came in when she needed a trim; it had to be a posh hairdresser in Aberdeen for her blonde highlights.

He heard a tiny sigh and noticed the brief compression of her lips, but she only said, 'That's fine, Dennis. You've done your best,' and gave him a little, gracious smile as befitted a doctor's wife. She'd got a lot grander since the days when she was married to an Irish navvy made good. She'd worked in the local Spar then, but now it was all voluntary work in the Shelter shop and charity committees in Aberdeen.

She was a good-looking woman, though. What age was she now – late forties, fifty, even? – but she was slim and toned-looking, with delicate features and clear blue eyes, and if the unwrinkled complexion owed something to Botox, it had been skilfully enough done for it not to be obvious.

He was just brushing the hairs off her shoulders when she raised her hand in greeting to a woman walking along the pavement who had stopped, peered in and then opened the door. Lilian gave a little worried sigh.

'That's my daughter Gabrielle, Dennis, late as usual! She can't seem to remember the simplest arrangement these days.'

Dennis smiled. 'She's not the only person with that problem. Ask any hairdresser!'

As her daughter came over, her face was reflected in the mirror above her mother's. There was a resemblance between them: they had the same shape of face with well-defined cheekbones and a clear, arching brow line, but in the daughter, you could see the Irish heritage – the pale skin, the dark-blue eyes 'put in with a sooty finger'. Terrible hair, though. Scraped back from her face into a ponytail like that it did nothing for her and inheriting Pat Curran's determined jawline hadn't done her any favours either. She looked strained, with dark circles under her eyes, and he remembered there had been rumours about a breakdown.

'Can't believe you're her mother. Sister, surely?' Dennis said, knowing his client.

'Oh, don't be silly!' She was laughing up at him when Gabrielle reached her. 'What happened to you this morning?' she said.

Gabrielle coloured. 'I was positive we said half past eleven. Are you sure you didn't make a mistake?'

'Of course not. I'd been thinking we could have a quick coffee before my appointment and that was for quarter past eleven. I wanted to speak to you, anyway. I texted but you didn't reply.'

'I know. Sorry – I forgot to switch on my phone.'

'Oh, I see.' She gave her daughter a sharp glance, then said, 'Well, I suppose we all do that from time to time,' in a bracing sort of way.

'Of course we do. How long are you going to be? I was just going along to the Co-op.'

'I've done my shopping.' Lilian paused, and Dennis guessed what she was going to say next – they'd been talking about the news that was all over the town. Was that an anxious glance she was giving the nervy daughter?

'There's a bit of a fuss in Forsich. Malcolm was speaking to the police surgeon today and apparently they've found a body up at the Mowat farm.'

Gabrielle stared at her. 'A *body*?'

'Oh, some tramp who seems to have been dossing down in one of the sheds, apparently. It's not at all pleasant, from what Malcolm said – you really don't want to know. Try not to listen to the gossip. You've had more than enough to cope with recently and you know David hates it when you get upset.'

'Yes – yes, I know. Right. I'll just get what I'm needing and head home.'

Her mother gave her an anxious look. 'You are all right, aren't you? You could come home with me if you like. I think maybe it would be wiser—'

'No, I'm fine,' Gabrielle said hastily. 'It's a lovely day. I'll go for a walk.'

'Don't forget the sunscreen. You know you burn easily. And you won't forget when David will get home, will you? He worries if you're not there.'

'I won't forget. Why should I?' Her daughter's voice was challenging.

'Of course you won't,' Lilian said too heartily. 'I'm just a fussing mother hen,' she said with a smile to Dennis.

'Enjoy your walk, darling. We have to make the most of this weather – they're saying it's set to break quite soon.'

At the door to the Co-op there was a group of people in animated conversation. It wasn't hard to guess what they were talking about; the local grapevine was certainly efficient if not necessarily accurate. There was something repellent about the avid expressions on their faces and Gabrielle determinedly shut her ears as she skirted round them to pick up a basket.

Somehow her mother's concern about how the news might affect her made her feel much, much worse. It showed that it was obvious how much she was struggling, and she hated it, too, when Lilian started being motherly. After all that had been said between them over the years she had lost that right. Of course, every child loves Mummy; they're conditioned to it, poor little sods. But when you grow up you start looking at your mother the way you would at any other person and Gabrielle had concluded a long time ago that Lilian was someone she didn't much like.

She'd made regular filial visits over the years – always brief ones, and she always stayed in the house that Pat had had built – an ugly, square block of a house with three bedrooms, bathroom, kitchen and a living room with a picture window that looked out onto the bogland, scarred by the abandoned drainage trenches and the derelict sheds where there were still some old vehicles they hadn't managed to sell off. It was flimsy, just thrown up without regard for kerb-appeal or permanence – now it was certainly showing its age – but she still preferred it, despite the draughts and the cracks and the leaks, to Lilian and Malcolm's grand Victorian pile, for all its expensive comforts. Anywhere was preferable to being under the same roof as Francesca and Lilian.

Once she'd done the shopping, she'd stop on the road just outside Forsich and walk up to the moors on the rising ground behind the town. She wasn't ready to go back to the empty house and there might be a breeze up there stealing in from the sea. Perhaps there was even a little healing magic left in the place where she and Paddy had walked together so many times.

CHAPTER FOUR

Detective Chief Superintendent Jane Borthwick called DCI
Kelso Strang into her office on Saturday morning.

'Curious one, this, that's just arrived on my desk. A bit
nasty, really. It's up in Caithness – body found in a derelict
cottage yesterday morning, but only after the ravens had
found it first.'

Strang winced. 'I've seen photos of what they do to lambs.'

'Then you get the picture.'

They were in Borthwick's office on the top floor of the
Edinburgh Police Headquarters, an ugly block in Fettes
Avenue. Her desk, as usual, was bare of everything except
a thin file open before her – a reflection, Strang thought, of
her own distaste for elaboration and clutter in any form. She
was always well-groomed and discreetly made up, usually
wearing a trouser suit so neutral that you never gave her
appearance a thought.

Her professional style was similar. Strang had worked closely with her for almost a year now; he respected her ability and was perfectly at ease with her no-frills approach, but he was wary too. When it came to policing, she was a political animal in a way that he wasn't – at least not yet. He knew she thought his idealism was naïve and even, perhaps, self-indulgent.

'I've got a meeting in five minutes, so I'll give you this to take away with you,' Borthwick said, tapping the file in front of her with one well-manicured finger. 'But the gist of it is that it was an adult male and the local force made the initial assumption that this was a down-and-out and most probably drug-related. They got him in to the mortuary in Wick last night and found that he'd actually drowned somewhere and been moved to the cottage afterwards. No ID, as yet.'

'Odd, certainly.'

'I want you to go up and assess the situation first. The body has been flown down to the Scientific Services lab in Aberdeen for further investigation, but they're closed over the weekend, so we won't get any answers till Monday.

'Get up there tomorrow, can you, Kelso? If you need a team I'll authorise that but we're tighter on budget than ever so keep it to a minimum. OK?' She was looking at her watch as she spoke, and she stood up, handing him the file.

'Yes, ma'am.' Strang got up too and moved to hold the door open for her then followed her out. She went along the corridor, but he headed downstairs to the domain of the less exalted beings.

The Serious Rural Crime Squad had been set up as a money-saving operation, to cut back on the costs of maintaining full CID services in country areas where major crime was rare. Strang was the only officer permanently

49

in place, with a recent promotion to DCI. As a senior investigating officer, he could be deployed to reinforce the detectives on the spot in the less complex cases, without drafting in extra support. The top brass liked that, so he'd still be operating as before; all the new position would do was give him operational rank over the local DI.

Borthwick had warned him at the start that he would have to be something of a maverick and he'd relished having the power to make decisions without needing to make his case to anyone else – in fact, he'd find it hard now to go back into a conventional team. Last year, when he had been scarred both mentally and physically by the road accident that had killed Alexa, the professional isolation had given him time to adapt to the new normal, to some degree, at least, and the demands of the case had let him shut it out.

For the time being, that was. Kelso hadn't given himself time to mourn and after it was over great waves of grief and rage swept through him until sometimes he felt he was drowning in despair. Yet the thought of moving on was almost worse; allowing Alexa to become his past not his present seemed a terrible disloyalty.

It was only the need to get up in the morning and go to work that had kept him sane, and gradually, with the inexorable healing of time, the cycles of despair recurred less often even if they did not disappear. Working for professional exams had occupied his evenings but now he would welcome a new investigation where again he would be on the spot, living the case day and night.

He went back to his office. It was tiny, on a back corridor and just beside a cleaning cupboard, but he didn't have to share it and he could retreat into it like a snail into its shell when he needed peace to think. He sat down at his cluttered desk, so unlike his boss's, and cleared a space to set down the slender file she had given him.

It covered the main facts. The village where the body had been found, Forsich, was about ten miles along the North Coast 500 road from Thurso and a mile inland, right on the edge of what they called the Flow Country, the largest wetland in Europe. From the preliminary pathology report, the indications were that the man had drowned in peaty water – a burn or perhaps even one of the bogs the area was famous for. Then for some unknown reason, the corpse had been moved to an abandoned croft house where, as Borthwick had said, it had attracted the attention of scavenging ravens, fortunately disturbed by the local farmer.

Strang finished reading and sat back in his chair. He was certainly getting about Scotland with this job. He'd never been to Caithness; it was famously grim, wasn't it, situated on that exposed northern coast with dangerous seas and storms from the Arctic sweeping in. He was familiar now with the villages and hamlets of the west coast, picturesque in their isolation, and presumably Forsich was like that too. It would certainly be interesting to see.

He reached for the phone to make the necessary arrangements. He'd got all the levers he would need to press in place already and he could have the SOCOs in position by this evening.

DC Livvy Murray had been opening the door from the CID room just as DCI Strang had walked down the corridor towards his office. She shut it again and shrank back; he didn't notice her. It was her practice to avoid him as far as possible. Not to any extent that would make it obvious and embarrass both of them, of course – if their paths crossed she smiled and said a polite hello, not meeting his eyes.

But she suspected that he was avoiding her too. When someone had risked his life to save you from your own stupidity, it didn't make for a comfortable relationship on either side. Every time she heard there was to be an SRCS operation she tensed up, but so far she hadn't been allocated to one. She'd begun to wonder if this was tact on the super's part, but since Borthwick hadn't actually spoken to her since she started at Fettes Row it was more likely coincidence than consideration of the sensitivities of a very junior DC.

Livvy had settled in to CID work with enthusiasm and her sergeant seemed happy enough, on the whole – or as happy as the dour bugger ever allowed himself to be – but she was having problems with Edinburgh. Her heart was still in Glasgow with its rougher edge and its friendly, down-to-earth folk, always ready to have a laugh with a stranger at the bus stop, instead of standing there like stookies and treating a polite enquiry about when the bus is due like a personal affront. And what sort of police station had Waitrose as its corner shop, for God's sake?

She'd found a wee one-room-and-bath flat down in Leith, which was more her kind of place, but she wasn't trying hard enough to make friends; the first few hours of her time off were always spent getting to the train station and back home to Glasgow. Only it wasn't her home any more; her old mates there were getting on with living their own lives – married now, some of them, and when you weren't around for the casual drink after work you sort of lost touch. She felt exiled, a bit of a loner. Ideally, she'd apply for a transfer, but she had enough contacts left in the Glasgow force to know that her name was still mud. She'd just have to sweat it out a bit longer.

Kelso Strang had disappeared along the corridor and she could safely go for her lunch break now. She ought to have a salad. Maybe she would. She always meant to until she got there and smelt the chips.

Calum Cameron was looking round nervously as he sidled into the Lemon Tree, Morven Gunn's cafe. It was always crowded on a Saturday and this morning the local gossips were out in force.

'They're not letting on,' he heard one woman say, 'but someone said to me it was just a tramp.'

'I heard it was old Rabbie,' another offered. 'He was fair stotting at the pub last Saturday and he maybe never made it home.'

Calum knew they'd be talking – the whole town was buzzing with what was probably fake news, mostly – but hearing for yourself what they were saying made it worse. At least there was no sign of Morven; from the clattering of pans she must be in the kitchen directing the preparations for lunch. That was lucky. She'd gone mental about him distracting Kirstie the last time he came in.

He spotted Kirstie clearing a table in the far corner. She didn't look round, even when she must have known he was coming over.

'Kirstie, can we talk?' he said in an urgent undertone.

She gave him a brief glance over her shoulder. 'Haven't time,' she said. 'Lunches are just going to start.'

Was she as worried as he was? It was hard to know with girls – they put on all this stuff, so you couldn't tell if they were pale and hollow-eyed, like he'd been when he looked in the mirror this morning.

'Later, then. You know what's happened—'

'Yeah, like I wouldn't? There's been police crawling all over the place ever since last night.'

'But they're saying it's been there for days.'

'So?' She still wouldn't look at him.

'But we know it wasn't.'

Kirstie was wiping the table with unnecessary force. 'And that's my problem – how?'

Calum could feel cold sweat forming on the back of his neck. 'The police – they're going to be questioning everybody. What are we going to say?'

She whirled round. 'Nothing!' she said fiercely. 'We're going to say nothing. Just zip it. No one's going to ask us, anyway – why should they? And if you open your big mouth and my father finds out about us going there, I'm so not speaking to you ever again.' She picked up the tray she had loaded and turned away.

'Wait, Kirstie,' he begged, then lowered his voice. '*He was lying on my mother's rug.*'

She froze for a moment, then with determined bravado said, 'And they'll know how? They're not going to look at it and say, "Oh goodness me, isn't that Calum Cameron's mother's rug?" Just shut up about it, pretend it never happened and everything'll be fine.'

'Suppose my mother sees it's missing and asks me if I know where it is?'

'Say you don't know. Or just lie – tell her you took it to have a picnic with some of your pals and left it behind or something – oh, I don't know! For God's sake think of your own effing excuse. Just keep me out of it.'

Kirstie went round him with a swing of her hips. Biting his lip, Calum turned away. It was all very well her talking like that, but he'd never been any good at lying to his mother and lying to the police was plain daft. Even not telling the police something important that you knew could get you in trouble.

As he weaved his way through the tables to the door, he could see the amused looks. It must have been obvious he and Kirstie were having a row. One plump, motherly lady even patted his arm.

'Och, don't you worry, laddie! She'll be ready to kiss and make up tomorrow, you'll see.'

Without looking at her Calum bared his teeth in what might pass for a smile and went out, the giggling of the old biddies ringing in his ears. He wasn't sure he even wanted to kiss and make up. Sure, Kirstie was hot. But she'd shown a nasty side he hadn't seen before, ready to dump him in it to save her own skin.

He wouldn't say anything meantime, but he wasn't making any promises. If it was all about looking after number one, two could play at that.

Kelso Strang had got packing down to a fine art, even keeping an extra toilet bag prepacked with shaving tackle and toothbrush ready for a sudden summons like this. He'd had plenty of practice as inquiries took him up and down the country, though over the past year there had only been two other murders since the big case in Skye and both of those were domestics where there was no doubt about the perpetrator.

When he got back to the old fisherman's cottage beside Newhaven Harbour, he packed a supply of clothes then added a thick sweater – you never knew what the weather in Caithness might throw at you – with his mind on the case. Why move a body? Because it was in the wrong place, had to be the answer. But why from a bog to a derelict cottage? Why not take it further into the wilds where it might rot away undetected? Unless you didn't want it to be undetected – but then, could you be sure it would be found in the cottage?

He chucked in a couple of books – a short story collection, the new William Boyd – and was zipping up his bag when the phone rang. It was the landline, the one most often used by his family, and he gave a guilty start. He'd meant to phone his mother. Mary Strang always liked to know where he was since he only took his police mobile with him on a case, but in the rush to get away it had slipped his mind. Now he'd have to pretend he was just going to do it and she'd have to pretend to believe him.

But when he looked at the caller ID, he saw it was his sister. Finella had said she might be dropping in; he should have phoned her too.

'Hi, Fin,' he said.

'Hi, kid. Are you around tomorrow? Betsy has a playdate after nursery – I hope they know what they're letting themselves in for but if it gives me a couple of hours' respite

I have no scruples. I'll be dropping her off at four and I'll have to pick her up about half five – will you be in?'

Kelso sighed. 'Sorry – no go. I'm driving up to Aberdeen and then on to Caithness.'

'Oh.' Her voice went flat, and he realised that the brightness of her tone had been artificial – remembered, too, that he'd thought she had something on her mind when he saw her at the party.

'You OK?' he asked.

'Oh, sure!' The brightness was back. 'Just thought we hadn't had a get-together recently. Caithness! You do get around. What is it this time, K? Or will you have to kill me afterwards if you tell me?'

He thought for a moment. There would be local reports today, the news media would have the full story tomorrow and anyway she wasn't about to phone the *Scottish Sun*. 'It's a bit gruesome. Someone was found dead, but the ravens got to him before anyone else did.'

'Aargh! That's horrendous. So – you'll be away for a while?'

'Couldn't say. Sometimes things that look complicated turn out to be simple enough.'

'Right.' Her voice had gone flat again. 'Be careful, anyway. No heroics, like the last time, OK? Give me a buzz when you get back.'

Finella rang off, leaving him uneasy. There was definitely something wrong. Things had been going well for her in the last year, he'd thought; money had been a bit tight when Fin was a stay-at-home mum, but she'd gone back to work part-time with her old law firm now Betsy was established at nursery. Her partner, Mark, had given up the management job at Tesco that his father-in-law so despised and was writing wills and conveyancing property in a firm in Linlithgow, working towards a partnership, so it ought to be easier now. They'd moved to a nice flat in Morningside recently, and last year they'd even had a holiday in Greece, so money obviously wasn't the problem.

Marriage, he wondered suddenly. Could that be it? Mark obviously had a problem with what he called 'the M word' in jokey conversation, and Fin had seemed happy enough with their present arrangement – though maybe resigned was a better way to put it? Perhaps that was starting to cause friction; she was a dutiful child, uncomfortable with disapproval from her conventional parents in a way he never had been.

Kelso hadn't married Alexa from any sense of duty. He'd joked to her that he wanted to tie her down as securely as possible, so he could never lose his precious girl. The ring on her finger hadn't given any protection, though, against a juggernaut crashing through a motorway barrier. Unconsciously he fingered the scar that ran from cheekbone to jawline on the right side of his face. It had healed completely now but touching the puckered line triggered a sharp stab of memory.

But he'd things to do and he'd better get on with them. Like phoning his mother, now he'd been reminded.

It would be fresher up on the moor. Gabrielle Ross turned off the main road into an old farm track and parked at the end of it. She didn't take the route Paddy had always taken, up from the house right along the edge of the bogland to what he called his secret loch – oh no, not that way, not that way.

Paddy had loved walking through the boggy ground, roaring with laughter when the tussock he had stood on sagged under his weight and his boots filled with water. From her earliest years she'd tagged along after him, hating the way the greedy ground grabbed at her feet, sucking and pulling so that sometimes she lost her wellies, hating the squelching of her feet in the wet boots, terrified that the bog would suck them both down. She knew all the stories about cows that disappeared, and she had nightmares afterwards, but it was worth it for an afternoon with Paddy all to herself and perhaps a share of a brown trout or two for tea as a reward.

But Paddy had a passion for the Flow Country. He had seen it at first as an enemy to be vanquished in his quest to make money out of the drained land, but then its weird beauty had somehow bewitched him – the birds, the strange insects and the stranger plants. Even after the dream came to nothing he had felt a paradoxical delight that the bog remained wild and untamed and when he came up from Aberdeen the first thing he did was find the rods and creel and set off.

Gabrielle jumped out, undoing her ponytail and pushing her hands through her hair to loosen it as she walked across the springy turf. She could smell wild thyme as it was crushed beneath her feet and hear the contented mumbling of the wild bees as they made the most of this time of plenty.

Mindfulness should be easier here. When she sat at home trying to listen to her breathing and relax into her heartbeat, there was still too much space for thinking and then the breathing got uneven and the pulse ragged. Now she could focus on the myriad shades of green of grasses and bushes, on the shimmering silver blue of the Pentland Firth in the heat haze away on the edge of the horizon, on the white flags of bog cotton fluttering gently in the light breezes; she could strain her ears to catch the trickle of song from the lark she could see spiralling up in the distance. There was a curlew somewhere; she could hear the mournful 'Whaup! Whaup!' that gave it its Scottish name. She gave a deep sigh and felt her tense muscles softening.

Gabrielle felt nearer to Paddy up here. The 'secret loch' lay ahead, its peaty depths navy blue under the summer skies. She could almost feel he was there, right at her side; he was much too vital a person to be just . . . snuffed out. She gave a small, involuntary sob. There was another ghost walking beside him too – the vital, optimistic girl she had once been. That girl had been snuffed out, certainly.

She'd let him down so badly. He should have had a thriving grandchild by now, even if he hadn't been there to see it, and she should have been nurturing his other baby too, the firm he was so proud of, his legacy. She hadn't even the strength to do that for him now: too much grief, too much pain, too much fear.

All she had to cling to was David's steadfast confidence that she could, given rest and the blunting of memories through time, get back one day to that ghost self. If that had really gone forever, there would only be despair and the voice in her head whispering quietly, 'Why go on?'

Her mind, so briefly quieted, began the old circuit of frantic, hamster-like scrabbling. The peace spell broken, she walked back to the car.

Her phone pinged with a text just as she got back to

the house – David, to say they'd landed at the Aberdeen heliport. By the time he caught the plane to Wick and drove home it would probably be four hours and he'd be hungry. She'd better make a casserole that could wait in the oven.

She unpacked the shopping bags, selected onions and carrots and went to get a knife from the wooden knife box that stood on the surface. There was an empty slot; the small vegetable knife was missing. She frowned. She must have put it in the kitchen drawer by mistake. That was unusual; she and David both enjoyed cooking, and these were expensive knives that would lose their edge, tumbled in with the other utensils.

She looked, but it wasn't there. Gabrielle paused to think. When had she had it last? Yesterday, of course; she'd made a salad for her supper – coleslaw, tomatoes, cucumber. Could it have got thrown out with the cabbage leaves? The compost bin was fairly full. She tipped out the smelly debris onto a sheet of newspaper and raked through it. No knife.

She was shaking now. She must have had another of these terrible blanks. She'd put it in some totally crazy place and now she had no idea where that might be. If David found it first . . . He didn't need evidence that she was getting worse, on top of everything else. Abandoning her preparation, she went through the house frantically opening every drawer, every cupboard. She couldn't find it. With tears of frustration in her eyes, she took a bigger knife and went on chopping.

It was only when she went to the cloakroom later that she saw it as she washed her hands – carefully placed near the basin. She picked it up slowly, feeling a chill down her spine. It was very shiny, very sharp. Very . . . attractive. Experimentally, she laid it against her wrist.

Was that what she'd been thinking? They said that cutting yourself gave you relief from stress; she'd read that somewhere. And she really needed relief from stress—

She increased the pressure just a little, until it was painful. Just a tiny slit, to see . . .

David would notice, would notice at once. She drew a shuddering breath, dropped the knife into the basin as if it had some toxic power of its own. She must stop this, calm down, control herself. Her hands were sweating so that they were slipping on the cold tap as she turned it on. She splashed her face, her neck, again and again, forcing herself to breathe deeply and regularly.

At last her hands were steady enough to pick it up and go back to the kitchen. *That never happened*, she told herself. *You're making a drama out of a careless mistake – you forgot you had it in your hand when you went through to the cloakroom and laid it down. A simple oversight.*

But as she put the knife back in its place her eyes went again to the blade. It had felt so neat, so cool against her skin . . .

At five o'clock sharp Morven Gunn made a production out of locking the door of the Lemon Tree cafe, a signal as pointed as calling, 'Time, gentlemen, please,' in a pub. She backed it up with a glare at the tables where a couple of groups were still lingering over their tea.

She was a big woman, lean and bony, with harsh features and a thin-lipped mouth that had an embittered downward slant at the corners, famous locally for her aggressive approach to the art of table service. Her scones, though, were equally famous and the lunches were good too; since there was no competition within the village, the cafe was seldom quiet and today she had been run off her feet.

She hovered round the occupied tables, pouncing from time to time on any empty plates and clashing them down loudly in the kitchen.

'She's in a right ill mood today,' one woman said in an undertone. 'What's eating her?'

'Doesn't need to be anything, with Morven. She's always in a right mood,' her friend said. 'Has been for years.'

'Worse than usual, I'd say. We'd probably better go before she lays hands on us and throws us out.'

'It's been known.' The group at the other table were leaving hastily, psyched out, and they gathered up their bags and stood up too. 'My turn to pay. But she's not getting a tip, mind.'

Morven rang up the bill and took the money with a cold nod, then ushered them out and locked the door again with a sigh that was almost a groan. She was tired to her very bones. The din made by customers high on the local scandal just hadn't stopped, her head was splitting, and it was all she needed that Kirstie had been in a silly mood too; she'd been clumsy and careless, and pert with it when Morven bawled her out. She'd sent her home early and told her she'd dock her wages. She'd been more bother than she was worth today.

It left her with a lot of clearing to do so it was late before she could lock up and set off wearily for home. It was getting on for seven now, but it was still hot and humid in the evening calm. It felt uncomfortable – unnatural, even –

but that was in keeping with the weird, febrile atmosphere.

The main street was still busy even though the shops were shut, and a police car came slowly along, heading to Mowat's farm, no doubt. They said there was lots of activity there today, with yellow 'Crime Scene Do Not Cross' tapes everywhere; half her customers seemed to have walked out there to take a look – probably the most exercise they'd taken in weeks, from the looks of them. She kept her head down and didn't even turn to look as it passed.

Her small rented flat was next door to the Crown Bar, the only pub in the village, and it opened directly onto the pavement. It was in full sun and she knew what it would be like when she opened the door: unaired, with a hot, foetid smell. It backed onto another property, so she couldn't open a window on the other side to get a through draught and there would be no respite until the shadow of the buildings opposite lengthened to reach across the road. Tired as Morven was, she couldn't face sitting in the stuffy front room, sweltering, hearing the chatter in the street outside as people gathered at the pub.

A terrible weariness came over her. She hated this, she hated it! The bitter unfairness of life with its multiple injustices brought the tears to her eyes. By rights on a day like this she should be sitting in the pretty garden under the shade of the apple tree with money in the bank and a future to look forward to.

All this was doing her head in: she wanted peace, solitude – though perhaps what she really wanted was respite from the demons inside her own head. She hesitated for a moment, then turned along one of the side streets that led to the old Free Church, deconsecrated and empty now.

Gary was there, in the graveyard – all that was left of him, her bright hope. They wouldn't let her put 'Murdered' on the headstone, as she'd wanted to, so all that was carved on the polished granite was his name, dates, and 'Beloved son of Morven Gunn' with plenty of space for her name below when she joined him in her own lair under the turf. She often came here and even the illusion of Gary's presence always made her feel calmer.

She left the path and as she picked her way between the graves it occurred to her that she should have brought a watering can for the row of dwarf rose bushes she had planted in front of the headstone. There was dampness in the air, certainly, but they hadn't had proper rain for a fortnight.

But when she reached the grave, she saw that there were flowers laid on it beside the bushes – a big bunch of tight yellow rosebuds with a card with the initials 'G. R'. She stopped short as if the sight of them had been a slap in the face. She knew who would have put them there and she could feel the rage building in her.

The shriek burst from her in a demented spasm of purest fury. The tears poured down her cheeks as she picked the bunch of flowers up and with frantic fingers broke and tore at the blooms, scattering petals and greenery all about her. Then she stamped on them, grinding them into the earth, just as she had been ground down by Pat Curran and his devil's spawn.

CHAPTER FIVE

Rhona Mowat bent over her iPhone, trying not to let her daughter see that she was studying her across the breakfast table on Monday morning. Unusually, Kirstie was out of bed early enough to have breakfast before she went to the cafe, but she didn't seem to want anything except coffee. The piece of toast her mother had insisted on lay on her plate with a single bite taken out of it.

The girl was pale under her make-up – plastered even thicker than usual this morning – and her eyes were heavy, as if she hadn't slept well. She'd come home from work early on Saturday looking as if she'd been crying, but when Rhona had asked her what was wrong all Kirstie would mutter was that Morven Gunn was a cow and she hated her.

She'd been subdued all Sunday, but she seemed to be planning to go to work this morning. Morven's bark was worse than her bite and if she hadn't actually sacked Kirstie, the storm, whatever it was, would probably have blown over.

She said, very casually, 'You going in today, Kirstie?'

Kirstie's chin came up in her usual defiant gesture. 'Course. Why wouldn't I?'

'I thought you had a bit of a run-in with Morven on Saturday?'

'So?' She shrugged. 'She's like that.'

'You're looking tired, that's all.'

'I'm fine.' She got up, tipped her uneaten toast into the bin and left her plate and mug on the draining board. As her mother opened her mouth to say, 'Dishwasher!' a police car drew up in the yard and Kirstie jumped and gave a little gasp.

Rhona looked at her sharply. She should have thought about it sooner; Kirstie might look fifteen going on twenty-five, but she was still just a child and it would hardly be surprising if a body found on her own doorstep had spooked her a bit. They hadn't told her about the ravens but there was little doubt she'd have been furnished with all the gruesome details by the gossip in the cafe. The sinister white-clad figures that went to and fro up the track to the cottage were a constant reminder and Rhona hadn't been sleeping very well herself, thinking about it.

She got up as the policeman came to the door. 'Oh, it's Jack,' she said to Kirstie. 'He'll be looking for a cup of coffee, probably.' They had got to know the lads working around the cottage quite well over the last few days.

'I'm just going.' Kirstie picked up her backpack from the corner, opened the door and said hello to the officer, then went quickly off across the yard.

PS Jack Lothian watched her go. 'She looks keen to get to her work,' he said.

'Makes a change,' Rhona said dryly. 'Coffee? There's some in the pot.'

'Thanks, but no thanks. There's a lot on today. Fergus about?'

She gestured vaguely. 'Somewhere around. I can give him a message when he gets in.'

'I was wanting to speak to both of you. There's a DI coming up from Edinburgh – inquiry's being scaled up. Apparently it's a murder investigation now.'

'*Murder?* But I thought it was just—'

'Yes,' Lothian said heavily. 'We all did.' He didn't look happy.

It was proving to be a busy morning in the Curran Services office. An order hadn't appeared for urgent delivery to a West Franklin rig and now Ailie Johnston was hanging on the phone trying to find out why. Then she'd have to try to find another supplier who could step in at short notice and that wasn't going to be easy.

She'd been planning to check up on Niall Aitchison first thing – she hadn't been able to get him out of her mind all weekend – but by the time she'd found a solution to the problems that seemed to multiply with every fresh call she made, it was late morning.

Had he appeared today? He certainly hadn't come to see her as he did most days, usually when he wanted to have a bitch about his latest problem with Bruce Michie. While she was too professional to join in, she was quite prepared to make sympathetic noises, and given that according to

Michie they'd had a set-to when last Niall was in, she'd have expected a visit.

Oh, she really hoped he was just stuck at his desk dealing with what had piled up last week. If not, whatever Michie said, she'd feel she had to give up her lunch break and trail away round to Niall's flat to find out what the problem was.

He wasn't. His office was empty and when Ailie went along to the main office to ask the secretary who most regularly worked for him if she knew where he was, the girl looked blank.

'Is he on holiday?' she said without much interest.

'*I* don't know, Donna,' Ailie said sharply. 'Is he? When did you last see him?'

Donna gazed into the middle distance. 'Couldn't really say. Maybe last week sometime.'

'He wasn't in last week. Did he say anything about going away?'

She shrugged. 'Could've, I suppose. Don't remember.'

'Thanks, Donna. That's a great help,' Ailie said with heavy sarcasm. She really was a useless quine, that one. But even when she asked other, less vacuous staff there was no more information.

Of course, it was possible there had just been a mix-up over holidays, but it still wouldn't explain why he wasn't answering his phone. Bruce Michie's facetious remark about the lifeless body and the cat had somehow stuck in her mind. She'd no reason to suppose Niall even had a cat, but the uneasy feeling she'd been trying to dismiss returned.

Gabrielle slept late. The sleeping pills left her feeling groggy and she staggered into the bathroom for a long shower with her eyes half-shut. That helped, though she was still feeling faintly nauseous as she dressed and went downstairs to breakfast.

David heard her and emerged from the study; after being offshore he'd be able to work from home for a couple of days. She'd be glad of his company to fill the empty hours, even though his nannying sometimes got a bit oppressive.

He was doing it now, his pleasant, open face creased into lines of worry as he looked at her. 'All right?' he said.

She stiffened. 'Is there some reason why I shouldn't be? Did I disturb you last night when I wasn't sleeping?'

'No, no,' he said hastily. 'Coffee? There's some in the pot.'

'Thanks,' she said, sitting down at the table where he'd laid out her breakfast for her as usual. She didn't believe him. He was running his hand through his fair hair now and after he'd given her coffee he made to go back to his study but was hovering. Yes, he was definitely anxious about something.

'David, is there something wrong?'

'No, of course not. I was just wondering if you had plans for the day?'

'Not really – a walk, perhaps. If you're not busy, maybe we could go somewhere for lunch.'

He seized on that. 'What a good idea. You finish your breakfast and then you're to have a rest. No housework for you today, my girl; you get so tired when you've had a bad night. You go out and sit in the sunshine They're saying the weather's meant to break soon so we have to make the most of it. Give me an hour just to do a couple of things and then I'll be ready.'

'You spoil me, darling,' she said, and he dropped a kiss on the top of her head and went back to the study.

Despite the sun pouring in through the kitchen window,

she felt a chill of dismay. He worried about her so much, she tried so hard to keep signs of her deterioration from him – only yesterday she'd retrieved her purse from the freezer just before he went to get ice for their drinks. But now there was definitely something. Something she'd done to worry him that she couldn't remember? And if she had, did she even want to know?

With a sort of dreary hopelessness, Gabrielle took a mouthful of the cereal, but it felt dusty in her mouth and she scooped what was left into the food compost bin. She picked up her coffee and dutifully went out onto the terrace at the back to do as she was told. The decking was rotting in places and it wasn't much of a garden either, just a badly kept lawn with a few straggling bushes beside the fence that marked the boundary with the rough ground beyond. The stillness was broken only by the insistent low hum of a million insects and the unnatural heat and the heavy, damp smell of stagnant water from the surrounding bogland was oppressive; she could feel a headache developing. Often at this time of day she would still feel doped and drop off again, though she hated doing it, feeling confused when she woke up. But today she was restless. She'd be better off inside, doing something to occupy herself, whatever David said.

She stood looking round the immaculate kitchen. A moment later, she heard David come out of his study and then the sound of the washing machine starting up. She frowned. What on earth was needing to be washed? In her enforced idleness she seized on things to do and dirty clothes barely hit the clothes basket before she whipped them away for laundering. As she went towards the tiny utility room, David came out.

He jumped when he saw her. 'Oh – I thought you were in the garden?'

'Came in. It's a bit sticky out there. What are you washing?'

'Er – just thought I'd wash the sheets.'

She looked at him blankly. 'But I changed them yesterday!'

'Oh well, I didn't know that, did I? Won't do any harm.'

Her anxiety was making her angry. 'David, you know you never change the sheets. What was wrong with them?'

David tried to say, 'Nothing,' then faltered under her fierce gaze. 'I-I didn't want to tell you.'

'Tell me what?'

'Look, promise me you're not going to worry about this,' he said, taking her hand and leading her back to the kitchen table to sit down. 'It was just that I woke up last night, well, early morning, really, and you weren't there – you must have disturbed me when you got up. I could see you weren't in the bathroom and when I went downstairs the front door was open and you were walking away, across the road and out into the bog. I called but you didn't pay any attention. When I caught up with you, your eyes were wide open, but you didn't seem to see me. So, I realised you must be sleepwalking – you didn't even jump when I took your elbow.

'I just guided you back up to bed and you seemed quite ready to lie down and go back to sleep. But the sheets were muddy – I thought if I washed them while you were outside you wouldn't have to know – unless you noticed your feet were dirty?'

Gabrielle shook her head. 'Just went straight into the shower.' She began to shake, and then the tears came. 'Oh God, what am I doing to you? Why don't you just put me away and have done with it? Resting isn't doing any good – I'm getting worse. What am I going to do next?' She smudged the tears away with her fingers, but they kept trickling down.

David picked up a box of tissues, then sat down beside her and pushed them forward. 'Come on, mop up. Worse things happen at sea, as my mother always used to say. Irritated the hell out of me, actually.' He tried to catch her eye, but her head was bent over the table and he put his hand below her chin and tilted it up. 'Hey! You're supposed to laugh at your husband's jokes – it's a wife's duty. Particularly if they're not very funny.'

She managed a watery smile but even though he was smiling too it didn't hide the concern in his blue eyes. 'Sorry,' she muttered, wiping her eyes with a tissue.

'Don't be silly. You only need to apologise for something you did deliberately. I understand what a strain you're under, darling. Now listen – sleepwalking isn't a big deal. It's not a sign of anything else, it's just a common manifestation of stress. Look at what you've had to cope with! And you take those sleeping pills, don't you? That could be a factor. And sometimes something as simple as being uncomfortable can put you into that sort of disturbed state – like being too hot, you know?'

'I suppose so,' she said, blowing her nose and then it struck her. 'David, you seem to know a lot about it. Have I done this before?'

He was taken aback. 'Er, no . . . er, I just looked it up on my laptop this morning.' He opened his blue eyes wide, the picture of innocence.

'You always were a rotten liar. I have, haven't I?'

David sighed. 'OK, OK. Only once, that I know of. Last

week. You'd gone downstairs and were standing looking out of the window in the sitting room. Not a problem. I guess we just lock the outside doors, so you don't go out and come to any harm.'

Gabrielle's lip trembled. 'But we never lock the doors here! It would be like being in a *prison*!'

He ran his hand through his hair again, looking helpless. 'Maybe you should talk to Malcolm about it.'

'Maybe,' she said, though she had no intention of doing it. She'd consulted her stepfather professionally when she first came back and after five minutes he had dashed off a prescription for antidepressants. They had lain in the bathroom cabinet, untouched – she took enough drugs already just to get a few hours' sleep.

'It's up to you, sweetheart. You know I love you and I'm behind you whatever you decide to do.' He leant forward to kiss her, then stood up. 'Just a couple more things to finish up. I'll be ready to go in five minutes.'

Gabrielle watched him go. Sometimes she'd felt he was too inclined to let her make all their decisions. She certainly had the stronger character, but he would do anything for her and what she had seen as weakness was the flip side of gentleness and kindness. Even if she lost it completely he would tend to her with care and compassion.

She'd kill herself first.

The pathologist who met DI Kelso Strang in reception at the Scientific Services lab in Aberdeen was a young Asian woman. She was small and slight in her white coat, but the glasses she wore had heavy tortoiseshell frames.

Were they, Strang wondered, specially chosen to counteract any impression of youthful inexperience? She certainly exuded an air of fierce competence, as if mutely responding to some argument it hadn't yet occurred to him to offer.

She introduced herself as Dr Kashani and led him through to a small office where there was no central desk, only a wide shelf down one side with an impressive array of equipment: he recognised the computer terminals, a microscope and, he thought, a centrifuge but the rest meant nothing to him. It was clinically tidy.

She swung round a couple of office chairs and waved him towards one as she reached into a filing cabinet and unhesitatingly pulled out a file.

'I can give you a brief summary of my findings. DI Hay has officially viewed the cadaver already, but you may want me to take you along to the mortuary to inspect it, just to put this in context . . . ?'

In the course of his service, in the army and the police force, he'd seen bodies in various states of dismemberment and decay, but it had not left him with any enthusiasm for viewing one unless in the strict line of duty, and from the report this one would be peculiarly unpleasant.

'That won't be necessary,' he said, ignoring Dr Kashani's look of disappointment – or was it contempt? 'I'd be grateful if you could talk me through it, as far as you can tell. In layman's language, if you would – I'm afraid I'm not a scientist.'

He had ventured a smile, but she only said, 'I see.' Now he was sure that it was contempt.

She consulted her notes. 'It was assumed by the police

doctor at the scene that the cadaver was that of a male who had been sleeping rough so cause of death was likely to be either overdose or natural causes. It was transferred to Wick Hospital where the pathologist carried out a formal assessment. His initial findings were of blunt force trauma to the back of the head and there were signs that death had been caused by respiratory impairment from being in or under a liquid.'

'Do you mean he drowned?'

'If you like,' she said stiffly. 'There was also evidence that the body had been moved post-mortem.'

She was beginning to irritate him. 'Evidence beyond the fact that he had been discovered in a place that was, as I understand it, perfectly dry?'

'I couldn't comment on that. The evidence I am talking about related to subcutaneous hypostasis – in layman's language, that's—'

'Where blood gathers after death. Yes, I know about lividity.'

For the first time Dr Kashani gave a nod of approval. 'Good. So, I was able to establish that when death occurred he was lying prone, but on his side when found.'

'I suppose if I ask you for an estimated time of death you will give me the standard "between the time when he was last seen and the time the body was discovered"?'

She permitted herself a small smile. 'I can do a little better than that, DCI Strang. He had been dead for at least two or three days, very possibly more, by the time the body was examined. And further, since the only sign of lividity was consonant with the prone position I can state that after death the body wasn't moved for some time, very approximately six to ten hours—no,' as he made to speak, 'I can't be more precise on how much longer than that it might have been left.'

Strang thought of crime scene pictures he had seen of other bodies after a few days. 'But if it was any length of time, moving it would be an extremely distasteful business?'

'Of course, but not to quite the extent you would imagine. A preservative process had begun, the result of the very low pH value of the drowning element, I would imagine, though we will have to wait for the test results to come in to get confirmation.'

'Low pH? Acidic? Do you mean the body was – was *pickled*?'

She gave a little grimace. 'No. But I suppose you might say that this was the very preliminary stage of a tanning process. It would decay quite rapidly once it was moved, especially in this heat.'

Strang thought about that for a moment. Flow Country – bogs – there was something about ancient bog bodies, wasn't there? 'Does that mean it is likely to have been in a peat bog?'

She recoiled. 'I couldn't possibly say that. Samples are being processed and I'm sure when you get the results—'

'Dr Kashani, I appreciate that you need to be cautious, but perhaps *you* can appreciate that in a murder inquiry I can't just say airily, "Oh, we can't do anything until the test results come through." I'll be going on up to Caithness today to set one in place. Would the peat bogs in the area be a useful preliminary focus?'

She pursed her lips and something in him snapped. 'Oh, for goodness' sake! A man has been killed. It's not a "cadaver", it's his dead body. It's my job to get justice for him to the best of my ability and time is the enemy. Witnesses forget, evidence gets destroyed. I'm not going to report you to the pathologists' union for making an intelligent guess!'

Kashani flushed. 'You're implying that I'm insensitive. I'm not. I'm professional. And part of my professional training is that we proceed only on the basis of scientific evidence. I'm in the justice business just as much as you are, and wild guesses won't get you a conviction in court.'

'No. I know that.' She'd wrong-footed him and now he felt annoyed with himself for his outburst. 'Let me try again. Do you have any real, "*scientific*" evidence' – he couldn't resist a tiny emphasis on the word – 'that might back up my wild guess that peat bogs might be a reasonable place to start?'

She got up and went over to one of the flush panel cupboards that ran right along the wall and took out a polythene bundle of clothes. It was sealed and labelled with the date and a number. She pointed to it. 'The dead man's number,' she said. 'Matching the tag attached to his big toe.'

Not 'the cadaver's', he noted, raising an eyebrow with a slight smile. Kashani didn't look at him, but the corners of her mouth did twitch as she cut off the label and opened the bag.

The stench was indescribable: corrupt flesh, dried blood, faeces, stale urine. He gagged, but under her cool, impassive gaze forced himself to swallow hard. And then he caught the underlying smell, the faint but unmistakable smokiness of peat.

'Is a smell scientific evidence?' he asked.

'We can't perform olfactory analysis yet, though there is an electronic "nose" that's showing promise, but it's a legitimate observation. Had enough?'

Strang nodded and she tied up the bag again. He suspected she had relished his discomfort and that she might now be more inclined to be helpful.

Strang said carefully, 'So, Doctor, are there any other observations that you would feel qualified to make?'

She seemed pleased by the form of words. 'He had expensive clothes. The shirt and jeans are both Burberry.'

'So, not a down-and-out, then.'

'I didn't say that!' She looked alarmed.

'Of course not. He could be a down-and-out who struck lucky begging at a house whose wealthy and eccentric owners regularly purged their wardrobe. On the other hand, it could be a useful hypothesis that the clothes he was wearing belonged to him. Fingernails?'

He didn't have to explain. 'Well-cared-for, with no evidence of manual labour on his hands,' she said. 'And there were no signs of substance abuse or disease.'

'Healthy apart from being dead, you mean.'

She was ambushed into a surprisingly hearty laugh. 'Yes, Inspector, I suppose you could say that.'

Strang chanced his arm. 'There, that didn't hurt, did it?'

Kashani gave him a sidelong look but otherwise ignored it. 'I'm sure you have a lot more questions, but I have a very heavy schedule today.' She took a sheet of paper from the top of her notes. 'The full report is online, but this is a brief digest of the most significant of my findings.'

'Ah, the Janet-and-John bit,' he said provocatively.

The pathologist sighed. 'DCI Strang, I'm happy to be frivolous when I'm not working. When I am, I'm serious.'

That threw him slightly, though not for the reason she

perhaps imagined it would. Yes, perhaps he had become more 'frivolous' lately. After Alexa's death he had been serious for a very long time, but Finella had said something recently about him being more like his old self. Recovery implied a lessening of the pain of loss and that in itself was painful.

'Sorry, Dr Kashani. I can appreciate that.' He speed-read the sheet. 'That's very clear. Thank you.' He got up and held out his hand.

She had small hands but a surprisingly powerful grip. 'Good luck. It's a very unusual case.'

She was certainly right there.

At one o'clock Ailie fetched her bag from her desk and left the office. No need to bother with a jacket: it was what Aberdonians call 'an awfie grand day'. The jet stream, allegedly, had got itself stuck in some particularly favourable position for the north of Scotland and they'd had clear, brilliant blue skies for more than a week now. Fine, settled weather being rare made you appreciate it more and there was a definite holiday feeling in the grey streets today with people sitting at tables outside cafes in short sleeves – even the odd Hawaiian shirt for the seriously venturesome. The flecks of mica in the pale granite sparkled and even the wind off the sea was no more than a pleasant breeze.

Ailie had never been to Niall Aitchison's flat. It was in one of the narrow streets leading off the top of Union Street, a desirably central area, and when she reached the address it was a handsome, substantially built tenement block. Victorian, from the look of it, and Niall's flat was main door with its own tiny strip of garden in front, so it was quite a pricey property – or at least it would have been until recently, when the bottom had fallen out of the market with the downturn in the oil business.

He'd probably open the door and explain he'd just taken a bit of unpaid leave without making sure people knew. Ailie told herself it was irrational to be feeling nervous as she rang the bell, but there was no reply even after she rang again, a longer, imperative peal, and she stepped to the side, leaning forward to peer in the window on the left of the door with her hand cupped to the glass. The front room was neat, unremarkable – a sofa and a couple of chairs on either side of an old-fashioned fireplace, a large-screen TV at one end. And empty. No sign of a body – or a cat.

'Are you looking for Niall?' a voice said.

Ailie turned round. There was a young woman with a child in a pushchair standing at the door to the upper flats with a key in her hand, just about to let herself in.

'Yes,' Ailie said gratefully. 'I'm from his office – he didn't come in last week and when he didn't appear today we were getting concerned. Is he all right?'

'Oh yes, as far as I know. I spoke to him – when was it? Oh yes, the Friday before last. He was just away off to Caithness, like he does at the weekend sometimes. Can't remember the name of the place—'

'Forsich,' Ailie supplied. 'He grew up there. His mother died quite recently.'

'That's right,' the woman said. 'He said he was keeping on the house, though, so maybe he's stayed on to sort things out.' From the pushchair came a little wail and she said, 'Oh, sorry, he's hungry. I'll need to give him his lunch. All right?'

'Of course. Thanks very much.'

Ailie walked back down the street. That was an answer of a sort: at least he hadn't been taken ill suddenly, as even quite young people were sometimes, and been lying there helpless or – well, worse, as she had begun to think he might be. But it still wasn't like Niall not to answer his phone, wherever he was. Not like Niall at all.

He'd been Pat's right-hand man, staying behind in Forsich at his mother's to handle the fallout when the drainage venture failed and Pat went off to Aberdeen to retrieve his fortunes, until such time as there was a place for him at Curran Services. She couldn't remember the details – it was near enough ten years ago – but the death of a teenager had featured and there had been boiling hatred for Pat, and by extension for the representative who'd been, in essence, the scapegoat. It was brave of Niall to keep on a property in the place now his mother was gone, though considering the virulence of some of the correspondence that had crossed her desk she'd call it foolhardy, herself.

As Ailie walked back to her office, her feelings of disquiet were stronger than ever. Niall had always been so utterly reliable; devoted to Pat and to Gabrielle as well – indeed, she'd sometimes thought his feelings for Gabrielle were more than just those of a loyal employee. Not that it would have come to anything; he was a quiet man, shy and, well, dull if she was being honest. She doubted if it had ever crossed Gabrielle's mind even to think of him in that context.

But now Ailie thought about it, there had been some big bust-up with Michie. She didn't know any of the details except that the boss had talked about giving Niall a flea in his ear. Was Niall sulking in his cottage, deliberately remaining out of reach just to be difficult? That seemed perfectly possible.

She'd have to report to Michie, though, and he wasn't going to take it well. Niall might have a seat on the board but with Gabrielle absent there would be nothing to stop Michie, as the second-biggest shareholder, sacking him from his job.

Niall ought to be warned. Ailie had been told that Gabrielle mustn't be bothered, but she could always phone David, ask him to go round to Niall's house and check out the situation. David was a nice lad, very supportive – he wouldn't mind.

She had almost reached the office. It was as she went into a shop to buy a sandwich to eat at her desk that a headline in the *Press and Journal* caught her eye.

MAN'S BODY FOUND ON CAITHNESS FARM, it ran with the subheading, RAVENS FOUND HIM FIRST.

She stooped to read it. The word 'Forsich' seemed to leap out at her from the page and suddenly she understood the clichéd phrase, 'my blood ran cold'.

CHAPTER SIX

After his interview with Dr Kashani, DCI Strang went along to the reception area where there was a bench he could sit on to study her summary, the starting point for establishing the victim's identity.

Height, 5'8", weight 145 lbs, estimated age – not very helpful, this last, since the only visible evidence related to the bone fusion, which is completed around twenty-five. There was no sign of age-related compression of the spine so, Strang reflected ruefully, it placed the victim somewhere between twenty-five and sixty. That didn't narrow the field much.

He had had brown hair, very slightly greying, and there had been enough left of one eye to show that they had been brown. No distinguishing features. Strang sighed. A defining birthmark might have been too much to hope for, but this was a description that could fit every other guy you passed in the street. Checking the list of Missing Persons hadn't given them any possibles either, so DNA test results would

out to grab a sandwich. Can I buy you one as a thank you?'

She gave another smile, but a more constrained one. 'No, thank you, Inspector.'

He felt rebuffed. 'No? Just a coffee?'

'Sorry. My husband wouldn't like it.' She went to the door, taking out a gauzy headscarf that she draped over her head as she stepped outside.

'Oh – sorry,' Strang found himself saying to her back. He sat down again, feeling faintly aggrieved. He hadn't noticed her wedding ring; he wasn't asking her out for a date, after all. It was only a friendly gesture between colleagues. And, of course, he'd have done the same if she'd been fifty-five and matronly. Of course.

He wasn't that much of hypocrite. Of course he wouldn't; Dr Kashani had rather intrigued him with her fierce professionalism and he'd enjoyed making her laugh. And again, there was that sharp pinprick of pain. It seemed disloyal to Alexa to find himself attracted, even in this very slight way, to another woman.

Strang gathered up his belongings and went out to have lunch. By himself.

Monday was a quiet day for the Lemon Tree cafe, usually. Not today. Today it had been almost as busy as it had been on Saturday. Looking out from the little kitchen at the crowded tables with a jaundiced eye, Morven Gunn scowled.

There were tourists there among a few regulars and from their conversation they weren't just dropping in for a cup of tea on their way round the North Coast 500 scenic route – ghouls! One, a fat man whose face was sweaty, red and peeling from too much sun and who looked as if he might at any moment burst out of his Rangers football shirt, had actually had the brass neck to ask her how to reach the farm where they'd found the body; she had shrivelled him with one look and stalked away.

Kirstie was taking the orders and serving, but she wasn't her usual self. She was smart enough to know that being smiley and chatting up the customers was the way to bump up her tips but there was none of that today. She looked wan and was moving among the tables like a robot. If this was some sort of sulky protest about getting her pay docked she'd better snap out of it soon or she'd be looking for another job and Morven would be looking for a new waitress.

She bent to get a fresh tray of scones out of the oven. The blast of hot air added to the heat in the tiny kitchen and she seized a length of kitchen roll to mop her sweating face. She hadn't been prepared for the extra numbers, so she was hard-pressed to keep up with demand, and lunch orders would be starting any minute. She was turning the scones out onto a rack and when she heard the bell on the cafe door jingle again her first thought was, *Bloody hell, how many more?*

The sudden stillness alerted her to the arrival of someone who wasn't just another ordinary customer and she went to the door and looked through. The newcomer was a uniformed policeman, though with his chubby face adorned with an unconvincing moustache he could have been a schoolboy dressing up. She heard him say, 'Kirstie Mowat? Can I have a word with you?'

Kirstie was carrying a loaded tray. She stared at him,

ashen-faced, and then she swayed and crumpled to the floor in a sea of coffee and smashed crockery. The customers at the nearest table jumped up and one woman screamed. The constable's jaw dropped and he stood looking helplessly around at the chaos he had caused.

Morven erupted from the kitchen. 'Could you not have caught her before she fell, you useless gomeril! Don't just stand there – clear up the mess, if you can't think of anything better to do.' She crouched over Kirstie as another woman came forward; recognising the local nurse she stood back.

'She'll be all right. Just leave her a wee moment,' the nurse said and indeed Kirstie's eyelids were fluttering, and she was struggling to sit up. 'Take it gently, now, pet. That's it – you're fine. Just let me put an arm round your shoulders – there you are! Now, up we go – let's get you onto a chair.'

A chair was pushed forward and Kirstie, coffee-stained and starting to cry, slumped onto it. Morven brought a glass of water from the back and the nurse took it from her.

'You drink some of that – that's better, isn't it? It's all this heat – we're not used to it. And I bet you didn't have a proper breakfast before you came – is that right?' Kirstie nodded, sniffling into a tissue a sympathetic customer had provided. 'Is your mum at home? You just finish your drink, then I'll take you back to have a wee lie-down – that's all you're needing.'

As Kirstie sipped obediently, the constable cleared his throat significantly. 'I'll still have to speak to you, miss—'

There was a swell of disapproval, a sort of growling mutter, and someone hissed. His face went bright red. Before anyone else could speak, Morven turned on him. 'Not done enough damage? You've no right to speak to a minor without her parents present. You were lucky she didn't hit her head on the corner of the table and kill herself or you'd be up for manslaughter. Now you can clear this up – you'll find a shovel through in the back.'

'I'm within my rights,' he said stubbornly. 'And it's up to you to clear up the mess.'

Morven advanced towards him, crockery crunching underfoot. 'We'll see who's got rights. We don't pay your wages to get rudeness. Get out my cafe! You've not heard the last of this.'

The ripple of applause settled it. Clutching the tattered rags of his professional dignity about him, the constable retreated with a sinking feeling in his inside. Maybe this was one of these things said in the heat of the moment that people didn't really mean, but he had a nasty feeling that the old bag had meant every word of it.

And he still had to interview the girl, at home this time. He could only hope her parents were more reasonable.

DCI Strang had just finished his lunch when a call came in from Angie Andrews, in Edinburgh. She was the Force Civilian Assistant allocated to admin for the SRCS and a constant source of stress for Strang, who was haunted by the fear that she'd be poached by someone who could pull rank on him; she had the rare talent of combining superb efficiency with an amused acceptance of the deficiencies of others. His only comfort was that she scorned any form of hierarchical respect and top brass tended not to like being treated as just another of Jock

Tamson's bairns – and not one of the brightest, at that.

'Where are you, Kelso? Still dossing around in Aberdeen? You're in luck, then. The station there's sent through details of a witness with something to say about your Caithness case and they're happy for you to follow it up, so you better get your ass over there before you go.'

Strang brightened. 'Great timing, Angie. Give me the details.' He wrote them down, then paused, frowning. 'Tell the hotel I'll be late, OK? I was hoping to get it all kicked off up there today but once I've spoken to this Ailie Johnston and called in at Thurso, I'm not going to have time to set up anything for tomorrow morning.

'Still, if she's got something useful to tell me it'll be worth it,' he said, adding darkly, 'If.'

Angie laughed. 'Cheer up, misery guts! Could crack it wide open, for all you know.'

'Oh sure. Maybe it could.' He was trying to feel more optimistic as he rang off. People who phoned in after a murder weren't all nutters. Just most of them.

She hadn't wanted the nurse to take her home. The last thing Kirstie needed was her parents to be given a dramatic account of what had happened in the cafe; it was going to be hard enough anyway to think of an excuse that would fob her mother off, especially since her head was still swimming.

When they reached the gate at the end of the short drive leading up to the farmhouse, she turned to her escort with her most charming smile. 'Thank you *so* much for looking after me. I'm feeling fine now – just the heat, you know, and I've learnt my lesson about not eating breakfast.'

The nurse glanced towards the house. 'Someone'll be in, will they? Just in case you have another funny turn.'

'Oh yes. Even if Mum's out, Dad'll be back soon for his lunch.' Not yet, with any luck, and if Mum really was out she'd have a chance to leave a note saying she wasn't feeling well and slip upstairs to bed. Then she could pretend to be asleep when someone came to check; that would give her time to figure out how to deal with the situation.

Kirstie waved an airy goodbye then let herself into the house quietly. She was in luck: there was no one in the kitchen. She scribbled her note then went upstairs and got into bed. Despite the sticky heat she was shivering – with shock, she supposed. She hadn't believed that Calum would tell but he had, obviously. The policeman hadn't wanted to speak to her for fun.

She had no scruples about lying if it worked, but if Calum had dobbed her in there'd be no point in denying his story – they wouldn't believe her. So, they'd want to know why she hadn't come forward like he did once she'd heard what had happened. So, what could she say?

It wasn't as if Kirstie had done anything wrong, not really – certainly nothing the police would care about. But if Dad and Mum found out she'd been sneaking out to meet Calum in the cottage in the middle of the night they wouldn't buy the idea that it had just been to sit and chat.

If she could get to the police, talk to them before someone came to the house, maybe she could persuade them not to clype to her parents. She'd seen them setting up in the village hall earlier on; she could go there and speak to them before they came to find her.

She heard the back door opening and a minute later footsteps on the stairs. She pulled up the bedcover and shut her eyes as her bedroom door opened. Her mother's voice said, 'Kirstie – oh,' then paused and Kirstie could feel that she was being looked at. She lay still, breathing smoothly and deeply, and heard her mother withdraw quietly without shutting the door.

Then her father's voice was calling from downstairs, 'Rhona? Are you in?' and her mother was saying, 'Sssh! Don't wake her. She's come back, not feeling well. I thought she wasn't right, these last couple of days. You know, I think she's been upset with all that's been going on here.'

'*She's* upset! We're all upset,' her father grumbled, though in a lower voice. 'Haven't been able to get around the farm this morning for folk getting in my way.' Then a door shut, and Kirstie couldn't hear any more.

The trouble was, they certainly wouldn't let her go anywhere this afternoon. But after the way Morven had set about the policeman this morning she didn't think he'd try again today – and anyway, if he did he'd be told she was ill. She could get up later today, say she was fine now and be out first thing to see someone and confess. It was the best she could do, but if Calum thought she would let him off being a treacherous little snake, he'd another think coming.

She yawned. She really was very tired. She'd hardly slept the last couple of nights.

When Rhona looked in later, Kirstie was snoring gently.

Ailie Johnston was nervous. Apart from anything else she felt uncomfortable about overrunning her lunch hour –

something she never did – but she didn't want the police turning up at the office. Bruce Michie might be annoyed if he went looking for her now and couldn't find her but if he realised what she'd done he'd go crazy, especially if it turned out to be just some daft notion of hers. She'd told herself it probably was, and the policeman might give her a hard time too and make her feel stupid – you heard bad things about them these days. Even though in any dealings she'd had with them herself they'd seemed nice enough, this maybe wasn't the smartest thing she'd ever done.

As she sat at a corner table in Starbucks where she had a good view of the door, she looked round the cafe. It was quiet at this time of the day apart from a couple of women finishing a late lunch and two men on their own, one working on a laptop and the other speaking on his phone. It wouldn't be difficult for the inspector to work out who she was – and that was him coming in now probably, given the way his eyes swept round, taking in everything. He was a good-looking lad, tall and well set-up with reddish-brown hair and hazel eyes – *Pity about the scar running down the right side of his face though*, she thought, as he turned his head towards her. You'd think they could do something about that, but maybe it didn't bother him.

He had a nice smile too as he came towards her. 'Mrs Johnston? DCI Strang,' he said, showing her a plastic ID card. 'May I sit down?'

Feeling a little flustered – should she shake his hand or just wave him to a seat? – she half-stood up, then sat down again. 'Yes – yes, of course.'

He didn't, as she had thought he would, get himself a

coffee. The barista had given him a sharp glance as he came in and had seen him produce his card, then turned away so ostentatiously that Ailie realised she'd better keep her voice as low as possible.

'Thank you for getting in touch with us.' Strang sat down and produced a small gadget from his pocket, setting it on the table between them. 'Do you mind if I record what you're saying? Easier than me licking my pencil and writing it down.'

She gave a little laugh, mainly of relief. 'That's fine. I'll just turn round so I'm facing it – that loon over there behind the counter has his ears flapping.'

Strang smiled again. 'I had noticed.' He switched on the machine. 'Right, Mrs Johnston—'

'Ailie.'

He nodded, identified himself for the tape then said, 'Ailie, there's something you want to tell us about the murder case in Forsich, is that right?'

He was very easy to talk to, making quiet encouraging noises, prompting her with a question when she hesitated. He showed no sign of impatience as Ailie told him the whole story – Pat Curran, the failed drainage company and local resentment, the success of Curran Services, even poor Gabrielle's problems – and she could feel his interest sharpening as she went on. The cold feeling that she'd tried to put down to an overactive imagination came back in force. Could it really have been Niall, lying there for the ravens to find?

At last she ran down. 'That was it, really.'

'You've been very helpful. Can you describe Niall Aitchison for me?'

highly visible if the media wasn't to start on again about the cuts to local CID. He'd been hoping that by now he'd have had a chance to second a couple of likely officers in Thurso instead of expensive imports from Edinburgh, but because the investigation looked like moving on a lot faster since the interview with Ailie Johnston he couldn't drag his feet. He'd have to phone the boss and brief her.

DCS Borthwick sounded harassed but was pleased that it looked as if there might be speedy identification of the body and agreed with the need for an immediate presence. 'Go ahead – I'll arrange authorisation for a DS and a DC, leaving ASAP.'

'Thanks, ma'am. I've another interview that sounds promising – the boss who had a barney with—'

She cut him short. 'Sorry, Kelso, I've got a meeting. Put it in your report – I want to be kept in the picture but you're in charge. You've got plenty of experience under your belt now and I have every confidence.' She rang off.

Feeling gratified if just a little nervous, Strang called Angie to ask her to make the arrangements.

'Told you so,' she said smugly. 'You'll have this whole thing wrapped up in a couple of days.'

'Smug isn't pretty. Any chance of Dave McAllister? I worked with him on the Ayrshire case – he's good.'

'On leave. If you want action today, you'll have to take pot luck. Beggars can't be choosers, sweetie.'

Strang grimaced. 'I suppose you're right.'

'I always am.'

'You can go off some people. Anyway, do your best. The idea is to get them up there and installed tonight and I'll get back to you with their orders for tomorrow morning, OK?'

He glanced anxiously at his watch as he ended the call. He'd have to hurry if he was to catch Bruce Michie at Curran Services before he went home, and he'd have to make his excuses and ask DI Hay to meet him at Forsich in the morning.

DC Livvy Murray was swearing under her breath at the screen in front of her, which had chosen this moment to freeze. Resisting the temptation to inflict GBH on the bloody thing, she grovelled on the floor to switch it off and switch it back on again, then had to wait while it put up stupid little welcome messages and demanded that she log in.

She was alone in the CID room with two more hours of her shift to go and no excuse for not clearing some of the backlog of reports her sarge had been trying to offload for days. When Angie Andrews came in, she looked up hopefully.

'Tell me I urgently have to go out to a call,' she begged. 'I was a sitting duck when that bastard Williamson was on the prowl and now I'm slave labour.'

'Better than that, Livvy,' Angie said. 'How long would it take you to throw a few things in a suitcase?'

Her face brightened. 'Tell me how many pairs of knickers I need, and I'll be ready in ten. Where's the job? Tell me it's a fugitive from justice who's on the run in Spain.'

'Not exactly. It's SRCS. Caithness – you know, the case where the ravens dropped in for a quick snack before they found the poor sod.'

'Oh.' Livvy's spirits, which had risen, suddenly sank. 'That . . . that's the one Strang's heading, isn't it?'

Angie raised her eyebrows. 'You said that like you think it's a bad thing. What's wrong with Kelso? Could quite fancy him, myself.'

She went pink. 'No, it's not that. Just . . . well—'

'Oh, I remember. Did the heroic bit for you, didn't he? He's probably forgotten about it.' Then she added, 'Well, more or less.'

'*I* haven't,' Livvy said darkly. 'Though I suppose this was bound to happen sometime. Am I on my own?'

'Not exactly,' Angie said. 'There's DS Kevin Taylor as well.'

Something about the way she said it made Livvy look at her sharply. 'Don't know him. What's he like?'

'Just came last week. He was in Bathgate before.'

'Even so, he *might* be all right. I'm broad-minded.'

'That's good. You'll have to be. Arrange the following words into a well-known phrase or saying: pig, chauvinist, male.'

Livvy put her head down on the desk with a despairing groan. 'Suddenly writing up reports looks strangely appealing, you know that? Oh well, give me the details and I'll go home and pack. Jerseys, mostly, I suppose. It's pretty much the Arctic Circle up there, isn't it?'

CHAPTER SEVEN

'Oh, don't tell me! I've got Ailie Johnston to thank for this, haven't I?' Bruce Michie's eyes were positively popping with rage at being subjected to the indignity of police interrogation on the flimsy grounds that one of his workforce seemed to have disappeared.

Without replying, DCI Strang looked stonily at the short, plump man with the damp, mean little mouth who was sitting behind a desk that looked much too big for him on an imposing leather chair that prevented his feet from touching the floor. It made him look like a schoolboy who'd been kitted out in his older brother's cast-offs in the forlorn hope that he'd grow into them.

After a moment, with a visible effort at control and a smile that didn't reach his eyes, Michie said, 'Oh well, you have to make allowances for her, I suppose. Her age, you know?' Then, sensing a lack of support, he hurried on, 'I blame myself, to be honest. When she was fussing that Niall hadn't been in contact with her I said something facetious about his dead body lying in his flat being nibbled by a cat and I could tell by the look on her face that the idea took hold, even though I told her not to be daft. He didn't even have a cat, for God's sake.

'Look, I'm not fashed if Niall's taken a bit of unofficial leave. He's had a difficult time lately with his mother's death and he's probably got a lot of stuff to straighten out.'

'Do you normally have such a relaxed attitude to your staff not coming in to work?'

Michie glared. 'No, of course not. But he's one of the shareholders – minor, admittedly – and considering the major shareholder has taken indefinite leave of absence, I can hardly call him out on that.'

'It's a private company, I take it? And the other shareholder – that would be Gabrielle Ross?'

He gave a little titter. 'My goodness, Ailie has been having a real heart-to-heart with you, hasn't she? Yes, Pat left Gabrielle forty-eight per cent of the company, I as the original financial backer have forty-five and Niall got the other seven per cent – probably to stop Gabrielle getting the bit between her teeth, or it could have been the pay-off for dealing with the fallout from Pat Curran's previous failure. Pat was always canny, to be honest.'

'I see. So, in Mrs Ross's absence you are running the company?'

'Yes. It's very sad – tragic, really.' Michie shook his head, his face composed into suitably sorrowful lines. 'She's completely lost the place. Of course, it's been hard for her. Very close to her father – too close, probably – and then the house fire and losing the baby she was expecting just pushed her over the edge, I suppose. To be honest, we're all wondering if she'll ever be fit to come back, poor lass.'

Expressing sympathy tended to be more convincing if you managed to keep the note of glee out of your voice and Strang also had a particular prejudice against people who said 'to be honest' too often. 'So that leaves you in charge of the business, yes?'

'Absolutely. It would have made more sense, really, if I'd taken over when Pat died, as I pointed out at the time, but Gabrielle would have none of it. She saw the whole thing as a sort of sacred trust, you know? There's no room for that sort of sentimentality in a modern business.'

'What precisely does that mean?'

It was a very direct challenge and now Michie was looking flustered. 'Oh . . . oh well, nothing specific, really. Just, you have to be hard-headed, not clinging to the way things were in the past.'

'Pat Curran wasn't hard-headed?'

'Oh God, yes! No one ever put anything over on him. It was just, Gabrielle . . .' He frowned.

He was clearly hunting for an example, Strang thought. Interesting, since he must have had something in mind in saying that, something that he didn't want to mention. But now his face had cleared.

'Ah, yes! For instance, I'm well known in Aberdeen; it would have made good business sense to add my name to the letter heading but Gabrielle wouldn't hear of that either. It was still to be Pat's baby, even now he's gone. Sentimental, you see.'

'And now you're in charge, are you going to put that in hand?'

Michie shifted uncomfortably in his chair. 'Not just at the moment, probably. We'll see.'

'Was Mr Aitchison in favour?'

'I've no idea. We never discussed it.'

'So that wasn't what you were arguing about on the last day he was in the office?'

The man's face darkened. 'Is that what she told you?'

Strang said nothing, letting the pause lengthen.

'This is ridiculous!' Michie burst out. 'You have professional disagreements in any firm and this was just one of them. If you must know, it was his job to look for new business and I wasn't satisfied with his results. He didn't agree, and we had a bit of a set-to. That was all, OK?'

'But you thought it was likely he was so upset that he didn't come in to work the next week?'

'That was what Niall was like! Sulky, difficult, not ready to accept that he wasn't Pat's little protégé any more. His problem, not mine.' Michie shrugged.

'I see. Thank you, Mr Michie. Now, just for the record, can you tell me your whereabouts over the past week?'

This time it looked as if his eyes really might pop out of their sockets. 'I don't believe this! You're asking me for an *alibi* because some menopausal woman has a fantasy that a body she read about in the papers is one of my employees? Who do I complain to about this?'

'You're entirely at liberty to refuse if you choose, sir, but this is merely standard procedure. It would mean we wouldn't have to trouble you later if there did prove to be some connection.'

'I'm a reasonable man, Inspector, but you are trying my patience.' He gave a martyred sigh. 'Still, it's simple enough. I worked here all last week and went home every night. I was there with my wife every evening except Wednesday when there was a Rotary meeting. All right?'

'And the weekend before?'

'Oh, for goodness' sake—' he protested, then seemed to think the better of it and said, with a certain bravado, 'Oh, I might as well tell you, though God knows how you'll distort this. I was in Caithness, actually, staying at a fishing hotel with a couple of friends.'

'And were you in touch with Mr Aitchison while you were up there?'

He suddenly shouted, 'No! I never went near the bloody man. All right?'

'Fine,' Strang said and stood up. 'Thank you for your cooperation, sir. If we need more details about the weekend, we'll be back in touch.'

Michie looked astonished at this abrupt conclusion. 'Is that all?'

'For the moment.'

As Strang drove away he had plenty of food for thought. If the victim was confirmed to be Niall Aitchison, the inner workings of Curran Services would certainly warrant close scrutiny.

But he wasn't going to be able to interview the person he really wanted to talk to, after what he had heard this afternoon – Pat Curran, silent in his grave, but still casting a long shadow.

* * *

DC Livvy Murray, holdall in hand, walked into the police garage where an unmarked car, and DS Kevin Taylor, should be waiting for her. She spotted the registration number she'd been given, walked over and saw that he was indeed in the driver's seat already. She slung her bag in the back and opened the passenger door.

He turned his head. He was a big man with a beer gut and ham-like arms exposed by his short-sleeved shirt. In the expanse of his moon-shaped face his small, piggy eyes barely featured so that when he smiled, Murray found her eyes drawn almost mesmerically to his wide mouth with teeth like tombstones.

He was grinning now. 'DC Murray? Well, well, they didn't tell me I was getting a girlie! Hop in, sweetheart.'

Murray's hands were curling into claws as she sat down and fastened her seat belt. Taylor revved the engine unnecessarily a couple of times and then pulled out of their parking slot a little too fast.

'Whahey!' he carolled as he pulled out into the traffic. 'All set for a holiday at the taxpayer's expense? And what happens in Thurso stays in Thurso, right?'

She could tell him to stop the car and file her complaint about sexism right now. And with the current political attitudes she'd get it upheld too – and then what? Yes, Taylor would be in for it, but she'd seen what happened to women who'd been dumb enough to think that just because they were in the right they'd get support. Oh, all the proper things would be said, and everyone would be terribly careful around you, but the easy camaraderie would disappear, and Murray wasn't about to jeopardise that for this pathetic loud-mouthed oaf – not until she'd a dossier on him that would totally nail him, anyway. And he was her superior officer, and it was a long way to Thurso. A long, long way.

'I don't think a lot happens in Thurso anyway, sir,' she forced out.

Taylor guffawed. 'It will once we get there! Oh, you got lucky today, believe me. And we've got plenty of time to get to know each other before we arrive. I'm Kevin – Kevlar to my friends.'

You have friends? She managed to say, 'Why Kevlar?' instead.

He struck his chest with his fist. 'Kevlar, like the armour stuff, as in, strong enough to stop a bullet. That's me.'

'Really.' Her tone was so acid that even he noticed. He gave a dramatic groan.

'Don't tell me – you're one of the tight-assed ones who can't take a joke. I'm going to have to watch my language or you'll have me up on a charge, right? Lezzie, are you?'

It could be easier if he thought she was. 'Do I have to answer that, sir?'

Taylor gave her an ugly look, but he seemed to have got the message that he was on seriously dangerous ground. 'No, Constable, as we both know, you don't.' He simmered in silence for a moment, then said sarcastically, 'But if it wouldn't compromise your principles too much, can I ask your name?'

'Livvy.'

'Livvy? What's that short for?'

'Olivia,' she admitted reluctantly. Being called after Olivia Newton-John by her star-struck mother was the cross she had to bear.

'Dead poncey name that.' He sniggered. 'Sort of name that makes you think you're better than us that are common as muck.'

Murray quite literally put her tongue between her teeth and trapped it there to make sure she didn't get provoked into a response. Silence was the only weapon she had, for the moment at least. She could amuse herself by trying to analyse his weak points, like a gambler looking for another player's 'tells'. Vanity, certainly, but his annoyance when she wasn't prepared to play along suggested insecurity and she could definitely work on that.

As they crossed the Forth Road Bridge, the frigid atmosphere seemed to be taking effect. Taylor glanced at her, then glanced again with what she hoped was unease and cleared his throat.

'Er . . . anyway, do you know anything about Strang? I gather he's in charge.'

Was the 'anyway' a peace offering? If so, she was happy to agree a truce – temporarily. 'He's a good officer. Clever. The DCS's blue-eyed boy. He's mostly fair but he's steely – can be pretty hard on you if you step out of line.' And she had the scars to prove it.

'You've worked with him, have you?'

'Just once, a while ago. When they were first setting up the SRCS.' Too much information, she realised, even as she spoke. Should have kept her tongue trapped.

'Where was that, then?'

'Skye.'

'Skye – right. Nice place.' Then he said, 'Hey, hang about. I've just remembered something. There was a big stushie, wasn't there – he got commended or something? Rescued a woman PC, didn't he? She'd done some daft thing. Did you know her?'

'Slightly.' The lie tripped off her tongue before her brain got into gear. Never tell a lie when the truth's on record, her reprobate one-time boyfriend had told her – the one now languishing in Barlinnie jail. She hurried on before Taylor could get in a follow-up question, 'They've sent through our orders for tomorrow, Sarge. I could check them now, if you like – save time later. It'll be late when we get there and we're on first thing tomorrow morning.'

'Might as well,' Taylor said gloomily. 'You're not going to be a barrel of laughs, anyway, are you?'

She seemed to have made her point. There was a lot more work to do towards the deflation of 'Kevlar' – huh! – but at least she'd made a start. Murray permitted herself a small smirk as she started reading.

'There's not much here. First off, we go to a house owned by Niall Aitchison – address supplied. No indication about questioning, just that we're to see him. Ask if he knows anything about the murder, I guess. After that, we report to the boss – there's an incident room set up in Forsich village hall.'

'I'm just off now Fran – OK?' the receptionist called as she went to the door. 'See you tomorrow.'

Francesca Curran said, 'Fine. Bye, Cathy!' She was working through a pile of repeat prescriptions; technically they could be left until tomorrow but unlike Cathy, who was hurrying back to get the supper ready for her family, she had no particular incentive to get finished up promptly.

She completed them and laid them ready for collection tomorrow, then sat back in her chair.

The evening loomed ahead of her. Gabrielle and David were coming round for supper and she'd have to sit there and watch him fussing round her as if she was so fragile and precious that she would break if he didn't personally wrap metaphorical cotton wool around her every time anyone said anything, and now her mother was just as bad, glaring at Fran last time when Gabrielle had said something stupid and she'd made a light-hearted remark about her being doolally. They seemed to be conspiring to make Fran feel uncomfortable.

Apparently jokes were out. She hadn't meant it; Gabrielle, in her estimation, had nothing wrong with her brain. She'd just found a way to hog the limelight in her usual manipulative way, being such a sensitive little flower that everyone had to be on tippy-toes all the time. It wasn't doing her any good, though, all this grieving and sighing about. She was looking awful and she'd clearly managed to convince herself as well as everyone else that there was a problem. If she just pulled herself together, the way Fran had had to do when things went wrong for her, there wouldn't be all this fuss.

And plenty had gone wrong. She lived daily with her regret that she'd never had quite enough energy to strike out and make a life for herself. Or was it courage she lacked? From her earliest days her father had made it clear she was a poor second best and it wasn't even as if she had been her mother's favourite, despite being the loyal one who'd stayed. Lilian somehow always seemed to suggest both daughters were rather a disappointment and didn't quite come up to her standards. She liked having Fran around, though, ready to help with entertaining or do little chores she didn't fancy doing herself.

Gabrielle had had it easy, escaping to Aberdeen with Pat while she was young enough to set up a social network and feel at home there. Fran didn't make friends easily. She had her own small group here, but she'd had to work at it and the thought of being friendless and starting from scratch had left her paralysed; she just didn't have the confidence to do it.

When she was leaving school, the receptionist's job in her stepfather's surgery had come up just at the right time – or was it the wrong time? Lilian encouraged her, and it had seemed obvious to do that until she decided what she really wanted to do with her life, but it had made it harder for her to say at any particular moment, 'Now, yes now, I'm going to make the break.'

And a receptionist's job elsewhere wouldn't pay for a decent place to stay. The Sinclairs' rambling Victorian house not only had space for a smart little self-contained flat for her but also housed the surgery – a ten-second commute to work was hard to beat as well.

She had to face it – her only hope for a home of her own, before the menacing ticking of the biological clock actually stopped, was finding a man. David had looked like the answer to her maidenly prayers and she liked to think she had been making progress until her sister ruined that for her too.

But if she was brutally honest with herself she knew that

he hadn't been that into her and what she'd felt afterwards was hurt pride not heartbreak. Even so, she couldn't forgive Gabrielle for annexing him when she had so many more opportunities than Fran did, up here in the sticks. The only man who figured in her social scene now was Niall Aitchison, and though she was finding it hard to work up the occasional pub supper at a weekend into a serious relationship, if she succeeded he would do.

Perhaps it was sad to think like that. He was hardly a knight in shining armour, but then she wasn't a princess. Not like Gabrielle. Francesca, the pathetic loser. Francesca, who could only ever be a poor second best, as her father had decreed.

It had been after six o'clock by the time DCI Strang was ready to head north, and much of it had been slow driving on smallish roads, so it was after eleven before he crossed the county border with its WELCOME TO CAITHNESS sign – and *FAILTE GU GALLAIBH* too, by government decree, despite local resistance to the infliction of Celtic Gaelic on English-speaking Picts.

Apart from a professional visit to Peterhead Prison, this was the farthest north Strang had been on the east side of Scotland and he hadn't known what to expect. Even this late it was still light, the sky clear apart from some slender golden clouds close to the horizon. Familiar as he was with the dramatic Highlands, he was taken aback by how flat the countryside round about was, with only a few low rises that you could barely call hills. Over to the west the peaks of Sutherland were visible in the distance, but north and east – nothing but that wide, wide sky, punctured occasionally by a village or the spire of a church, like a van Ruisdael landscape. It was – Strang looked for the word – *uncompromising* country. There was little that was picturesque about the small towns that he drove through either, no different from the small towns in the central belt or the hinterland of Fife.

It was almost midnight when he reached Thurso. The hotel – he checked the address Angie had given him – was on the outskirts of the town, a forbidding-looking grey stone building called the Masons Arms. Promising, that – not. Yawning, he parked in the street outside, picked up his holdall and his laptop and crossed the pavement to the entrance.

There was no light on in reception and the door was locked. Strang swore. He was tired, and he wanted to get his head down; Angie had said she would alert the hotel to his late arrival and if Angie said she would, she had. So why wasn't someone waiting up for him? He looked for a bell to ring.

There wasn't one. Swearing again, he took out his phone, looked up the number for the hotel and dialled. He could hear it ringing inside, and then it cut out to an answering service. 'Please leave a message after the tone . . .' It would be unwise to leave the message that would adequately express his feelings.

What now? Sleep in the car? Not that he hadn't done it before, but he had no wish to do it again. Without much hope he went back to dialling the number again, ringing off when the message cut in, dialled, rang off, dialled, rang off, dialled.

And at last, a light came on. A sullen-looking girl in

a loose T-shirt and tracksuit bottoms, pulled on over her pyjamas by the look of it, plodded across the hall, unlocked the door and opened it.

'Yes?' She still seemed to be half-asleep.

'DCI Strang. Weren't you warned I'd be late?' He walked past her into the gloomy hall. It was high-ceilinged, large, and empty apart from an uncomfortable-looking settle against one wall and a reception desk at the back. An open door behind it showed a couch with a pillow on it and a sleeping bag thrown back.

'Oh.' She plodded back to the desk, switched on a lamp and looked about her vaguely. 'There was a note, but I thought that was them that came earlier.'

Presumably the pair from Edinburgh – that was something, anyway. For a moment he thought of finding out who they'd sent but the girl was yawning her head off and he was keen to get to bed himself.

'My key?' he prompted.

'Oh – yeah.' She unhooked a key from a board behind her. 'First floor. Breakfast from half seven.' She gestured towards a door on the left, which opened on a dark cavernous space, and was turning away as he took the key from her.

He gestured towards the staircase leading into upper darkness. 'Perhaps you could put the lights on?'

It took a moment for that to sink in, then, 'Right,' she said, lumbering over to press a switch at the foot of the stairs. 'There's one when you get to the first floor as well.'

As he reached the stairs she was already shutting the door to the back room and would, Strang reckoned, be asleep before he reached the top. It didn't give him much hope for comfort over the next few days, but as long as the bed was flat enough to lie down on he didn't think he'd have much trouble falling asleep.

As usual, Gabrielle had taken her pills when she went to bed, but at two o'clock she woke up, coming to the surface reluctantly through the mists of sleep.

She was alone. David was going offshore again and had decided to leave after supper rather than get up in the middle of the night to make an early flight in Aberdeen.

'You need your sleep,' he had said. 'I don't want to disturb you – the early morning's often when you're sleeping most soundly.' Then he added nervously, 'And you'll be sure to lock up properly?'

She had felt a little sick at what that implied, but smiled and promised – though, if it was she who locked the doors, might she not remember where they now kept the keys even if she was asleep? Lilian had brought her home, asked three times if she would be all right, then mercifully was persuaded to go and leave her alone.

It had been an evening of slow torment. David and Lilian were watching her all the time, ready to leap in with unnecessary reassurance if she so much as hesitated over a word. Their anxiety made her even more anxious; she was sure he was telling Lilian about the sleepwalking when she saw them having a murmured conversation. Or was she telling him about the mix-up over time yesterday? Or – horrible thought – had she done some other crazy thing that they hadn't wanted to tell her?

Malcolm had been pompous, Francesca had been

acid – situation normal. To be fair to Fran, she'd been set about last time by Lilian and David for the sort of flippant remark to her sister that was common currency in their relationship and the result was a resentment so intense that you could see it was almost choking her. Gabrielle would have sympathised if it wasn't for the fact that she didn't seem to have any real emotions any more.

Once she had locked the doors and put the keys in the bowl in the sitting room, she'd hurried upstairs to take her pills, desperate for a few hours of oblivion.

Few enough. Gabrielle sat up to look at the clock then sank back on her pillows in despair. David was right – she needed her sleep. But something had wakened her, some unidentified noise.

And now she heard it – the sound of stealthy movement close by. She listened, straining her ears. An animal in the garden, a fox, perhaps? She'd often seen one, brash and busy, trotting across on its nocturnal business. A badger, even? But the top predators that had the night hours to themselves were confident, unafraid. This wasn't an animal.

The sound she was hearing was hesitant, furtive, as if whoever was making it was constantly checking for fear of discovery. But where was it – inside or outside?

Thank God she had locked the doors. But then, she thought, she hadn't locked the windows – in fact there were windows open all over the house for air on this warm humid night. The locked doors were only intended to keep her in, not to keep someone else out. She was too afraid to move; all she could do was listen with frantic intensity.

She could make out actual footsteps now, towards the

front of the house. Outside on the paving, or inside in the hall? If they came up the stairs there was one that would creak – the third or fourth step, she thought. If she heard that she would scream, grab for her phone, call the police . . .

It wasn't inside. The next footsteps were quick, running now, and certainly going away. As Gabrielle leapt out of bed she heard a car door slam and a car being driven off, fast. Then it was out of sight from the window and she ran downstairs to fling open the door.

There was a bloody pile of – something – on the doorstep. She screamed, convulsed with horror and shock. But there was no one to hear her. She was on her own. She had to calm herself, control her panic, look at the thing, whatever it was.

It was offal – heart, liver, lungs, the detritus of a butcher's shop. The sort of thing people used to buy to feed their dogs but was now probably consigned to a refuse bin round the back. The stench of flesh rotting in the summer heat made her gag.

She knew that as Paddy's daughter she had enemies in the village, but who hated her enough to send the message 'You're dead meat'? Its brutal cruelty took her one more step along the road to despair.

CHAPTER EIGHT

DC Livvy Murray came into the dining room looking around her hesitantly. It was a huge room, panelled in gloomy pitch pine with several long tables down the middle, obviously set up for bus parties. The North Coast 500 route round the top of Scotland – promoted as 'the Scottish Route 66' – was bringing the tourists in their droves, but none of them were having an early start today, apparently.

There were smaller tables round the edge near the windows and only a couple were occupied, by single men; reps, possibly, from the neat short-sleeved shirts and ties. They looked as if they didn't view the day of selling ahead of them with sunny optimism.

It was early yet, not much after half past seven, and there was no sign of either of her colleagues. Good! She'd no wish to spend more off-duty time than she had to with the loathsome 'Kevlar' and she might feel more ready to cope with meeting Strang after a Full Scottish and several cups of coffee.

As she chose a table, a waitress went past her with a plate – soft, greasy bacon, a frizzled egg, a grey-looking sausage, a dry disc of black pudding, tinned tomatoes and watery-looking baked beans with a fried tattie scone curled at the edges – and she changed her mind. 'Just toast and coffee,' she said when the waitress came.

The coffee was grey and lukewarm, but she gulped it down anyway for the caffeine hit, such as it was. She emptied three of the tiny packets of butter to spread on the leathery toast and had topped it with two packets of some indeterminate red jam when she saw DS Taylor coming in. As he reached the table she picked up her toast and stood up.

'Morning, Sarge,' she said. 'Just going to finish up a few things so I don't keep you waiting. See you in the hall in ten? Strang's probably along there already.'

Taylor glared at her. 'You can wait till I'm finished here. You needn't think I'm going to miss having a proper breakfast just so's we look keen.' But he didn't look happy at the thought that she might show him up.

'Let me know if you find one.' Murray went out munching her toast, satisfied with her tactics so far. She'd got Taylor feeling edgy and she hadn't had to sit at the breakfast table with either him or the boss. And tomorrow, she vowed, she'd find a wee cafe that would do her a decent bacon butty, even if she would have to pay for it herself.

Kirstie Mowat was feeling sick as she walked to the village hall. She tried to blame it on the poached egg on toast that her mother had forced her to eat before she would allow her to leave the house, but she knew perfectly well that it was anxiety making her stomach churn.

At least the policeman hadn't come to the house yesterday so maybe, just maybe, her parents wouldn't need to hear about it at all. But that left the problem of how the police were going to react to her not telling them about finding the man there right at the start. The fear that was haunting her was that the man might not even have been dead, that if they'd checked to see he might have been saved. She'd had nightmares about that.

There were cars and a big van in the car park outside and the double door was standing open. The hall was cluttered now with chairs, tables with computer terminals and screened-off areas like little rooms. There was a group of officers in uniform standing in the middle listening to a tall man wearing a light jacket over a shirt and tie.

Kirstie hesitated on the threshold and when one of the policemen said, 'Sir,' and nodded towards her, he turned his head. The first thing she noticed was that he had a scar down the right side of his face, the second that he had the sort of gaze that made her feel that she wouldn't need to tell him anything because he knew it already. She gave a little quiver.

He saw that too, then came across. 'I'm DCI Strang. Can I help you?'

'I'm–I'm Kirstie Mowat. I think you wanted to speak to me.'

Strang turned to the group. 'Anyone know about this?'

She recognised the policeman who stepped forward, the one with the pathetic moustache who'd come to the cafe. He had turned bright pink and she suddenly realised that he didn't want to talk about that any more than she did.

'A witness reported that she might have information relevant to the discovery of the body. I was going to get a statement—'

Kirstie jumped in, 'Yes, so I thought I ought to come in to see you myself.'

The policeman seemed relieved. Strang looked from one to the other, then said, 'Right, Constable, leave this with me.'

He led her to one of the screened-off cubicles; he sat on one side of the table and waved her to a chair opposite. 'All right, Kirstie, what did you have to tell me?'

She hadn't quite expected this. She'd thought they'd ask questions that would tell her what Calum had told them already, but this way she could be volunteering stuff they didn't need to know. She hesitated.

Strang smiled. 'Will it help if I tell you we'll find out anyway and there's no point in trying to work out a story?'

She gave a little gasp. 'I wasn't . . . I wasn't—'

'I think we both know you were.' He wasn't smiling now. 'I've a lot to do today. Don't mess me about.'

Kirstie gulped. 'Well, me and Calum – Calum Cameron – kind of meet up sometimes, just to like, hang out, you know?' She had a nasty feeling that he did know, but she went on, 'That old empty house where they found the body? Well, it's up near our farm and we all used to muck about there when we were kids. We went up there on Thursday night—'

'What time would that have been?'

She could feel her face getting hot. 'I don't know – midnight, maybe?'

'Midnight? After your parents were asleep, perhaps?'

'Mmm.' Then she burst out, 'Will you have to tell them? I'll get in so much trouble.'

'We don't make any promises. Go on.'

'The door was standing wide open, but we never thought anything about that except maybe we hadn't shut it properly the night before—'

'Stop there. The night before? You went the night before and there was nothing there?'

'That's right. But that night, when Calum went in he saw this man and he went, "Oh!" and stopped. I looked over his shoulder and saw him too – it was gross, he was all, oh, dirty and smelly. We didn't think he was *dead*, though.' She stopped. 'Was he – was he still alive then? If we'd checked he was all right, could we—?' Her voice quavered.

'No, Kirstie,' Strang said. His voice was more sympathetic this time. 'He was definitely dead. There was nothing you could have done. And it definitely wasn't someone you recognised?'

'Didn't look, really. But – but might it have been?' she faltered.

'Probably not,' he said smoothly. 'And after that?'

'We just went home.'

'And you didn't say anything to your parents about this? Not even after your father had found the body?'

Kirstie hung her head. 'No. My father would kill me if he found out I was there with Calum. Please don't tell him!'

'I think you know that he wouldn't. He might very reasonably be worried and angry. What age are you, anyway?'

'Fifteen. And a half.'

'I see.'

'Oh, you needn't worry. It's all over with him,' she said, venom in her tone. Indeed, when this was over his might very well be the next murder they'd be called on to investigate.

Strang's mouth twitched. 'Well, Kirstie, I'm not going to seek out your parents and tell them. On the other hand, I have to warn you that some of the information you have given me is highly significant and you might even be called as a witness at some future trial. If you want my advice, tell them yourself.'

'Mmm, thank you,' she said, almost as if she meant it.

'DCI Strang?' a voice said behind her and she turned her head. It was an older man with a small, bristly moustache and a rather red face. 'I'm DI Hay.'

'Oh yes.' Strang half rose. 'Can you give me one minute and I'll be with you? Thanks.'

The man withdrew but somehow Kirstie had the impression that he was none too pleased.

'Very quickly, then, Kirstie. Can I check two things? The body was not there on Wednesday but was on Thursday night – you're sure?'

'Absolutely.'

'Second, the door. You said that was standing wide open and that was unusual?'

'That's right. You see, it has bars nailed across it, so no one can go in, but actually the nails were worked loose ages ago and all the kids knew you just pulled and it would open. But we didn't want grown-ups finding out because they'd go and barricade it properly.'

Strang got up. 'Thanks. I'll send someone in now to

record a statement. Tell him exactly what you told me and then it'll be brought back to you to read and sign. OK?'

'OK.' She gave a deep sigh of relief as she got up. It hadn't been as bad as she'd feared. He wasn't going straight to clype on her and everyone knew trials took ages to come to court. She might even have left home by the time her parents found out.

Ailie Johnston wasn't looking forward to work that morning and sure enough the receptionist told her when she arrived that Mr Michie wanted to see her at ten o'clock. She nodded and went on to her office with a feeling in her stomach as if she'd swallowed a stone.

She tried to get on with the list of priorities she always drew up before she left at night, but she wasn't able to concentrate. She could feel herself getting more and more nervous, and at quarter to ten she decided she'd had enough. If he was going to sack her he could do it at her convenience and not his, and since she had half a mind to walk out anyway it hardly mattered if he was annoyed. She jumped up and walked down the corridor to his office.

She had just raised her hand to knock when she realised he was on the phone. She was about to turn away frustrated when she heard what he was saying; in this modern building the doors weren't very thick. It was her moral duty not to listen. She listened anyway.

'I've spoken to Chris, Tom. Make sure you've got it straight – this needs to be watertight or we're in big trouble. And you know not to mention—Yes, that's right. OK?'

There was a listening pause and then Michie said, 'Right,

right. And be careful. A real bastard he could be, if you ask me. And keep in touch.'

Ailie retreated along the corridor. She waited at her desk, turning over what she had heard, then went back at ten o'clock precisely. She wasn't sure now that she wanted to be sacked. If Niall really had been murdered and Bruce Michie was involved, she would do her level best to find out anything she could and pass it on to the nice DCI Strang, starting with that last conversation.

In fact, Michie seemed surprisingly calm about it all. 'Ah, Ailie. Good,' he said. 'I hear you went to the police with your worries about Niall?'

She could feel her cheeks getting hot. 'Well, I was—'

'No, no. That's fine. Of course, I'd prefer that you'd come to me first, but you did your civic duty and I'm the last person to find fault with you for that.' He gave a little chuckle, which she immediately assessed as phoney.

'That's good, Bruce. I was sure you'd be supportive.' She could do phoney too.

'Of course, I'd hate to think this really was anything to do with Niall, but I got the impression the inspector was taking this quite seriously. Was that your impression too?'

It gave Ailie a sick feeling even to acknowledge it, but she had to agree.

'I know that you were close to him, so I think you should prepare yourself in case it is indeed bad news. And as a firm, of course, we should be ready for that too. For instance, do you know if he had any relatives?'

'His mother died recently. I think he mentioned a sister, but I don't know more than that.'

'You don't know her name or where she lives?'

Ailie thought for a moment. 'No, sorry. I don't think they were close.'

'Pity. So important for the employer to be able to offer support. If you do remember, be sure to let me know. Now, I know this has been distressing for you. Are you all right to work today?'

Ailie assured him she was and left with her head spinning. When had Michie ever shown the smallest concern about what anyone else was feeling – and why had the man who had been utterly scornful of her worries about Niall changed his stance so completely after the visit from the police?

Niall Aitchison's house was a white-painted harled cottage just on the edge of Forsich. It stood in a row of houses in one of the back lanes of the village, with a pleasant outlook over the fields and some scrubby woodland. It had a pretty garden, very well maintained, and the paintwork was fresh and the windows shining in the bright sunshine.

DC Murray had put on one of the thick sweaters she'd brought with her before she left the hotel; now as the sun got higher in the sky she was sweltering.

'I thought it was supposed to be cold up here in the north. It's far hotter than Edinburgh. Sticky too.'

'You'd better strip off, then,' Taylor said with a leer. 'Not that it looks as if you've much to flaunt.'

Murray's lips tightened. Oooh, she'd have him once they got back, and to hell if the lads in the station didn't like it. This was going in a log; she looked at her watch to check the time.

Fortunately, she had put on a white Gap T-shirt

underneath. She took the sweater off and chucked it in the back as she got out of the car.

There was no answer when she rang the bell. They walked round into the back garden, also neat, with a table and bench set up on paving outside the back door.

'Not a bad wee place,' Taylor said. 'No one here, though. Best get back to report to Strang.'

God, he was sloppy. 'Shouldn't we check the neighbours to see if anyone knows where we might find him?'

He looked huffy. 'Oh, I suppose we could. Bet we don't get any joy, and anyway we won't know what to ask until we see Strang. I'm going to put him on the spot about that.'

Rather than laughing in his face, she said, 'Why not?' as she led the way to the house on the left-hand side.

There was no one in and Taylor looked triumphant. 'Told you it was pointless. I don't know what you're hoping to find out, anyway – the man'll be out at work and we'll get him in later, once Strang's got round to briefing us.'

Murray paid no attention, walking along the lane to the house on the other side. This looked more promising; there was an outer front door that was standing open and when she rang the bell an elderly lady with a sour expression, leaning on a stick, opened it remarkably quickly.

Before Murray could speak, she said, 'Saw you there at the house. Do you know where he is?'

'Mr Aitchison?' Murray asked.

'Aye, him. Just went off without a word to me. Expecting me to go on feeding the cat – at my own expense, mind you – until his lordship decides to turn up again.'

Taylor had caught up on the doorstep. 'Gone away,

127

has he? Thank you very much, madam.'

He was turning to go when Murray said, 'Could we maybe come in and talk to you for a minute? We're police officers.' She held up her warrant card.

The woman peered at it for a moment, then said, 'No.'

It didn't sound like the opening bid in a negotiation. Taylor was already walking down the path when Murray said, a little desperately, 'How long have you been looking after the cat for him, Mrs . . . ?'

'MacFarlane. Nine days. I'm counting, and if he's not back by five the night, it's ten I'll be charging him for. Fair enough, I said I'd look after Agnes's cat when he was away at work, but he paid money down first.'

'Agnes?'

She gave Murray a look of contempt for her ignorance. 'His mam, of course. When she passed on, I'd to do it for him so the wee beast comes to me if it's hungry. I'm not wanting a dead cat on my conscience, but you can tell him he'd better get back here or else I'll shut the door and ignore the yowling. Someone else can take a turn.'

Murray was doing a calculation in her head. 'So – Mr Aitchison's been missing since a week past Saturday?'

Mrs MacFarlane sniffed. 'If you call it "missing" when he just drove off in his car. I was having my elevenses and he could have come in and told me when he'd be back.'

She asked, though not hopefully, 'Do you know the registration number?'

'Me? I've better things to do with my time. You mind and tell him what I said.' With a surprising turn of speed, she withdrew inside and slammed the door.

Taylor said, 'If that old bat thinks we're passing on messages about a bloody cat, she's another think coming.'

The look of contempt Murray gave him was worthy of Mrs MacFarlane herself. 'Work it out. Why do you think we weren't told what to ask him? We were meant to find out if he was here. And he wasn't, was he? What does that tell you, *sir*?'

'That he doesn't think about his mother's cat when he decides to go off on a little holiday,' he said sulkily.

As he drove off, she said, 'I'll just contact the DVLA, then.'

He only said, 'Hmph,' but she chalked it up as another victory.

DI Drew Hay had a thin, crackly voice as if everything inside him had dried up. His hair was thin too, mouse fading to grey and combed in careful strands over the top of his head. His eyes were an indeterminate blue-grey and he was at present surveying DCI Strang with a jaundiced expression.

'I'm entirely at a loss to understand why the powers-that-be should have decided that we weren't competent to deal with whatever crops up on our patch. I've personally been doing that for the past twenty years.'

And in that time, apart from the odd domestic, how many major investigations had he even taken part in, let alone directed? Strang wondered. One of the prickly ones, obviously.

'Oh, I can quite sympathise,' Strang said smoothly. 'It's the old story – budget cuts, I'm afraid, and this lets us bring in the extra skills when needed without funding them year-round. But I'll be relying on you and your lads a lot – there's no substitute for local knowledge.'

He finished with a placatory smile that had no effect. Hay glared at him.

'And how do you expect my detectives to have local knowledge when they're not local? Most of mine were moved to Wick and the few they've sent up here won't ever have set foot in this place.'

That was a definite blow. 'Right, I can see that. You don't know anything about a man called Niall Aitchison, by any chance?'

'No. Sorry.' The satisfaction with which he said that didn't suggest he was.

'Right. We're waiting for DNA results, but a witness report suggests that Aitchison, who has a connection with Forsich, has been missing for a week from his job in Aberdeen. I have a team up from Edinburgh going to check on a local address we have for him. I'm going myself to the cottage where the body was found to hear how the operation there is going. Would you like to accompany me?'

Hay got up. 'I've too much work of my own to attend to without intruding on what has been deemed to be your investigation. Whatever the chief constable may think, this is no rural paradise. Crime is still a thriving business and with a brutally diminished staff I have plenty to keep me busy.'

'I'm sure. But I can draw on whatever manpower I may need?'

'I understand you have that authority, Chief Inspector. But I have a job to do as well, a job that is my first priority, whatever the high heid yins may decree.' With a curt nod he got up and walked out.

Strang pulled a face at his back. The good news was that he wouldn't have a resentful Hay peering over his shoulder and making carping remarks, but the bad news was that if he wanted local CID backup, endless difficulties would obviously be made. He'd have to rely on the team from Edinburgh; he just had to hope that Angie had found him good ones. He hadn't stopped to check this morning before he left the hotel.

At least Lothian, the uniformed sergeant he'd been speaking to earlier, seemed young and keen. He'd arranged for him to escort him to the crime scene and he was presumably waiting for him now.

As Strang left the interview booth, the door of the hall opened. The man who came in wasn't prepossessing – paunchy, blubbery-faced – and the woman behind was slightly built with pale skin and hennaed hair.

With a sinking feeling he recognised her as Livvy Murray, so nearly his nemesis on Skye. She'd been in uniform then, a loose cannon, and even though she'd made it into CID now, she had minimal experience. *Gee thanks, Angie*, he muttered inwardly, then went forward with a smile.

He didn't look exactly pleased to see her. But then, Murray hadn't chosen to come and work with him either and her hackles rose just a little bit.

She introduced Taylor, then hurried on. 'Sir, we've just been at Niall Aitchison's house. There was no one in and we established with a neighbour that he went off last Saturday in his car and she said he'd never been back. She's properly ticked off because he's left her looking after his cat, that was his mum's.'

131

Strang looked amused, for some reason. 'So, he had a cat after all, then. Oh, sorry, nothing. That's interesting – it may be very significant.'

'You didn't tell us what we were to ask him if we found him, sir.'

Taylor's tone was accusatory, and Murray stared at him. He still didn't get it, even after what she'd said before, and he certainly didn't get Strang, who had raised his eyebrows and was giving Taylor a look that would have made Livvy squirm if it had been directed at her.

'The objective was simply to establish whether or not he was there. That's answered it, which is in line with information received that he might possibly be the victim. We have a very strong witness who's been concerned for a week that he hasn't been responding to her calls and emails – it's out of character, apparently. He has a flat in Aberdeen and CID there applied for a search warrant last night, so we can hope for DNA evidence shortly.' He thought for a moment and then said, 'Right – get on to Aberdeen and ask them to arrange for Bruce Michie of Curran Services to go and view the corpse, Sergeant. If he can identify, it would be quicker. And there's a computer free over there – log in and read the reports that have come in so far. Once you're both up to speed I'll brief you on the next tasks. I'm going now along to the croft where the body was found, and I'll be back shortly.'

Taylor turned obediently. Murray hung back. 'Would you like me to come along, sir? Might be helpful getting statements or something.'

The long, cool look he gave her was familiar. She'd sounded too eager, almost needy. She wanted to kick herself.

'Thanks, Livvy, but I'd rather you familiarised yourself with the background too.'

As he turned away, a uniform came forward and Strang said, 'Right, Sergeant, lead on.'

Bitterness swelled in Murray. She'd thought that now she was CID she'd be involved with whatever was going on, but it looked as if she'd be held at arm's length just as much as she had been when she'd been a PC. She knew that whatever the official version might be she'd messed up last time, in Skye, and though he hadn't said anything she was pretty sure he was disappointed she'd been allocated. He wouldn't have taken to Taylor either – who would? What you saw was what you got.

It wasn't her fault. And she'd been sent with a job to do; she wasn't going to let him get away with shutting her out, any more than she had last time. Only this time she'd show how much she'd learnt and she wouldn't make any of the stupid, impulsive mistakes that led to disaster. Certainly not.

CHAPTER NINE

The croft house was up a stony track just off the narrow road that ran past Fergus Mowat's farm. It had a commanding position not far from the top of a steep rise and there was a small area at the front, once a garden but now untended, full of rank grass and nettles. At the back there was a concreted yard where weeds grew through the cracks, and a small, tumbledown shed.

PS Lothian parked the SUV beside it and they both got out. Strang slung his jacket into the back of the vehicle. 'Not quite the weather I'd expected up here,' he said. 'Quite oppressive.'

Even in his white summer uniform shirt Lothian looked hot. 'We're not used to it, sir. Nice for a bit but it's gone on so long it feels a bit weird.'

With the warm, humid air and the low, constant hum of insects, it seemed more like Greece than the north of Scotland. Uncanny, uncomfortable. Strang walked around the cottage, looking at the gaping window spaces and at what was left of the corrugated iron roof – just one panel still precariously balanced on walls that were crumbling away. A home where people had lived and loved, now no more than a relic of a bygone age. He would have found it depressing, even without the image in his mind of the dead man with the great black birds gathering.

The front of the building was still protected by Do Not Cross tape, but the SOCOs had done their work and left. Strang ducked under it and studied the door, now closed. The wooden bars had been nailed across it in workmanlike fashion but, as Kirstie had said, the nails no longer held. He pulled it back and stepped inside.

It smelt dank, earthy, but there was little to see apart from stone debris. If there had been any signs of any previous occupation, they would have been cleared away and he would have to study the photos to see how it had been – one drawback of the clever new SRCS system. It would only be occasionally that he would be in a position to see a body at the scene of crime.

He stepped back out again and looked around. A couple of hundred yards below and off to the right was a solid-looking farmhouse in grey stone with a huddle of well-kept outhouses round about a wide stockyard. 'Mowat's farm?'

'That's right,' Lothian said. 'He's the one found the body.'

Strang turned his head. 'If the door was shut, no one would look inside. But suppose the door was left standing open . . . You could see it clearly from the farm, or from the track, of course. Or even from the road, right?'

Lothian nodded. 'And Mr Mowat walks up this way

pretty much every day to check on his sheep, he said.'

'So, if you knew that, you could be pretty certain that he would notice if the door was standing open?'

'Aye, likely. But look, that's him going across the yard now. Do you want to ask him yourself?'

'Fine. I'm finished here, anyway.'

As they went back to the car, Strang stopped, looking at the track that ran on past the croft house. 'Where does that go?'

'On to the moor – I think there was an old shepherd's bothy up there. Then it just ends up in the bogs, I think.'

If you were transporting a body – and, Strang suddenly realised, in broad daylight at this time of year when there was no helpful darkness – you'd want to bring it in at the back so the building itself concealed you from anyone on the road below. And you'd have a fine vantage point to check that you were unobserved as you dragged the body in the door at the front. 'Get someone to check that out for me, can you?' he said as they bumped down the hill to park in the yard.

Fergus Mowat came across to meet them and was introduced to Strang. He was burly and greying, with bright blue eyes like his daughter Kirstie's. 'How's it going?' he said.

'Early days yet, sir. Look, I've read your statement and I don't want to drag you all through it again. There's just a couple of things. Do you own the property?'

Mowat shook his head. 'The old folk died twenty years ago, and the family had no use for it but neither did I. So, it's just been left.'

'But the door has always been kept shut – is that right?'

'Absolutely. Nailed shut. The place is a death trap – falling stones, rusty metal – that bit of the roof that's left could go any time. You don't want bairns scrambling about there and hurting themselves – or vandals breaking it up for the fun of it, either. Once they start that kind of thing they'd be looking round for something else to trash.'

'So, you could be guaranteed to notice if it was standing open?'

'Oh aye. Apart from anything else, I'd be feart the sheep might wander in and get trapped if the wind blew it shut again.'

'I can see that. Mmm. One other thing – I take it you didn't recognise the man?'

'Recognise him? I . . . well, I have to say I didn't really look much. He was in a right mess with those damned birds, and it was just a tramp—' He stopped. 'Here, hang on! You're not saying that I might've?'

Strang hesitated. He had no direct confirmation yet, but he had little doubt now that it would come soon. He was going to risk it. 'Mr Mowat, I would ask you not to discuss this with anyone else. Do you know Niall Aitchison? Is it possible he could be the man you saw?'

'*Niall Aitchison?*' Mowat was struck dumb for a moment. 'But . . . but he was dirty, stinking—'

'His build?' Strang suggested.

'His build – well, I suppose . . .' He frowned, as if trying to recapture the scene. 'He'd dark hair – muddy, but . . .' Again, he stopped, and Strang waited patiently. At last he said heavily, 'I take it you've a reason for asking me that?'

When Strang nodded, he went on, 'I certainly can't say it was Niall. Like I said, I didn't look at his . . . face.' He gave a little shudder. 'But the rest – yes, could be.'

'Thank you. I know this isn't easy for you. How well did you know Mr Aitchison?'

'Known him since he was a wee boy, though it'd probably be more accurate to say I knew who he was. We were never friends and our paths didn't cross – he's a good ten years younger. And after the business with Pat Curran . . .' He shook his head.

'Yes, I know there was ill feeling about the collapse of the drainage business—'

Mowat snorted. 'Ill feeling? That's one way of putting it. Curran slithered away and left half the village to fight for what they could get back – and it wasn't much.'

'You?'

Mowat grinned. 'Not me. I'm too canny. Sleekit, that was what Pat was – all Irish charm but I wouldn't have trusted him to shake my hand if I wasn't holding the other end. Plenty did, though, and it was Niall who was the mug left here to pick up the pieces. Made himself a lot of enemies . . . Oh—' He stopped with a little gasp.

'Mr Mowat, we're not jumping to any conclusions. Identity still hasn't been established. But is there anyone—'

'Anyone? There's just about everyone, even his own sister.'

'And she is?'

'Morven Gunn. Runs the Lemon Tree cafe. Look, I'm not saying—'

'Of course not. We won't be taking things any further until we have more confirmation. Don't worry about it.'

But as Strang thanked him and they drove away, he could see from Fergus Mowat's face that he was worrying that he'd said too much. That was the trouble with rural communities; they tended to hang together in a neighbourly conspiracy. It was one he was somehow going to have to infiltrate.

Ailie Johnston, summoned to the boss's office at ten o'clock for the second day running, gave a sigh of annoyance. Bruce Michie knew perfectly well that this was the busiest time when the urgent requests and problems piled in, all demanding action immediately and preferably yesterday. She was pretty sure she knew what it was about; being busy had kept her from thinking about Niall but now her stomach was churning again as she walked along the corridor.

She could see he was ill at ease. He looked up and licked his lips before he said, 'Ah, Ailie. Good,' and he was fiddling with the paperweight on his desk, a miniature oil rig sitting on a heavy granite base.

If he'd called her in to pat his hand, he could forget it. Nursemaid duties weren't covered in her job description and she didn't try to hide her irritation. 'Yes, Bruce, what is it? The phone's going crazy this morning—'

'Yes, yes. But the thing is, I've had a call from the police. They've asked me to go and – well, view the body.'

'Oh.'

'Yes, "oh". They've jumped straight to the conclusion that this is something to do with us, thanks to . . .' He didn't finish his sentence.

He didn't need to. Ailie could feel herself turning red,

139

though she'd nothing to blush for. 'If it isn't Niall, I'll apologise for causing a fuss. But if it is, they would find out anyway.'

He always backed off from confrontation. 'I know, I know,' he said hastily. 'It's just . . . Well, anyway, the thing is I've got this big meeting this morning—'

'With Ron Barclay, yes. I'll phone and postpone it.' She got up.

'No, no. The thing is, we've a major decision we need to take, the sooner the better. I was just thinking, maybe you could go instead. You knew Niall better.'

'*What?* You're joking! Not a chance.' She folded her arms and glared at him. 'They asked you, it's you they want.'

Michie had come out in a light sweat; he produced a handkerchief and dabbed his forehead with it. 'I-I don't like these things,' he said feebly. 'He was – *mutilated*, you know.'

'Yes, of course I know. You think it would be my idea of fun? You think because I "knew him better" I'd be fine with looking at—' she gulped, 'what happened to him.'

'No, no, of course not. It's just . . . well, you told them about us having that wee disagreement. To be honest, you dropped me in it, when I told you it was nothing. They've probably got me down as a suspect now and—'

Ailie looked at him with horror. 'You're not saying you're afraid you might give yourself away?'

The handkerchief came out again, wiping forehead, upper lip, back of neck. 'No, of course I'm not effing saying that. The thing is—'

'There seem to be an awful lot of "things" that it is. No, Bruce, do your own dirty work. You know where to find me if you're wanting to sack me but if not, I'll get on with the work I'm paid to do.'

Michie might be sweating; Ailie felt icy cold. There was that old superstition that if the murderer approached the body of his victim, it would start bleeding again. She didn't believe it – but did Bruce?

When DCI Strang and PS Lothian got back to the incident room, DC Murray jumped up from the computer terminal and came over to him with a piece of paper in her hand.

'Sir, we've got the number from the DVLA. Shall I pass it on to uniform to put out a bulletin?'

'Yes, fine. Good work, Livvy. Where's Kevin?'

'Kevlar, he likes to be called.'

'*Kevlar*? What's that supposed to mean?'

'Like the body armour, you know? "Strong enough to stop a bullet." That's what he says.'

'I . . . see.'

'I just call him "sarge", if that helps,' she said, deadpan.

He managed not to smile. 'Not a lot, Livvy, as you well know. Where is he anyway?'

'Taking a break. Catering's arrived.'

There was a burst of laughter as he looked round. Taylor was clutching a bridie and the woman pouring tea had just said, 'Cheeky monkey!'

Strang walked across. Taylor swung round as he approached.

'Hello, sir. Let me introduce you to Mairi, tea lady *extraordinaire*.'

'I'm sure. Hello, Mairi. Just coffee please. Thanks. Kevin,

if you don't mind eating while we work, there's a couple of things we need to get on with.'

He picked up his mug and went back towards Murray, looking round for somewhere he could hold a briefing.

The hall was busy with uniformed officers going to and fro and the screened-off cubicles were in operation; at least they'd found some witnesses ready to come forward. There was one woman he noticed, a big, raw-boned, sour-faced woman; her body language was belligerent, and she was being escorted across to Sergeant Lothian by an anxious-looking constable.

'This lady wants to make an official complaint, sir,' he said.

It was a phrase they all dreaded. Strang saw Lothian square his shoulders and pin on the sort of hopeful smile that suggested goodwill. 'How can I help you, madam?'

It all came out in a torrent of rage. 'Help me? You can help me by sorting out the officer who came barging into my cafe and terrified a minor to the point where she fainted, causing serious damage to my property – and then gave me cheek, I may say. That's him, over there, standing behind that silly wee moustache.'

Strang followed her gesture and saw the young constable who had brought Kirstie to him earlier, shrinking into a corner as if impaled by her pointing finger. The moustache was, indeed, the only distinguishing feature in his plump face.

Lothian looked as if he was having a problem in reconciling the image of threat and intimidation with the mild reality, but he said very properly, 'If I may just take your name, madam, we'll find somewhere where we can formally log your complaint.'

'I should think so too. Morven Gunn. I'm the proprietor of the Lemon Tree cafe.'

Strang studied her with considerable interest as there was a little flurry finding a vacant space. Niall Aitchison's sister. And it wasn't hard to figure out who the 'minor' was, or even why she might have seen a routine question as a threat; he'd sensed at the time that something was going on there that neither the constable nor Kirstie had wanted to mention.

He stepped forward. 'Do you mind if I sit in on this, Jack? I've got a bit of background that might be useful.'

Lothian gave him a look of relief. 'Oh thanks, sir. That would be great. Do you want to take it yourself?'

'No, you do the formal bit. I'll observe and chip in if there's something I want to ask, if that's all right with you.'

'Any time.'

As he waited for Mrs Gunn to be installed in a cubicle, he looked round. Murray was standing at a tactful distance, awaiting instructions, but she'd stationed herself so she could hear every word. Taylor, on the other hand, had drifted off and gone back to chatting up the tea lady. Strang suppressed a sigh. The sergeant was clearly going to be a liability; he'd have to rely on Murray and hope that lessons had been learnt in the last year.

'Go and talk to that constable, would you, Livvy? Just a casual chat – find out his side of the story. Don't get involved, just listen. Can you do that?'

'Of course, sir,' she said stiffly.

'And would you ask Kevin when he can tear himself away to go along to the hotel and arrange a room to be an office for me. I can set up my laptop so tell him not to let them charge us for anything elaborate – just a table, a few chairs. I don't want to make demands on the Thurso police station but there's no privacy in this place – anyone can eavesdrop.' He put emphasis on 'anyone'.

'Yes, sir. I'll tell him.'

She didn't look abashed. In fact, she looked smug and Strang knew he'd tacitly authorised that with what he'd said about Taylor. It hadn't been wise; there was clearly bad blood there already and even if from what he'd seen of 'Kevlar' – *Kevlar?* – it was hard to blame her, Livvy didn't need encouragement.

Gabrielle Ross became gradually aware that the phone was really ringing, that it wasn't somehow part of her confused dream. She'd no idea what time it was; she felt awful.

Her mother's voice at the other end of the phone sounded concerned. 'Are you all right? You took forever to answer the phone. I was just checking that you remember it's Francesca's day off and I'm not in the Shelter shop till later so we're going to the Castle of Mey cafe for lunch? I thought you'd be here for coffee first.'

Gabrielle squinted at the clock by her bedside. Half past eleven, for heaven's sake! 'Yes of course,' she lied. It was becoming harder and harder to get a grip on reality – what she knew and didn't know. 'I just slept in a bit so I'm running late. What time are we leaving?'

'You know as well as I do how long it takes to get there.

144

But your voice sounds very croaky. You're not ill, are you?'

'No. I'm fine. Be with you in half an hour.' She put down the phone before her mother could interrogate her any more.

Her throat was indeed rough. It was raw and painful; she had vomited several times as she shovelled the offal out onto the ground across the road, boggy ground that had swallowed it up eagerly like some obscene monster feeding. She'd scrubbed the doorstep with bleach as if that could somehow sanitise the vile emotions that had prompted such malevolence.

Afterwards Gabrielle had crawled into bed, taking another pill. She was taking too many these days and increasingly she felt she was spending her days in a kind of fog but blest oblivion, even for a few hours, was worth it.

She wasn't going to tell her mother. She wasn't going to tell David, who would go into a protective frenzy. She wasn't going to tell the police even though she could make a shrewd guess at whose car door must have slammed and roused her to hear those terrifying, stealthy movements around the house. Explaining why she believed that would mean going back to the time she did not want to think about, the accident for which she didn't feel guilty, not in the least. And yet somehow, as if the acid of years of directed hatred had worn away her shield of justification, she was starting to feel it now, another addition to the load of misery that was driving her to despair.

When Gabrielle went into the downstairs cloakroom, the little silvery knife was lying beside the basin. She'd got so used to finding everyday things in odd places that though she didn't remember putting it there it didn't surprise her;

she'd found the idea of the little sharp blade cutting a scarlet line across pale skin coming into her mind more and more seductively. Would the letting of blood really bring some sort of relief?

She picked it up. Just a little tiny cut, somewhere David wouldn't see? She knew it would be painful, but if she hurt it would prove she was alive, not just a walking shadow of her one-time self. She held up her left arm to expose the armpit then took the knife in her right with a great, shuddering sigh.

'You're to go and arrange a room at the hotel to be an office for the boss,' Murray said.

Taylor was eating a chocolate biscuit. He gave her a dirty look. 'Who says?'

'The boss.'

'When did he say that?'

'When you were off chatting up your friend over there.'

'And what are you going to be doing meantime? Dossing around here? I don't think so.'

'No, I'm to talk to one of the constables and report back.'

'Why should you be doing that? You're the skivvy, not me. Get along to the hotel and I'll speak to him. Which one is he?'

'Sorry, Sarge – boss's orders. Just a wee room, table and chairs. And you're not to let them charge us for installing tech stuff – he just wants a bit of privacy and there's not a lot around here. OK?'

Taylor's piggy eyes narrowed. 'Got something going, the two of you? When you said you knew him, I didn't realise you meant you *knew* him.' He sniggered.

She resisted the temptation to slap him, but her palm itched. 'I didn't,' she said, as disdainfully as she could. As she turned and walked away from him, she still wasn't sure that he'd obey Strang's order, but she certainly wasn't going to invite more discussion by looking back.

There was an almost visible black cloud engulfing the young constable who was still sitting in the corner, looking as if Morven Gunn's accusing finger had held him transfixed. He looked up nervously when Murray approached.

She gave him a reassuring smile. 'Hi. I'm DC Murray – Livvy. What's your name?'

'Craig Davidson.'

'My boss has asked me to have a wee chat. Tell me why Big Scary Lady is so pissed with you.'

He didn't quite smile, but he relaxed a little. He really was very, very young. She wasn't exactly old, but she had to stop herself from calling him 'sonny'. As she took a seat beside him, out of the corner of her eye she saw Taylor stomping out, throwing a darkling glance at her over his shoulder.

'I didn't do anything, except my job.' Davidson was clearly aggrieved. 'I didn't barge in, like she said, just opened the door like you do. I was told to interview Kirstie Mowat at the cafe – she's a waitress there and all I did was ask if I could have a word with her and she just took one look at me and then fainted. Don't know what she'd done to have such a bad conscience. She came in here early this morning to speak to the DCI and she was putting on to him that she'd been going to come in of her own accord – oh yeah, sure she was! I didn't get a chance to tip him off.'

'He's pretty smart. He probably realised. But what happened when she passed out?'

Davidson groaned. 'It was mega. Dropped her tray, knocked over a table, broken cups and spilt coffee everywhere. And the cafe was full too, and there were all these folk muttering at me like it was police brutality. Then the old bat started yelling at me, and when I said I'd still need to speak to the girl she went radge and someone began hissing. But I was only doing my job.'

Murray could just picture him, burning with embarrassment but still dogged. 'Good for you,' she said. 'What was the bit about giving her cheek?'

'I didn't! She ordered me to clear up the mess, but it wasn't me made it, and I just said it was up to her. Didn't go down well.'

He gave a rueful grin and she warmed to him. 'Lousy job sometimes, isn't it? But I can't see you did anything wrong.'

'She'll lay it on thick, though. Don't know what the DCI will think – he'll maybe believe her not me.'

'I'll tell him. I'm sure you'll be OK. But it was kind of funny she turned on you like that.'

'Nothing funny about it. Terrifying, more like. God help anyone who has to interview her, if that's what she does when it's just the waitress.'

'Serious overreaction, wouldn't you say?' Murray thought for a moment. She'd done what she'd been tasked to do – find out Davidson's side of the story – and there was no need to do any more. She glanced across, but Strang was still sitting in on the interview and she couldn't resist. 'Why were you to interview Kirstie, Craig?'

'Her boyfriend made a statement yesterday, something about them being at the croft and seeing the man there. I was to ask her about it.'

The statement had been one of the reports she'd read. 'But she didn't come forward till she knew we were on to her? So, did Big Scary Lady know all about it – was she protecting Kirstie, do you think, when she went for you?'

Davidson seemed struck by this idea. 'Could be, yeah. A bit OTT, otherwise.'

'Maybe this is all about trying to scare us off? Sort of "mess with me at your peril" kind of thing.' She was getting quite excited with her own theory. 'Anything else you know about the local background, Craig?'

He shook his head regretfully. 'I'm not from round here. Forsich's only a wee place anyway, and even if you were from Thurso you'd probably not know a lot about it.'

That was certainly disappointing. But she did have an idea to play with now and she said, 'Would you ask around, see if anyone knows anything? Just casually, you know, not officially or anything. Come directly to me.'

Even as she said the words, she had slight misgivings. Strang had specifically told her not to get involved, but he needn't find out. If Craig did come back with anything useful, she'd get the brownie points for grafting while Taylor mucked about. Knowledge was power. That was the theory, anyway.

DCI Strang had drawn his chair into a corner to observe while Sergeant Lothian sat across the table from the complainer. He saw Morven Gunn's eyes flick to his own face, then quickly away when she saw that he had noticed.

Her glance was watchful, guarded: the blustering anger she had displayed earlier wasn't in evidence now. Had it been synthetic, he wondered? And if so, why?

Lothian was taking down the details when his own phone bleeped, signalling a text message. He looked at it. From the DI in Aberdeen, it read, *Body ID'd as Niall Aitchison by Bruce Michie of Curran Services*.

Morven Gunn was watching him again, He kept his face impassive as he met her gaze, holding it until she looked away. Of course, she couldn't possibly read his mind, but it was a strange feeling to be looking at Niall Aitchison's sister, knowing that her brother was dead when she didn't.

Unless, of course, she did.

She sat back down, a guarded 'who-wants-to-know' expression on her face. 'Yes.'

'Then I'm afraid I have bad news for you. The body that was recently found near Mowat's farm has been identified as your brother Niall.'

He heard a slight intake of breath, but her face didn't change. 'Are you sure?'

'I'm afraid so, yes. Are you all right? I can get someone to take you home—'

'No need.' Her voice was harsh. 'As no doubt someone will helpfully have told you already, there was no love lost between us. The people you'll need to break it to gently are Pat Curran's women.' She spat his name. 'He took the brother I had, and the mother. They've both been dead to me for years.'

She got up. 'And now, unless you insist on detaining me against my will, I'm leaving. I've got work to do.'

There were more questions – Curran's women? – but in the circumstances, with someone who looked all too ready to complain about any lack of respect, real or imagined, it wasn't wise to try to ask them. He said, 'We will have to talk to you later, but not right at the moment.'

By the time Strang finished his sentence, he was speaking to empty air. The two men stared at each other and Lothian gave a low whistle. 'Well, what do you make of that, sir?'

'Hard to say.'

Francesca Curran was on the sofa in her mother's sitting room, painting her nails on the low table in front of her. Her mother had taken away the coffee tray since there was still no sign of Gabrielle.

She was beginning to think there really might be something wrong with her sister after all. She'd been weird last night, hardly able to finish a sentence and with Mum and David trying so hard to cover up and pretend everything was fine. Even Malcolm had noticed and come over all professionally soothing like he did when he'd some patient that was losing it.

It gave her a sick feeling in the pit of her stomach. What if Gabrielle had inherited her grandmother's gene for early dementia?

Francesca had been in her teens when it started, when Granny got – well – random. Then it had happened hideously quickly, the deterioration from being smart and self-sufficient to being bewildered and helpless. She'd been scared of her – no, not scared exactly, more so embarrassed it was painful and she'd go to ridiculous lengths to avoid so much as looking at her. She felt ashamed of that, but if Gabrielle went the same way and if it ended up that they were all having to look after her she wasn't sure she'd cope any better now.

And Gabrielle's granny was her granny too. What if Fran started losing the plot herself?

She had finished painting her nails and waved her hands to dry them. She didn't really know why she'd bothered; it was her day off but all she had in prospect was going out to lunch with her mother and sister – how sad was that? Suppose she did start forgetting things and getting all withdrawn like Gabrielle, suppose she too had some awful twilight zone ahead of her, without ever having had a proper life, a lover, children – it would be so cruel! Her eyes filled with self-pitying tears and she dashed them away hastily as her mother came back into the room.

'Gabrielle's on the way. She slept in, I suppose. She just seemed worn out last night. I promised David we'd try to cheer her up today, try to take her out of herself. Sometimes you're not really as kind as you might be, Francesca—'

The old feelings of resentment flared up. 'Why is it always about Gabrielle?' she cried. 'Am I supposed to nanny her? All she needs to do is rest and stop stressing. Can't Malcolm give her a prescription?'

Lilian sat down on the sofa beside her and reached out to take her hand. Fran drew back with a yelp. 'No, no, they're not dry.'

'Oh, sorry.' She let her hand drop, but she leant forward to look her daughter in the face. 'Francesca, I think you need to understand. Gabrielle isn't – isn't really well at all. She's not just forgetful, she's doing odd things too. Poor David's worried sick. She was sleepwalking the other night, went right outside onto the road. And there's other stuff I know he isn't telling me. She's just, I suppose, depressed – well, the fire, and losing the baby so soon after Pat died, you know. But we have to look after her really carefully because I think she's getting closer and closer to despair. Malcolm prescribed something for her, but David is afraid she isn't taking it. And you know what can happen with depression . . .'

'Yes, of course I know. I work in a doctor's surgery, remember.' She spoke brusquely. It wasn't something she wanted to hear: there had been a girl at school with depression who'd gone out and drowned herself and if

Gabrielle went and did that, she'd have made sure they all ended up haunted by guilt for the rest of their lives. There was a bitter little voice in her head saying, *Typical!*

The room at the hotel Taylor had commandeered was a pokey little office at the back of the hotel and its dispossessed occupant was looking flustered as she struggled to gather up papers from the desk, piling them on top of the in- and out-trays. Taylor was standing tapping his foot and the look she directed at him as she went out was withering.

Clearly, he hadn't been exactly tactful but at least he'd been effective. Strang took his place behind the desk and gestured Murray and Taylor to the chairs facing him while he set up his laptop. Taylor slumped down looking sulky, signalling irritation that he should have been tasked to do something he felt was beneath him.

The chief inspector's lips tightened. Taylor had a lot to learn but right at the moment he had neither the time nor the inclination to teach him. He gave no sign that he had even noticed.

'You've had time to catch up on the reports, so you know the background to the case. I'm aware that the introduction you've had has been less than ideal but my original plan for a briefing last night fell through, thanks to an important witness statement that meant I had to spend unscheduled time in Aberdeen – time well spent, as it turns out. So, listen up, because you're going to have to get on top of this fast.

'I've requested a formal statement from the neighbour you spoke to and we've had evidence from two teenagers that the body was not in the cottage until the day before it was discovered. We now also have a positive identification of the body as Niall Aitchison.'

'I thought that!' Murray exclaimed. 'When the wifey next door said he'd been missing since Saturday—'

'Didn't take a mastermind to work it out,' Taylor said, his tone patronising.

Murray glared. 'Oh? I wasn't sure you were with me on that, Sarge.'

'Whatever,' Strang said flatly, and Murray subsided. 'Morven Gunn, the woman who came in to make a complaint today, is his sister. She appeared completely unmoved when we told her, said that the people who would need to have the news broken gently were "Curran's women". We don't as yet know who she meant – she made a point of leaving and, in the circumstances, we couldn't detain her.

'I have information that Patrick Curran's daughter, Gabrielle Ross, is in Forsich at the moment, suffering from some sort of nervous breakdown. If she is fit to talk to us – which she may not be, from the sound of it – she may be able to tell us who the others are. PS Lothian is getting hold of an address for her.

'Apparently we're spoilt for suspects. Pat Curran had a drainage business here that went bust after he'd persuaded half the village to invest, whereupon he moved to Aberdeen, set up a new, very successful business but didn't feel he owed any sort of reparation – which technically, of course, he didn't. Niall Aitchison was the fall guy, as far as I can make out.

'Background is our problem. According to PS Lothian none of the uniforms involved at the moment have connections in the village. So, we need to find a source—'

Taylor perked up. 'Mairi,' he said. 'She's a local lassie. I could go and have a talk with her. I bet she can rattle the skeletons in the cupboards.'

'Good,' Strang said, and became aware that it was Murray who was now looking less than pleased. Liked to be centre stage, did Murray, but he hadn't any more time for her sensitivities than he did for Taylor's. At least Lothian showed no signs of being a prima donna – as yet, anyway.

'You go on and see what you can find out from her then, Kevin. Once Lothian comes back, he can take me to see if I can get an interview with Mrs Ross. Livvy, the uniforms have been out knocking on doors and I think one or two witnesses have stepped forward, so you can sift what's come in and work out what follow-up is needed. All right?'

'Sir.' She didn't move, though, as Taylor got up and went out, only bending down to fiddle with her shoulder bag. Once he had gone, she said, 'Could I just ask about the body, boss? I read the PM report and it said he'd drowned, but then he was found in that cottage. Do we know why?'

Strang grimaced. 'Sixty-four-thousand-dollar question, Livvy. Why indeed? Now, you'd better get back to the hall and see what you can come up with.'

It was the old story yet again. She was going to be sidelined, kept away from the heart of the investigation. He must be still holding it against her that she'd screwed up in Skye and now he was going to take a uniform along with him when by rights it should have been a detective. Admittedly, she wouldn't have seniority and if Strang had taken Taylor instead it wouldn't have been any better – worse, in fact. It was maddening enough that he'd come up with a source of local knowledge from chatting up the tea lady while he stuffed his face, when that was where she'd hoped to get an advantage by way of her new chum Craig.

Taylor had waited for her with a bad grace and drove off to Forsich almost before she had shut the door. 'What were you saying to him after I left?' he demanded. 'Get it straight, Murray, I won't have you undermining me.'

'Perish the thought, Sarge,' she said sweetly. 'Your name wasn't even mentioned.'

'Hmm,' he grunted. 'Anyway, you can sit in while I interview Mairi. Got her tongue hung in the middle, that woman – I should be able to get some useful stuff. Watch and learn, Murray, watch and learn.'

At the hall they found Mairi more than ready to abandon her post and be drawn into a corner to dish whatever dirt she could come up with.

'You can take notes, Constable,' Taylor said. 'Mairi knows all about everyone here. Don't you, pet?'

'Oh aye,' Mairi said, giving Murray a wink. She was a cheerful-faced middle-aged woman who looked as if she had embraced the principle of 'one scone for you, one scone for me' in her working life. 'What I could tell you about this place would make your hair curl, right enough.'

She beamed as she settled back in a chair, crossing her arms across her ample stomach and preparing to enjoy herself. 'Hope you can write fast, dearie.'

'Just watch me.' Murray got out her notebook. Before

Taylor could say anything, she asked, 'Would you know who were "Curran's women"?'

Taylor bridled, but before he could say anything Mairi was off. 'Curran's women? It's a bit of a funny way to put it, but there's his daughters, Gabrielle and Francesca. Kind of fancy names, but that's Lilian all over. That's their mother – maybe you could say she was one of Pat's women, though of course he wasn't good enough for her. The minute the new doctor came she was all over him like a rash. And he couldn't believe his luck – she's a bonny-looking woman if you can take the highfalutin ideas that go along with it.

'But maybe you'd still call her one of Pat's women too, despite being his ex. He left his mark, did Pat. He—'

'How do you mean?' Taylor interrupted.

It stopped the flow. 'Oh, he just . . . did,' she said lamely. 'You know, he was kind of a character . . .'

Murray looked up from her notes to step in before he could mess up further. 'Lilian and Francesca – do they both live here?'

'Well, of course!' She seemed astonished at Murray's ignorance. 'At Dr Sinclair's house. He's got the surgery there and Francesca's one of the receptionists – and a right sour-faced besom she is too. Told me I was wasting the doctor's time when all I needed was exercise, as if it was any of her business.'

Viewing Mairi's comfortably upholstered figure and double row of chins, Murray conceded that Francesca was probably right, but plain speaking seldom won you friends.

As Taylor said, 'So there's three of them, then,' Murray spoke across his statement of the obvious. 'What about the other daughter – Gabrielle?'

Taylor was going red with irritation. 'Murray, can I remind you that you're here to take notes, not to conduct the interview?' he said, but Mairi, having been offered a juicy topic, was off again.

'Well, now you're asking!' she said. 'She was the one went with her father after the divorce. Like as two peas in a pod – tough as old boots, the pair of them. At least, that was her till he just dropped dead, like that. And then she'd a bit of bad luck down in Aberdeen – I'm not right sure what it was, but she's back here and some kind of not well, they're saying. Not the best place to come, to be honest – her and her father's not popular around here.'

'Now that's what I wanted to talk to you about,' Taylor said firmly. 'Can you pin that down for me – who was involved, what was their problem?'

Murray groaned inwardly. Could the man not see that she was going to give him the answers to his questions if he just let her talk on, and probably some answers to questions he didn't yet know needed to be asked? Mairi liked telling it her own way, and now she was struggling to try to fit what she had to say into the template he was imposing.

From where Murray was sitting, she had a view of the hall door and as it opened she glanced up. Strang came in and it was obvious from his face, and the way he let the door swing back behind him to slam shut, that he wasn't pleased. Like a schoolchild, she had an automatic guilt reaction, but a rapid review of her recent behaviour didn't throw anything up.

He marched across. 'It seems that DI Hay needs PS Lothian this afternoon. He's given me directions for the address I wanted so I'm going there now. Oh – I'm sorry to interrupt, madam.'

He must be in a temper. It looked as if he'd only just realised they were in the middle of an interview. Now he looked from one to the other.

'DS Taylor, you're conducting this, right?'

Taylor could see what was coming. 'Well,' he said, 'DC Murray could—'

Strang went on as if he hadn't heard. 'Once you've finished, carry on with the review we mentioned. Murray, you'd better come with me. You can take your lunch break later.'

He stalked off with Murray trotting in his wake, trying to keep the smirk of satisfaction off her face.

Strang drove along the Forsich high street in silence, his expression grim. He was aware of Murray at his side glancing at him nervously once or twice, but he didn't trust himself to speak. PS Lothian had been both annoyed and embarrassed about being called back: it was clear this was a quite unnecessary summons and merely part of a power play by DI Hay.

'I'm really sorry, sir,' Lothian had said. 'One of the lads must have told him I was taking you round and my boss thinks this should all be done by your guys.'

'That's not quite the situation now. I can overrule him but that would put you in a very awkward position, wouldn't it? You still have to work with him when this case is over.'

Lothian looked relieved. 'Well, I suppose . . .'

They had left it like that, but now Strang really was thrown back on the team that Angie had sent up – and he'd have words with her about that when next he saw her. Taylor was a useless barrel of lard and Murray – he didn't trust her. She'd landed him in a situation before where he'd been forced, if not exactly to lie, certainly to peddle a cynically spun story. He hadn't liked doing that and he hoped never to have to do it again. On the other hand, she wasn't stupid, and she had the sort of lively curiosity that made for a good detective.

She and Taylor had embarked on a turf war, so he'd have to balance up the tasks to keep the peace. If one of them decided to make a complaint about insubordination and the other one complained of sexism, he'd have no energy left to investigate Niall Aitchison's murder.

Murray stole another glance at him and tentatively cleared her throat.

He seldom stayed angry for long. 'Yes, Livvy?' he said.

'It's just, well, I think I know who Curran's women are, boss.' She repeated what Mairi had said and he listened with interest.

'Shouldn't be hard to find the doctor's house. We can head over there after we've talked to Mrs Ross – if she's at home. Kevin seems to have got some useful stuff out of Mairi.'

Murray bridled. 'Actually, it was—'

He didn't let her complete the sentence. 'It was his idea to talk to her, and his interview. Right?'

Murray drooped. 'Yes, sir.'

They drove in silence again, along past Mowat's farm. They were right out in country now, moor and bogland stretching on either side with not a house in sight. Strang had just begun to wonder if the directions were right when Murray said, 'Oh, that must be it.'

The house she was pointing to had plastered walls painted white, though not recently from the looks of it. There were rust stains around the drainpipes and the paintwork was blistered in places. Perhaps its inherent ugliness – a two-storey box with windows and a door poked into it in the style of a child's drawing – had made it unloved. It certainly looked it.

Strang parked outside and they stepped out into the clammy heat. Opposite the house on the other side of the road there was only blanket bog, a landscape of muted greens and browns under a wide, wide sky. The sun was glittering on pools of stagnant water spiked with rushes and bog cotton and as they looked a huge, iridescent dragonfly drifted languidly across.

Murray shuddered. 'I hate insects. You can hear them all the time here and there's just clouds and clouds of flies over there. How could anyone live here? It's . . . creepy.'

Strang laughed. 'Not really a country girl, are you? Doesn't speak to me, either, though I can see it's got a sort of bleak beauty. Anyway, we may not like it but presumably Mrs Ross does.'

There was no car outside, which wasn't encouraging. There was no bell by the front door; Strang knocked, then after a moment knocked again, louder this time. There was still no response.

'Out or just not answering the door?' Strang walked round to the back of the house while Murray cupped her hand on the glass to peer in the windows, then followed him.

'Can't see anyone, boss. Furniture's pretty sparse – no pictures or anything.'

'It looks as if it hasn't been regularly occupied. The garden's running wild and the decking's starting to rot. No sign of anyone in the kitchen, either. Pity. I daresay we'd better leave it for the day.'

They were walking back to the car when Strang noticed that a little further on there were what looked like drainage trenches, long parallel lines of heaped-up soil, dried out now in the sun.

'Hang on,' he said. 'It was a drainage project that caused all the trouble with Pat Curran. Maybe that's why this house is here, out in the middle of nowhere.'

He walked on down the road. Wide tracks, deepened into ruts by some kind of agricultural machinery, led to smaller tracks and paths out along the drained land, but water had seeped in again and had pooled at the bottom of the trenches. There was a small plantation of trees still in their protective tubing, but they looked stunted and sickly; several had fallen over and been stripped of their leaves – deer to blame, most likely.

A cluster of rudimentary sheds, mainly just wooden struts surrounded with chain-link fencing and roofed with corrugated iron, still held abandoned equipment and a couple of vehicles with wide, heavy-duty tyres. It looked as if someone had hoped that one day they might come in useful again.

Strang went to the gate of one, closed with a bar and a heavy padlock, and shook it. 'Lucky those are still here. There's a lot of agricultural theft these days.'

Murray was looking around her. 'Probably not a lot of people come along here these days – oh, geroff!' She started swatting frantically at a cloud of tiny black flies that were gathering round them.

'It's this humid heat. They've smelt our sweat,' Strang said, marching briskly back to the car. He was waving his hands too. 'You have to watch these little bastards – they have a filthy bite. And that's a cleg now too.' He flapped away a bloated-looking horsefly. 'Had a bite once and my whole arm swelled up.'

Back in the car with the air-conditioning on full, Murray examined her arms. 'They've got me a couple of times,' she said, displaying two small red spots.

'Get some antiseptic onto them whenever you can. And we'll need to find some repellent before we go anywhere near there again. Now, the doctor's house – easiest thing is just to ask in the village, I suppose.'

Morven was in a funny mood today, Kirstie Mowat thought, eyeing her boss warily. She'd been late opening up the cafe; having got up early to see the inspector, Kirstie had been putting in time, just hanging around till it was time to start work but then had found herself waiting on the doorstep for quarter of an hour.

Morven never gave much away but she was never one to keep her bad temper to herself either. So, she wasn't actually out of temper today, just a bit grim-faced, which wasn't unusual, but today she looked as if she had something on her mind. Something dark.

She didn't even mention what had happened the day

before, didn't ask if Kirstie was all right. She didn't, to Kirstie's relief, ask why the policeman coming to look for her should have made her faint. She'd had the 'bad-time-of-the-month' excuse all lined up, in case she did, but it looked as if Morven had forgotten all about it.

The cafe hadn't been so busy today – just a couple of the usual suspects and three or four drop-ins. One lot were Americans and Kirstie made a point of being particularly charming to them – always great tippers, Americans – as she explained that the lunch wasn't quite ready yet but was being freshly made right now. They seemed to like that.

Weirdly enough, when she went back into the kitchen to see how much longer it would be, she heard Morven chuckle and when she went in her boss was setting a quiche down on the table with a broad smile. It vanished as she saw Kirstie and her face was grim again.

You'd almost think Kirstie had imagined the chuckle and the smile. She knew she hadn't, though.

CHAPTER ELEVEN

'Scottish baronial run riot,' Strang said as he pulled into the car park at the surgery side of the Westerfield House. It wasn't busy; there were just three or four cars outside.

Murray didn't like to say she'd no idea what that was, but it certainly was a toff's house. Built of red sandstone, it sprawled over about half of a huge garden, with turrets everywhere you could stick a turret and half a dozen different roof levels. Oh, and a great enormous weathervane on the tower in the far corner that had a huge eagle with outstretched wings, looking as if he was trying to pick the whole thing up and not quite managing.

'Can you imagine anyone doing this on purpose?' she said. 'It's like Disney – the Beast's castle.'

'Height of fashion at the time, no doubt, and said "serious money" to anyone who looked at it. And then of course it's been extended and extended at different periods – the surgery bit here is a lot more recent.'

'Do we go to the surgery or the house, boss?'

Strang thought about it as he got out of the car. 'Surgery, I think. It looks as if consulting's over for the day and if the news is likely to come as a shock to any of "Curran's women" it might be as well to have a medical man on hand.'

The receptionist was a dark-haired woman with an overenthusiastic perm. She didn't look the type to be called Francesca, Murray thought, and anyway she was wearing a wedding ring. Mairi hadn't said anything about the other daughter being married.

She looked startled when they produced their warrant cards, but then said, 'Oh – oh yes, of course. I'll see if Doctor Sinclair is free to see you now. DCI Strang, did you say?' She came out from the enclosed reception desk and crossed the empty waiting room to knock on a door at the far end.

A voice said, 'Oh, I see. Yes, certainly,' and a tall man came out. He had probably been quite good-looking when he was younger, but the regular features were blurring round the edges a bit and his colouring suggested he was no stranger to the gin bottle. His pale-blue eyes were still quite striking, though, and the smooth dark hair had no sign of grey.

His manner was self-assured – like a very sleek tomcat, thought Murray, who if he didn't have the cream right at the moment was reckoning it would appear pretty soon. It was probably going too far to say he was faintly sinister, but she certainly didn't like him.

He came across the room to hold out his hand to Strang. 'Chief Inspector Strang? Malcolm Sinclair. Come through and tell me what I can do for you.'

He had ignored Murray completely. She trotted along behind like a puppy as he led the way into the consulting room.

'This has come as a blow to the whole community,' Sinclair said solemnly, sitting back and spreading his hands across a stomach that was starting to expand. 'We've been very fortunate in that we haven't been burdened with too many of these people in the past, but I suppose we have to expect urban problems catching up with us now they've started this ridiculous "Route 66" promotion to send yobs on motorbikes roaring round the coast road. I don't know what they're thinking of nowadays.'

Pompous prat, Murray thought.

He went on, 'But what did you want from me?'

'I'm afraid this wasn't a rough sleeper, sir,' Strang said. 'In fact, it's possible he may even have been one of your own patients – Niall Aitchison.'

It seemed as if Sinclair hadn't heard. It was a moment before he said blankly, '*Niall Aitchison* – are you sure? I heard it was a dropout who was dossing down in that abandoned cottage.'

Strang shook his head and Sinclair went on, 'But what in hell was Niall doing in that place? It's been boarded up for years, ever since the old MacRoberts died. And how am I going to tell the girls? He was – he was in and out of the house here all the time. In fact, Francesca—oh dear God!'

'Are any of the family here at the moment?' Strang asked.

Sinclair had got out a handkerchief and was mopping his forehead. 'I can't remember – let me think. Sorry – this has been such a shock. My wife has a committee meeting in Aberdeen – no, that's tomorrow, of course. Sorry. Oh – oh yes, they should be, I think. There was some plan for the three of them to have lunch at the Castle of Mey cafe – nice little place, you know, attached to the Queen Mother's Highland retreat. Worth seeing—' He stopped. 'Oh God, I'm babbling. It's the shock. What time is it? Yes, we should just catch them. I must break it to them before they leave, and some idiot comes up and just blurts it out. This'll go round the town like wildfire and my wife is very sensitive.'

He jumped up and hurried them out of the room and across the waiting room, under the curious gaze of the receptionist, through a door that opened onto a hall that looked straight out of a Gothic novel. Murray, her existence still unacknowledged, followed them through.

She'd be willing to put a fiver on Dr Sinclair not having known the body in the cottage was Niall Aitchison. If he had, and put up a performance like that, he wouldn't be a GP in a wee town in northern Scotland. He'd be giving David Tennant a run for his money.

Although, of course, she could be wrong.

The sitting room where they found 'Curran's women' reflected the hectic style of the exterior – a huge room with an inglenook by a monumental fireplace and alcoves, recesses and window seats built into the thickness of the walls. It had been decorated in a style that betrayed uncertainty, relying mainly on swagged curtains, multiple cushions and several vases of silk flowers to convey opulence.

The manner of Sinclair's entrance had been enough to convey alarm to the women who were sitting there; while he stumbled to find the appropriate words and they stared at him, Strang took the chance to observe them.

The older woman, Lilian presumably, had honey-blonde hair and Strang knew enough to recognise an expensive tint. Even if her neat-featured style didn't appeal to him personally he could see that she was quite attractive, and she certainly didn't look old enough to be the mother of the woman sitting next to her – plump, mid-to-late twenties, thin mousy hair. Francesca or Gabrielle?

His mental question was answered when he looked at the third woman, sitting huddled into the corner of the sofa opposite as if for protection. There was no doubt at all that this was the one with the problems; he could see the signs in the dark circles below the eyes and the heavy, slightly swollen lids. She looked as if she was doped at the moment and there were the signs of personal neglect as well in the lack of make-up and the hair dragged back into a ponytail – that had to be Gabrielle, who had lost her father and her unborn child in a short space of time and had failed to find the strength to cope with her grief. Strang knew all about grief and his heart went out to her.

Sinclair had gone to sit beside his wife, wedging himself in awkwardly so Lilian and Francesca had to shift up to make room for him. He put his arm round her and held her close to him as he said, 'Er . . . there's something I have to tell you.'

Lilian twisted to look up at his face. 'Darling, what's wrong? You're frightening me!'

'I know, I'm sorry.' He looked around the women. 'It's bad news, I'm afraid. The body they found the other day – well, I'm afraid . . .' He stalled again and gave a helpless look towards Strang, who stepped forward.

'I'm DCI Strang. I'm sorry to have to tell you that the victim has been identified as Niall Aitchison, who was I gather a close friend.'

Utter shock registered on Lilian's face. 'But-but they said it was just a tramp!' she cried. 'Someone sleeping rough – Oh my God! How could it be *Niall*? That's . . . that's awful. Oh, Malcolm!' She gave a sob, turning to bury her face in her husband's shoulder.

Francesca seemed to take a moment to understand. Then she screamed, a high-pitched wail that gathered in intensity. 'It can't be – not Niall! He was all I had left and that's been taken away from me now too.' She was struggling to get the words out. 'And then, his eyes . . . I'm going to be sick.' She leapt to her feet and rushed from the room.

Gabrielle hadn't said anything. Was she so spaced-out she hadn't absorbed what had been said, Strang wondered, and then realised that tears were silently pouring down her face. She said brokenly, 'He was . . . he was such a nice man. We owed him so much.'

She was making no attempt to wipe her face. Murray, a silent observer, picked up a brocaded box of tissues lying on the coffee table and gave Gabrielle a handful. She looked at them as if she was uncertain what they were for, then put up her hand to wipe the tears.

'What did Fran mean, his eyes?' she said slowly.

Lilian jumped up and came across to her. 'She was just upset, talking nonsense. We need to go to her. Come along.' She took her daughter's hand and led her, unresisting, from the room.

Sinclair stood up too. 'I'm sure there are questions you

173

are entitled to ask, Inspector, but as you can see it would be totally out of the question at this time. Perhaps you can come back once the ladies have had a chance to recover from the shock.'

'Of course,' Strang said smoothly. 'But since we're here, perhaps you could give us a bit more background about your family's connection with Mr Aitchison. Clearly it's been a close one.'

For a moment he wondered if Sinclair would refuse, but then he said wearily, 'Oh, I suppose. You'd better sit down. Do you want a drink? I need a brandy.' Barely waiting for their refusal, he went to one of the alcoves which housed a lavishly equipped drinks trolley, picked up a decanter with a silver label that said 'Brandy' round its neck and a heavy crystal tumbler. He half-filled it, took a swig, then a second one, and topped it up before carrying it back to his seat on the sofa.

Strang and Murray sat down on the sofa opposite. At a nod from Strang, Murray discreetly took out a notebook.

'Your stepdaughter seemed particularly distressed,' Strang said. 'Did they have a relationship?'

'Oh, wishful thinking, I'm afraid. It's hard for her, you know. There is a positive dearth of really *suitable* young men around here and she was disappointed too over young David. He'd been around here a bit and it had been looking quite hopeful until of course Gabrielle appeared on the scene.

'Spoilt brat, if you want my opinion, and hard as nails. Fran's a good girl, always very loyal to Lilian, but Gabrielle, I'm sorry to say, takes after her father and quite frankly he was a complete bastard. Of course, to her he could do no wrong and she went off with him to Aberdeen without a thought of what losing her meant to her poor mother. And the moment she saw David, she just set her cap at him and stole him from right under Fran's nose. She hasn't a lot of confidence, poor girl, and that really knocked her back. Personally, I think that was what was behind it – a spiteful pleasure in taking something away from her sister. Not a nice person, Gabrielle.

'And Fran—' He sighed. 'I doubt if there was ever anything at all between her and Niall – one of nature's non-combatants, if you ask me, but well, you know, *faute de mieux . . .*'

'Did I gather that Mr Aitchison was Mr Curran's representative up here after the failure of the drainage company?' Strang asked.

'His patsy, you mean.' Sinclair leant forward confidentially; the level of brandy in his glass had dropped considerably. 'I'm not going to try to wrap this up in clean linen. Curran was a swindler but smart enough so no one could prove it. If you ask me, he engineered the bankruptcy so that Lilian got nothing – not a penny, after all she'd had to put up with all these years. And he was never man enough to face the people he'd sweet-talked into investing their hard-earned cash, so that poor old Niall was left facing the music. He couldn't just run off and hide in Aberdeen – his mother was still living here, and he was a good son.'

'What sort of a man was he?'

Sinclair paused for a moment, thinking. 'A decent enough chap, I suppose. Hadn't the imagination to be anything but, to be frank. He got twisted by Curran to the point where it broke up his family – Mum supported him and the sister was left out in the cold having lost everything. It was tragic and she's very embittered now, but it's no wonder.

'Niall was a lot more loyal than Curran deserved. It's possible he carried a bit of a torch for Gabrielle – though for heaven's sake don't mention that to Fran. She'll be crushed enough by this.'

He looked at his watch and shifted restlessly in his seat. 'Look, I'm worried about the girls – they're going to be working each other up into a state. I really need to go and see what I can do to calm them down.'

'One last thing,' Strang said quickly. 'You mentioned Gabrielle's husband, David Ross. Where would I find him?'

'Offshore at the moment, as far as I know. He gets called out to the rigs when they've a computer problem. We'll get in touch with him and let him know what's happened and tell him you want to speak to him. Now—' Sinclair stood up.

Murray tucked her notebook away and they left him to his unenviable task.

The police had been in with Bruce Michie for some time. Ailie Johnston had shown them in then retreated with some reluctance. It wouldn't really do to be caught with her ear pressed to the door but once she was back at her desk she found it difficult to concentrate.

There had been a lot of incoming phone calls lately from the two men she knew sometimes went off with Michie for boys' weekends, fishing or doing a bit of rough shooting up in Caithness. She only kept his work diary so that was no help, but then she remembered, of course, that he'd told her he was going and afterwards she'd asked if he'd seen Gabrielle. That had definitely been the week before last. The Saturday when according to his neighbour Niall had gone up to Forsich too.

Ailie knew them – Tom Morrison, whose company dealt with hydraulic repairs and Chris Brady, who was in the services industry like themselves. Most of Michie's friends were.

It had struck her before as odd that Michie should be pally with Brady, a direct competitor; he was a rather brash, overbearing man who had made the mistake of trying to patronise Gabrielle when he came to the office, officially to condole with her after her father's death. He had come out with all but visible claw marks, looking shaken. Now she was wondering if there was some sort of conspiracy going on while Gabrielle was ill.

That row between Michie and Niall: Ailie didn't know what it had been about but there was no doubt that in any power struggle Niall would have supported Gabrielle. He was totally loyal to her, just as he had been to Pat – who had, Ailie was forced to admit, taken shameless advantage of that.

She had left the door of her office open and now she heard someone coming out of Michie's office and the police walk past on their way out. She looked round her desk for something she could use as an excuse to go and see Michie, but before she could find anything her buzzer went and she was summoned.

Michie was looking a bit on edge, she thought, but not rattled. When she asked brightly if he'd had a grilling, he

177

said, 'No, no, very civilised. Just wanted to know the guys' addresses and the name of the hotel where we were staying so they could check I was where I said I was and they could eliminate me from enquiries. That was all, really.

'I wanted to get in touch with Niall's sister, so I could offer her appropriate sympathy from the company, as you know, but of course they weren't at liberty to give me her details. Still, they said they would pass on our details and invite her to make contact. So, if someone calls in this connection, put her straight through to me, all right?'

Ailie bridled. 'Yes of course. I'm not in the habit of screening your calls unless you ask me to.'

'No, but you might start gabbling on to her about her brother. I don't want that. Straight through, all right?'

Ailie gave a curt nod, then went out. What was it that Michie didn't want her to say to Niall's sister? Then it struck her: she would be Niall's next-of-kin, set to inherit, among other things, Niall's shares in Curran Services. If Michie could get hold of them, he would have the majority shareholding – and suddenly the connection with Chris Brady started to make sense.

And just how far would they go to get what they wanted?

DCI Strang was scribbling notes to himself as he read through the reports that were coming in. He'd skipped lunch; it was after two already and after a hectic morning he needed things straight in his mind to write the press statement he'd be making this afternoon. He'd hoped to speak to DS Borthwick beforehand, but she was unavailable. It wasn't a real problem since it was going to be short and uncontroversial, but it never did any harm to make sure she was kept on board.

DS Taylor and DC Murray were detailed to come for a briefing at three. Murray was definitely the more useful officer and today it had looked as if she'd learnt a bit since last time. Her besetting sin had been trying to chip in with her own questions when he was conducting an interview but this morning she'd waited till afterwards and hadn't butted in with a question that would have been unnecessary and disruptive.

Details had come in from an interview with Bruce Michie in Aberdeen about the fishing hotel he had visited with his friends, along with their names, and he was keen to check it out after he made the statement. But if he took Murray with him this afternoon in preference to her sergeant, Taylor would definitely resent it. He didn't want to provoke open warfare.

He didn't want to provoke open warfare with DI Hay either, but he was irritated that the man was being deliberately obstructive. If he could have taken Jack Lothian with him this afternoon it would have got him off the hook.

He was still brooding on the problem when there was a tap on the door and Lothian himself appeared.

Strang brightened. 'Good to see you. I thought I'd lost you to DI Hay.'

'I found that the problem he had called me back to deal with was very easily sorted out, so I left a message telling him and came back,' Lothian said with professional blandness. 'A couple of things had come in that I felt you should know about at once.

'There's a report from the Forsinard Flows visitors centre that a car had been sitting in the car park there since the previous Saturday. It's got Niall Aitchison's number plate.'

'Where is that?'

'It's on the A897 – that's the road we went on to Mr Mowat's farm this morning.'

Strang digested that. 'So, it's not far from the house where Gabrielle Ross is staying?'

Lothian looked blank. 'Couldn't tell you, sir. But I can find out—'

'No need. We can get my team onto it this afternoon and call in some forensic help to check out the car.'

'There was another thing too. Someone called David Ross contacted the incident room at the village hall to ask if you would phone him back urgently. Wouldn't leave a message.'

'Ah,' Strang said. 'Gabrielle's husband. I'd better take a minute to call him now. She's in a highly nervous state and my information is that he's offshore, so he may be anxious about her.' He called the number Lothian gave him.

Ross was indeed anxious. 'I'm gutted about Niall, of course, but it's my wife that's my big worry. They were very close, you know, both of them utterly devoted to my father-in-law. She's had a bad time and she's not well – fragile, you know? Right on the edge, frankly, and police questioning when she's so shocked could tip her over.

'OK, you've a job to do and Gabrielle will want to help any way she can, but I think she'll need a lot of support. I can't get off the rig until Thursday morning. Could questioning wait till I've seen how she is?'

180

Strang gave an inward sigh but having seen Gabrielle he could understand the man's concern. 'Yes of course, sir,' he said. 'We'll be wanting to interview you as well, so it would be helpful if you could make yourself available on Thursday. We can assess your wife's situation then.'

Ross seemed suitably grateful and Strang rang off, pulling a face. 'Not ideal, since she's likely to know more about Aitchison than anyone else, but driving her into a complete breakdown wouldn't be great for PR.

'Now, Taylor and Murray are coming for a briefing at three. You should be in on that and then after I've spoken to the media I'll be wanting you to come with me to the hotel where Gabrielle Ross's business partner was staying for a fishing weekend with some of his pals on the weekend when Aitchison was last seen. All right?'

Once Lothian had gone, Strang, his problem solved, went on to prepare the press statement. Ideally it should give the impression that the police were keen to be totally frank in so far as they were able while sadly not being able to be very frank at all.

When DC Murray got back to the incident room at the village hall, it was very quiet with just a couple of uniforms working at computers and one on a phone call. There was no sign of Taylor and the tea trolley was unattended, but there was a box with sandwiches and crisps, so she helped herself, looked dubiously at the filling, then found a free terminal and logged on.

She'd been hoping that PC Davidson might be around, bursting with useful information, but there was no sign of him. Taylor had definitely gone one up for thinking of interviewing Mairi and Strang had slapped her down when she'd tried to claim the credit that was due to her for asking the right questions.

She should have redeemed herself a bit, though, when they'd gone to Sinclair's house. She had been a model of unobtrusive efficiency and hadn't said a word, even when she'd really wanted to probe a bit about the weird stepdaughter's background – just as well, as it turned out, since when she said that to Strang afterwards it was obvious that he knew about it already. A double bereavement, he told her. And judging by her reaction, finding out what had happened to Aitchison was going to make things even worse.

Murray logged on to see what Taylor had managed to collate from the door-to-doors – not a lot, as far as she could see. As yet there was nothing useful, but he'd checked barely half of them. What time had he gone off for his lunch break, she wondered, as she gave a sigh and settled down to work through them.

Still nothing. Apart from Aitchison's neighbour, no one had seen the man since that Saturday morning. So, though they knew when his body had been placed in the empty cottage, they had no real idea when the man had been killed and the autopsy report hadn't helped – not even a guess. And what did 'preservative process' mean? Embalming? There were some dead weird features to this case.

Absorbed in her work, she didn't notice PC Davidson's approach until he tentatively cleared his throat just at her shoulder. She jumped and looked round. Just for a moment she didn't recognise him; the little moustache had disappeared – a great improvement, even if it did make him look more like a teenager than ever.

'Ah, Craig! Got something for me? Come on, sit down.'

He sat down opposite her, looking awkward. 'Don't want to get your hopes up too much – it's not a lot, really. I was just doing house-to-house asking if anyone had seen Aitchison in the week before we found him. There was this female – she hadn't, but all she wanted to talk about was a Pat Curran. That mean anything?'

'Oh yes. He's dead, but he won't lie down. Go on.'

'She went into a rant about the whole family. He was a conman and there's a daughter, Gabrielle – she's a murderer, according to my source.'

'A murderer?' Thinking of the broken creature she had seen that morning, Murray was astonished. 'Who did she murder?'

'She was so worked up by this time, she was gibbering. It was something to do with Morven Gunn.'

He spoke the name with venom, and Murray smiled. 'Your friend? She can't have been the victim – she's certainly alive and kicking.'

'Oh yes, and then some. But that was about it. A male heard the woman was shouting and came to the door. He told her she'd to calm down or she'd get in trouble and said to me not to pay any attention. As he shoved her back in she said over her shoulder, "You look in the graveyard." That was all.'

Murray's eyes were shining. 'Sounds good to me. You're a wee stotter, Craig.'

He grinned. 'Happy to help. And by the way, Lothian

told me Gunn's dropped the formal charge. Said your boss put her right in her place.'

'He's good at that,' she said with feeling. 'Thanks again, Craig.'

'I'll get my report in now,' he said, standing up.

'Er . . . could you hold it back for a bit? Just give me a chance to check it out and then I'll get back to you, OK?'

He looked a little puzzled, but said, 'Sure,' and went off.

She knew she shouldn't have done it, but she needed to convince Strang that though Taylor might outrank her she could out-think him every time. She could go to the graveyard right now, if she knew where it was. Taylor, of course, had the car keys but it could be in walking distance.

There was no one here who looked as if they would have local knowledge. She went out into the high street and into the Spar shop, three doors along. The girl at the till tried to send her to the crematorium in Thurso, but when she insisted it was a graveyard she was looking for, an older woman came forward.

'There's one just along the road on the right, by the old Free Kirk. Can't miss it.' She smiled. 'Looking for your ancestors, are you? We get a lot of folk doing that around here these days. It's that programme about who you think you are that does it.'

Murray didn't correct her, only thanked her and went off to follow her instructions. She'd been right; it wasn't hard to find. The church was boarded up, but the graveyard was still well-tended; a peaceful spot on sloping ground, very natural with the graves planted in the mossy turf with rocky outcrops and straggling trees whose tops were barbered by the prevailing wind.

It was still today, though, still and clammy. Even the slight incline made Murray sweat under the midday sun as she walked around, checking the headstones as she went. They mostly seemed to be old graves, some leaning and even lying flat, covered with moss.

As she looked around, a flash of colour caught her eye – pink, from a row of little rose bushes on what was obviously a more modern grave; its headstone was shiny grey granite with the lettering in gold. She bent to read it.

'Gary Gunn, beloved son of Morven Gunn,' it said, with a date of death some nine years previously.

Murray bit her lip. Never judge someone else; you don't know what has made them the way they are. No wonder Morven was angry and aggressive, especially if she believed her son had been murdered, as Craig's source suggested. She stood thinking for a moment, then turned to go.

There was litter nearby: green striped paper, torn into shreds that looked as if it had wrapped a bouquet of roses – yellow, probably, though now it was reduced to a scattered pile of browning petals and brutally broken stalks.

Despite the heat, Murray felt a chill. It was worrying evidence of fury, of violence and, yes, of real hate.

Where else had that hatred been directed? Morven Gunn had been totally unmoved by her brother's death.

CHAPTER TWELVE

It was almost quarter to three when DC Murray got back to the village hall, where Taylor was waiting for her with unconcealed irritation.

'Where the hell were you? I was only going to wait another minute before I drove along for the briefing myself. You can explain to Strang that it's your fault if we're late.' He strode out of the hall, throwing open the door and leaving it to swing back in her face.

She hurried to catch up with him. 'Where were you anyway when I got back here? I've been working on the reports you hadn't finished and then went out for a bit of air.'

'None of your business where I was,' he snapped.

As if she needed to ask! The beer breath just about knocked her over as she joined him in the car and they drove in hostile silence along to the Masons Arms.

It gave Murray time to think about what she was going to do with the interesting information that had come her way.

She knew what she should do: tell Strang whenever she saw him. She'd have to do a bit of fancy footwork about how the information had come to her, but the well-constructed fictions she'd been telling her mother all through her adolescent years had sharpened her wits and she could always think of something, even at short notice.

On the other hand, knowledge was power and secretly hoarded knowledge was even more satisfying. She wanted to impress Strang to the point where he would have to ignore Taylor's seniority; if she quietly found out a bit more about the 'murder' accusation against Gabrielle Ross, she could present him with a neat package of information instead of just a line that he – and even Taylor – could follow up on.

She was having misgivings about that by the time they reached the hotel car park. Perhaps if she and Strang were working on their own this afternoon, she might be better to tell him anyway – she could say PC Davidson had happened to mention the information and that she had used her initiative and checked out the graveyard. Only he hadn't ever been exactly keen on her using her initiative, really.

Murray was still in two minds when she went into Strang's office. When she heard that Lothian was to go with him to do interviews at the fishing hotel while she was stuck with Taylor checking on an abandoned car, that settled it.

The hotel, rather coyly called the Angler's Rest, wasn't quite the traditional fishing hotel Strang had expected. His father, in favour of killing things in general, had taken him a couple of times to a fishing and shooting hotel on the west coast, which had been the ancestral home of the owner, fallen on hard times. Nothing much had changed since the days of Victorian hunting and shooting parties: the furnishings were shabby, the ancient curtains all but in tatters and the more modern comforts non-existent, but there were blazing fires, menus that featured roasts and school puddings, and a help-yourself bar that had an eclectic range of whiskies and an honour box. The stone-flagged hall was always littered with waders and its walls were lined with stags' heads and glass cases with remarkably un-lifelike fish.

The Angler's Rest wasn't quite like that. Its position near Halkirk, about ten miles from Thurso, was certainly ideal for access to the trout fishing at Loch Watten and Loch Calder, but it was just a grey stone villa-style house with an unappealing two-storey block extension and a white-painted conservatory on the front. The signboard featured a very large salmon leaping on a line above a very small man.

There was no one about when they walked in. The entrance hall was a bar and presumably the counter also acted as a reception desk. There was no one visible but Lothian found a buzzer to press while Strang looked around.

The carpet was an aggressive orangey tartan with bar stools to match. There was a wooden stand on the bar counter crammed with leaflets about boat hire, ghillies, organised fishing days and tackle shops and there were framed angling cartoons on the beige and cream striped vinyl wallpaper. Strang had a suspicion that the fish mounted on the wall behind the bar might, if prompted, sing 'Don't Worry, Be Happy'.

They waited, then Lothian pressed the buzzer again. When there was still no response, they walked on through the conservatory dining room and into the kitchen behind.

The back door was open, and they could hear voices from the garden beyond.

A heavily built man in rather grubby chef's whites was sitting in the sun smoking along with another man in jeans and a grey T-shirt and a girl, who looked about eighteen, in a pink overall. She saw them first.

'Oh!' she exclaimed. 'Police!' and then the men turned too.

The chef put his hands above his head. 'It's all right, Officer, I'll come quietly!' he declaimed, to laughter from the others.

How often had he heard that one, Strang thought, wearily. 'Thank you, sir. DCI Strang and Sergeant Lothian. Is one of you the proprietor?'

'Nah!' the chef said. 'He's off in the afternoon. Want me to buzz the flat?' He picked up the mobile that was on the table beside him.

'If you would.'

As the chef turned aside to make the call, Strang said, 'There's a couple of questions I want to ask you too. Were any of you here the weekend before last?'

'Chef was,' the other man said. 'I was off. Why are you wanting to know?'

'Just some routine questions.' The girl hadn't spoken and Strang asked her directly, 'You here?'

She gave him a long, cool look that implied distrust. 'Yeah, I think so.'

'I understand there was a party of men staying the weekend before last. Three men on a fishing weekend?'

'We get a lot of them.'

She obviously wasn't inclined to be helpful, but he persisted. 'Three on that weekend?'

189

'Yeah, could have been.'

The chef came back, saying Jeff – 'He's the boss' – would be right down. Strang put the question to him but got nowhere with that either; the chef had nothing to do with the guests. He returned to the girl.

'So, there could have been this party of three? Do you remember anything about them?'

She did at least admit she might have done. 'It was them had another man come in later, when we'd really stopped serving but I'd to get him something.'

'Hayley, you're just confusing the officers.'

The voice came from behind them. A squat man wearing a black T-shirt proclaiming 'Just another sexy bald bloke' had just come out of the house and he spoke sharply. As Hayley shrugged, he said, 'Jeff Baxter. What can I do for you? No problem about the licence, I hope?'

'Just a couple of routine questions,' Strang said, as usual. 'Perhaps there's somewhere we could talk?'

Somehow, he got the impression that the man wasn't surprised by their visit. It would be interesting to see if he would admit to that once they were all sitting down at the table in the dining room he had taken them to.

He didn't. He said, 'Would you like coffee – a soft drink, maybe? Don't suppose there's any point in offering you a drop of the hard stuff these days?'

Strang agreed that there wasn't but asked for water, and Baxter summoned Hayley with a bellow to fetch it along with a Coke for himself.

Baxter sat back in his chair. 'What can I do for you then, Chief Inspector? Or do I know you well enough to call you Inspector?' He gave a fat little giggle.

Strang ignored it. 'It's straightforward enough. Three men—' Lothian without prompting had accessed the details on his phone and he gave the names.

Baxter listened, nodding. 'That's right. Bruce Michie and Tom Morrison are old mates of mine – been coming for years and a few months ago Chris Brady joined them. Come up now every few weeks for a lads' weekend away from the ladies, God bless 'em. No one to tell them when they've had enough!'

'When did they arrive?'

'Oh, couldn't be that specific. Two came in the late afternoon, as far as I remember, and one checked in nearer dinner time. Bruce was one of the earlier ones, and then Tom. Oh, Chris had a lot of catching up to do by the time he got here, I can tell you that.'

'So, they came separately?'

'That's right. They all like to be independent – say you think the fish aren't biting at Loch Watten, you can always head over to Loch Calder and see if they're taking over there.'

'Did they have much success?' Strang asked. 'I'd have thought it would hardly be worth taking a fishing weekend with the weather the way it's been. The trout are never very hungry when it's hot and the water level must be low too.'

Baxter looked vague. 'Oh well, you never know. An excuse for a break, anyway.' He definitely wasn't comfortable.

'Did they spend much time out there trying?'

'Oh, I expect so. I can't really say – I work, I don't hang out with the guests during the day.' He looked round impatiently. 'Where is that girl? Hayley!'

Lothian, with a glance at Strang for approval, said, 'What kind of fishing did they do, sir? Fly-fishing individually, or out in a boat together?'

Baxter was visibly irritated. 'Oh, I don't know. Both, probably. You'd better ask them. Oh, here she comes at last. Hayley, I don't know how it can possibly take you so long to open a can and take a couple of bottles out of the chiller.'

As the girl handed them the water, Strang said, 'Hayley, you mentioned another man who joined the party we were talking about, a bit later. Is that right?'

Baxter butted in. 'Hayley, what did you have for your supper last night?' Hayley looked blank and Baxter gave a short laugh. 'Your average goldfish is a mental giant compared to her, Inspector. Can't remember yesterday let alone ten days ago. There were only three of them together, though there were other guests in the hotel, so maybe one of those came in late.'

'Is that right, Hayley?'

She looked sullen. 'I dunno.' Without waiting for any more questions, she went back into the kitchen.

Strang stood up. 'I think that's all for the moment then, sir. I'm grateful for your cooperation. Do you mind if we take the water with us?'

Baxter jumped up with alacrity. 'Not at all, not at all. Be my guest.' He showed them out, chatting volubly about the astonishing weather and how it was going to break any day now.

Back in the car, Lothian said wryly, 'Pretty happy to get us off the premises, I thought.'

'And who was Hayley's man that Baxter was so keen

192

to convince us didn't exist?' Strang said. 'I think we need to get her for a chat when she's not on duty.'

At last, Francesca retreated to her bedroom in a state of collapse. Gabrielle and her mother were in the smart little sitting room of her flat, the one Lilian had done up for her in a tasteful palette of grey and pink and which said nothing at all about Fran's personality.

It had been a difficult afternoon. Sinclair had brought up the decanter of brandy and had plied Fran with it so that she went from hysterical sobbing into full suttee mood, acting as if it was only the lack of a funeral pyre that stopped her flinging herself upon it in self-immolation.

'My life is over!' she kept declaiming. 'Niall was my future and now he's gone, he's gone.'

Gabrielle listened in silence, while inside she was screaming, *It's not about you, it's about Niall!* The brandy helped, in fact; she was feeling more and more removed from everything and everyone, as if she was watching them through a sheet of glass. Twice when her mother spoke to her she failed to reply because all of it seemed nothing to do with her.

Anyway, she didn't want to talk now of all that Niall had been to Paddy and to her: totally loyal, endlessly supportive, warmth and kindness personified. She had always known he was in love with her, without ever expecting her love in return. She'd seen his pain in an unguarded moment when she'd announced her engagement to David, but even so he had stood as an usher at the wedding. He'd even told her that all he wanted was her happiness, and to be there at her side to see it. And he had been, he had been, until . . .

Yet here was Fran, playing the role of grieving widow and everyone in this make-believe world was behaving as if her imaginary relationship with Niall had actually happened. No wonder Gabrielle felt unreal.

Sinclair was worried about Lilian too. He was fussing round her like a mother hen and indeed she too looked in shock, staring straight ahead while Fran ranted on. The brandy did at last pull her together and she began on her own mother-hen act.

'You go off and have a lie-down, darling,' she said to Fran. 'Grief is very tiring, and you need your strength. There are going to be difficult days ahead. Malcolm will give you something if you need it, but I think you'll be able to sleep once you're in bed.'

Clutching a box of tissues, Fran stood up and hiccupped her way to her bedroom. Sinclair, perching on the arm of Lilian's chair, said, 'What about you, my darling?'

She leant her head into him and gave a sigh. 'Oh, I'm all right, truly. It was just the terrible shock.'

Gabrielle averted her eyes. She always did. Watching her mother snuggle up to the man who had replaced her father disgusted her. Each time it felt like a betrayal of Paddy all over again.

'What happened with the police?' Lilian was saying.

'They won't bother you, meantime. I've given them a bit of background about our friendship with Niall, but they know you're away tomorrow – though I wonder if you should go, I really do.'

'I wouldn't, if I wasn't the chair, but going would be less stressful than trying to cancel. Of course, I'm very upset but

he was an old friend, not a member of the family, after all.'
She turned to Gabrielle. 'But you were close, I know. We've
all been worrying about Fran but are you all right?'

Gabrielle heard her voice as if it came from a long way
off – 'Yes, I'm all right. I'm always all right' – and saw the
others exchange a look.

'Gabrielle, I think you should stay here. I don't like the
thought of you being at the house on your own. Malcolm
spoke to David and he can't get back till the day after
tomorrow. You and Fran could be company for each other.'

If Lilian hadn't been going away Gabrielle might very
well have stayed; her own empty house, with all that had
happened, wasn't appealing. But sit around listening to Fran
wailing all day? 'Oh no, no,' Gabrielle said. 'I'll go home. I
just want peace, really.'

Sinclair stood up. 'I'd better get back to the surgery. Do
you need anything to make you sleep, Gabrielle?'

'No, I have some pills still.'

'Good, good,' he said heartily. 'Be sure to take them. You
need your rest.' He kissed his wife and went out, clutching
the almost empty decanter.

Gabrielle got up. 'I'm going to go now.' She suddenly felt a
desperate compulsion to leave and had to stop herself running
to the door. She couldn't stand this for a moment longer, this
weird world of illusion where she felt so utterly detached. If
she got out, perhaps she could connect with the real Gabrielle
again. She picked up her bag and was heading to the door
when she realised her mother was looking at her oddly.

'What did they say?'

'What did who say?'

'The voices. You just said you were hearing voices.'

Gabrielle froze. 'I didn't say that. I didn't hear any voices. I'm sure I didn't!'

'But—' Lilian said, then, apparently registering her daughter's look of shock, went on hastily, 'No, no, don't worry. I must have misheard what you said. Are you sure you're fit to be on your own?'

'Yes, of course I am. I just need to get away. It's been difficult, with Fran and everything . . .' She blundered her way out of the room, aware of Lilian following her down the stairs.

'How much brandy did you have, darling? Should you be driving, if you're confused . . .'

'I'm fine, I'm fine.' She couldn't stop herself bolting for the door as if she feared being recaptured then slammed it behind her and jumped into her car. Her head was ringing; were those voices that she was hearing, speaking in some language she did not understand?

There were several cars in the car park across the road from the Forsinard Flows RSPB visitor centre when DS Taylor and DC Murray got there. Murray got out, checking the number plates and pointed. 'That one.'

It was a black Audi A3 and from the plate it was less than six months old – certainly not the sort of car you would leave unattended for days on end in normal circumstances. 'I wonder why no one called in sooner? It's just asking to be nicked.'

'Wouldn't mind nicking it myself. It's a Sportback – great spec.' Taylor bent down to peer in the window.

'Don't touch it!' Murray said sharply.

'I wasn't going to! And anyway, loads of people probably have.'

'Adding more prints won't make that any better,' Murray said over her shoulder, walking across the road to the centre.

It was a low, grey stone cottage that to Murray's surprise was right beside a railway line, sharing the platform with the station. Inside, its walls were covered with the sort of information that the kind of people who spent all their time hiking about the countryside would want but which, frankly, left Murray cold. There was a video presentation running at the moment that showed a purplish, fleshy-looking plant shaped like a steel trap with spikes round the edges suddenly snapping shut on a fly crawling on its edge while a voiceover discussed the digestive process of the Venus flytrap that would strip the flesh and dissolve it into mush. It had a horrible sort of fascination.

'Yuck, that's gross!' Murray said. 'It's like that *Little Shop of Horrors* film. I never knew plants like that really existed. Makes you feel sick.'

'Don't look at it, then.' Taylor walked over to the desk where a woman wearing a blue RSPB T-shirt was pointing out something on a map to a young couple in shorts and hiking boots.

'Miss!' Taylor interrupted. 'Could we have a word? DS Taylor, DC Murray.'

She looked annoyed. 'Can I just finish explaining to these people where to go? Then they could get on with their walk.'

'I'm afraid—' Taylor began, when Murray broke in, 'Oh, I'm sure you'll only take a minute. We can watch the rest of the film. Come on.' She drew Taylor away.

'And why would I want to waste my time with this? Murray, I'm warning you, you're way out of line,' he snarled.

'Don't think the boss would be happy about us antagonising people needlessly. Maybe it's the way it's done in Bathgate, but—'

She knew she was living dangerously and she was quite glad when she was cut short by the woman calling over, 'I'm free now,' as the young walkers left.

'About the car, is it?'

Taylor took control, ready with his retaliation. 'Yes. Why was it left unreported for so long? It's a valuable car – why would anyone have abandoned it out here in the wilds?'

The woman looked flustered. 'I don't know! I wasn't here all the time.'

'But you did see it there earlier and didn't do anything?'

'Well, no. Why should I? It's a public car park.' She was gathering confidence. 'People take the train in to Aberdeen or Inverness for the day sometimes and leave their cars there for when they come back.'

Taylor pounced. 'Ah! For the day. But this, as far as we know, was here for a week, not just a day.'

'How was I to know how long they'd gone to Aberdeen for?'

'But on Saturday, you decided they wouldn't have gone to Aberdeen for more than a week and called in?'

Taylor was sounding triumphant, as if some how he'd won an important point. Murray despaired of him. The woman was defensive now, ready to argue about it. She chipped in, 'We're grateful that you did, anyway. Do you by any chance remember the owner leaving it – a male on his own, probably, 5'8", brown hair, brown eyes?'

The woman shook her head. 'I didn't see who left it there but no one like that came in here on that Saturday. We only had about half a dozen visits altogether. I suppose he might have gone round onto the platform without me seeing him, but there aren't a lot of trains and I always glance out of the window when one comes in. There's never more than two or three people on the platform and I certainly didn't see him.'

Taylor drew breath to speak and she could read his mind: he was just about to ask why, then, she thought the car belonged to someone who'd taken the train and hurried on.

'So, you know that the car was left on the Saturday – is that right?'

'Yes. It was the only car in the car park when I left. I'm off Sunday and Monday and I noticed it when I came back last Tuesday.'

Taylor got his word in at last, with a look at Murray that dared her to interrupt. 'So, what made you *eventually* decide to report it at the weekend?'

'Just, it had been a long time, I suppose. And we've got a bit of a stroppy element around here, making protests and stuff because they don't like what the RSPB is doing to bring more visitors in and they might do something.'

Taylor was looking interested about the stroppy neighbours. Before he could go off on another tangent, Murray said, 'So if he didn't come in here, and he didn't go off in the train, why would he have parked here?'

'People do, if they just want to go out on the Dubh Lochan trail or just to the Lookout Tower. There's a boardwalk that takes you there and you can climb up and see the pattern of the Flows. It's very pretty, you know, almost like a tapestry.

You can see some of those insectivorous plants you were looking at just now too, and there's the birds as well . . .'

'Thank you, madam,' Taylor said firmly. 'We've established that you didn't see the man in question, so we don't need to take up any more of your time. There will be a forensic team coming to take the car in for examination, tomorrow probably.'

Suddenly, the woman said, 'Oh my goodness! Is it that man – the one who got murdered? And those ravens – what a terrible thing!'

They both made the sort of noise that neither confirms nor denies, then left. Taylor turned towards their car; Murray had already set off down the road.

'Where are you going?' he called.

'I want to see where Aitchison went when he left the car. There's the tower she talked about, look – it isn't far.'

The Lookout Tower was a stark, modernistic two-storey erection clad in pale wood, almost like a guard post and totally out of keeping with its rustic setting. Murray had never been inspired with a desire to protect the countryside herself, but she could understand why those who did might have got a wee bit upset about it.

'For goodness' sake, what do you expect to see? The murderer's footprints? By all account it happened over a week ago and that was before the body was moved. Let's wait and see what Strang wants us to do.'

Murray paid no attention, striding off down the boardwalk that ran across the bogs and pools. 'It'll tell me what Aitchison might have been looking at. Maybe he arranged to meet his murderer here. It won't take long.

And anyway, I want to see one of these plants.' Grumbling, Taylor followed her.

It was a quite extraordinary landscape, a world of water where such ground as there was, was half-water itself, treacherous in its solid appearance. In the heat the black, peaty lochans and pools glittered like so many mirrors, reflecting back the sky, and of course there were insects everywhere, buzzing, humming, even moving on the surface of the water with long, oar-like legs.

Sinister was the word that came to Murray's mind. Step off onto one of those brilliant green patches and it would suck at your feet, drag you down and down into the muddy depths. Ugh! The hot, damp air seemed to rise to envelop her and she was beginning to regret having suggested this. Taylor was probably right that there wouldn't be any fresh evidence. She'd have liked to see one of those plants before she gave in, though, and she was peering at the plant growth around the boggy hummocks as she went. She hadn't seen anything at all like the huge, bloated thing on the screen.

As she was peering down, she noticed a small plant that weirdly moved to close its leaves together suddenly, and she recognised it for what it was. The Venus flytrap, when not subjected to serious magnification, was actually rather dull. The tower was a lot further away than it looked and the swarms of little flies were starting to gather too. Remembering what Strang had said about them, Murray was ready to admit defeat. If she was ordered back she was going to wear a hoodie with long sleeves and smother herself in Jungle Formula.

She was just turning round when there was a yell from Taylor. 'That bastard just bit me!' He was flapping his hand at a huge fly that was soaring lazily out of reach and when he held out his arm she could see a red mark already forming.

'Looks nasty,' she said.

'Yeah, it does. Thanks very much – it's your fault. I'm going back to the car.'

Murray trotted after him meekly. 'You should go in to the chemist when we get back to Thurso and get something for it.'

Taylor only grunted as they drove off. Twenty minutes later they passed the abandoned drainage scheme site and then they approached Gabrielle Ross's house.

'Look!' Murray exclaimed. 'There's a car there. I know it wasn't there when we came past earlier, because I looked. Strang was wanting to speak to her when we came here before but there was no one in. We'd better stop and have a word.'

Taylor slowed down reluctantly. 'We weren't told to see her.'

'Yes, but if we don't use our initiative we'll just end up having to come back another time,' she argued. 'And I don't like this place. There's something really nasty about it.'

'Yeah, the wildlife,' Taylor said darkly, rubbing his arm. 'It's sort of sore itchy now, if you know what I mean.'

He stopped, though, and she jumped out and went up the path to knock on the door.

CHAPTER THIRTEEN

Morven Gunn put up the CLOSED sign and locked the door of the Lemon Tree cafe. She had just gone through to the kitchen to finish up the clearing when she heard a knock and muttered imprecations under her breath. As if ten till five wasn't long enough to ask her to put up with the public! Which part of the word 'closed' didn't they understand?

But the person standing on the doorstep now peering in the door was wearing a uniform, a plump grey-haired woman who when she saw Morven approaching smiled encouragement through the glass in the door.

Grudgingly, Morven opened it a foot or two, holding her hand round the side ready to close it again. 'What do you want?'

The policewoman's smile widened. 'Hello, dear. Hope I'm not disturbing you. I know it's been a terrible day for you, but I'm your police liaison officer – PC Barnett, but call me Margaret. And you're Morven, is that right? Can I come in just for a minute, to see what support you're needing?'

Morven opened the door another few inches without saying anything and Margaret wormed her way through, looking around.

'Oh, it's a lovely wee place you've got here! I think you've just got yourself another customer!' Unasked, she sat down at one of the tables, patting the seat of the chair beside her invitingly. 'It can't have been easy, working on today after hearing the terrible news. That's so brave! Were you and your brother very close?'

Morven sat down. She took a vindictive pleasure in saying, 'No, we weren't. I disliked him quite intensely. He'd been dead to me for years,' and relished the look of shock on the woman's face.

'Oh, I see,' she said nervously. 'That's . . . that's sad.'

'Not really. The way he behaved turned every decent person against him. Oh, no doubt they'll all say the right things now, but I'm not hypocrite enough to claim that I'm sorry he's dead.'

Margaret obviously didn't know what to say. Pink with embarrassment, she blurted out, 'I . . . I suppose you won't want bereavement counselling services, then.'

Morven gave a sarcastic laugh. 'You worked that out? Well done.' Then her face changed. 'They were rubbish anyway, these folk, when I really needed them. They know nothing – *nothing* – about true grief. And your lot know nothing about justice.'

She stood up, her face bright with fury, pointing at the quailing constable like an avenging angel. 'You'd better get out. I've no more time to waste on this. And take the message back to your boss to leave me alone, too. All right?'

Margaret scrambled to her feet. 'Right, right, of course, if that's how you feel.' She made for the door, then remembered her other commission. Feeling she was taking her life in her hands, she said, 'Just one more thing. There was a message passed through asking you to phone someone. Can I give it to you?' She fumbled in the pocket of her uniform and produced a note, holding it out with the nervousness of one offering a biscuit to a savage dog.

Morven took it without thanks and the policewoman was barely out of the door when she locked it again. She looked at the note, then with a tight little smile tucked it into her pocket while she finished up in the kitchen and went home to the small, stuffy flat in the high street.

The heat had built up inside. If she drew back the net curtain and opened the window to get what air there was, the passers-by could peer in – and they would, they would, particularly today. She switched on the fan that didn't really make a great deal of difference, except that the hot air moved round.

She sank thankfully into a chair, feeling limp with exhaustion. Whatever she might have said, the day had been a real strain and for a moment she leant her head back and shut her eyes, letting herself dream for a moment of the cottage with the pretty garden on the outskirts of the village. She could be sitting there enjoying the cool of the evening, under the apple tree she'd climbed as a child.

It was so near she could almost touch it. Surely someone as young and healthy as Niall wouldn't have got round yet to making a will – surely? And she could imagine what Mr Bruce Michie, of Curran Services, wanted with her, and it wasn't to offer his heartfelt condolences – she'd heard about the way Pat Curran had left his shares. This could be her opportunity to shaft Gabrielle Ross. That would be some slight compensation, even if nothing could pay her out for what she did. Except an eye for an eye, a tooth for a tooth.

Gabrielle Ross's mobile had rung as she was driving home and she saw David's number with a sinking heart. She didn't want to talk to him – she didn't want to talk to anyone – but she drew into the side to take the call. He'd spoken to her after Malcolm had told him the news, but she knew he wouldn't leave it at that. She must sound calm, and not as if she was straining to hear voices that weren't there.

'Don't worry, I'm all right. I can handle it.'

'It's just—' he said, and she interrupted him.

'I know, I know. I don't blame you. Coping with me if I completely lose the plot is a scary thought for all of you.' She couldn't help the edge coming into her voice.

'Oh, for goodness' sake, Gabrielle! Stop thinking like that! Given what you've had to cope with, you're amazing. I wish I could get back sooner but there isn't a space on tomorrow's schedule for me to get taken off. I don't like you being on your own out there, though. Stay at Westerfield with your mother, all right? I'll pick you up there when I get back—'

'She's away tomorrow. I'm not staying there alone with Fran while she performs a five-act tragedy.'

'Oh. Can't Lilian just cancel whatever it is? You need her—'

Her control snapped. 'No, I don't! Stop treating me as if I'm an imbecile! Life's hard enough without that.' She could feel her eyes stinging.

'Oh, my darling, I didn't mean it that way, truly! I can't bear it when you're upset and I'm not there to do something about it.'

She felt guilty and very, very tired at the same time. 'I know, I know, I'm sorry. It's been a hellish day. I'm just on my way back home to have a long bath and a bit of peace and then I'll have an early night.'

'You do that. I've spoken to the inspector in charge of the police investigation and he wasn't a problem. He'll wait to speak to you till I can get back, so you won't be bothered now. Get a good sleep.'

She was relieved about that. It would give her time at least to get her head straight before all the questions came in. 'I'll try. It'll all look different in the morning, as Paddy used to say to me.'

David laughed. 'That's my girl. Hang in there. Speak soon. Love you, sweetheart.'

Gabrielle had driven on again and parked outside the house. She let herself in then stood in the hall to listen to the silence she'd been craving, but somehow the air seemed alive with her teeming fears and imaginings. She ran her hands through her hair in a despairing gesture.

Make tea. That was what you did as a displacement activity for distress. Dragging her feet from sheer tiredness she went through to the kitchen and switched on the kettle. She made a little ceremony out of laying out a china cup and saucer instead of a mug and fetching an old brown teapot from the cupboard along with loose-leaf Earl Grey instead of a tea bag. As she was warming it up she could see the knife block out of the corner of her eye; the little knife was still there today, and she looked away hastily before it could send out those evil, tempting messages again, and poured in the boiling water.

It was, indeed, a soothing activity. She laid out a tray and carried it through to the sitting room, set it on the table by the window then sat sipping her tea. At last she could feel her mind beginning to quieten, her scampering thoughts slowing down.

Now, as she sat there, a car drew up outside and a man and a woman got out – the woman who had come that morning to Westerfield House.

The police. Gabrielle gave a wail of purest dismay. This must surely constitute cruel and unusual punishment, after David being so reassuring. She couldn't deal with questioning, not today. She wouldn't answer the door – but they had seen her. They were standing on the doorstep waiting for her to let them in. Very slowly she hauled herself out of the chair and walked through to open the door.

It was the woman who spoke, bright-faced, with dark red hair in a pixie cut. The man a few steps behind her was round-faced, bulky, and was for some reason staring at his arm as the woman said, 'Mrs Ross? Could we have a word?'

PC Margaret Barnett went back to the incident room in the village hall feeling considerably shaken by her encounter with Morven Gunn. She'd been encouraged to become a police liaison officer because of her kindly, motherly nature and she'd never before had a reaction like that from any of the families who had been victims of some sort of trauma. Admittedly, she'd no experience of dealing with someone whose brother had actually been murdered but most people who had lost someone close to them were more than grateful for her care.

There was a shift finishing so there were quite a lot of officers milling around on their way off duty. A little circle had gathered round PC Craig Davidson, the banter all about his moustache, or rather its disappearance. He was taking it in good part but Barnett when she joined them took his side.

'You leave him alone. He was picked on by that Mrs Gunn. She's a fiend, that woman. I'm just back from there and I'm still shaking.'

She had a fascinated audience for her description of the encounter. 'The thing is,' she said at the end, 'I can't imagine anyone saying that about their own brother. Oh, I'm not daft, I know there's plenty folk don't get on with their families, but they wouldn't come out and say it like that.'

'Especially when she's a suspect,' someone pointed out.

'Who's a suspect?' PS Jack Lothian had come in unnoticed, with DCI Kelso Strang behind him.

'Morven Gunn, Sarge. Margaret here went to see her to give her support and she got mauled.'

Strang was interested. Barnett, a little bashfully, repeated what she had told the others already about Mrs Gunn's opinion of her brother, then elaborated on what had been said afterwards.

'From what she was saying, she seemed to be going back to something else that had happened, sir. It was about her having had a bereavement of some kind and she didn't think it had been treated right. She didn't say what it was, though.'

Davidson cleared his throat. 'I think I maybe know

something about it. I spoke to one female this morning – she wasn't very coherent, just sort of ranting, and then her husband stopped her. But she was accusing Gabrielle Ross of being a murderer and it was something to do with Morven Gunn.'

Strang looked startled. 'Gabrielle Ross? No more detail than that?'

'Not really, sir. I've just put in my report. Oh, and I mentioned it to DC Murray at lunchtime,' he added helpfully.

Strang did not seem impressed by that. 'Did you indeed,' he said grimly. 'Are she and Taylor back?'

'No, sir, I don't think so.'

Strang turned to Barnett again. 'Did Mrs Gunn say anything else?'

Barnett thought about it. 'Not really. Oh yes – right at the end she said to tell you not to bother her.'

'Right. Thanks very much.' He walked away, then came back to check who was going to be on duty and asked them to tell Murray and Taylor that he would see them in his office at the Masons Arms when they got back.

'I-I don't really feel ready to speak to the police,' Gabrielle Ross said.

The woman – she couldn't remember her name – sounded very sympathetic. 'I know. You've had a dreadful shock. But if we could just have a word with you, even for a few minutes . . .'

And somehow Gabrielle was stepping back and there they were in the hall, with the woman introducing DS Taylor and reminding her that she was DC Murray, 'since I'm sure you couldn't remember it, with everything that was going on.'

Then somehow, they were all in the sitting room and Murray had spotted the tea tray and said Gabrielle must drink her tea while it was hot and somehow, she was asking them if they'd like some too and Murray was thanking her and saying she'd just fetch a couple of mugs. 'Kitchen through the back?' she said brightly and disappeared, leaving Gabrielle with the round-faced, bulky man who seemed preoccupied with his arm.

He said morosely, 'Got bitten. Don't suppose you've got any stuff for that, have you?'

It seemed easiest just to say no, and he lapsed into silence. Then Murray was back again, pouring tea into the mugs and sitting down.

Helpless as a trapped animal, Gabrielle waited.

'You were all very fond of Mr Aitchison, weren't you?' Murray's voice was warm and friendly. 'Were you particular friends?'

'Yes,' she said. 'It went back a long way. He was my father's right-hand man for as long as I remember.'

'But your sister claimed he'd had a relationship with her?'

Gabrielle had felt angry about that all day and she couldn't let it pass. 'No, of course he didn't!' she said scornfully. 'Fran was desperately trying to build it up into something. I know he felt a bit hunted because she kept wanting him to take her out. Being Niall, he was too kind to say no. Niall was – always kind.' She gave a little gulping sob.

Murray said hastily, 'I don't want to upset you. Now, we believe he came to the Forsinard Flows visitor centre on the 24th June – the Saturday before last. Did he call in here on the way?'

Everything went very quiet and inside her head the moment seemed to go on for ever. She didn't know how long it was – three seconds, five? – before she heard her own voice, quite steady, saying, 'No. Though I did go out for a brief walk, I think – yes, that's right, so I can't say whether he did or not.'

'But you didn't see him after that, any time that week?'

'No.' She didn't know how much more of this she could take. 'Look, I'm not really feeling very well. Can't it wait?'

Murray was immediately soothing. 'Of course. We'll be asking you to make a formal statement later on, so we won't take up any more of your time now. You look as if you're needing a rest.

'There was just one more thing. This may be distressing for you, but I think you should know that someone has accused you of murder – something to do with Mrs Morven Gunn's son Gary? These rumours can be very persistent and unpleasant so maybe we can help you quash it—'

Gabrielle felt stunned for a moment. This was like a nightmare, but she was awake – awake and furious. In the first spontaneous reaction she'd had for weeks, pure rage took over and she jumped up. 'How dare you! You come here and repeat those lies to my face! Get out of my house – get out, right now!'

Murray went pale. 'I didn't mean—'

'I don't care what you didn't mean. Get the hell out.'

The man had got up. 'That's enough, Constable. I'm sorry, madam. We're on our way.'

'Sorry,' Murray was saying over her shoulder as he escorted her out in front of him. Gabrielle heard him say as they walked down the path, 'Well, that was clever, wasn't it?'

She put her hand to her head. God, would the horrors of this day never end?

Murray couldn't blame Taylor for being livid. He wasn't half as livid with her as she was with herself. She'd screwed up there, big time, and there wasn't a chance that he wouldn't grass on her to Strang. Indeed, he was enjoying himself outlining what he was going to say to the boss when they saw him – the way she'd bulldozed him aside at the visitors' centre, then insisted on the ill-starred visit to Gabrielle Ross, not to mention dragging him out into the bog to get attacked by wild insects. 'It's swollen, look,' he said, pointing.

Murray didn't try to defend herself. There wasn't any point and all she could think about was how angry Strang would be. She'd been determined to show him that she'd learnt her lesson and yet here she was, making exactly the same kind of mistake again. Perhaps he was right to tell her not to use her initiative – but something in her rebelled at that. This was the job, to get information and act on it.

After all, she'd found Gary Gunn's grave using her initiative. And from Gabrielle's reaction, too, there was at least some foundation for the accusation. They just needed to find out the details and having another chat with Mairi might be the answer; if there was gossip going around she'd know what it was, or at least would know a woman who did. That might give them some sort of insight into the feud between Morven and her brother – if she believed, rightly or wrongly, that Gabrielle had killed her son and Niall had stayed best friends with her, it certainly would sour the family relationship. You could develop some fascinating theories from this.

If she was going to be allowed to. Her heart sank at the thought that Strang could take her off the case – send her back to Edinburgh with a black mark, even. The best she could expect was doing the menial stuff while Strang took Lothian along on the interviews or even Taylor, after this. Strang had been professional discretion itself but she could tell he didn't rate Taylor any more than she did. He was going to be so mad at her, though, that all her plans for being his go-to officer had crumbled to dust.

Taylor said, 'I'm going to go to Thurso before we report in at Forsich. I need to find a chemist's to get something for the bite – it's looking bad.'

She knew that. He had given a progress report on it every few miles, but feeling to some extent responsible she had refrained from making sarcastic replies.

He parked outside the shop and went to the door. She saw him try the handle, then bend to peer in, then look at his watch. She looked at her own. Twenty to six. Oh dear.

Taylor was in a towering temper when he got back in. 'This is all your fault! If you hadn't insisted on going in to see Mrs Ross I'd have been in time. Now what do I do?'

'Just wash it with soap,' she said helpfully. 'And if it's really sore I can give you some paracetamol.'

'Oh great. If I come down with septicaemia that'll be your fault too.' He got back into the car and drove towards Forsich but as they passed the Masons Arms Murray said, 'Look, there's the boss's car. He must be back in the office. We'd better stop here.'

As they walked through reception Murray was trying to think of the best slant she could put on what had happened. She wasn't looking forward to seeing his face change as it was explained to him what had happened.

She didn't have to. When they went in, Murray for once meekly behind Taylor, it was obvious from Strang's expression that he had heard at least part of it already.

DS Taylor got his version in first. DCI Strang listened with increasing anger, compounded by an unpleasant feeling of helplessness. His first instinct was to send Murray back to Edinburgh and ask for a replacement but that would cost money and it wouldn't be well received. He couldn't go on using Lothian all the time either: the SRCS would be billed for that too and DI Hay had already made difficulties.

'All right, Constable. Explanation for all this?'

'I screwed up, sir. I'm very sorry.'

At least she wasn't trying to make excuses. 'As I understand it, you heard about the accusation of murder against Mrs Ross before the briefing this afternoon but said nothing – is that right?'

'Yes, sir.' She bowed her head.

'Why was that?'

'I . . . I just wanted to find out a wee bit more about it first. And I did – I went along to the graveyard and found Mrs Gunn's son's grave. Gary he was called. And—' She stopped abruptly, biting her lip.

'Yes? Go on.'

'It's . . . it's only going to make it worse for me when I do.'

'Pleading the Fifth Amendment won't do you any good,'

he said dryly. 'What else did you decide not to tell me at the briefing?'

He saw her look at him under her lashes as if to see whether that could be showing some lightening of his mood. She wasn't stupid; the abject apology had been the smartest thing she could do.

'There was a bunch of flowers there – roses, I think, and it had been torn in shreds, really viciously – not just the flowers torn off, but all the stems snapped, and it looked as if it had been stamped on too.'

'And from that you deduced?'

'Not exactly a deduction, sir. I just guessed maybe Mrs Ross had put flowers on the grave and Mrs Gunn didn't like it. Maybe.'

Strang sighed. 'Moving on. You both established that the car was left at the centre on the Saturday, so that at least confirms our theory about the time of death. Now let's go on to the visit you paid to Mrs Ross – a visit which, in view of her obviously fragile state, I had promised her husband would not take place until he got back from the rig.'

Murray went pale. 'I didn't know that, sir! It was just that we'd tried to speak to her earlier in the day when she was out and when I saw the car I thought if I had a word with her it would save time.'

'But as I understand it what you questioned her about was the accusation of murder, in a peculiarly tactless way, presumably to add to this little private case you were building independently?'

'I know I did, sir. I'm sorry, I think I just . . . Well, you know.'

He knew, all right. They both also knew what had happened before when she just . . .

She was going on. 'Like I said, I'm really sorry. But, sir, I didn't just ask about that. I asked whether Aitchison had stopped in at her house on the way to the Visitor Centre, and that threw her.'

'Did it?' Taylor said. '*I* didn't see that. She just paused to remember what her movements that afternoon had been.'

'Caught her breath,' Murray said flatly. 'Ten seconds before she said "No".'

Strang didn't doubt that she was right. That was the infuriating thing – she had real ability, if only he could rein her in, while Taylor was a waste of space. He took a sudden decision.

'Kevin, I'll let you go now to see if you can find someone with a first-aid kit who can give you something for that bite. They're nasty dirty creatures, clegs. Livvy, you stay for a minute.'

She was biting her thumbnail as Taylor went out. When the door had shut, Strang said, 'What's it all about, Livvy? Why are you trying to run a separate operation?'

'I just wanted to prove to you that I'm good enough to do more than filter reports. If I'd been able to come to you and say, "This is what the trouble between Morven Gunn and her brother is all about," you'd have been impressed.'

'I see. Well no, Livvy, I wouldn't have been. I'd have been thoroughly irritated. You don't have to prove to me that you're observant and you have good ideas. You have to prove to me that you're not going to suddenly rush off and do something that fouls everything up. There could quite legitimately be a complaint from the Rosses now.

'Tomorrow I'm going to interview Mrs Gunn, who seems curiously keen on not being interviewed. Kevin will be coming with me. You can liaise with Aberdeen to set up interviews with Bruce Michie and the other two fishermen for the day after tomorrow and get Angie to book two seats on the plane from Wick. We'll have a briefing at eight-thirty. Right?'

'Yes, sir. Sorry again.'

Had that done any good? Strang sighed again as she went out. He wasn't convinced that it had and he was faced with taking Taylor around with him tomorrow. At least he wouldn't have to worry about him interrupting with questions he had just thought of. Strang had serious doubts as to whether Taylor thought at all.

Gabrielle's moment of rage had fizzled out as fast as it had flared up. Her tea was cold now, with the lemon slice sitting limply on top; she was standing staring at it with an odd sort of absorption when the panic attack struck.

She'd felt strangely detached all day; now she was floating, above and away from her body. Her heart was pounding so that she could barely breathe, and she was hot, far too hot, sweating and trembling. She was possessed by a sense that something terrible was going to happen, something even more terrible than what had happened already. She was dizzy and sick; her knees wouldn't hold her up any longer and she collapsed back into the chair panting while the world spun about her.

It felt as if she was dying. She could just let go, drop into the dark abyss, into the silence and the blessed peace. But the force of the attack was waning already and gradually it passed. She was still shaking but her racing heart steadied and slowed, and her breathing became at last easier. She was still here, then. She hadn't escaped. All the problems were still waiting for her and despair, the enemy she had kept at bay for so long, flooded through her.

But Paddy had bred her to be hard and resilient and she owed it to him not to give way. She had to take back control – of herself, of the betraying thoughts. She closed her eyes, summoning up her strength. She'd always had a talent for shutting her mind to what she didn't want to think about, a talent that had stood her in good stead recently, but now her hard-won detachment was under siege.

Of course, Gabrielle knew she and Paddy had been hated in the village and she was scared by Morven – she could still all but smell the stench of the offal. But it had been a shock to be confronted directly with evidence that not just Morven but others in the village, too, still considered her a murderer even after all these years.

She wasn't. Of course she wasn't, and she had vowed long ago not to let them define her morality. For years she had barely thought about it but now she found herself unable to resist the memories that were forcing themselves upon her, clamorous and strident.

CHAPTER FOURTEEN

She'd been defending darling Paddy, that was the thing. Her heart had ached on his behalf. He'd had so little left, despite all he'd done to set up the business and then to try to save it, not just for himself but for the community who'd invested in it.

Not that they were grateful. When they'd thought they were going to make money on the back of his hard work, he was a hero; now Gabrielle was getting spat on at school.

'It wasn't his fault!' she would cry, but no one would listen. The girls she had thought were her friends whispered in corners and walked away if she approached. They didn't know how many hours he spent at the computer late into the night to try to find work that could replace the drainage contract after the government decided that saving the bogland for the newts was more important than providing employment for the community. Or how depressed he got when nothing worked.

And then Malcolm Sinclair had appeared on the scene. How could her mother choose someone so flabby and boring in preference to Pat, all whipcord muscle with a gift of the gab that meant he could make you laugh till you cried?

As if she didn't know. Lilian's dreams of Pat's success, of the day when they'd have lots of money and could move out of the shoddily built box near the drainage works into something more aspirational, weren't going to come true now and in her usual cool, practical way she'd moved on.

Gabrielle despised her. She wasn't going to be swept off to the glories of Westerfield House along with Francesca, as Lilian had expected. She was fourteen now; she'd always been a daddy's girl and she certainly wasn't going to leave him at the moment when he needed someone to be on his side. Anyway, how could she stand the boredom?

She'd never forgotten her mother's fury, or the row that followed. With Pat's reputation in tatters there had been sympathy in the village for Lilian, but one of her daughters choosing to stay with him risked damaging her image of being in some sense wronged – and to Lilian, image was all.

As the business imploded and went into administration, Gabrielle suffered every indignity along with her father – Paddy, as she'd started calling him. She was fiercely protective and developed her own hard shell when it came to coping with the anger and contempt from the community.

At the end, Paddy owned the house and some of the original equipment he'd saved for to set up the business, but that was all. Selling the machines and borrowing against the house should give him enough to make a new start in Aberdeen and Gabrielle couldn't wait.

She'd stopped going to school. Everyone there was hateful to her and she'd be leaving anyway with Paddy. He'd tried to persuade her to stay with her mother until she got her Highers, but she wouldn't listen.

'I don't need Highers. I'll be working for you,' she said. It was only later she realised it made her another burden for Paddy, but he never let it show.

That afternoon she was anxious. Paddy had gone to try to persuade someone to back him for a share in the firm; she'd stayed alone in the house. She didn't go into Forsich any more because there was so much rage and hatred for Paddy that it frightened her. She'd been inside at the sitting-room window – just where she was sitting now – when she saw Gary Gunn running past.

Gabrielle knew him from school, though he was younger – thirteen, maybe. She knew too that he was Niall Aitchison's nephew. Niall had been the only person who'd stayed loyal to her father and when she saw Gary look up at her she smiled and waved. His face contorted into an ugly mask of hate and he gave her the finger and shouted something, then ran on.

It felt like a slap in the face and she shrank back out of sight, crying, though she should be used to it by now. It took her a few minutes to start wondering why he should have been running past when he lived in the village. The drainage works! Was he going there, planning on some sort of vandalism, perhaps?

He wasn't going to get away with it. Grabbing up from the hallstand the old blackened Irish bogwood stick with its thickly gnarled knob for protection, she hurried out of the house but by that time there was no sign of him. It wasn't far to the drainage site, abandoned now.

Just as she reached it, she heard a throaty roar and ran the last few yards. Gary was in one of the sheds, sitting perched high in the cab in a tractor with giant wheels. Somehow, he'd got it started – knowing Paddy, the key was probably still in the ignition – and now it was lurching unsteadily out of the shed, across the dried-out ground. The boy was stealing it!

That mustn't happen. It was one of the few assets Paddy had left and he needed every penny he could scrape together. Yelling at the top of her voice, she ran after it.

Gary heard her and replied with the same insulting finger as he trundled slowly on, right across the dried-out, pitted terrain. She drew level with him, then got ahead, but she dared not get too near those massive wheels. She didn't trust him anyway not to drive it straight at her. In desperation, she hurled the stick, aiming at the windscreen.

The heavy knob, hard as iron, struck it four-square. It didn't break but splintered, leaving Gary driving blind. He didn't stop, though, lurching on, refusing even now to give up his prize.

Gabrielle turned to see where he was headed, then shouted and waved in frantic warning. The edge where the drainage stopped and the bogland began was a deep ditch, with an expanse of water at the bottom.

'Gary!' she shrieked. 'Stop! Stop! You're going to crash!' but he showed no sign that he had heard her, bumping forwards with fatal determination. The huge machine went straight over the edge then toppled slowly, almost majestically, into the dubh loch beyond. The engine cut; the only sound now apart from the surging waves was Gary screaming.

She scrambled down into the ditch, sick with horror, feeling the pull of the bog as she reached the bottom. The great wheels towered above her and the cabin beyond was sinking deeper, deeper into the loch beyond. Even if she could have reached him the door to the cabin was on the underside.

'Push out the windscreen,' she shouted. 'You could climb through, Gary! Kick it out!'

But he was panicking now. 'Help me!' she heard. 'Help me!'

There was absolutely nothing she could do. His cries faded behind her as she ran to fetch help, though she knew by the time anyone got there it would be too late.

It really wasn't her fault. She'd only been trying to stop him stealing what belonged to Paddy when she hurled the stick. Breaking the windscreen was just an accident, really. He didn't have to drive on when he couldn't see. He shouldn't have stolen the tractor anyway. He'd brought it on himself, the whole thing.

No one ever found the Irish bogwood stick. The inquest brought in a verdict of accidental death but in the village she was blamed. That hardened her determination not to blame herself, so effectively that she had believed it to the point where she imagined that with the passing of time everyone else would believe it too.

They didn't. And now, alone in this isolated house, she began to be very afraid.

* * *

On Wednesday morning DC Murray found a cafe in the high street that did a good line in bacon rolls, and the coffee wasn't bad either. Even if you could get grey bacon and watery coffee in the hotel at Police Scotland's expense, this was worth £3.50 of anyone's money.

When she got back to the hotel she looked into the dining room but there was no sign of DS Taylor. It was still twenty minutes till their morning briefing session with DCI Strang but remembering his cleg bite she had slight misgivings and went up to his room. When she knocked on the door, his 'Come in' sounded a bit feeble.

He was up and dressed, but he didn't look great, flushed and sweaty, and she could see his arm was very swollen.

'Oh dear! You're not looking well,' she said uncomfortably.

Taylor glared at her. 'No, I'm not, thanks to you. Didn't get a wink of sleep last night. I think it's infected. I'll go along to the surgery in Forsich when it opens, but you'll have to drive me. And I certainly can't work today and the way I'm feeling I won't be fit for tomorrow either.'

'Have you told the boss?'

'Not yet. It's taken me half an hour just to get dressed.'

Murray went to the phone. 'I'll buzz his room, see if he's there.' Given that it was her fault in a way, even though she hadn't actually asked the cleg to bite him, it wasn't very nice to feel pleased that it wouldn't be Taylor who would be going to interview Morven Gunn this morning or, possibly, flying down to Aberdeen on Thursday.

Strang answered. 'Morning, sir,' she said, 'I'm afraid Kevin's not very well.'

* * *

Strang heard the news with mixed feelings. In the first place, it meant he was short on manpower just as the case was opening up, and it also meant he had the problem of Taylor's welfare to deal with. From what Murray said it was clear he'd need antibiotics, which with any luck would clear up the problem. But it was not unknown for bites like that to turn very nasty indeed. He followed Murray along the corridor to Taylor's room.

Seeing him lying back in a chair blowing out his breath as if this was almost too much of an effort to make somehow reminded Strang of a stranded whale. He was definitely running a fever; his eyes were too bright, and his face was flushed. The arm, too, didn't look good; it was very swollen, fiery red and with pus oozing out. Sepsis was obviously a danger if it wasn't tackled right now.

As Taylor told him how bad he was feeling, Strang made a lightning calculation. If he ended up hospitalised here it would create all sorts of problems. The man was a liability anyway: this gave him the perfect excuse to fly him back to Edinburgh to get any further treatment and ask Angie for a replacement who might actually be of some use. Meantime he could make do with Murray and since her gas was on a peep after the foul-up yesterday, she might actually be quite useful.

'I'll see if we can pull strings to get you an urgent appointment with Dr Sinclair,' he said. 'If he can start you on antibiotics now we can get you on a flight back to Edinburgh. You don't want to be stuck in hospital up here if it turns nasty.'

Making a sudden recovery Taylor sat up, his face

brightening. 'Oh, thank God for that. The sooner I get out of this bloody place the better. Can Livvy take me along to the surgery now?'

Strang shook his head. 'I want her at the briefing along with Jack Lothian. I'll get him to put the arrangements in hand for you and you can get on with your packing. Livvy, I'll see you in quarter of an hour.'

Taylor's holdall was already open on the floor by the time they left.

Back in his office, Strang looked at the time – quarter past eight, worth trying DCS Jane Borthwick. She'd made it clear he was on his own with this one, but it was good politics to keep her in the picture even if there wasn't much progress to report as yet.

JB was there and listened with what Strang felt was interest rather than commitment – supportive in a general sense but making no suggestions. He told her what the situation was with Taylor.

She sounded mildly amused. 'I had no idea you were risking life and limb up there. You'll be asking for hardship allowance next. But you're right, he should be sent back.' Then, to Strang's dismay she baulked at the idea of a replacement.

'You've . . . what? Half a dozen or so principal interviews that you'd want to conduct personally, but beyond that it's the sort of foot-slogging the locals can do with a bit of support from the station at Wick. You've got DC Murray, haven't you? She's a bright young woman. That should be enough direct backup for the next few days.'

It was money, of course. It was always money. And if

the investigation foundered, it wouldn't be the lack of manpower or the lack of cooperation from the locals that would be blamed, it would be him. He was brutally exposed on this one.

JB was right about Murray – she wasn't lacking in intelligence. He was being forced to have her partner him on this investigation, in which case he had to do a swift strengths and weaknesses analysis before she arrived for the briefing – facing up to his own too – if he was to make it work.

The landline rang while Kirstie Mowat was still at the breakfast table drinking her coffee. She ignored it; all her friends called her on her mobile, and it rang a couple of times before her mother got up from the desk where she was working at the other end of the room.

'Even if it's for me, it wouldn't hurt you to answer it, you know,' she said as she picked it up. 'Hello? Oh yes.'

Kirstie, seizing the opportunity to take the rest of the mandatory slice of toast to the bin and sit back down before her mother saw, wasn't really listening until she heard, 'Right, no problem. I'll tell Kirstie.'

'Who was that, Mum?'

'That was Morven. She's not opening the cafe today, so you won't be needed.'

Kirstie's eyes widened in indignation. 'Well, thanks a whole bunch! Why couldn't the woman have told me last night? I could still be in bed. What's she closing it for, anyway?'

'It's probably because of her brother's death,' Rhona said. 'Seems the right thing to do.'

'Really? Why didn't she shut it yesterday, then? And she didn't exactly seem overcome with grief about it, either.'

'You wouldn't necessarily know. She's a very private person.'

'Yeah, maybe.' Kirstie pulled a face. 'But she was sort of pleased about it too, you know. She was giggling about something when she was by herself in the kitchen.'

Rhona was startled. 'Was she? Maybe it was about something else – and anyway, grief takes people different ways. They weren't close. So – what are you going to do with your unexpected day off?'

'Dunno. I'll have to call round, see who's about.'

Aware she was on dangerous ground, Rhona said casually, 'Is Calum working today? We haven't seen him for a day or two.'

'Calum?' Kirstie said the name as if she'd never heard it before. 'Oh, I dumped him.'

'Really? Did you have a row?'

'No. I just discovered he was a total, utter snake.' Kirstie got up. 'It's too early to call anyone. I'm going back to bed.'

Amused, Rhona looked after her. Fergus would be pleased; that relationship was a wee bit too intense for his liking. At least she hadn't shown any sign of being heartbroken and with the police finishing up at the cottage now Kirstie had seemed much more relaxed.

It had been a blow to DC Murray when Strang had said Lothian would be at the briefing. He'd made it humiliatingly plain in the last couple of days that he rated the sergeant above his detectives, which was at least part of what had made Murray decide to strike out on her own, but when she arrived in Strang's office it was clear there was no question of Lothian replacing Taylor for the Morven Gunn interview. He had to do his own briefing for the uniforms shortly and as well as the arrangements for Taylor, Strang had just added the tasks that Murray had been given the previous day. Yes, she was definitely in on it and this time she was going to make sure that she got it right. She sat silent with her hands demurely folded in her lap until Lothian left.

Strang raised his eyebrows. 'All right, Livvy? You're very quiet.'

'Just thinking it feels a bit weird having a briefing one-to-one,' she said. 'It's usually a bit of a rammy with everyone piling in.'

'I was thinking that too. But it does give us a chance to work things out ahead of the next interview. Look, I know you've felt in the past that I don't want your input—'

And in the present too, she thought.

'—but it's not because I think your ideas don't have merit. It's that I try to have a clear idea of what my objectives are and if you put in an unrelated question it can break the thread and make it hard to get back on track.'

She hadn't considered it that way. 'Right,' she said slowly. 'Sorry, boss.'

'I genuinely wasn't asking for an apology. I want to develop a system where we communicate better so that you understand the direction it's going in and can come in when you have a relevant idea.

'This morning, say. What line are we going on when we speak to Mrs Gunn?'

Murray thought for a moment. 'Can't think she'll cooperate. She's hell-bent on scaring us off even coming near her – all that stramash about PC Davidson, just for a start. She was just kind of spelling out that she's the kind who'll kick up.'

'She's scared of pressure because, the thing is, she has to be a major suspect. She's told us herself she hated her brother. She claims Gabrielle Ross murdered her son and Niall went on being pally with her even so. We can really pressure her on that – it means she's got a big grudge at him already. And we know their mother died recently and maybe she's angry because he's got the house. She's his next of kin, so if he was out of the way she'd get his money . . .' She realised Strang was looking at her with a slight smile and faltered.

'What are you doing, Livvy?'

'Oh.' She looked down. 'Trying to establish a motive.'

'And do you remember what I said about that the last time we worked together?'

In a small voice, she said, 'It was putting the cart before the horse.'

'Right. Let's reset this. You built your hypothesis on her trying to warn us off. She could have other reasons – like that she's allergic to the police because we didn't prove her son's death was murder. The point is, we don't know and we don't need to know.

'I agree it would be helpful to know more about the case—'

'I checked out the records, sir. Gary Gunn was trying to steal a tractor because his mum had lost money when

Curran's went bust. Gabrielle Ross tried to stop him, and the tractor went into a wee loch and he got drowned. Straightforward accident verdict brought in.'

Strang was impressed. 'That's good work, Livvy. Use your initiative that way and I'll be a happy man. Now, let's work through the angle.

'We know that Niall Aitchison was last seen driving away from his house around eleven on that Saturday morning. We know that the car was in the car park at the Forsinard Flows centre on the Saturday evening, though we don't know if he drove it there.

'So, what is the line of questioning when we speak to the people most closely involved?'

'We try to establish their whereabouts.' She was feeling a little crestfallen.

Strang smiled. 'Not very exciting, is it? We're relying on the house-to-house as well, of course, to check if he was seen anywhere else, but it's not looking hopeful. My gut feeling is that he went straight to a date with his murderer and never went back to his car.'

'So, where he was killed would have had to be within walking distance of the centre?' Murray had brightened up. 'That would point to Gabrielle Ross – or her husband, for that matter.'

'It could also be that it was somewhere else entirely and the murderer drove it there afterwards to divert suspicion onto someone who was held by the locals to be a murderer already. Maybe we'll get a nice neat forensic answer once they've taken the car apart and maybe we won't. What else do we need to establish?'

Murray's mind went blank. 'Don't know, boss.'

'Who was where last Thursday when the body that had been drowned in a bog mysteriously appeared in the cottage.'

How could she have forgotten that? She'd got too caught up in the whole Gabrielle stuff, that was the problem. 'Right enough. But it might never be discovered if you left it there, so why would you want to move it to—'

'Livvy!'

'Oh. Sorry. Motive, again. So, we need to know where they all were then too.'

'Good. You're learning. Now let's get on and see Mrs Gunn.'

'Maybe we'd better put in for our *Kevlar* jackets, boss.' She was walking behind him, so she couldn't see his face, but she reckoned he was smiling.

The phone call came in at one minute past nine, just as Ailie Johnston was sitting down at her desk.

'Oh, Mrs Gunn! I have instructions to put you straight through to Mr Michie, but he's not at his desk just yet. Can I ask you to phone back a little later?'

Mrs Gunn wasn't inclined to be helpful. Ailie took down the message that she was driving to Aberdeen and would call at the office when she arrived in the afternoon.

When he came in half an hour later Bruce Michie was annoyed that he had missed her call but mollified by the information that she had responded so keenly.

'Excellent, excellent!' he said, rubbing his pudgy little hands together. 'Clear my diary, Ailie. I want to see her whatever time she arrives.'

'Yes, of course. I'll stand ready to make tea.' Then she added, with malice aforethought, 'Would you like me to bring through a box of tissues? She may be very emotional when you're talking about her loss.'

Michie looked alarmed. 'Do you think so? Well of course, I could buzz for you to come – more of a woman's thing, you know?'

'And should you maybe be wearing a black tie?'

'Black tie?'

'It's been a sad loss to the firm.' Ailie's tone was as pointed as a sharp stick jabbed in his ribs. 'You wouldn't want her to think you were lacking in respect.'

'Oh, I suppose so. Maybe you could—'

'You can pop round to John Lewis in your lunch hour,' she said firmly. 'I'll just away and sort out your appointments.'

She went out and shut the door, but she didn't go back immediately. She heard Michie make a telephone call, just as she had thought he would:

'Keen, yes, definitely. She only got the message yesterday and she's on her way here already. Couldn't be better.'

At that point one of the secretaries came along the corridor. 'Is he there?' she asked Ailie, who had smoothly moved off towards her office. 'What sort of mood's he in?'

'You're in luck,' Ailie said. 'Quite cheery, actually.'

A long day loomed ahead for Gabrielle, a long day when she had to resist the little knife as she practised mindfulness and embarked on displacement housework despite the house being still gleaming from her efforts yesterday. She was keeping the TV on, showing endless vacuous programmes that she couldn't bring herself to watch, just for the sake of having other voices that might prevent the intrusion of those inner voices that could frighten her into another panic attack.

But the dark thoughts still kept intruding. Curran Services – that was what lay behind it all. Paddy had been so proud of his success and the business had been all she had left of him, his memorial. It had been all-important. She'd sacrificed everything to it, even her sanity, but she'd accepted that she had to shut it out, along with everything else, to try to get her health back.

It wasn't working. She was getting worse, she knew she was. What she had gone through, what she was still suffering was dragging her down and down. She was finding it hard to see a future for herself, let alone the business. There were other uses for the little knife besides making tiny, discreet slits in hidden places for the sake of momentary relief. Could she find the courage of despair?

The phone rang while she was trying to frame an answer. She didn't recognise the number and she said, 'Hello?' cautiously.

The voice at the other end spoke for some time. Then she said, 'Oh no! No!' and began to cry.

CHAPTER FIFTEEN

It was annoying to find the Lemon Tree cafe closed. There was no explanatory note on the door and Morven Gunn wasn't at her home address either.

'Done a runner,' Murray said darkly.

'Or she could just be out shopping, having closed the shop as a mark of respect,' Strang pointed out. 'I know. I'm no fun. At kiddies' parties I go round bursting the balloons too.'

She grinned. 'What next, boss?'

'Westerfield House.' As they set off in the direction of the surgery, he went on, 'We've given them time to get over the shock and now we can afford to start asking the question, the one that always gets the response from the middle classes: "You're not suggesting that *I* could have had anything to do with it?"'

'Sort of the same as "It wisnae me", only posher.'

'That's about it. I'd like to start with the mother, Lilian. What's your take on her?'

Murray considered it. 'Bats her eyelashes.'

'Did she? I didn't notice.'

'Not literally. Just she kind of plays up to Sinclair – "Oh, poor wee me, but you're so big and strong". He just slurps it up. Men do.' Then she added hastily, 'Present company excepted.'

As always, it was the unexpected things that got you. Strang had a sudden vision of his Alexa, who'd had a fine line in mockery for any hint of machismo, and his 'Mmm,' covered up a shaft of pain. He went on hastily, 'You've read Ailie Johnston's statement? She suggested that Gabrielle hadn't been close to her mother after she walked out on Curran.'

Murray nodded wisely. 'Lilian would fairly be put out at Gabrielle choosing him not her. She'd want to be the queen bee and if you think about her daughters' names she's got pretty fancy ideas too. I'm sorry for Francesca, though. Living with your mum at her age, stuck in a wee place like this – you'd go pure mental.'

When they arrived at Westerfield House, Strang was pleased to see a police car in the surgery car park. 'Looks as if they've managed to slot Kevin in – that's good. We'll go to the house this time and hope to get Lilian there.'

It wasn't their lucky day. The woman who opened the front door was wearing a navy overall and told them Mrs Sinclair was out.

'Will she be long?' Strang asked.

'Oh aye, she's away to Aberdeen. She'll not be back till late. She'll mebbe stay over – it's an awful long drive.'

'Right. Is Miss Curran in?'

The woman hesitated. 'She's in, but she's likely none too keen on visitors.'

'We're police officers,' Murray said. 'We're needing to talk to her.'

'I'd a suspicion you mebbe were. You'd better come in, then, and I'll tell her.'

She showed them into the room they'd been in before and went off. Murray looked round about her, at the pastel colours and the heavy drapes and the multiple cushions on the elaborately upholstered sofas.

'Rooms like this make me want to run around messing them up,' she said. 'I tell you what I'd start with – ripping up that cushion.' She pointed.

'"All you need is Love, Laughter and Prosecco". A bit twee, I agree. I think I'd go for the two lovebirds one first, myself, but—'

He broke off as Francesca Curran appeared in the doorway. She was wearing black as if to demonstrate her bereavement but the roll-neck wool sweater looked too hot for a day like this and there was a thin film of perspiration on her forehead. She went past without speaking and collapsed onto a sofa as if her legs wouldn't hold her up for another minute. She was holding a lace-edged handkerchief in her hand, the kind people give at Christmas when they can't think of anything else.

'I'm sorry to have to trouble you at a time like this but I know you'll be anxious to give us whatever help you can to find the person who did this,' Strang said.

'Oh – oh yes, of course,' Fran said with a deep sigh. 'But whatever you do, it won't bring him back, will it?'

Strang agreed that it wouldn't. 'Did you and Mr Aitchison have – well, an understanding?'

She sat up, bristling as if it had been some sort of veiled attack. 'I don't know what you're driving at, but we certainly understood each other. Of course we did. We were spending more time together, but neither of us is young and impetuous and Niall had his job in Aberdeen, so we couldn't see each other as often as we'd have liked. And to tell you the truth, his mother was very possessive. Once she died, I thought . . .' She gave a little gulp and dabbed at her eyes again.

'When was the last time you saw him?' Strang asked.

'It was a Friday, about three weeks ago. I saw him in Thurso and he took me for a drink. He was up at the cottage.'

Strang saw Murray look at her with raised eyebrows and he nodded encouragement.

'Did you see him again over the weekend?'

Fran went pink. 'Not that time, no. I said to him I'd be in if he wanted to phone and arrange something, but he was very busy, you see, trying to sort things out so he could have a real home up here, where he could settle down properly.'

'Did he not like his job in Aberdeen, then?'

'Oh – I . . . I don't know.' She seemed flustered. 'It was just, well, he wasn't valued. He was nothing but a dogsbody for my father and then of course for *Gabrielle*.' She put a scornful emphasis on the word.

Strang said, 'And did you feel he resented that?'

'Of course he did! He must have, but he wasn't the sort to talk about it behind their backs and he was too nice to confront them the way he should have. He needed someone to encourage him to stand up for himself, get proper recognition instead of Gabrielle grabbing everything for herself, like she always does.'

'You and your sister don't get on, then?'

Francesca paused, looking down at her hands that were picking at the lace edge on her hanky. 'We could've – she is my sister, after all.' She sounded wistful. 'Sometimes I think we might, if . . . but she was my father's favourite and she got accustomed to thinking she could just have anything she wanted. David, her husband – well, he was my friend first. He used to come round here a lot when he'd those friends working at Dounreay – and then, of course, she swanned in and that was it. And she treats him like a dogsbody too.' She sniffed, then leant forward confidentially.

'I shouldn't tell you this, maybe. But she's got real problems. She's doing seriously weird stuff and David and Mum both think she's having a breakdown. Either that, or she's going doolally, like my gran did.'

Strang and Murray exchanged startled glances. 'Dementia, you mean?' Strang asked.

Francesca nodded. 'I hope it's not or that could be me too.'

It was a fine example of sisterly concern. Strang went on, 'So you met up with Niall three weeks ago. Did you see him at all after that, even just driving past?'

Fran gave a little sob. 'I never saw him again.'

'And were you here during that time?

'Oh yes.' She gave a bitter little laugh. 'I don't go anywhere. I don't do very much, frankly. After work I'm mostly just stuck at home. Mum and Malcolm took me out with them for supper on Thursday but that was all I did.' Then she shuddered. 'That was the night before they

240

found – him – in that awful cottage. Then the ravens—'
She gave a sobbing gasp.

Strang said hastily, 'You know the cottage?'

'We all do. Used to play there as little kids. Don't know why. It was just an old ruin – a bit smelly, but I suppose we went there because we were told not to. I'd forgotten about it, until—' Fran shuddered again. 'Why would anyone do that? Put him there for the ravens to find?' She was getting visibly distressed.

Strang said, 'I don't want to upset you, Miss Curran. You've been very brave. But just one last question. Did Mr Aitchison have any enemies that you know of?'

She stared at him. 'You mean, you don't know? Niall didn't do anything to make enemies, but my father and Gabrielle did, and they made him do their dirty work. He'd no friends here, except us.'

Francesca didn't get up as they left, only sinking back further into the cushions of the sofa for another bout of crying. As they walked back to the car, Murray said, 'Is there something wrong with the water in this place? They all seem to hate each other.'

'If there's poison in the atmosphere, it all seems to come back to one person – Pat Curran,' Strang said soberly.

It was half past eleven when the buzzer Bruce Michie used to summon Ailie Johnston sounded twice, then after a two-minute break, three times more.

Ailie scowled at it. 'Keep your hair on,' she muttered as she went through, and her 'Well?' as she went in was definitely truculent.

'That woman – Morven. Have you got her phone number?' Bruce Michie was in a state of some agitation.

'No, I don't. Why would I?'

'She phoned earlier. Can you not dial 1471?'

'I've had about thirty calls since then. If I dialled the recall number all I'd get is the one I put through to you ten minutes ago.'

'Oh yes. Well, no need for that. When did she say she'd be here?'

'Wasn't specific. Middle of the afternoon, I would guess. It must be a five- or six-hour drive.'

'We've got to put her off.'

Ailie stared at him. 'Put her off? Why?'

'Oh – just, I don't think it would be suitable, after all. Might upset her to come here, maybe? You said it yourself, about the box of tissues. It would be kinder, you know?'

She gave him a cynical look. 'Really? Anyway, I don't see how we could stop her. She's just going to turn up here.'

'Then it's your job to tell her I can't see her. Just say something's cropped up and I couldn't arrange it. Ask her to call me tomorrow.'

Ailie didn't stop to argue. 'Fine,' she said, and scurried back to her office. She just might be in time to dial 1471 on that last call before another one came in.

She was in luck. The number came up and when she dialled it, the voice at the other end said, 'Russell and Macfarlane. Can I help you?'

'Sorry, wrong number,' she said and put the phone down. She knew the name; it was a firm of solicitors just across the town, in Belmont Street – a street Niall would have walked along every day on his way to work.

And what had Russell and Macfarlane had to say to Bruce that had suddenly made him so much less keen to express his condolences to Morven Gunn?

The police car wasn't in the car park when they left Westerfield House so with any luck Taylor was on his way back to Edinburgh.

'What next, boss?' Murray said as they walked along. They'd probably send up a replacement but at least she had today to play herself in and it was all going pretty well this time, as far as she could see. She'd even been allowed to ask her own question in one of his sacred interviews. Whahey!

'We've been a bit stymied this morning, haven't we? I think we can presume the Lemon Tree won't be opening today, but we might check whether Mrs Gunn has come back home – ask a couple of neighbours if they've seen her. David Ross doesn't come back from the rig until tomorrow and we can't question Gabrielle again until then, particularly if there's some question of mental illness.

'But I want to call in at the incident room to check that we can get into Niall Aitchison's house – I've been wanting to look around that. There may be some new lab reports in and I've got a loose end I'd like to tie up before doing the Aberdeen interviews.'

Yes, she was definitely getting her feet under the table. Murray was in a good mood as they walked along the high street and into the hall.

PS Lothian was there, talking to a woman constable but he broke off when he saw Strang. 'The team that was dealing with Aitchison's car has got it shipped off for forensics to examine, sir. They've done a preliminary check for prints but from the handle on the driver's side and the steering wheel it looks as if it was driven most recently by someone wearing gloves. There was a fibre in the catch that looks like wool, though the lab will have to test it.'

'You don't wear woolly gloves in weather like this – not to keep your hands warm, anyway,' Murray said.

'No,' Strang said slowly. 'No, you don't.'

They picked up coffees from the tea trolley and while Strang talked to Lothian about the door-to-doors – disappointing, from what Murray could hear – she checked for forensic reports that might have come in from Edinburgh. There was one that looked interesting and she called, 'Sir!'

Strang came across to read it over her shoulder. It was an analysis of the head wound: it had been caused by a blow from something rounded and smooth, as Dr Kashani's initial report had stated, but more detailed analysis had established that it had also been extremely heavy and applied with a force that suggested the weapon must also have had a handle.

'A cosh, maybe,' Murray suggested and Strang said, 'Mmm,' but she didn't think he was really listening. She could tell that his mind was elsewhere. What had he picked up that she hadn't?

'Right,' he said. 'Let's move. We'll check on Mrs Gunn first.'

When Gabrielle's phone rang again she barely responded. She'd no idea how long it had been since the previous call; she'd sat shrivelled in a chair, suspended in a vortex of misery where time had no place.

It went on to the answering service and after a few minutes she got up and found it. It was showing her mother's number, and when she accessed the message Lilian's voice was sharp with anxiety. 'Gabrielle? Why aren't you answering? I worry so much, you know. With everything, I'm afraid of what you might do. Are you there? Phone me back, or I'll have to get Malcolm to come round and see if you're all right. Don't do anything stupid, will you?'

Malcolm – oh, for God's sake, anything but Malcolm, being paternal. She knew what his advice would be when she told him what had happened, and he would probably be right, but she wasn't ready yet to admit she'd have to give up. Her mother's fussing phone call had rubbed her up the wrong way and she wasn't going to give her the satisfaction of hearing her crumpling under the strain. Do what Paddy would do, she thought, tell them to fecking take a running jump.

'Mother?' she said. 'Thanks for phoning. Sorry it took me a minute to answer – I was out in the garden. Yes, I'm fine, honestly.'

She was proud that she'd managed to keep her voice steady, that she had sounded, as she thought, normal. Though perhaps she couldn't remember what normal was, because her mother still sounded worried.

'It's been such a shock for you – well, for us all,' Lilian said. 'And he propped up the business for you as well. But you mustn't let that prey on your mind – remember you promised David!'

With a hollow feeling inside Gabrielle said, 'Yes, of course. Was there anything else?'

'Not really, darling. No more funny voices in your head, then?'

This time, she knew she hadn't managed. Her voice was shrill as she said, 'No, of course not. Bye.' She switched the phone off and sank her head in her hands.

Mrs Gunn wasn't back home, and Murray found a neighbour who said he'd seen her leaving in her car at about half past seven, and no, she hadn't had a suitcase or anything with her.

When she reported back to Strang he seemed to find that interesting too. 'That would figure,' he said, but he didn't explain further. She was to drive, and he settled back in the passenger seat as he checked the messages on his phone.

He gave her directions to head towards Halkirk. She'd read the report on the interviews at the fishing hotel but when she asked if that was where they were going he said no.

'I'm just going to key in the address Jack's found me into the satnav. I want to speak to a young woman called Hayley and if possible at home, when she isn't at the hotel where she works. With our luck today, she'll probably have gone there already but it's worth a try.

'I want you to do this interview, Livvy.'

'Me?' Murray was so surprised that she took her eye off the road for a moment, then hoped he hadn't noticed that she'd taken a slightly unusual line into the corner ahead.

He didn't comment, anyway. 'I'll tell you why. I don't think she likes police officers very much and someone nearer her own age might get more out of her. Her boss treats her as if she's stupid, but I don't think she is – I think she's smart enough to reckon she gets away with more that way.'

'Playing the daft laddie?'

'Exactly – too clever is dumb. The thing is, when she happened to mention that someone had joined Bruce Michie's party of fisherman, her boss was anxious to suggest she was too vague to know what she was talking about. I don't think she liked that, so it might give us a way in. Unfortunately, they haven't managed to turn up a decent photo of Aitchison – we'll just have to see what she says.'

Murray was thinking furiously as she drove on. It was vital to get her tone right on this one. 'Do we think it was him, then?'

She heard mild impatience in his voice. 'We don't know, Livvy. That's why we're asking her.'

Oh dear. She was doing it again – trying to develop a theory ahead of the facts. 'Yes, boss,' she muttered. But even so, it could be Niall Aitchison and whatever he said she was going to be thinking of his description when she was asking this girl her questions.

'One of the things I'd most like to establish, if possible, is how she saw the relationship between the men – who talked the most, who did the others listen to. She may not have noticed, of course, but it's worth a try.'

They drove on for a while in silence, Murray's mind busy with the task ahead. Then Strang said, 'What do you make of what we've learnt today, Livvy?'

What had they learnt? That Fran Curran had a miserable life, that the car had likely been driven by someone else after Aitchison was dead, that the murder weapon would have had a handle. She'd noticed at the time that this was saying something to him, something more than the bare facts.

'Not sure, boss.'

'We've got clear indications now of malice aforethought. It's occurred to me before that moving the body might have been a clumsy attempt to cover up what had perhaps been an unintended fatality, but as you said yourself, no one would happen to be carrying woollen gloves. It would have to be planned beforehand. And the description of the weapon – again, planned. The killer didn't just lose their temper and pick up a stone.'

'Could be a baseball bat, maybe? I've known that be used before.'

'Yes, we all have,' Strang agreed, but she had a feeling he was thinking of something else.

Now the bossy voice from the satnav was directing her down a lane on the outskirts of the village of Halkirk to where there was a small circle of council houses, built in the seventies from the look of them and badly in need of renovation.

Hayley's house was one of the better kept, with a neat front garden. As they walked up the path Hayley appeared round the side of the house, wheeling a bicycle. She stopped when she saw them, then said, looking at Strang, 'Oh, it's you again. I'm just on my way out.'

Murray stepped forward. 'Going off to work? I know, we're a nuisance, but I swear it'll only take a minute. You're Hayley, right? I'm DC Murray, but just call me Livvy. Can we have a wee chat? My boss says you're someone who notices things. Here, let me park your bike and then you can let us in.'

Hayley, looking bemused under the onslaught, allowed

Murray to wheel the bike over to lean it against a fence and duly opened the door leading straight into a room dominated by a huge TV, with the furniture – a corner sofa and an armchair – arranged to give the best view of the screen.

'Nice house! Do you live here on your own?' Murray chattered on.

Hayley's expression was still hostile. 'No, with my mum and dad but they're out at work. You said this was only going to be a minute. What are you after?'

Murray grinned at her. 'Don't like the polis, do you?'

'You wouldn't either, if they'd put your boyfriend in jail,' she said sullenly.

'They did, actually. Well, ex.' As Hayley, and Strang too, gaped at her, she went on, 'Did me a real favour, in fact. Best thing that ever happened to me. Anyway, this isn't about your friend, this is about a guy that got killed. You do remember the weekend you were asked about when these men came up for the fishing, don't you?'

For a moment she thought Hayley was just going to shrug but after a moment she said, 'Yeah. Course I do. I'm not a *goldfish*, whatever Jeff says.'

'Didn't think you were. Michie, Morrison, Brady – are those the names?'

This time she did shrug. 'I just call them the boring old farts. They come up every wee while. They're pals with Jeff.'

'Who would you say is the big man, of the three?'

She actually looked interested. 'There's a ginger. He's the one they all listen to. The wee fat one sucks up to him.' Then she hesitated. 'Jeff wouldn't like me saying anything. Look, I've to go, or I'll be late.'

'Just one more thing. Jeff rubbished what you said about a man who came later. What was he like?'

Hayley looked blank. 'Don't remember. Just, he came in late when I was finishing up and I told him service was over, but Jeff told chef to make something for him.'

'Dark, fair? Tall, short? Young, old?'

'Didn't notice. Old, though.'

For the first time, Strang put in a question. 'Old like me, or old like your grandad?'

'Old like you, I suppose. If he was young, I'd've noticed.'

Murray had to turn a laugh at the unthinking brutality into a cough. 'Were they pleased to see him?'

'The ginger was. Got up and clapped him on the back. Look, that's all I know. I'm going.' She went to the door and held it open for them.

'Thanks, Hayley,' Murray said. 'Don't let Jeff put you down – and have another think about the boyfriend, OK?'

Back in the car, Strang said, 'Respect! Well done, Livvy.'

She glowed, but all she said was, 'Didn't tell us much, did it?'

'Oh, this and that,' Strang said. 'The ginger one – we'll get a look at him tomorrow. The "wee fat one" was a pretty fair description of Bruce Michie too. Can you write all this up today, Livvy?'

'Yes, boss.'

'Sometime, you must tell me about your chequered past,' he said.

'Don't hold your breath,' she said cheekily. As she drove off she asked, 'Is it Aitchison's cottage now?'

'That's right. Not sure how much it will tell us when it's

been searched already, but we don't know much about the man and it can be a revelation of someone's character.'

But Niall Aitchison was an exception. When they let themselves into the house Murray had looked at before from the outside, it was obvious that the character they were being offered insight into wasn't Aitchison's, it was his mother's.

Apart from papers spread out on a small repro desk in walnut veneer there was no sign of the 'sorting things out' that Francesca had claimed he was doing. The sitting room was relentlessly old-fashioned with its reproduction dark wood furniture, beige sculpted carpet and gold velvet curtains. In the hearth there was a fan of paper to cover up the grate and on the mantelpiece beside the brass candlesticks and the oak clock were a few photos of successively a toddler, a schoolboy and a rather blurred one of a youth in a V-necked Shetland pullover with his arm round a middle-aged woman.

They both looked at them with interest.

'Looks the kind of boy who'd be good to his mother. See how neat his hair is in that one,' she said with obvious scorn, pointing. 'Can't be much more than eighteen or nineteen but he's middle-aged already.'

'Not much sign of teenage rebellion,' Strang agreed. 'Seems to have been very loyal to Curran too, despite the way he was left to take the flak. Loyalty instilled at an early age, perhaps?'

'He's kept the house clean too,' Murray pointed out as they walked through the hall opening the doors on a couple of rooms with suites of bedroom furniture and beds still made up with candlewick covers and satin quilts. The third bedroom was obviously Niall's: smaller, and its single bed had a dark-green cover and a tartan rug folded across the foot. It too was neatly impersonal, apart from a bookcase that held a collection of books made up of boyhood favourites and more recent purchases that were mainly non-fiction.

Murray took out *The Compleat Angler* by Izaac Walton. 'This one's about fishing – but look, it's got a misprint, right in the title.'

'I think it wasn't a misprint at the time,' Strang said, scanning the rest of the shelf. 'They all seem to be on what they call "country pursuits". Hmm.'

He walked off and headed through to the back of the cottage. The kitchen was fitted with Formica cabinets and work surfaces and against one wall there was a small table with a plastic tablecloth printed with flowers. On the draining board beside the stainless steel sink an upturned mug propped up a plate.

There was something very pathetic about that, Murray thought; the poor sod doing the washing-up after his breakfast, just like he'd always been taught to do, then going out to meet his death in a bog.

Strang had opened a door that led onto a small lobby by the back door. She heard him say, 'Ah!'

When she went through, he was holding a fishing rod. There were three or four others in a rack beside a row of hooks with weatherproof kit and a couple of tweed hats with fishing flies stuck into the hatbands. Green waders stood on the floor beside a couple of wicker fishing creels.

'I thought I might find this through here,' Strang was saying but Murray was eyeing a neat steel cabinet in one corner.

'Is that what I think it is?' she said.

Strang looked over his shoulder. 'Oh yes,' he said. 'Shotgun cabinet. He's on record as having a licence. A lot of people do round here – switch from fishing to shooting once the weather turns.'

He put the rod back then bent down. 'I wondered if this would still be here,' he said and took down a scarf from one of the hooks to cover his hand to pick something up carefully. It was about twenty centimetres long and had a shiny metal handle and a thick, blunt rubber top, a murderous-looking thing.

Murray gaped. 'Whatever is it?'

Strang was weighing it in his hands. 'It's a priest – so-called because after a fish is caught this is used to deliver the last rites.'

'Is that—'

'I doubt it. We'll get it tested, of course, but I doubt if the murderer would have risked coming to put it back here,' he said, putting it into an evidence bag. 'But you never know – I wonder if anyone in the fishing party has inexplicably managed to lose his?'

He was very quiet on the drive back. Murray could almost hear him thinking but she couldn't work out what he'd made of the morning's work. Still, as far as she could tell he'd been pleased with her interview with Hayley. Maybe he'd start seeing her as an asset rather than a liability if she didn't screw up again. And, of course, she wasn't going to.

CHAPTER SIXTEEN

It was half past three when Ailie's buzzer went. It was Bruce Michie, his voice high with nerves.

'It's that fool Sadie. She buzzed me to say that Mrs Gunn has arrived instead of telling you,' he raged.

'Usually if people say they've an appointment that's what she does and then she just brings them up,' Ailie pointed out.

'I've told her to wait for a minute, but the woman must've heard my voice! She'll know I'm in. You'll have to go down and tell her I can't see her, that I'm with someone for the rest of the afternoon.'

Ailie held her ground. 'When am I to say you're available, then? She's come all the way here because you said you wanted to see her. She's not just going to say, "Dearie me, that's a pity," and go all the way back again. You better speak to her and get it over with.'

But Bruce stood his ground. 'You're my secretary. It's your job to deal with things like this.'

She looked mutinous, but it wasn't an argument she was going to win. As she walked down the stairs to reception she was framing her letter of resignation in her head.

The woman who had been sitting in one of the chairs by a small coffee table got up when Ailie appeared. She marched over to her and, ignoring the receptionist who was trying to introduce them, said, 'Right. You can take me up to see him now. I've no time for mucking about. It's a long drive back.'

She was a big woman with heavy features, an ill-tempered expression and such aggressive body language that Ailie, not large herself, felt like a child again confronted by the playground bully. As firmly as she could she said, 'I'm sorry, Mrs Gunn, I'm afraid he's not available this afternoon. I didn't have your phone number to warn you—'

Morven gave a short, harsh laugh. 'Don't be daft. I heard his voice on the phone. He's up there – if there's someone with him they'll have to wait. Not me.'

It hadn't worked with the bully either back then. To avoid physical contact Ailie stepped aside as Morven swept past her and up the stairs. Ailie followed and when the woman turned at the top and said, 'Where is he?' she had no alternative but to indicate Michie's office.

It was possible that he might fire her, but she knew he wouldn't actually beat her up and she wasn't at all as confident about Mrs Gunn. She retreated into the safety of her own office and shut the door, wondering how a man as gentle and peaceable as Niall could have a sister like this. Maybe she'd knocked all the fight out of him at an early age.

She sat at her desk nervously eying the buzzer in case Michie wanted – what, help? Protection? There was no doubt in her mind that it had to do with Niall's shares in the business – something about his will, perhaps? She did wonder what was going on there in his office.

Did she dare just creep along and listen outside? She could pretend she was on the way to one of the other rooms further down the passage if the door opened suddenly. But Ailie had only just stepped out of her room when she heard it – a scream of what was unmistakably violent rage. She shot back in, closing over the door but leaving a crack she could peer through.

She heard the door of Michie's office open, and then a torrent of abuse. A moment later Mrs Gunn stormed past, her face a twisted mask of fury. Behind her Michie appeared, looking pale and shaken and Ailie opened the door wider to let him in.

He sank into a chair. 'Oh my God, what a terrible woman! I really thought she was going to attack me. It wasn't my fault that Niall had made a will when she'd thought his shares would come to her as his next of kin.'

And you had, too, Ailie thought. 'So, who's got them?' she asked, as if she couldn't guess.

'That's the worst of it.' Michie was sunk in gloom. 'You might as well know – he's left them to Gabrielle, and now there's nothing I can do to stop someone who's lost the plot having full control of our future. Mind you, I really wouldn't like to be her when that woman finds out.'

'She'll have David to protect her,' Ailie said, but she felt uneasy even so. Morven Gunn had looked as if she was capable of doing anything – and the last person who'd owned those shares had ended up dead.

* * *

Kelso Strang had spent the afternoon working in his office while Livvy Murray wrote up her reports along at the incident room. He finished up, then went downstairs. He'd suggested they meet in the hotel bar for a drink after work, but it was a dismal place, dark and gloomy with a beery smell, probably emanating from the brown-and-amber patterned carpet that looked as if it had been specifically designed to conceal any spillage. There was no one behind the counter and even after Strang had pressed the buzzer there was no response.

Originally, he'd been dismayed to find Livvy Murray allocated to the investigation but after today he was feeling more optimistic and he'd surprised himself by suggesting a drink tonight on impulse. As JB had pointed out, she was a bright young woman and she was enthusiastic too. What she'd done on her own initiative – with the notable exception of interviewing Gabrielle Ross – had been useful stuff and she'd conducted her interview with Hayley with some skill. With Taylor now out of the way, this might be a good chance to persuade her to renounce the temptation to go for 'Ta-dah!' moments, with their attendant risks.

Still no barman appeared. He pressed the buzzer again irritably. The hotel really was depressing, which did nothing for morale.

This was also, if he was honest, the most isolated he had felt on an SRCS case. JB was getting twitchy; she seemed to be expecting the sort of progress that just couldn't be made immediately. She was pushing him to get things wrapped up in the next couple of days, so he could hand over the legwork to the local force and mastermind the rest from a computer in his Edinburgh office – a cheap solution, but he'd no confidence that it would work. In previous investigations he'd worked closely with the people on the ground, but DI Hay's hostility had made that impossible. Any handover would be fraught and good cooperation afterwards was unlikely.

In Skye, JB had been around too. Now he was in sole charge, they were under the cosh and he'd have to rely on Murray to an uncomfortable degree. He'd have to spell out to her what needed to be done and stress the importance of doing what she was told.

When she came in she cast a disparaging look around the bar. She drew her hand across one of the tables as she passed, looked at it and pulled a face. 'Sticky. They obviously don't even wipe up.'

'They probably don't wash the glasses properly either. Anyway, it's too nice an evening to spend inside. I heard someone saying something about a good place down on the beach. Let's go.'

They found a low, white-painted building wrapped around with a veranda and they were able to sit with their drinks looking north-west over the tranquil sea, its shot-silk surface hardly rippling as lazy waves rolled in. It was still broad daylight and a glorious evening, the sky hazy gold with pink streaks, with only a few blue-purple clouds low on the horizon.

'I got kind of scunnered with scenery when I was in Skye,' Murray said, 'but this is awesome. Is the sky bigger here, or something? You never see anything like this in Edinburgh.'

'It's just that there's nothing to see between us and –

well, Iceland, I suppose it would be. Better make the most of it, anyway. See those clouds there – that's a change in the weather coming.'

'I won't mind much. It's fine here by the sea but when you're in beside the bogs with the insects and everything it's not. Look at poor Kevin.'

'Don't forget the Jungle Formula next time, Livvy. Now – tomorrow. I've decided to go to Aberdeen by myself.' He saw the disappointment on her face and went on hastily, 'We can't spare the time to have both of us tied up. Believe me, you'll be busy enough while I'm away.

'The lads in Aberdeen have done a good job with the preliminaries so I'm set up for the interviews with Hayley's boring old farts.'

Murray, looking a little happier, laughed. 'Hope she dumps the boyfriend.'

Strang gave her a quizzical look. 'That's a good career move, is it?'

She wasn't to be drawn. 'Definitely,' she said primly. 'Anyway, what do they reckon to Ginger?'

'Seems to be the Big Man, like Hayley said. Definitely something to probe there. And I'd an email from Ailie Johnston just before I came out with some interesting stuff. It all seems to relate to Niall Aitchison's shares in Curran Services. Pat Curran arranged it so that Gabrielle was the majority shareholder, though if Aitchison teamed up with Michie they could outvote her.'

'Must have trusted him.'

Strang thought about that for a moment. 'Or distrusted her – or maybe just felt she would need advice and support?

But in any case, if Michie got his hands on those shares he could outvote Gabrielle and take over the company and Ailie claims that at first he and his pals thought that Morven Gunn would inherit as next of kin.'

Murray turned to look at him. 'But she didn't?'

'No, and judging by his attempts to avoid meeting her, Michie only found out later, according to Ailie. Mrs Gunn barged her way in, then left in a furious temper.'

'So, who did he leave them to, then?'

'Gabrielle, it seems – the shares, anyway. Don't know about the property.'

'If Fran's not in the will it'll be a right punch in the mouth, especially after her carry-on about their relationship. And if it all goes to Gabrielle – well, she'll be fit to murder her!'

Strang winced. 'Don't even joke about that! We're looking for confirmation from the lawyers, but it does seem more likely, you'd have to say. Of course, it would leave Gabrielle with full control of the firm, which wouldn't exactly please Michie.

'Anyway, it gives me an angle for the interviews tomorrow.'

Murray nodded eagerly. 'If the other guy who arrived later was Niall, that could have been what the fishing weekend was all about – some kind of business deal.'

'Or of course it could just have been a fishing weekend and some other guy just happened to arrive late. Open mind, remember, Livvy?'

'Oh, sure,' she said meekly, if not quite convincingly.

'I'll be triangulating the evidence, focusing on inconsistencies. Ailie Johnston thinks Michie's been phoning round so I'll be looking out for that – it's very difficult to avoid using the same words when a story's been agreed beforehand. After I get back I want to see Gabrielle, if at all possible, or her husband at least – he should be back from the rig later on. I want another look at the drainage works too.

'But tomorrow morning I want you to try for an interview with Morven Gunn again. Find out where she was that Saturday afternoon.'

'Do I get danger money?'

'Use your charm and you won't need it. Then I'd like you to have a talk to Fergus Mowat at the farm. You'll have seen his formal statement and it didn't offer us anything so I'm not looking for an interview, just a chat, all right? I want you to focus on his movements around the farm during the twenty-four hours when the body could have been placed in the cottage. Did he see anything, hear anything out of the ordinary?

'I'm hoping I might be back later on but if it takes longer than I think, you'd better try for Lilian Sinclair – she should be back home by then. Get her separately from her husband and then push him for an account of their movements on the Saturday too. Watch out for agreed statements there.'

Murray nodded. 'Right. Nothing more from Francesca?'

'I don't think so, unless you're looking for confirmation of something her mother said.'

He noticed with approval that she had dived into her bag and brought out a notebook to jot down her tasks. As she wrote, he went on, 'But no flights of fancy, now, Livvy. Stick to the script, OK? We'll have to pack in as much as possible.

I spoke to DCS Borthwick and she'll be expecting us back in Edinburgh very soon.'

Murray looked dismayed. 'Back in Edinburgh? But we can't possibly have tied this up in that time—'

'No, but anything else can be done by the lads here.'

'But Craig Davidson says the CID's rubbish!' she wailed. 'There's only the inspector and a couple of DCs. And we won't have the chance to follow up on anything we might get from the interviews tomorrow.'

'It's all about money – isn't it always? We're just too expensive to keep on site in our luxurious accommodation.'

While they were sitting there the blue-purple clouds had thickened, puffing up into a mass that was slowly spreading. The sky was looking threatening now and a chill little wind had started blowing in off the sea.

Murray rubbed her bare arms. 'I should've brought my sweater. Can I get you the other half, boss?'

Strang shook his head. 'Thanks, but no thanks. I've got work to do tonight.'

She walked back to the high street with him but when he turned towards the hotel she muttered something about a pub where one or two of the Thurso lads sometimes went and said goodnight.

He was glad she'd made some friends, at least. It could be pretty lonely for her on a job like this, without even Taylor to talk to – though she'd made it pretty obvious that she preferred her room to his company.

Being on his own had never been a problem for Kelso. His service as a sniper had made him self-sufficient and it had been Alexa who had driven their social life. While he missed her desperately, he didn't miss the evenings he'd often spent talking to people he'd nothing in common with. Now he'd pick up a pizza and when he'd got through his work he'd settle down with a book and a nightcap from the bottle of Scotch he always stashed in his bag.

As he waited for his pizza he found himself thinking about Murray again. She'd obviously developed a sense of ownership about the case and was bitterly disappointed at the thought of being dragged away.

He could see it from JB's point of view – she was under money pressure all the time. They had managed to establish a time frame for Aitchison's murder and by the end of tomorrow he could hope to have statements about the movements of the persons of interest and a plan for the follow-ups needed. The trouble was that they still seemed to be skirting round the elephant-in-the-room situation: the body being moved from the murder site to the cottage. It simply didn't make sense and it would rile the hell out of him to leave without at the very least finding a theory to explain it.

What Strang was always saying to Murray, that motives weren't their business, was only true in part. He was laying it on thick with her because of her tendency to fall in love with a theory and then look for confirmation. But, of course, managing to work out the 'why', especially on this point, would be a major step forward.

The Flow Country was an ideal place to get rid of a body. If you chose an area where there was no footpath you could just walk away with a reasonable hope that if it was discovered it would be years later, by which time there wouldn't be much left.

In theory, that was the smart thing to do. The most favoured method of disposal, burial, more or less ensured preservation but leave a body out in the open in some very secluded spot and Mother Nature, with her army of undertakers – the predators, the insects, the maggots – would do the job for you.

Unless, of course, you chose a peat bog. Mummified bog bodies going back to the Iron Age have been discovered in Europe; perhaps that would have been Niall Aitchison's fate. So had the murderer, perhaps, returned to the site and seen what was happening – and then moved it? Why?

Suppose that, for some reason, you only realised later that you needed proof of death. If a body wasn't found, getting a legal declaration of presumed death could take years and until then Niall's property, including the crucial shares, would be frozen. But why the cottage? Why not lay the body at the roadside where it was bound to be discovered? It was a new line to consider.

But it was true that he could consider it just as well from Edinburgh. There were a couple of things he wanted to do himself but there wasn't much excuse for staying here after that. There were lab reports still coming in, admittedly, and it was possible he might have to make another visit. He'd be glad enough to get home, though.

His sister Finella was on his mind. He'd even, to her surprise, given her a 'social' call last night which was unusual when he was working. She'd immediately assumed he'd phoned to say something had gone wrong that she would have to break to their parents – his practice since teenage days – and when he'd said he'd nothing to confess, she'd been puzzled.

'Just wanted to touch base,' he'd said. 'You OK?'

'Oh,' she'd said. 'Yes, absolutely fine.'

But he'd detected a hesitation and her voice was flat. 'That's good then. I just wanted to say we're almost at the stage where the local lads can take over, so it shouldn't be long before I'm back.'

'I'm glad. That's good.' There had definitely been relief in her voice but immediately she said, 'It'll get Betsy off my back – she's always on about when she is going to see Unkie.'

'I'll give you a call when I get home and brace myself for a session of playing slave.'

He'd kept it light, but he was more worried than ever now. Something was definitely wrong, but he wouldn't get it out of her over the phone.

Yes, in some ways it would suit him to get back to Edinburgh, particularly if the remarkable spell of weather was breaking. The north-east coast was famed for the savagery of its climate and courtesy of the jet stream they'd been lucky to have seen it in such a benign mood – even if Kevin – *Kevlar!* – probably didn't see it quite like that.

It was very late when Morven Gunn got back to Forsich. For the last two hours the journey had been under lowering skies, with dark clouds driven briskly on a north-east wind. Her mood was stormy too. She had left with such high hopes this morning when it had looked as if it was all going her way, as if at last she had actually achieved – perhaps not justice, but the recompense she believed was her due.

From the start she'd understood that Niall might have a will, of course. But even then, by rights any will he made would have left her, his only sister, at the very least their mother's house – the mother who had gone completely over to the enemy despite her own grandson being murdered. As Niall, the traitor, had done.

It was Niall who'd encouraged her to invest in Pat Curran's business. Admittedly, he hadn't told her to borrow against the house she'd kept after the divorce from Gary's father, but when it was all going so well it had seemed foolish not to capitalise on its success. But she'd never even have thought of it if it hadn't been for Niall, who claimed he was doing her a good turn. So, he owed her.

Not that he saw it that way. He hadn't even agreed to give her more than the 'bairn's part' of their mother's estate, enforced by Scots law. She had thought she hated her brother as much as she could, but she'd been wrong. After that refusal the impotent fury she had felt had festered like a boil needing to be lanced. He should pay for what he had done to her; that would only be justice.

And when she'd got the message to phone Bruce Michie she believed it had all come right in the end. There was only one reason he could want to contact her: either Niall being a young man hadn't yet made a will or he had, but with belated shame had made her the beneficiary. She knew about his shares in the business and if Michie wanted to buy them back she was ready to drive a hard bargain.

Morven hardly noticed that Bruce Michie was wracked with embarrassment as he told her what her brother had done, with a halting apology for dragging her all this way for nothing. He didn't tell her who had benefited instead of her, but he didn't have to. She knew.

It struck her as viscerally as a knife blow and her scream had expressed an agony of shattered hopes. Then the tempest of rage took her, and she had flung herself from the room and down the stairs to reception, blindly knocking a woman out of the way so hard that she fell back into one of the chairs there.

As she returned to her car she didn't notice the curious stares that followed her as she passed, muttering curses like some crazy woman and shaking with anger and the frustration of realising that though she might wish her dead brother would rot in hell, there was nothing she personally could do to ensure it.

As Morven drove off there were blasts on the horn from other motorists, but she barely noticed them. It was only when, in a moment of blind impatience, she pulled out to overtake a car that was dithering and found herself nose-to-nose with a juggernaut that she realised that rage could be as dangerous as drunkenness. She swerved back to her own side of the road with her heart thumping and drove on more cautiously.

It was pouring now, heavy silver curtains of rain that glittered and dazzled in the headlights. The sweep of the wipers was becoming mesmeric and she was lightheaded with exhaustion and hunger too; she hadn't eaten since seven o'clock this morning and had spent more than nine hours on the road already – for nothing.

It was Curran's spawn Gabrielle who filled her mind, Gabrielle with her bloodstained hands and black heart;

Gabrielle, who should never have felt able to return to Forsich. Knowing that she was there, just down the road, seeing the insolence that allowed her to leave flowers on Gary's grave, had been fuelling her anger and she'd given her fair warning that if shame wouldn't drive her away, worse would follow.

But Niall, her own flesh and blood, the little brother she'd loved and looked after once, had played traitor again. Now her future panned out before her in merciless clarity: her days spent slaving in the cafe to pay the rent on it and on the miserable hovel she had to call home while Gabrielle could move into the cottage Morven had grown up in, glorying in her ultimate, total triumph.

She was tired, so tired! Morven's eyes drooped and, feeling the car swing across the road, she startled awake, wrenching at the wheel. She saved herself from disaster, but she was close to the end of her tether now. She opened her window wide, letting the stinging rain and wind buffet her. She must get herself home safely and sleep, then in the morning she would make her plans. After everything, this wasn't going to be the end.

The time had come for justice to be done and for Gabrielle Curran to pay for her sins.

CHAPTER SEVENTEEN

Kirstie Mowat splashed along Forsich high street in a thoroughly bad mood. The rain was unrelenting, her fashionable parka was soaked right through, she had slept in and her mother had stood over her while she ate a piece of toast. Now she was late, and she'd get a bollocking from Morven too.

The cafe was open, one of their regulars was in already and there was a smell of bacon cooking. As Kirstie came in, pushing back her hood, he looked up and said, 'Don't worry, dearie, it may never happen.'

'You think?' she said bitterly and went on through to the little kitchen at the back. She could feel the atmosphere before she even opened the door: brooding, like that odd heavy feeling you get before a thunderstorm.

She braced herself and went in and said, 'Sorry I'm late,' as she waited for the thunderbolt.

Morven, buttering a roll, didn't look round. 'I'm docking

your wages,' was all she said. 'Make a cup of tea and take it out to him.'

Kirstie did as she was told, with a nervous glance over her shoulder as she went. It wasn't like Morven to hold back. She busied herself with folding paper napkins and when Morven came out with the bacon roll she stole a glance at her face. Kirstie wasn't particularly imaginative but as she looked the image that came to mind was one of those primitive African masks, rigid with an ugly emotion she couldn't read. There was something quite frightening about it and she was glad when a few more customers arrived.

It was quarter past nine when a young woman wearing a yellow oilskin jacket came in. Somehow, she didn't look like the normal clientele and when she took off her hood to expose dark red hair and asked to speak to Morven Gunn the penny dropped, even before Morven appeared from the kitchen to be shown the warrant card.

'DC Murray,' she said. 'Could I have a word?'

Kirstie held her breath. She'd seen Morven erupt before when the police dared to intrude and with the funny mood she was in today, anything could happen.

Instead, with a zombie-like calm Morven said, 'Yes, of course. I'd rather you came across to my flat, if that's all right.' She took off her apron and turned to Kirstie. 'I won't be long. Just say breakfast is off but there's scones there if folk are wanting them.'

The two women went out and the silence that had fallen in the cafe was broken by half a dozen voices. 'Here, Kirstie, do you know what's going on?' one of them asked.

She thought of telling them Morven was being

arrested, just for fun, but thought the better of it. 'Me? How would I know? Anyone wanting a scone?'

It was a horrid little flat, DC Livvy Murray thought, as Morven Gunn unlocked the front door for her and she stepped straight into the living room. It ran across the front and it was narrow like a railway carriage and cluttered so that she had to weave her way through between occasional tables and overstuffed chairs that looked as if they were accustomed to more spacious surroundings. But the covers were grubby now and the cushions limp and shabby. There was a damp, fusty smell of stale air that made her want to throw open the window, despite the rain.

She had last seen the woman giving vent to a tirade about the hapless PC Davidson and she'd been steeling herself for a violent reaction, verbally at the very least. Morven was looking terrible this morning, the shadows under her eyes so dark they looked bruised and her eyelids thick as if she hadn't slept, so it was disconcerting that she was so calm, waving Murray to a seat in the corner and sitting down on the couch herself.

'Did he complain?' she said.

Murray was puzzled. 'Did who complain?'

'Did he not? I thought it was that man, Michie.'

'Bruce Michie? What would he have to complain about?'

For the first time, there was a spark of emotion. 'God knows. But folk do.'

'Am I right that you had a meeting with him yesterday?'

Morven's face was blank again. 'Yes.'

'Why?'

271

'He asked to talk to me.'

'About?' This was heavy going. Murray saw Morven's hands tense into fists; she was finding it hard to maintain the appearance of being unruffled.

'He had an idea that I might have inherited my brother's shares in Curran Services.'

'And had you?'

For a moment her control slipped, and she spat out, 'No!'

'And who did?'

Her nails were digging right into her palms now and her jaw was locked rigid. 'He . . . didn't tell me,' she managed.

'Upset, were you?'

'Yes!' Again, that flash of anger. 'I may have raised my voice a bit, but I was hurt. Wouldn't you be? Your own brother, who knew you'd lost everything, your home, your son—' She choked on the word.

Murray softened her tone. 'I'm sorry for your loss. That was a great tragedy.'

If she was hoping to draw Morven into talking about it, she was out of luck. The shutter came down again and she only compressed her lips and nodded, without saying anything. Mindful of her mistake with Gabrielle Ross, Murray wasn't about to raise the subject of blame for Gary Gunn's death unless Morven did.

And, apparently, she wasn't going to. She was back in control, saying calmly – too calmly? – that it had been an overreaction and she realised afterwards that Niall had been entitled to do what he liked with what was his. 'I was disappointed, of course, but I've rebuilt my life already without any help from him.'

Morven might be saying the right things but her whole demeanour was screaming something completely different. It looked as if it was almost killing her not to let rip. But so far, she had managed, and Murray moved on.

'This is just a routine question. Can you tell me your movements on the Saturday before last – the 24th?'

Morven gave a short laugh. 'Same as they are every Saturday. Closed up the cafe after the lunch service, at two o'clock, then came back here. I don't remember exactly but I probably went along to the Spar. I usually do.'

'You didn't go anywhere in your car?'

'No, I came back here to rest. When you work as hard as I do you get tired. You probably won't know about that.'

That was a glimpse of what Murray reckoned was her normal aggression. The rest was an act, for whatever reason, and she was nettled into saying, 'You didn't walk up to your son's grave? It's a lovely place on a hot summer day.'

The mask slipped. 'Oh my God, you've gone snooping there too? Is nothing sacred? Get out my house – you've had all you'll get from me.' She stood up, looming over Murray, who got to her feet quickly.

'I'd finished, anyway. Thank you for your cooperation.' She tried not to scuttle like a frightened rabbit as she left.

She didn't hear Morven give way at last to the rage she had been suppressing, because her head was buried in one of the shabby cushions to stifle her screams.

It was the sound of someone moving about the house that woke Gabrielle next morning and she sat up with a gasp. It

273

was oddly dark outside but the digital clock by her bedside was showing 11.38.

She sat bolt upright, her heart racing, and there was panic in her voice as she called, 'Who's there?'

'Only me, Gabrielle!' her mother called. 'Are you still in bed?'

Gabrielle collapsed again, her mind still fuddled from the pills she had taken the night before. She'd slept soundly for once, perhaps because the rain that was drumming on the windows now had provided a lullaby as well as sparing her the relentless brutality of constant light. She'd locked up carefully last night but here was Lilian coming into her bedroom looking almost offensively bright and organised.

'Oh dear, bad night, sweetie?'

Propping herself up again, Gabrielle said, 'How did you get in?'

'David gave me a key. He thought it was . . . er . . .' She hesitated, then said awkwardly, avoiding her gaze, 'Just in case there was, well, some problem.'

In case I was lying here dead of an overdose, you mean, Gabrielle thought. God, how she hated her husband discussing her problems with her mother! But she said only, 'I thought you were in Aberdeen?'

'I woke early and decided just to get back here immediately. I usually get Nico to touch up my tint because Dennis is absolutely useless at that, but I'm so worried about my girls I decided just to come home first thing.

'Is everything all right? I was glad to see you'd locked up properly – awful that it's come to that in our little backwater, but David won't be back till later and after what happened

274

to poor Niall you mustn't take risks. I haven't even been home yet. I thought I'd just check that you were OK and see if I could coax you to come back with me until he gets here. I'll tell him to pick you up from Westerfield House, shall I?'

Lilian's style of motherliness always made her cringe. 'Thanks, but I've got things to do here.' She'd tried to speak crisply but her throat was still dry, and her tongue felt thick in her mouth.

Lilian smiled. 'What you need is coffee. Are you getting up, or shall I bring you some here? You need your rest.'

Gabrielle was still feeling dizzy, but she swung her legs out of bed and grabbed her dressing gown. She didn't want her mother working in her kitchen: what if she found the milk in the cupboard under the sink or the phone in the fridge, as had been known to happen? And where had she left that knife?

'No need,' she said hastily. 'I'll come down and make some.'

'I'll put the kettle on, anyway,' Lilian said. 'Then I'll just take a comfort break – it's a long drive.'

Gabrielle was able to check on the kitchen before her mother came back. There didn't seem to be anything out of place, though the knife wasn't in its slot. She remembered thinking about it a lot yesterday, but she couldn't with any certainty say what she might have done with it. She made the coffee and put the bread in the toaster, still feeling nervous.

She didn't want to talk to anyone until she'd made up her mind about where Niall's will had left her, not even David. Perhaps, particularly not David. She'd have to face up to it eventually, but she needed time to get her bearings, think calmly – if she could still think calmly – about what she wanted to do. About what, realistically, she was mentally and physically capable of doing. Loyalty was a heavy burden.

The toast had popped, and she was getting out plates when she heard her mother come back in. She didn't speak and when Gabrielle glanced over her shoulder Lilian was looking at her with an expression she couldn't quite read – shock, pity?

'Darling . . .' She sounded very hesitant. 'The cloakroom – what is that about?'

Gabrielle went cold. 'What – what do you mean?'

Wordlessly, Lilian turned and led her back across the hall. The cloakroom had a clutter of coats on the hooks behind the door and shoes and boots standing together on the floor below. Gabrielle's eyes went to the basin and yes, there was the little knife. But her mother wasn't looking at that: she was pointing to the dark-blue towels draped over the rail beside it. They had been quite neatly sliced into rags.

She felt her face flood with colour. Lilian was staring at her, waiting for her to say something.

'Oh – that!' She made an attempt at a laugh. 'I'm properly caught out, aren't I? I'm afraid I was just in a really bad temper – I'd burnt a cake I was making, and I felt destructive. Silly, I know, but we were needing new ones anyway and it was a great way to relieve frustration.'

She was proud of her quick thinking, but Lilian was still looking at her very soberly. 'I suppose I can understand how you felt – heaven knows, after Dennis has made a mess of my haircut, "frustration" doesn't begin! But Gabrielle, this

276

isn't normal. This is so weird, so violent! What else might you do, when we're all under such stress? I really don't think you should be alone.'

Gabrielle tried to make light of it. 'Oh, you're exaggerating. If it was as bad as that don't you think I'm better on my own? If one of you annoyed me I might turn dangerous.'

Lilian sighed. 'Don't be silly, I'm not worried about that. What I am worried about, darling, is – well, to put it bluntly, I'm frightened you might turn it on yourself. Have you been having thoughts about that?'

'No. I absolutely haven't.' Gabrielle had never found it difficult to lie to her mother. 'I'm fine here. I've things to do before David gets back tonight – like make another cake.'

Lilian sighed again. 'I can't force you to come. But Malcolm's insisting that you go and have a professional chat with him. He's just as concerned about you as David and I are. There's no need to struggle on your own, you know.'

'Thank him very much,' Gabrielle said. 'But no thanks. Here's your coffee, and I've made toast—'

Lilian was walking out of the cloakroom. 'I think I'd better be getting back. When I phoned Malcolm last night he said poor Fran is still very distressed.'

'Yes, poor Fran.' She went across the hall and opened the front door. *Just go, just go*, she said to herself.

And then she was on her own. She went back into the cloakroom, picked up the little knife and stared at it. Despair, the enemy she had kept at bay for so long, was slowly, steadily gaining ground.

* * *

277

There was a car waiting for DCI Strang at the heliport at Dyce airport. A DI was waiting at the gate; he'd met him before – Steve MacLean.

'Thanks, Steve,' Strang said. 'Your lot are doing a great job for us.'

'All part of the service. We've arranged for them to be at home for interview, like you asked. Tom Morrison lives in Airyhall, just ten minutes from here. Chris Brady's one of the fat cats – lives out at Cults. Bruce Michie lives in one of the new "executive" estates in Westhill.'

'Know anything about them?'

'Tom's a tiddler – old pal of Bruce Michie's. Brady's a bit of a shark in the business community – he's swallowed up a couple of smaller firms in the last two years. Michie—' He shrugged. 'Don't know much about him. Just standing in for Pat Curran's daughter. Curran himself was in the Brady league.'

'Really?' Strang said. 'That would figure.'

As they walked through the airport MacLean hesitated as they passed a news-stand. 'I wasn't sure if I should point this out to you. But – well, forewarned is forearmed.'

Strang looked at the paper he was indicating – the *Press and Journal*, the long-established newspaper for the North-East. So far, they had only printed a straightforward version of the statement he had given himself; today they had gone to town with a graphic description of Niall Aitchison's mutilated body – enough to bring on a feeding frenzy from the tabloids. There was his name, as investigating officer, as well as a mention of the 'new' Serious Rural Crime Squad. And a rather stiff quote from DI Hay in Thurso, stating that CID there was being bypassed.

He swore. 'I suppose it was inevitable. But I'd been hoping we'd have a bit more progress to talk about before this hit us. The press aren't inclined to be indulgent to Police Scotland right at the moment. I wonder how long I can afford to wait before I phone my boss?'

MacLean made a sympathetic face. 'The *P&J* probably isn't the first thing he reaches for in the morning. It'll depend on how long it takes the news media to pick it up and run with it.'

'She, actually,' he said. 'And she's usually snowed under with meetings. I reckon I can risk doing the interviews first in the hope that I've got a bit of proper red meat to offer her at the end of them.'

When they reached the car with the waiting driver, MacLean said, 'Keep me up to date with what's happening, but I'll leave you to it now. I've a pile on my desk like you wouldn't believe.'

'Oh, I'd believe you. Thanks for taking time out to meet me. I'll text you the outcome later.'

As he was driven to Airyhall, Strang had a sinking feeling in his stomach. With the Police Scotland top brass hypersensitive about the headlines at the moment, he was dangerously exposed. JB was in general a good boss but she had her own bosses breathing down her neck and she'd given him a big promotion. Reasonably enough, she wasn't going to sacrifice her career for his, so he'd better deliver. That remark from Hay wasn't going to help: if they decided the SRCS wasn't working they'd be ruthless and there wasn't a lot in his life just at the moment, apart from the job.

He knew the city centre in Aberdeen, but he'd never been in the residential areas before. They did love their granite, though today in the pouring rain it looked gloomy and colourless. There seemed to have been an agreement, too, that all the houses would be built to more or less the same pattern: rooms to either side of the front door and steeply pitched roofs with windows inset. The one the driver had stopped outside was in the middle of a long, monotonous street with few front gardens to add colour; almost all of them had a paved area for cars instead.

The doorbell was brass and highly polished and the woman who opened the door was grey-haired and very neat in a floral dress with a white cardigan. She was obviously expecting him, but she scrutinised his warrant card and looked him up and down before she said, with a little sniff of what he guessed was disapproval, 'Come in, then. Mr Morrison will see you now.'

It sounded as if she had once been a receptionist and saw formality as a way of putting him in his place. Strang thanked her with suitable humility and was shown into the front room, where a plump, balding man with a neat rim of grey hair and high colour in his cheeks got up to greet him from one of the lug chairs that stood on either side of a fireplace that boasted a large arrangement of artificial flowers.

He was also very nervous and almost too cooperative. At the first question about the fishing trip, he embarked on an exhaustive description, detailing virtually every cast he had made. But when he was asked if he had a priest, he looked puzzled.

'No, we're Church of Scotland. Well, sort of.'

Strang laughed. 'I meant for stunning the fish – you know, a sort of baton.'

'Oh, is that what it's called? No, I don't. I just pull them out and leave them on the bank. I don't like handling them while they're squirming – bad enough just taking them off the hook. I think Chris maybe has one, I'm not sure.'

What he was very keen to emphasise was that it had just been a perfectly ordinary fishing morning and they had all gone their own way as they usually did unless they'd decided to take a boat. He repeated this later using, Strang was interested to note, almost exactly the same form of words. He also denied that there had been another man who joined them; if anyone said there was, they were 'confused'.

He wasn't comfortable, though. Strang looked at him for a long moment. Then, 'I don't think you're very sure about that, are you, Mr Morrison?' he said.

Morrison's face flared. 'Yes – yes of course I am! Well, if there was it was nothing to do with me. Chris and Bruce sat on in the bar after I'd packed it in and gone to bed. They looked as if they were settling in and I haven't the stamina. Not as young as I was, you know!' He attempted a casual laugh.

Strang said, 'Did you know Niall Aitchison?'

Morrison jumped as if he'd bitten him. 'Niall Aitchison – no. Why should I? He's the one that got killed, isn't he? No, of course I didn't. Is that what this is all about?'

'Yes, Mr Morrison. I'm investigating his murder.'

'Then why for heaven's sake are you questioning me?' Morrison's cheeks flushed. 'I've never met the man in my life!'

'You're an old friend of Bruce Michie's, aren't you? Did you not know Mr Aitchison was one of his partners at Curran Services?'

'No, I did not! I knew about Pat Curran – met him a couple of times, and I knew the daughter had taken over. But we never talked about work. We went fishing to get away from it.'

Strang raised his eyebrows. 'All of you?'

Morrison gulped. 'Well, maybe Chris and Bruce did talk shop, a bit. They're in the same line, you know.'

'Oh yes, I know. I think you're well aware that something was going on. I think you were told what to say when I came to ask you questions.' Morrison was gaping like one of his hooked trout and his colour was such an alarming shade of burgundy that Strang hurried on, 'I think you were told that this was highly commercially sensitive, and you had to make sure that nothing suspicious seemed to be going on.'

'That's right! I don't understand about business, except my own – I'm one of Curran Service's suppliers, that's all.' Morrison was gabbling in his haste to get it out.

'So, can I ask you again – did someone join the group?'

Morrison hesitated. 'Well, it wasn't a lie, what I said. There was someone arrived, but it was just after I'd got up from the table on the way to my bed. Chris said you'd be asking about that, because someone said another man had joined them, but it just wasn't true.'

Strang sighed. For a moment there he'd thought he was going to get a description but that was too much to hope for. His next question, about their movements on the Saturday, produced only a long and tedious complaint about the weather being poor for fishing and his own lack of success.

Losing the will to live, he got up suddenly. 'Thank you, sir. That's all I need. You've been very helpful.'

At these words Morrison's relief was palpable. He sagged back in his chair, looking as if all the air had been let out of him and Strang added hastily, 'Don't get up, I can see myself out.'

At least he could score off one of the 'persons of interest' in the case. In fact, 'person of extreme boringness' would be more accurate, but at least he'd got some useful ammunition for the Brady interview. That might be a lot more fruitful.

CHAPTER EIGHTEEN

There was no one in when DC Murray arrived at the Mowats' farmhouse. She walked round into the yard, but there was no one about there either. A little at a loss, she looked around her, then thought that at least she could look for the cottage where Aitchison's body had been found. The track that ran past the farm looked promising and she didn't have to go far before she saw it, perched on rising ground.

There was still a bit of crime scene tape attached to one of the gateposts, but it was broken and drifting in the wind and she walked through. There were two dead birds, large, black, and hanging like rags from the fence at the side – ravens, presumably, executed for their crimes and she shuddered. The battered-looking door to the cottage was standing open and she stepped inside but there was nothing to see; the SOCOs would have cleared anything lying about and now it was just an old, decaying building, almost roofless. She went back out again and looked down towards the farm and the main road.

Anyone passing along there would be able to see the door standing open. Had the local uniforms checked for people who might have been passing? she wondered. It might be worth checking. But it was baffling that someone should take the risk of being seen – and in broad daylight, at this time of year – just to leave the body here for the ravens to find.

Unless it was to implicate someone? Fergus Mowat, even? She must ask if there was anyone who had it in for him. She walked round the back to the paved yard, but there was nothing to see there either, though it must have been where a car had been parked to unload the body. She decided to walk on up the slope beyond it.

The track itself, muddy today, would have been hard as concrete during the dry spell, so no helpful tyre marks as evidence. At the top of the rise – you couldn't really call it a hill – the track bore off down to the right in the direction of the village through fields where sheep were grazing. To the left there was only rough grass and heather and the land dipped away there too. If you didn't want to drive up past the farm, you'd have to come across country and it was rough terrain – and bog too, when you got down into the Flow Country. You'd need a sturdy vehicle for that.

Despite her wet-weather gear, the rain was managing to find a way round the collar and down her neck and her hands were red and freezing cold. The temperature must have dropped fifteen degrees since yesterday. She considered her options: wait on in hope for a bit longer, wait in the car or go and see Lilian Sinclair first. She was starting to shiver now, so scrub option one.

Murray was on her way back to the car when she heard someone whistling a tune. She turned to look: you never heard anyone doing that these days when someone else made the music for you through a plug in your ear. But the man who was coming up the track from the sheep fields towards her, wearing an Indiana Jones hat and a heavy waxed jacket, was whistling as if there was nothing made him happier than getting soaked and frozen.

He stopped when he saw her and called, 'Hello, there! Looking for me?'

'Mr Mowat? Yes. DC Murray.' She fumbled for her card.

'Och, don't bother with that. I'll trust you.'

He beamed at her and she smiled back. 'You seem cheerful, anyway, despite the rain.'

'Not despite – because of! We're not used to all that heat and I'd have been toiling up and down with water for the sheep in another day. What can I do for you?'

He peered at her – he had very blue eyes – and before she could say anything he tutted, 'Lassie, you're perishing with cold. Come on ben the house and I'll make you a cup of tea.'

Murray followed him gratefully and as he shed his coat and hat she stationed herself beside the Aga, snuggling against its warmth as she thawed out her hands. 'I know you've given a statement already, Mr Mowat—'

'Fergus. And what's your name? Seems daft to go calling you "constable".'

'Livvy. I didn't want to go through the details again, just to focus on times when you could definitely say that no one had been up around the cottage. You can't actually see it from here, can you?' She walked over to look out of the kitchen window as he took the kettle off the hotplate and made their tea.

'No, but we'd fairly see anyone who drove up that way. Jack Lothian said it would have been on the Thursday, right? You'd need to ask my wife Rhona as well – she's a bookkeeper and that's where she works.' He pointed to an office table with a computer and a filing cabinet beside it in one corner of the big room. 'Can't say if she was here that day. I was out for quite a bit of it myself in Thurso for a meeting about the support payments the government promised but needless to say they've never delivered – but don't get me started!'

'Would you have gone up past the cottage at any stage that day?' Murray asked, sitting down at the big wooden table and cupping her hands round the mug Mowat gave her.

'Only in the morning. I did my usual walk round the sheep and came back at this sort of time, I suppose. I was late back, and I didn't do an evening circuit, like I sometimes do. I'd have noticed the door then, but I hear it wouldn't have made any difference to the poor bugger.'

'No,' she agreed. She hadn't really expected him to say, 'Oh, now you mention it, I did notice . . .' but it was a bit disappointing. Whatever Strang might say, she still hoped for a breakthrough moment. Just as she said, 'I don't suppose you'd have any idea why—' She heard a car door slam.

'That'll be Rhona, I expect.' Mowat got up and looked out. 'Yes, that's her. Now you can ask her as well.'

Murray's hopes rose again. Mrs Mowat hadn't made a statement; perhaps they'd slipped up there and there was

287

something she could tell them that would crack the whole thing wide open – well, a girl can dream.

Rhona Mowat was more than willing to be helpful but unfortunately had nothing useful to add. She'd been out a lot of the time herself, she hadn't walked up to where she would have seen the cottage, and her daughter Kirstie had been out all day working at the Lemon Tree cafe.

Neither of them said anything about Kirstie finding the body; they obviously didn't know, and it wasn't Murray's business to tell them. Instead, she went back to the question she'd been going to ask before. 'You wouldn't have any idea why the body should have been moved to there, would you?'

They looked at each other, then Rhona said, 'We've been talking about this. It's totally bizarre. You'd have to know the cottage was there, in the first place. And Fergus said it didn't really look as if it had been broken into. He'd nailed up the door himself when we noticed a couple of kids going in there ages ago and it was dangerous with the roof falling in and everything.'

Mowat said, 'The bars I put across were still in place, it was just that the nails weren't properly holding. The little buggers must have carefully worked them loose, so you couldn't tell – going by some of the rubbish in there they'd been using it for years without us happening to spot them.'

Rhona chimed in, 'So maybe it could be someone who'd mucked about there as a kid, or else who'd been told about it by someone who did, and knew the door was loose?'

Murray was impressed. 'That works. But it doesn't explain why, really, does it? Fergus, does anyone have a grudge against you?'

They looked startled. 'I'd like to think not, Livvy,' Mowat said slowly. 'I suppose there's always someone you could have offended without knowing you had.'

'Did you have anything to do with Pat Curran's drainage business?'

They both shook their heads. 'We're lucky here,' Rhona said. 'Being out of the village we don't get so involved. Pat Curran was a conman – you only had to look at him, but some folk still fell for it. If Niall's murder was to do with that I can't think anyone would see Fergus as a good person to try to blame.'

Murray couldn't either. It didn't look as if there was anything more they could tell her, but she decided to take a punt. 'Look, I shouldn't really ask you this – my boss would have a fit – but you know this place and I don't. Strictly off the record, who do you think killed Niall Aitchison?'

They looked at each other and then at her, as if they were trying to decide whether to trust her. She said quickly, 'I promise it won't be used for any official purpose – cross my heart and hope to die.'

It was Rhona who spoke. 'I'm not going to say she did it, but I can't think of anyone who has been more violent in their anger about what happened than Morven Gunn. She'd more reason than most to hate the Currans and Niall made himself an extension of the clan. She lost her home and her son, and her own mother didn't support her. Niall was the baby and the boy, always her favourite, and he did well for himself when Morven couldn't even keep her marriage going. She always seemed a difficult person to me, but then favouritism's a rotten thing in a family.'

'Just as well we only had the one or our Kirstie would have to shape up,' Fergus said darkly. 'Look, Livvy, I'm not accusing anyone. But she's kind of the obvious one, isn't she?'

Murray thought of her interview with Morven, the violent hatred she clearly felt poorly concealed by the unconvincing mask of calm. Suddenly she blurted out, 'If you put a body in there, could you be sure that the ravens would come?'

They looked at her aghast and she could have bitten her tongue off. This was just the sort of thing that got her in trouble with Strang, and Rhona said stiffly, 'No, of course you couldn't.'

But Fergus said slowly, 'It was just carrion, I suppose. Looking for it – well, that's what they do.'

It gave Murray a lot to think about as she drove back to Forsich.

There was no doubt that Chris Brady was Hayley's 'Ginger'. He was a powerfully built six-footer with hair that was the classic flaming orange-red, receding a little from his temples but curling wildly where his chest was exposed by his open-necked shirt; his skin was pale and freckled. He greeted DCI Strang with a smile, but the pale-blue eyes were watchful and cold as he ushered him into the open-plan kitchen and family room that ran right across the back of the sprawling, ranch-style house in an expensive residential area.

'Thank you for agreeing to meet me, sir,' Strang said. 'This is just an informal chat to get a few details clearer.'

'Oh good, I'm so glad about that,' Brady said with heavy sarcasm. 'I'd hate to believe this was some sort of interrogation, Chief Inspector. Do take a seat.'

He sat down himself in the seating area on a large cream leather chair on a dark wood, swivelling base with a footstool in front of it and waved Strang to its counterpart opposite. 'Now, ask away. I have nothing to hide.' He spread his hands wide as if to indicate openness. He had very large hands, with fine gold hairs across the backs.

Strang said, 'Do I understand that you know what this is about? I assume that Mr Michie will have told you about his business partner's death.'

'Yes, he did. But I don't quite get how it affects me.'

'Did Mr Baxter warn you that we had been asking at the hotel about your fishing weekend?'

Strang saw his eyes flicker as if he was weighing up the implications of a 'yes' or 'no' before answering the question.

'Yes, he did. It's not just the normal thing for the polis to come calling and he was wondering what we'd been up to. "They're onto you, Chris," he said. I got a bit of ribbing about it.'

'And what had you been up to?' Strang asked politely.

There was just a flash of temper. 'You know perfectly well that we were on a fishing weekend. I don't appreciate being mucked about.'

'A fishing weekend in what sense? I understand you run a similar sort of operation to Curran Services, in which Bruce Michie is a minority shareholder though acting CEO at present. So, was it only the kind of fishing done in a body of water that was the object of the expedition?'

Brady looked at him with narrowed eyes. 'What's that supposed to mean?'

'Are you in the market for a merger?'

Strang thought the man was taken aback, though it was hard to tell. He didn't reply, just looked back at Strang with a challenging gaze.

'You see, Mr Brady, the reason we are taking an interest in your little fishing trip is that you and your friends were in the vicinity when Niall Aitchison was murdered. I know that Mr Aitchison and Mr Michie had a violent row in the office the day before. You and Mr Michie are long-standing friends and you might both see a merger as an extension of that friendship. With Mrs Ross, the majority shareholder, incapacitated you might have hoped that Mr Aitchison could be convinced to go along with that plan.

'Someone joined your party late that Friday evening. Was that Niall Aitchison?'

Brady had listened with careful attention. Now he gave a short laugh. 'Flying a kite, Inspector. No one joined us.'

Strang raised his brows. 'Eyewitness account.'

'Mistaken. Probably confused.'

'Let's go on to Saturday morning. Talk us through it.'

'We all went fishing, obviously. That's what we came to do.'

Strang sat back in his chair and waited. Brady waited too, but his was a tense silence. Eventually he burst out, 'Oh, for God's sake! All right then: we had breakfast. I had bacon, sausage, fried eggs – two – and a double helping of black pudding. Oh, and toast – two slices with marmalade – no, I tell a lie, it was honey. Would you like me to try to remember what the others had too?'

'That's all right. We can ask them.'

'Oh good,' he said mockingly. 'I wouldn't want to take

up too much of your time. I'm sure you're a busy man.'

Strang smiled. 'I have all the time in the world, Mr Brady. Let's move on to the fishing part. Did you fish together from a boat or fish from the shore?'

Brady gave a thin smile. 'If we'd known we were to be under some sort of suspicion we could have arranged to alibi each other all day. Since the thought never occurred to us, it was a perfectly ordinary fishing morning and we went our own way as usual, except when we decide to take a boat and fish on one of the lochs.'

'Ah,' Strang said. 'That's exactly what Mr Morrison said. Interestingly enough, in exactly those words.'

That threw him. 'Well – well, he would, because that's exactly what we did,' he blustered. 'Anyway, we all have our favourites – I like Loch Calder but Tom, for instance, prefers Loch Watten. I left right after breakfast and no, I didn't make a note of the time so that you could write it down in your notebook.'

'What equipment did you take?'

'For goodness' sake! What does that have to do with anything? Oh, if you insist! A couple of rods, reel, line, bait. Waders, a fishing creel, a fly box, camping stool. Packed lunch. Have I forgotten anything?'

Strang said, 'A priest?'

There was a frozen moment before Brady said slowly, 'Oh yes, a priest. Am I to consider that significant?'

'Do you still have it?'

The man rose abruptly. 'Follow me.'

He walked the length of the room and opened a door leading from the kitchen into a large utility room. Besides the normal laundry machines there was a locked metal cabinet.

'Guns?' Strang said. 'I take it you have a licence?'

'Of course.' Brady was opening a full-length cupboard, which held the fishing equipment he'd just detailed to Strang, neatly organised. He leant forward and unhesitatingly picked out a small but solid-looking priest made of some dark wood with a club-shaped head.

He held it up with a triumphant smile. 'Here it is. All right?'

It was wiped off his face as Strang produced one of the plastic evidence bags he always kept available. 'With your agreement, I'll take this. I'll give you a receipt, of course—'

'*What!*' Brady yelled. 'I don't believe this. Have you got a warrant?'

'Certainly not – I would have told you that. But presumably you could have no objection to having it checked?'

Brady paused, frowning. Then he said, 'Should I be calling my lawyer?' But he dropped the priest in the bag.

Strang secured it, though he was fairly certain that it would be clean. 'You're perfectly entitled to, of course. But it will save us both a lot of time and trouble if we can talk this through now.'

Again, Brady hesitated, but after a moment he said, 'All right. Like I said, I've nothing to hide. Let's get it over with.'

They returned to their seats. Before Strang could ask another question, Brady said, 'On that Saturday I drove straight from the hotel to Loch Calder, where I spent the entire day fishing. I arrived back at the hotel around five.'

'Witnesses?'

'For God's sake! Why would I have witnesses? I saw a few people in the course of the day, yes, but I didn't pay any attention to them and they probably didn't notice me. All right?'

'We can check if necessary. Did you catch anything?'

Brady gave a put-upon sigh. 'No, I didn't, since you ask.'

'Hardly surprising, given the weather. Not really the best time to arrange a fishing weekend. Unless you had some other reason. Or had arranged to meet somebody.'

Brady only stared at him, stony-faced. 'Right, I'm going to ask you again,' Strang said. 'Was Niall Aitchison the man who joined you? Think very carefully about your answer.'

'No, he bloody wasn't,' he snapped, goaded, then added hastily, 'Like I said before, there wasn't any man. Or if there was, he wasn't anything to do with us.'

Strang took out a pad of paper and scribbled on it. 'Your receipt,' he said as he got up. 'Thank you for your cooperation, Mr Brady. That's all.'

'Oh, thank you. Thank you very much. I thought you'd be bringing out the hood and the bath for water torture any time now. You've built up a wonderful theory, Inspector. It's just that it has no basis at all in reality and I can't imagine why you think it should.'

Strang looked up at him. 'Something to do with the fact that you're still lying about the man who joined you,' he said. 'But we'll leave it there for the moment.'

He went back to the car. He hadn't made any great breakthrough though there was something niggling in his mind that he couldn't quite pin down right now. Still, he had the Bruce Michie interview ahead. A weak man, he'd thought when he met him before; he was a lot more likely to crack under pressure than Brady, who was both tough and careful.

Strang had just opened the car door when his phone buzzed, and it was JB's number that appeared. He swore under his breath. He shouldn't have taken the risk; it would have been better if he'd got his word in first. It was with some trepidation that he said, 'Yes, boss?'

Back at Westerfield House, Lilian Sinclair parked the car and then went in through the surgery entrance. The waiting room was busy, and a couple of people were queuing at the desk. The receptionist was looking harassed and though she greeted her employer's wife immediately, she had to break off to answer the phone, so Lilian had to wait.

The two women ahead of her in the queue exchanged glances as Lilian leant forward whenever the receptionist came off the phone.

'Could you just tell the doctor that I'm back before he sees his next patient, Cathy?'

'Yes, of course, Mrs Sinclair,' the woman said. Then she added, 'Is Fran going to be coming in today? We're a bit stretched, you see.'

'I've no idea. If I see her I'll ask her,' Lilian said and walked away through the door to the house as the receptionist sighed pointedly and got sympathetic smiles from the women waiting.

When Lilian reached the hall the door to the sitting room was open and she could see Francesca sitting there on one of the sofas. The curtains were closed; she wasn't doing anything except staring straight ahead and she was wearing the same black clothes that she'd had on the day before. At least they were a bit more appropriate today when it was so much colder, but it was still the sort of exhibitionism that was really irritating.

'Goodness me, Fran, whatever are you doing here, sitting in the darkness?' she said, going over to draw back the curtains and let the daylight in.

Francesca shrugged her shoulders. 'Just mourning, I suppose. I didn't want people looking in and seeing me, but I thought you'd be back before long. I feel worse when I'm alone upstairs.'

'What you need is something to take your mind off it,' Lilian said briskly. 'Why not go back to work? They're busy today and Cathy's struggling.'

Her daughter looked at her in horror, tears springing to her eyes. 'How can I?' she cried. 'It would be so humiliating if I broke down in public.'

'Perhaps you wouldn't when you had something to distract you. It might make you feel better.'

'You're not taking this seriously, are you? You just don't accept that Niall and I had something special and now I have no future. I can't just go on as if nothing had happened when we haven't even had the funeral. When's that going to be, anyway?'

Lilian stared at her, then sank onto a chair. 'Good grief, I hadn't even thought of that. I don't know who will be arranging it. We'll have to find out somehow.'

'Lilian? Where are you?' Malcolm Sinclair appeared in the hall. 'Oh, there you are, sweetheart! I've missed you.'

She went to be embraced. 'It's good to be home. I got up at crack of dawn and the roads were quiet, but it's a long way.'

'How was the meeting?'

She brushed aside the question. 'Oh, fine. But Malcolm, Fran here was asking about Niall's funeral. Do you know anything about it? I think she feels that it might give her some sort of closure.'

Sinclair hadn't noticed his stepdaughter sitting there and when he did he looked uncomfortable. 'Oh, that could be ages, Fran. The police will have to agree to release—' He realised he was about to say, 'the body' and coughed instead. 'Well, it may take some time.'

'But who will be arranging it?' Fran demanded. 'He and his sister weren't speaking.'

Sinclair looked more uncomfortable still. 'Well, his lawyers, I suppose.'

Lilian looked at him narrowly. 'Malcolm, there's something wrong, isn't there? What is it?'

He looked from one to the other then said awkwardly, 'Look, this is only a rumour. But they're saying his cleaner had a phone call from the lawyers saying that . . . er' – he ran his finger round his neck to loosen the collar – 'Gabrielle will be her boss now. He's left her everything.'

The women were transfixed. Then Francesca gave a great wail. 'That bitch – she's done it to me again! I'll kill her! I'll kill her! Oh, it's not fair!' She collapsed face down on the sofa in a tempest of tears.

Just then the doorbell rang.

CHAPTER NINETEEN

DCI Kelso Strang got into the car, putting the phone back in his pocket. 'Change of instructions,' he said tersely to the driver. 'Dyce airport, please.'

Detective Chief Superintendent Jane Borthwick had not been happy. 'I think we need to talk. I want you down here for a review.'

'Right,' he had said hollowly. 'Is – is there a problem?'

'Have you read the *Press and Journal* today?'

'Not read, exactly. I did catch the headlines as I passed through the airport.'

'We need to talk through the next press statement. The media are on our backs already, so we have to thrash out what we can give them. As it happens, the chopper's still in Aberdeen so if you go to the heliport now I'll clear a space late afternoon. Then it can take you back up tomorrow morning.'

It clearly wasn't the moment to mention that he wanted to do another interview first. 'On my way, boss,' he had said and now he was trying to think through what he would be able to offer her. Livvy Murray should have done at least one of the interviews by now – two, if she'd been lucky in finding people in.

She sounded cheerful when she answered the phone but when it got right down to it there didn't seem to be much there to soothe an anxious DCS.

'Morven Gunn was seriously weird,' she said. 'She was trying to seem calm and normal, but it came over as sort of rigid, like if one wee titchy thing went wrong she'd fall apart and go completely radge. Oh, she said she was OK, right enough, and that Niall didn't have to leave her anything if he didn't want to – oh, and that she didn't know what the will said. Like I believed her! She didn't come out with anything we didn't know already, though – got quite aggressive at the end too.'

'Right.' He hadn't seriously thought anything would come of it. 'Did you see Fergus Mowat?'

'Yes, and Rhona as well. Wanted to help, but there wasn't a lot that was useful. He did say that it looked as if whoever put the body there must have known the door wasn't really secured.'

'That ties in with what we said before – that a passing stranger probably wouldn't have even registered that the cottage was there. What are you doing now?'

'Just going to grab something to eat. Are you going to get back soon? If not, I'll go and see if I can get hold of Mrs Sinclair.'

'Fine. Do that, and then I'd like you to put in reports on the interviews ASAP so the DCS can see them by the end of the afternoon. Emphasise the positive – it's all going to hit the fan any minute. The *Press and Journal* has done a big spread on it and we'll have the tabloids onto us any time now. She's asked me to go on down to Edinburgh – I'm on my way to the heliport – and they'll bring me back first thing tomorrow.

'So, after you've done that, go back to Gabrielle Ross's house. I'm hoping that her husband will be back by then and she won't even answer the door – doubt if you're flavour of the month where she's concerned. And even if she is prepared to speak to you, I don't want you to interview her – that's something I want to do myself. Understood?'

'Yes, boss.'

'Ideally, it'd be Ross you have to deal with. Make an appointment for me to see him and Gabrielle there late morning tomorrow. Any worries and you know I'm always at the end of the phone. All right?'

'No problem, boss.' She rang off, sounding very upbeat, which made Strang nervous. This was giving her a lot of responsibility and he hoped it wouldn't go to her head. Still, it was out of his hands.

He bought a copy of the *Press and Journal* at the airport and depressed himself further by reading it on the trip south. The one bright spot on the horizon was that he'd have a night at home and once JB was finished chewing him up and had spat him out he could phone Finella and see if she was on for a drink.

On the phone to Strang, Murray had been feeling fairly pleased with herself. At last she was getting the sort of respect from him that she'd always wanted; overnight at least she was sort of in charge of the murder investigation. It was only when she thought of the implications that she began to get cold feet. It was all very well for him to say he was at the end of the phone, but he was also in Edinburgh. The saying, 'Be very careful what you wish for because you just might get it,' came forcibly to mind.

She just had to follow instructions, and hope for the best. There was a lot to get through; she'd no time to go back to the incident room in Thurso for her break, so she bought a sandwich in the local Spar in Forsich instead and ate it in the car on the way to Westerfield House.

When she rang the doorbell, she was aware of a movement beside the curtain of the room to the left of the front door, the sitting room she had been in before. She couldn't be sure who had peeked out, but she had the impression it was a woman and there was an appreciable pause before the door was opened by Lilian Sinclair. She was looking flustered and as Murray stepped into the hall she saw Malcolm Sinclair leaving through the door that led to the surgery. She could also hear the sound of someone sobbing from the direction of the staircase – Francesca Curran, most likely.

Lilian greeted her warmly. 'Do come in. I remember you came with the inspector but forgive me, I don't recollect your name. Of course, we were so absolutely shocked at the news about poor Niall that I wasn't taking anything in. Malcolm said you would be wanting to talk to us again, but I'm afraid he's had to go back to the surgery – it overran this morning. Now, come this way.'

Murray introduced herself again as they went back into

the sitting room. On one of the sofas, the cushions that were so neatly primped on its opposite number were disordered and squashed.

Lilian noticed Murray's glance and sighed. 'Oh dear. Perhaps you heard my daughter crying. She's been quite distraught lately. I think Malcolm told you the position with her and poor Niall.'

'That's right. I can see she'd be upset.'

'Indeed, we all are. Now, what did you want to ask me – but wait, I'm forgetting my manners. Would you like a cup of tea, coffee?'

The condescending lady of the manor, recollecting her social duty to the serfs. Trying not to grind her teeth visibly, Murray said, 'No thank you. I'm a bit pushed today. Can you tell me your movements on Saturday 24th June?'

If she'd hoped to dent Lilian's self-possession she was out of luck. 'Oh dear, is that when poor Niall was actually killed? I didn't know.' She said it as if 'poor Niall' was the man's name. 'Actually, that's very straightforward. Malcolm's off on a Saturday and we always like to do something together. For the last three weeks of this wonderful weather we've been walking – that Saturday I remember we went up round St John's Point, for the views, you know? It was really stunning. Then we had lunch in the tea room at Castle of Mey – very good, you should really try it, Constable Murray! Then we came back for a nice relaxing evening here. Malcolm works so hard it's important that he eases up at the weekends.'

Murray had taken out a notebook and scribbled an entry. 'You were all very close to Mr Aitchison, were you?'

Lilian sighed. 'There's a lot of history there, Constable Murray. I don't want to bore you—'

She was clearly expected to say, 'I'm sure you won't.' She said, 'Carry on.'

'All right, then. You need to understand that it all stems from my ex-husband, Pat Curran. He came here and started up a drainage business – oh, I suppose it must have been almost thirty years ago. I was a local girl and he was so unlike the boys I knew here – much older, of course, and that seemed sophisticated to me at the time. He had the sort of dreams that would never have entered their heads. And he had charm – oh, in bucketloads! Charm was Pat's stock-in-trade.' She sounded bitter when she said that. 'Of course, my mother was horrified – "just a jumped-up Irish navvy" she used to say. Naturally, I didn't listen. I didn't see the rough side of his character until much later.'

'Rough side?'

'Oh, he didn't actually hit me. I'd have walked out there and then. I'm not the sort of woman who puts up with physical abuse.'

Murray wondered what 'sort of woman' it was who did, in Lilian's eyes. Weak, powerless perhaps? So that made her strong and powerful – and perhaps she was.

Lilian was going on, 'He was so coarse, mocking anything I did to try to live a civilised life. He even moved us out of the village to that terrible shack my daughter is so fond of, right by the works so that he could bring the mud in and expect to sit down at the table in his filthy dungarees – "I'm fecking going out again, so what's the point?" was all he'd say when I talked about decent standards. And I could see it rubbing off on my daughters.

'He drove a wedge between me and my girls. We'd been more like sisters than mother and daughters before, you know. But Gabrielle could do no wrong in his eyes so of course whatever I said was ignored as she got older. She was a very difficult teenager and very . . . well, I hesitate to say this about my own daughter, but very hard. And, of course, Francesca was hurt and jealous and that got between them too. You know, Constable Murray, that's my great private grief – that my daughters don't get on.' She pulled out a handkerchief and sniffed delicately into it.

Murray wasn't paid to listen to Lilian Sinclair's private griefs – whether genuine or not. 'Mr Curran was very successful at first, though, wasn't he?'

'Oh yes. He was smart, no doubt about that. But he financed the business expansion on the back of people in the village and then when it all failed off he went to Aberdeen, taking my older daughter with him and leaving poor Niall here to clean up his mess. Even his own sister was bankrupted, and it drove that family apart too – Pat Curran's poison at work again. You know poor Morven hated Niall – absolutely hated him—'

Then she stopped, putting a hand over her mouth. 'Oh dear, I shouldn't have said that! Of course, I really don't mean—'

'Of course not,' Murray said dryly. 'But you were divorced by that time, right?'

'Oh yes.' Lilian sighed again. 'I just couldn't take it any more. Malcolm had recently come as doctor here and I was just living on my nerves. He listened to me – so kind, so understanding, just such a wonderful man. Quite simply, we fell in love. Perhaps it was selfish of me – and Gabrielle certainly blamed me, no doubt about that. But Pat, quite honestly, didn't care. He let me go without a backward look and since then I've discovered what a real marriage is like. I'm a lucky woman, Constable Murray.'

'I'm sure. But your family's relationship with Mr Aitchison—?'

'I'd known Niall since he was a little lad – such a solemn wee thing, bless his heart! Very much an afterthought, fifteen years younger than Morven. When Pat took him on at seventeen he was around the house all the time, so he more or less grew up with the girls. Then thanks to Pat he was ostracised here, and I was sorry for the boy – told him we were there for him any time he wanted. He was very good to his mother, you know, but she wasn't what you'd call lively company.'

This was enlightening stuff. 'So – this was when his relationship with Ms Curran developed?'

'Poor Francesca certainly thought so.' Lilian's lips tightened. 'But I always knew that Niall preferred Gabrielle – all the young men did – and now, apparently, he's left her everything in his will.'

It was useful to have confirmation. 'I see,' Murray said. 'But I hear Mrs Ross isn't very well at the moment?'

'She's had a very difficult spell and she needs some time to get over it, that's all. She's very lucky that she's like me, with a good husband. David would walk over hot coals for her.'

Lilian spoke very firmly, and it was clear there wasn't going to be any useful gossip about that. With three reports still to compile, there was no point in prolonging the interview and Murray got up.

'Thanks, Mrs Sinclair. Will the doctor be in the surgery now?'

Lilian gave a little laugh. 'Oh dear, how very *Midsomer Murders*! You're going to have to corroborate my "alibi" aren't you?' She made quotation marks with her fingers. 'I'll take you in.'

With Murray at her heels she went across the hall to the door Sinclair had gone through just as Murray arrived. The waiting room was empty now and the receptionist was tidying up the desk.

'Malcolm's working in his room, is he, Cathy? I'm just taking Constable Murray through.'

She went to the far end and opened the door and Sinclair looked up from some paperwork and got up. 'I'm just about finished, sweetheart. I'll be through for lunch in a minute – oh!'

'Constable Murray, darling – you may recall. She just needs you to confirm that I wasn't telling porkies when I said that we went walking the Saturday before last – remember? See you soon. Goodbye, Constable Murray.'

She'd given him a firm nudge there. Annoyed, Murray said, 'I'm sure you were entirely accurate. Can I just have a brief word, Dr Sinclair?'

From Sinclair's expression, he'd have liked to say, 'Forget it!' Instead, he said, 'As long as it's a brief word. I'm running late already.' He didn't ask her to sit down.

'Mrs Sinclair's told me what you did. For the record, can you just confirm it?'

He looked hunted. 'Saturday before last – we'd have been

walking. Leaving here after breakfast, lunch out somewhere, back here in time for tea. All right?'

'Where did you go?'

'Oh, for heaven's sake! Well, that would be the day we went to John o' Groats and walked towards Duncansby Head. Fantastic views of the Stacks that day – you should go, Constable!'

Murray held her breath. Had he forgotten what he was supposed to say and was about to demolish his wife's alibi?

He was going on, 'They're these very dramatic geological formations – piles of rock, out to sea. Very interesting and well worth the effort of the walk, I assure you – good exercise, too.'

Murray took out her notebook. 'May I just jot that down, sir?'

'I hope you can write at dictation speed, then,' he said grudgingly, as if he hadn't wasted time already giving her a lecture on the local landscape. 'We set off after breakfast, about eleven, I suppose.' Then he stopped. 'Oh, hang on! You said the Saturday before last, did you? The 24th? I'm sorry, I was confused. I was describing what we did *last* Saturday. You were talking about the one before, weren't you? That was when we went to St John's Point. We'd hoped to see the Merry Men of Mey – that's a sort of tidal feature, Constable, can be quite dramatic, but we couldn't see anything much. Perhaps it was the weather. We got good views, though. And then we had lunch at the Castle o' Mey tea room – you get a very nice lunch there, you know.'

Yes, she knew. She'd heard his commercial for it

before and she had three reports to type up. Profoundly disappointed, she cut him short as soon as she could without blatant rudeness and left.

It was just after four o'clock when Kirstie Mowat came back to the farmhouse. Her mother was working at her desk in the kitchen and her father was sitting at the table doing something fiddly to the handle of some shears with baler twine when she came in. She took off her sodden parka, shaking it as if that would make any difference.

Rhona looked up. 'Take it over to the Aga. It needs to dry out – I told you it would be useless when it rained at the time you bought it.' Then she saw that her daughter's lip was trembling; she'd obviously been crying already, and she jumped up. 'Oh, sorry, Kirstie, I didn't mean to upset you! What's the matter?'

Fergus swung round. 'What's happened? Have you been crying, pet?'

'Well, like – yeah!' she said, trying at an offhand manner even while the tears were rolling down her cheeks, but when her father stood up she cast herself into his arms and sobbed.

'Here – you're freezing cold,' he said as he patted her back. 'Come and get warmed up while you tell us what's been going on.'

Kirstie allowed herself to be led to the chair by the Aga and began a mop-up operation with the wodge of tissues Rhona had shoved into her hand.

'It's Morven.' She sniffed.

Her parents exchanged glances. 'Aye, I thought it might be,' Fergus said.

'I honestly think she's going mental. She was just really, really weird today.'

'Losing her temper?' Rhona suggested.

'Like that would be weird! That's just standard – happens all the time so it doesn't faze me. No, she wasn't like she usually is. If I was a wee bit late, like I was this morning, I'd get a mega bawling-out but today it was like she just hadn't noticed. So that was OK, sort of, but then it got really strange. She was going around just as if she wasn't really there, like she was a zombie. Even when a policewoman came in to talk to her she didn't flip, like she did the last time.'

'The last time?' Fergus asked.

'Oh – oh yes.' Kirstie took refuge in a bout of nose-blowing. 'It was just a policeman came in wanting to ask questions and she told him to get lost. That was all.'

Rhona, nobody's fool, said, 'Funny you never mentioned it.'

'I just forgot. It was no big deal. Anyway, this time she went off with her, to her flat, I guess, and then just came back and went on the same way. But I could see she was sort of holding herself in and it was bit scary, so I tried to do everything really well – not doing any of the things to wind her up, like talking to a customer when she was wanting me to clear a table.

'Then she suddenly decided she was going to shut up early. It seemed – well, it was like she couldn't stand it much longer. She started muttering at the customers, trying to hurry them up – she often does, a bit, but not out loud like this. Folk were gulping their tea just to get out. So, then she

310

started clearing everything like a whirlwind – I've never seen her move so fast. And I was hurrying too, and I dropped a plate on the floor. It didn't even break but she just went absolutely crazy, screaming at me, and then she took me by the shoulders and shook me. My neck still hurts. So, then I just grabbed my coat and left.'

'And you're not going back,' Rhona said firmly. 'That's it.'

'That's it?' Fergus said. 'That woman assaults my daughter, and you say, "That's it?" I'm going to phone the police. She's a public danger! Remember what the constable was saying this morning.'

Kirstie looked up. 'What was that?'

'Oh, just a discussion,' Rhona said. 'Fergie, it wasn't Livvy who said anything about Morven, it was us, and I feel bad about that. She's a woman under a lot of strain and you know I told you what they were saying in the village about Niall having left everything to Gabrielle Ross. In the face of all that, no wonder she's in a state. Kirstie wasn't really hurt, just scared, isn't that right, Kirstie?'

With a certain reluctance, Kirstie agreed, and Fergus compromised. 'I'm going to make a point of going along to the incident room to have a chat with Livvy tomorrow, though. She ought to know.'

When Kirstie Mowat had gone, in floods of tears, Morven locked the door and put up the CLOSED sign. Then, as the red tide of irrational rage ebbed, she slumped exhausted against the wall. She was stupid to have lost it like that, when she'd tried so hard all day not to give way to the anger boiling inside. Even when the policewoman came asking her daft

311

questions she'd managed not to show how stressed she was, to seem quite cool and relaxed. If it hadn't been for that silly, hashy girl – she could feel the irritation mounting again.

She fought it down. Now, above all, she needed to remain perfectly calm. She sat down on one of the cafe chairs, shut her eyes, drew deep, soothing breaths. Then she forced herself to work methodically through the rest of the clearing-up; she didn't even react when two customers, hopeful of tea and ignoring the sign, rattled the handle and tapped on the door. She just very firmly ignored them.

At quarter to five Morven left, locked up and went across to her flat to fetch her car. She drove, deliberately slowly, out of the village along the road past the Mowats' farm. When she reached Gabrielle Ross's house she parked and got out. The car outside told her she was in. It was the only car, which told her that she was alone.

She knocked on the door. There was no immediate reply; she knocked again. When Gabrielle came to the door, she hardly recognised her at first in this pale, gaunt, strained-looking woman – Gabrielle, who had always been so offensively glossy and unassailable. She looked very, very tired too – worn out. Perhaps now, at last, she was suffering for her sins and Morven felt a surge of unholy joy.

'Gabrielle, we need to talk,' she said, quietly and confidently.

Gabrielle had opened the door little more than a crack. She started closing it as she said, 'You and I have nothing to say to each other, Morven.'

Morven stuck her foot in the opening. 'Oh, I think we do,' she said, and pushed.

The other woman made only token resistance and

Morven stepped inside, shutting the door behind her. 'Let's sit down and be civilised.' She pointed to the sitting room and Gabrielle obediently went in and collapsed onto a chair, shaking her head as if to wake herself up.

She was looking scared. Good! It made Morven feel confident, powerful. She sat down herself opposite, in a small chair with wooden arms. 'What we have to talk about is what you owe me for the death of my son.'

It was as if she had touched a nerve. Gabrielle suddenly sat up straighter. 'I owe you nothing,' she said with something of her old arrogance. 'If you've come here to try to blackmail me, you're wasting your time. I've said I'm sorry a dozen times about what happened to Gary—'

'Don't! Don't dare mention his name with your filthy lips, you with your black, evil heart!' Morven hissed at her.

Her loss of control seemed to give Gabrielle energy. She stood up. 'I said we had nothing to talk about, and we don't. I know what you did before – that disgusting message you left on my doorstep. I'm not having you sit in my own house and abuse me. I want you to leave, now.'

Morven subsided, clenching her fists in frustration. God, what a fool she was! She had vowed to have a civilised discussion about natural justice and she'd failed. Could she master herself long enough to retrieve the situation? The words almost stuck in her throat but she managed, 'Sorry. Sorry, I shouldn't have said that. It's just – well, I suppose I'm not really rational when it comes to my loss.'

Gabrielle was hesitating. Then she sat down again and said, a little awkwardly, 'I can understand that. All right, what is all this about?'

Oh, as if she didn't know! And she was on her guard now. Morven said, watching her carefully, 'It's about Niall's will.'

'What – what about it?'

She'd been right; she could read it in Gabrielle's face. The bastard had left it all to her. To them that hath, shall be given – it said that in the Bible, didn't it? And Gabrielle had everything before and had more now.

'You must see that it's just not right. The house, my mother's house, the house we grew up in – he should have left it to me, not you. And the shares in the company – that would have been at least some restitution for what your father did—'

It was a bad mistake. 'What my father did? What my father did was to try to bring employment and prosperity to this godforsaken little place and it wasn't his fault that government policy changed. No one made you invest in his business and if you lost your house through greed, that wasn't his fault either. And can I remind you that what your son was doing when he had his *accident*,' she laid heavy stress on the word, 'was trying to steal property that didn't belong to him.'

And from them that hath not, shall be taken away even that which they had. That was in the Bible too. Morven felt as if something had burst in her head, like a volcano erupting. She could hear her own breath becoming ragged as Gabrielle went on, 'Curran Services is my father's memorial and if you think I'm going to give you a chance to destroy it, you can think again. I wasn't sure what I was going to do. I wasn't sure I was strong enough to go on fighting, but by

God, I am now! Thank you for that, at least. And that's it, Morven. I'll show you out.'

Calmness, control: Morven had known she needed them because at heart she was afraid of what she might otherwise do. And they had vanished now. She sprang up, making some incoherent sound of fury, and as she launched herself on Gabrielle she heard the other woman's terrified scream as they fell to the ground.

CHAPTER TWENTY

Feeling much the same emotions as he had experienced when he had been summoned to the headmaster to account for some misdemeanour at school, DCI Kelso Strang tapped on the door of DCS Jane Borthwick's office.

She looked up from the file, which was the only thing on her otherwise pristine desk. He never understood how anyone managed that; it felt like a form of intimidation, and he wouldn't put it past JB to know that and do it on purpose.

'Ah, Kelso. Good,' she said. 'No problem getting here, then?'

'No ma'am, none.' He sat down opposite her.

'Brief me on this. I've got the latest reports – you've seen them?'

He nodded. He'd accessed them on the way down and Murray had performed quite an effective bricks-without-straw job.

'Read between the lines for me on the direction of the investigation. We can't afford to give the media any more ammunition right at the moment – we've got to get this one right.'

She was, he noticed, looking uncharacteristically stressed. The line between her brows looked deeper than it had been when last he saw her. No wonder, given the long-running problems with Police Scotland, but it wasn't reassuring. She'd given him solid backup on the last murder case but this time he sensed that he was in a situation where he might become the sacrifice on the altar of public opinion, if it proved necessary.

'It's a complex case,' he began.

She raised an eyebrow. 'Defensive, Kelso?'

'Maybe, but it's true. As you'll have seen, we're on pretty firm ground with what looks like a convincing time frame for the murder and we have solid proof of the time slot within which Aitchison's body could have been placed in the shed. But I'll be honest – we have no link between the two. We can speculate on the rationale for moving it, but I can't say any of the theories I've come up with are convincing.

'You know the Pat Curran background. Plenty of people had a motive to hate Aitchison because of that connection but it was all a long time ago – why now? He had very few social interactions with the village in the recent past and it's made sense to me to focus on the ones he had.'

Strang glanced at her to see how this was going down but her expression gave nothing away. He went on, 'I've established four definite areas: his work at Curran Services; his social life in Forsich, which seems to be mainly with the Sinclair family; his relationship with Gabrielle Ross – and then there's his sister.'

Borthwick picked up his tone. 'The sister?'

'Plenty of motive there, as you'll have seen. She's a difficult character, very volatile. Livvy Murray thinks she's right on the edge.'

'Yes, I saw that. Doing all right, isn't she, Kelso?'

That was a little dig at him; Murray had been something of a protégée of Borthwick's. 'Shaping up,' he said. 'The situation at Curran Services – since you asked me to read between the lines, I'd put good money on a takeover bid being cooked up there. As far as I can make out, Aitchison seems to have been against it and may have gone to the fishing hotel to make his point. Chris Brady's the driving force and he's a hard man. Wouldn't put anything past him, if it came right down to it.'

She looked at him keenly. 'You're not putting all your money on him, though, are you?'

'Not yet, anyway – don't know why. There's something niggling at me.'

'Just male intuition?' she said blandly.

He grinned. 'Something like that. Gabrielle Ross, now. She's key, but I haven't managed to speak to her yet. There are strong implications that she's either on the verge of a breakdown or having one already, and her sister thinks she could have Alzheimer's.'

'Alzheimer's? At that age?'

'Granny had early onset, apparently. Francesca didn't seem too bothered, unless she gets it too.'

'Very sisterly!'

'Yes. Their father played favourites and set them against each other.' Then he paused. 'It sounds – well, fanciful to say this, but while Pat Curran's dead, he's not quite dead enough. He seems to have had an extraordinarily poisonous effect on the relationships in that place and it's still going on. Old sins cast a long shadow, as they say.'

She grimaced. 'Indeed they do. All right, you seem to be covering the bases.'

That sounded as if she approved. He was just allowing himself to relax when she went on, 'What I'm not happy about is your use of local resources.'

They were always being nagged to watch the budget and he was moved to protest. 'But I've hardly used them at all! Uniforms, of course, for the legwork, PS Lothian took me round for a bit at first, but that's it. Latterly it's only been Livvy Murray and me.' He was tempted to add, 'Since you didn't replace Kevin Taylor,' but was wise enough to resist.

'That's the point. The DI in Wick – what's his name, Hay. He seems to be making waves about that. You know we have to rely on local goodwill for this kind of operation to succeed, Kelso. You can't be a one-man band.'

Strang felt a burning sense of injustice. 'I saw DI Hay the first morning I was in Forsich. He told me in no uncertain terms that he was far too busy to take any part in my investigation – apparently Thurso is a positive hotbed of crime, contrary to what one might imagine. He obstructed any further use of Lothian. When I asked if I could draw on him for manpower he said he knew I had the authority, but he would give priority to his own patch.' Would it sound too much like clyping if he added, 'whatever the high heid yins said'? What the hell. He said it anyway.

Borthwick assimilated that. 'Ah, I see. Well, you're in

charge. It's up to you how you handle his complaints to the media, but it might be as well to neutralise the situation by drawing him in. He's setting you up to take the flak for anything that might go wrong. We're very exposed.'

At least she'd said 'we', not 'you'. Strang said hollowly, 'I can see that. Any suggestions, boss?'

The frown between her brows grew deeper. Then she said, 'We've got to work out this press statement. I think, if I were you, I'd invite him along for that. Make a big thing out of how much you have appreciated the support you've had from the local force – talk about all the hours of door-knocking, that sort of thing. Stress how helpful the background information has been—No, Kelso,' as he opened his mouth to speak, 'surely there's been something, and anyway, can I remind you yet again that press statements aren't delivered under oath? You need to make sure his fingerprints are all over this.'

She saw the distaste on Strang's face and shook her head. 'Oh dear. You really are a purist. Should DI Hay be allowed to get away with telling blatant lies? Oh, of course you could simply call him out on it but in the first place they wouldn't believe you and in the second place it would descend into a slanging match that wouldn't do Police Scotland any good.'

Strang felt trapped. Of course she was right, but it was underhand, and he didn't like it. And the worst thing was, he knew that however uncomfortable he might feel, he'd end up doing it anyway.

She was going on, 'Now, this statement. How do we present what we have so far?'

Present – she meant 'spin', he thought in silent

disapproval. But then, hadn't he done exactly the same when he asked Murray to tart up her reports to Borthwick? His principles were more flexible than he would have liked to think they were.

'We've got a lot of good forensic stuff,' he said. 'We could major on that to begin with.'

Kelso Strang left Borthwick's office feeling somewhat mauled but reassured that she was onside – so far, at least. He went back downstairs to his own basement office and checked that nothing new had come in, then sat for a moment, thinking.

One remark of JB's had particularly stung – the remark about the one-man band. Unfair criticism is hard to take, sure, but in fact fair criticism hits much harder. He could see how possessive he had become about his cases. It wasn't surprising; with the vacuum at the centre of his life that Alexa had left, the job had expanded to fill it. It constantly occupied his mind.

There wasn't much else. He had his family, of course – and he must phone Finella today. Friends had been loyal, but their well-meant invitations always left him feeling more lonely, not less. Being absorbed in a case quietened the insistent pain of loss.

Looking at it objectively, he could see control-freak tendencies coming out. It was partly because for one reason or another he felt such support as he had was unreliable: the result of Livvy Murray using her initiative in Skye made him shudder every time he thought of it. This time he'd been nervously directing her every move, which meant that he was getting no fresh input. JB had been closely involved in the last murder investigation and there had been good backup on the ground too but this time he was indeed trying to do the whole thing himself – and God help him if it all went pear-shaped.

As JB had pointed out, this time Livvy was doing all right – more than that, she'd been doing very well. Maybe he needed to tell her a bit less and listen to her a bit more. He still wasn't happy that he'd been called away; it was putting a lot on her shoulders and he could only hope that there were no new developments before he got back tomorrow morning.

There wasn't anything he could do about that, so he might as well call Finella now. Of course, at this time his niece wouldn't be at nursery, so he'd probably have to schlep over to Morningside.

To his surprise Fin didn't welcome that suggestion. Yes, Betsy was at home, but she could dump her on a friend for a bit. 'If she's around, her Unkie won't get a moment's peace,' she said but for some reason it rang false.

He didn't pick her up on it, saying only, 'Let's meet somewhere civilised, then. My car's still in Caithness so I'll take a cab. You say where.'

She mentioned a bar he hadn't heard of and when he got there, he was surprised; it wasn't the smart wine bar he'd expected but a rather downmarket, impersonal-looking pub in one of the backstreets, mainly empty at this time in the evening.

Finella swung in, tall and blonde and smiling, and greeted him as brightly as usual. 'Still in one piece, I see. Always preferable. Now swear to me, cross your heart and hope to die, that you'll never let Betsy find out I've seen you. She wouldn't speak to me for a week and when Betsy's not speaking to you it's like someone constantly shouting in your ear.'

Kelso laughed, promised, then fetched her a gin and tonic and himself a Scotch. He let her chatter on, talking about their parents, their brother, who had actually managed to get round to phoning from the States last week to speak to his mother, until she ran down. Then he said quietly, 'Fin, come on. Level with me. You didn't want to see me to tell me family gossip. Why are we in this odd place? Why didn't you want me to come to the house – and don't give me the crap about Betsy. What's wrong?'

To his dismay, her eyes filled. Finella wasn't a crier: he could count on one hand the number of times he'd seen her in tears.

'I just wanted to make sure no one would interrupt us.'

'No one,' he said. 'You mean Mark.' Mark would never be seen in a pub like this.

She blinked hard, not meeting his eyes. 'Yes, I suppose so.'

'Oh dear. Is it the "M" word?'

She looked up, surprised. 'What's the "M" word?'

'It's how Mark describes marriage when you're not around.'

'Oh yes, of course. Stupid of me. Oh Kelso, I wish it was! Mum and Dad care about marriage – I don't. It's—' She broke off. He didn't say anything and after a moment she went on, 'What I really want is for you to tell me I'm being ridiculous, that I'm being suspicious about nothing.'

His heart sank. Another woman. Well, he'd never rated Mark; a bit too pleased with himself and too flash for

323

his liking. 'What makes you suspicious? Receipts, phone calls . . . ? Nights away?'

Finella gave a short laugh. 'Oh, you think it's a woman? I could deal with that.' From the way she said it suggested that she'd dealt with it before. 'No, it's – worse.'

'Tell me.'

'Oh God, how can I say this! You know we moved to the flat in Morningside, after Mark left Tesco and got the job in the law firm. Well, of course you do. You helped us move in. Sorry, I'm just—'

She broke off and he realised she was shaking. What on earth was coming next? Was it about the flat – persecution from a neighbour, a structural problem . . . He squeezed her hand and tried to sound confident. 'We'll sort it, whatever it is.'

Finella got it out at last. 'It's – it's just there's too much money.'

'It's not a problem you often hear people complaining about,' he said gently. 'What do you mean?'

'When he got the new job, it paid better than the previous one, I know that. But even so, it was a bit of a stretch to pay the mortgage on the flat we had. And then he got a big bonus, the first Christmas, and he said we should look for something in Morningside, and I was really excited. Much better catchment area for Betsy when it comes to schools and it's such a lovely flat too. And the mortgage payments didn't seem to be too much of a problem any more.'

Kelso felt sick. He knew what was coming now; he'd seen the pattern professionally all too often before.

She was going on, 'And he started splashing money

around. That Greek holiday – well, it was fabulous, really, but that was when I started worrying. The firm I'm with is just a wee firm – conveyancing, mainly – and I'm paid a pittance. He's with a top commercial chain, right enough, but it's not as if he's a partner or anything. I can't see how they could be paying him as much as that.'

'Have you tackled him about it?'

'I tried, very tactfully, but he just got angry – really angry. Asked me if I was accusing him of something – and I couldn't, I really couldn't, not to his face, Kelso. Then later he calmed down and said he should have told me he'd been put in the way of some good investments and with the stock market doing so well he'd made quite a bit that way. And I wouldn't know about that – he's always been very secretive about financial stuff.

'So perhaps it's true. It's what I really, really want to think. Because, if it isn't . . .'

If it wasn't, Kelso could see all too clearly what it would mean. Very few people were clever enough to get away with embezzlement for ever and when they were caught . . . He felt sick at the thought of what that would do to Fin and, worse still, to trusting little Betsy, so happy in her nice home with her mummy and daddy.

Finella was looking at him hopefully. He said, 'You know I can't tell you that of course you're wrong, that everything's fine. I can't tell you either that he isn't making money on the market – perhaps he is. I don't like to suggest that you should snoop, but maybe there's a paper trail for the investments—'

She gave him a scornful look. 'Do you really think

I haven't? Nothing in the flat – he even keeps his bank statements in the office.'

'Look, Fin, you don't actually know there's anything wrong. It's probably pointless to tell you not to worry too much, but don't push it until I get back from Caithness. I'll make some cautious enquiries about the firm, put out a few feelers to see if there's any gossip. If you're still not happy, I'll talk to Mark myself. If he's in the clear he'll probably clock me one, but it won't exactly be the first time that's happened to me. If he isn't, he may even realise he's getting in too deep and want advice.'

She gave him a watery smile. 'Thanks, kid. It's helped just to tell you. Don't say anything to Mum and Dad, though, will you?'

'Oh, just as well you warned me,' Kelso said with heavy sarcasm. 'I'd just been planning a long cosy session with Dad to get his advice. Don't be daft – and drink up. All your ice has melted.'

DS Livvy Murray took the road out of Forsich, past the Mowats' farm once more. The rain was still teeming down so hard that it was bouncing back up off the tarmac and every so often the car shuddered as a gust of wind took it.

She was feeling tired. She'd pulled all the stops out to get the reports in and hadn't even taken a proper break, so she was starving now. Still, this visit shouldn't take long – she'd basically been forbidden even to exchange the time of day with the Rosses – and it was quiz night in the pub she'd been to last night. It had a good line in steak pies.

It would be good if the husband was there. She'd

screwed up with Gabrielle before and she didn't want the embarrassment of being reminded of it. She liked to think she'd learnt from it and that she was improving – the boss had texted her a pat on the back – and as long as nothing went wrong while he was away she could feel she'd made some progress in wiping out her sins of the past. With that history, it wasn't exactly surprising that he was keeping her on a tight rein, but she'd produced some useful stuff so maybe he'd listen to her idea about the ravens' attack being almost planned, not an accident. The more she thought about it, the more convinced she became.

That was the house now. As she slowed down she saw with relief that there were two cars at the house, a 4x4 and a BMW 5 Series. A five-minute conversation and she'd be on her way back to Thurso to have a bath and change before she went out. She parked in behind them.

Murray grabbed her weatherproof jacket and draped it over her head as she got out – for all the time it wasn't worth putting it on properly. She slammed the door, glancing up at the big window and a man's figure appeared. He looked agitated and when he saw her, he gave a sort of frantic wave then hurried out of the room, appearing a moment later at the front door.

'Come in, come in!' he called. 'It's my wife – she's been attacked. Help me!'

She raced up the path. 'Police,' she said as she pushed past him and went into the front room.

Gabrielle Ross was lying on the floor. She was grey-faced and unconscious; she had a bloody bruise on her left temple and there were scratches on her face. She was lying against the stone fender that went around the fireplace and there was an injury to the back of her head as well, to judge by the blood staining the sharp edge. A small table was lying on its side nearby.

Ross was babbling. 'I've just got back from Aberdeen. I walked in two minutes ago and I called, and she didn't answer and then there she was – she's not dead, is she? She's breathing, I think – tell me she'll be all right!'

Murray dropped to her knees and put a hand on either side of Gabrielle's head to stabilise it as she checked the airway – you had to assume there might be a spinal injury. It was clear, but the breathing was shallow and when she took her pulse it didn't feel very strong; she was no expert, but the woman's condition looked alarming. Even as she did it she was reaching for her phone, dialling 999, snapping, 'Priority! Ambulance. Woman assaulted.' As she gave instructions she fetched a throw that was draped across the sofa to put over Gabrielle.

When she had finished she saw that Ross was wringing his hands and he seemed to be swaying slightly. There was nothing more she could do for his wife now; Murray stood up and took his arm, leading him to the chair by the window.

'Sit down, sir,' she said. 'Lean forward and put your head between your knees.'

He obeyed, slumping forward as if he had no strength left. Murray waited for a moment then let him sit up again.

'Just take it easy,' she said. 'They won't be long. She'll be all right – a bit of concussion, I'd say.'

'It's just – just the shock,' he said feebly. 'I feel cold – so cold.' He shivered.

'Would you like me to make a cup of tea?' she offered. Doing something – anything – would be better than sitting here wondering if Gabrielle's breathing was just going to stop.

'Brandy. Somewhere in the cupboard off the kitchen.'

Murray went through, deciding to make tea anyway. She could do with it herself and if she brought brandy as well he could lace his mug with it if he felt like it. While the kettle was boiling she rooted in the cupboard for it, thinking about the man waiting next door. It was certainly common enough for a man to claim his wife had been attacked by some stranger and he'd just come in and found her – known as the 'a-big-boy-did-it-and-ran-away' defence.

But the man was plainly shocked – and now she thought of it, she'd heard the sort of clicking a car makes when it's cooling down as she went past the Audi. And he looked surprisingly unmarked for someone interrupted during a violent assault and the scratches on Gabrielle's face – they had looked like nail marks. She'd be taking a good look at his fingers.

When she came back Ross was looking better. He was sitting beside his wife, studying her face, and gave a deep sigh as Murray came into the room.

'It's so cruel! She didn't need this, after all she's been through already. How could someone do this to my poor girl?'

She made a sympathetic noise as she handed him the tea and the brandy bottle; as she looked at him she could see that his hand still shook as he tipped some in, though he seemed a bit steadier. There was an anxious frown between his brows, but he was a pleasant-looking man, with fair curly hair and blue eyes. Perhaps there was something weak about the chin; having met Gabrielle briefly and heard a lot about her, Murray was prepared to bet that she'd be the one who wore the trousers. She got a good look at his nails: perfectly clean and neatly trimmed.

Ross sipped the tea then looked up at her with a smile – a very attractive smile, even though it was strained. 'I'm sorry, I don't know your name. You just said, "Police", which was something of a relief, I can tell you.'

'Oh, I'm sorry. I should have told you at the start – DC Murray. I think you spoke to my boss, DCI Strang, about an interview. He'd been hoping to arrange it for tomorrow but of course—'

'Yes, of course,' he said heavily, glancing down again at Gabrielle. She hadn't shown any sign of returning consciousness, but the breathing didn't sound any more laboured, either. With a restless movement he got up and went across to the window, as if somehow that would make the ambulance come more quickly. 'How long do you think it'll be?'

'They're giving it priority, sir, and there was one available. Coming from Wick so twenty-five minutes from the time I phoned, perhaps?' She glanced at her watch – still ten minutes to go. It was amazing how slowly time passed when you were waiting anxiously.

Ross was drumming his fingers nervously on the window ledge. To distract his attention she said, 'Perhaps you can tell me again exactly what happened?'

He turned and went back to take up his place again beside Gabrielle. 'I'd been out on a rig – I'm the go-to man for any computer problem – and they brought me back to Dyce this afternoon. I drove up, parked my car, came in. As I said, I called to her, then came through here looking for her. I-I don't know exactly after that. I can only remember the horror. I thought she was dead. I bent down to check and I could see she was still breathing, and it was just then that I heard your car door slam. Thank God you came just then. I was panicking.'

'We'll get the details later – name of the rig, time of the flight, that sort of thing,' Murray said. 'But do you have any idea who might have done this?'

Ross gave a sigh that was almost a groan. 'You probably know that the Currans weren't exactly popular around here. But Niall – and now this. His sister was all but deranged about her son's death and Gabrielle's mother phoned me today about Niall's will – he left nothing to Morven and everything to Gabrielle. To be honest, I'm only surprised she didn't make absolutely sure Gabrielle was dead before she left.'

It chimed so exactly with her own thinking that Murray found it quite hard to sound non-committal. Morven Gunn probably thought she had killed her before she left. This was going to be an open-and-shut case, though any half-competent brief would go for diminished responsibility.

Ross suddenly sprang to his feet. 'That's it! Thank God,' he said, crossing to the window. Hearing the siren now, she joined him.

But it wasn't the ambulance. A police car, lights flashing, drew up outside and to Murray's dismay the unhelpful DI

Hay emerged, dapper in a suit and tie, and strode up the path.

She went to meet him. 'DC Murray, sir. We're just waiting for the ambulance.'

He looked round. 'Is DCI Strang here?'

'No,' she admitted, without adding that he was in Edinburgh.

'This is my patch. I'm in charge. Is that clear? A domestic, I take it?'

He didn't give her a chance to reply. His little Hitler moustache was positively bristling with importance. As he strutted into the sitting room, she heard him say, 'So you're the husband?' just as sirens announced the arrival of the ambulance at last.

CHAPTER TWENTY-ONE

DC Murray had a hollow feeling in the pit of her stomach as she left the police station in Thurso and only part of it was hunger because it was ten o'clock and she'd only had a sandwich since breakfast. Mostly it was because of what she was going to have to tell the DCI.

She'd had to deal in the past with a superior officer who was stubborn, and it certainly wasn't the first time she'd had one who was stupid. But she hadn't had pig-stubborn and pig-stupid together before and it was a bad combination.

Even while Gabrielle was being carried out on a stretcher, DI Hay had started bullying David Ross. His opening gambit was, 'So what's this story about an attacker who seems to have disappeared?'

Ross looked shell-shocked. 'What do you mean? Look, I need to go with my wife—'

'She's in good hands now – nothing you can do. What

333

you do need to do is explain to me what happened. Had a row, did you?'

'Are you accusing *me* of doing this? Look, I'd been away. I just got back, came in and found her like this.'

'Oh aye? Heard that one before.'

Ross was getting angry. 'I can't believe this. Ask the officer – she arrived just after me.'

'And how would she know that?' Ignoring Murray's, 'Sir—' he ploughed on, 'You've got a story to tell, I see. I think the best thing would be to take you down to the station and get it all on tape. You see, unlike some people I don't believe in going round and round in circles before I take action.' This was said with a sideways look at Murray.

She tried again. 'Sir, there's one or two things—'

Hay glared at her. 'Not now, Constable. Later. Maybe.' He turned to one of the two uniformed officers who had come in with him. 'Take Mr Ross out to the car.'

She looked at him in surprise. He hadn't arrested Ross, but he hadn't told him either that he was entitled to refuse – it was a distinctly unprofessional con game. Ross had gone white – with rage? Murray wondered.

'Do I need a lawyer?'

Hay smiled. 'That's entirely up to you, sir. There's only one defence lawyer in Thurso and his office will have closed at five. Of course, we can wait till tomorrow, but you'd probably prefer not to have to kick your heels at the police station all night.'

Murray thought Ross might explode. But his voice was very, very calm. He turned to her. 'I want you to witness that this is outrageous behaviour. I am in a state of extreme anxiety about my wife, and I am being bullied. I will accompany you now, but I will be making a complaint at the highest level.'

Hay threw a sideways glance at Murray. 'Leave the room, Constable,' he said. 'I have noted your comment, Mr Ross. This officer will show you to the car.' He turned to the other PC. 'Secure the house. I'll be getting it fingerprinted first thing tomorrow morning.'

Murray did as she was told, but as Ross was escorted through the hall she stepped forward to intercept Hay. 'Sir, I think there's some things you should know about this.'

He glared at her. 'While I may not have enough experience to be considered competent to investigate a case of murder, I have ample experience of domestic violence – thirty years of it – and it has trained me to recognise it when I see it. He's a plausible-looking fellow and it's easy for someone as young as you are to be taken in.

'And perhaps you can inform the DCI that this has nothing to do with him. I am still in charge of local affairs and I will be handling it.'

'But, sir, I think it's linked to Niall Aitchison's murder.'

'When I want your opinion, Constable, I'll ask for it and you may have to wait a good while. You can give my officer a lift back to the station.'

When they had gone, the constable looked round about him helplessly. 'How'm I supposed to secure it? Haven't any crime scene tape or anything.'

'Just lock up and take the key in to DI Hay,' Murray suggested. 'I'll write a note to put on the door.' There was a big question mark over whether it was legal to deny Ross entry to his own house, but it looked as if details like that didn't bother Hay a lot.

As she drove back to Thurso she tried to pump the constable for information, but he was a stolid young man and his most revealing admission was that Hay was a pretty tough boss.

Then she had waited in the foyer. And waited. Eventually she had asked at the desk when she might be able to speak to DI Hay and was told to make an appointment for the following morning. She was in a thoroughly depressed state when she phoned DCI Strang.

After the drink with his sister Kelso Strang had gone home to the fisherman's cottage by the harbour in Newhaven. He was tempted to go along to the nearby pub for a meal, but he'd eaten so much junk food lately that instead he went across to the fishmonger's by the harbour. He liked to cook, and he'd savoured the sea bream with chilli lime butter, eaten by the window looking out towards the sea. The peace of the silent house was soothing; it was only occasionally now that he felt oppressed by its emptiness.

He was worried about Fin but there was nothing he could do about that at the moment and his mind turned inevitably to the investigation. He spent some time working on the press statement; when he was as satisfied with it as he was likely to be, he sat back and looked across the Forth, past the slim white column of the lighthouse at the end of the pier to where the lights on the Fife shore were just starting to come on in the dusty rose of gloaming. The rain sweeping across Caithness hadn't reached this far south and it was a pleasant evening. A good view to think to.

When he had been talking to JB about Chris Brady, he'd been aware that there was something he had subconsciously registered. He'd assessed the man as both unprincipled and, if necessary, ruthless – an obvious suspect. Yet he'd felt he wasn't, somehow. Why?

The answer came to him suddenly – of course, a man like that would have called in his lawyer at once if he'd anything to hide, yet he hadn't. And there had been something else he'd noticed too, later in the interview. It was irritating him now – what had it been?

That was when the phone rang. He listened in dismay as Murray poured out the story. He assured her there was nothing more she could do except get something to eat and go to bed.

Now he had his own phone call to make. JB would not be happy. She had summoned him because she was fussing about the PR slant for the press statement and the result had been that it was shaping up to be a disaster that wouldn't have happened if he'd been on the spot. Having to tell your boss that she'd got it badly wrong wasn't a comfortable position.

DCS Borthwick was still at her desk, though it was well after ten o'clock. She sounded weary and the silence that followed his report was eloquent.

'I'm sorry, ma'am,' he offered nervously.

She gave a sigh. 'No need. I'm justly punished – management by media reaction is bad management. I'm in your hands over this, Kelso. I can make time and come up tomorrow myself, but would that make things better or worse?'

It was at times like this that Strang realised how fortunate he was in his boss. 'Let me check out the situation first,' he said. 'If you can authorise a chopper for 6 a.m. I can be up there before anything further happens. If Murray's right, Hay's making a terrible mistake and I may be able to get him to see that before real harm is done. Checking out the husband in a situation like this is standard, but from the sound of it he's handled it very badly. The main problem may be to stop Ross going to the newspapers—'

Borthwick gave a short laugh. 'There we go again, being jerked around. The trouble is, we can't afford to ignore it. Yes, of course – I'll put the authorisation through now. Do you want more manpower up there?'

Strang paused to think. 'Again, let me see how things stand. It all depends on the poor woman's condition – not good, according to Murray. I certainly have a prime suspect for the attack and we may get that wrapped up fairly quickly.'

'That would take a lot of the pressure off, certainly. Is it too much to hope that we might be able to kill two birds with one stone?'

'Mmm. "Blessed is he who expecteth nothing for he will not be disappointed,"' he quoted, and she laughed.

'Isn't that the truth! Thanks, Kelso. I'll wait to hear from you.'

Strang ended the call with a mixture of relief that he wasn't being hung out to dry and concern at what would be facing him tomorrow morning. He put in a call for a taxi at five and went to bed, hoping that the soldier's gift of falling asleep whenever the opportunity offered was still operational.

It was almost midnight when David Ross was dropped off at Caithness General Hospital. Hospitals at night were strange places, without their bustling daytime atmosphere. Empty corridors loomed dark and empty on either side as he went through to the ward they had indicated. Not intensive care, then. He had thought it possible she might not even be there, but airlifted off to Inverness or even Aberdeen.

When he reached it, a sympathetic nurse directed him to a small waiting room. 'The doctor's with her just now but he'll be in to speak to you shortly and then you'll be able to see her. Her mum's here already.'

Ross had phoned Lilian while he was waiting at Hay's pleasure to be interviewed. She was alone in the room and jumped up to embrace him. 'You poor boy! You're looking absolutely shattered!'

He hugged her back. 'God, what a nightmare,' he said. 'Oh, Lilian . . .'

'I know,' she said. 'Sit down, love. Malcolm's here – he's just gone to get some coffee from the machine. He'll be back at any moment—'

The door opened as she spoke, and Sinclair came in carrying two plastic cups. 'Looks revolting,' he said, then, 'Ah, David! They've let you go at last – what a shocking thing!'

He nodded. 'How is she?'

'I've had a chat with the registrar. Not as bad as it

looks, apparently. You can go in to see her in a bit. They'll be monitoring her closely tonight, of course, but they seem to think no lasting damage, though concussion's a funny thing.'

Lilian looked anxiously at her son-in-law. 'What happened? Malcolm was asking me for the details and I had to tell him you were too upset to explain.'

Sinclair sat down beside Ross and handed him one of the coffees. 'Here, take mine. Not sure I fancy it, anyway. So – she'd been attacked when you got back home?'

Ross shuddered. 'Lying there against the fireplace, head all bloody. There'd been some kind of a struggle and her face had been scratched. There was a ruddy great bruise on her forehead too – the Gunn woman had obviously hit her again once she was on the ground. Probably thought she'd killed her.'

'Ah well, tough cookie, Gabrielle,' Sinclair said heartily. 'Chip off the old block.' Then, encountering a look from his wife, he added hastily, 'Sorry, darling. Didn't mean to be flippant. But she's going to be all right, you'll see.'

'But don't the police understand?' Lilian said to Ross. 'How could they possibly imagine it was you?'

'God knows,' he said bitterly. 'The man was deaf to reason of any kind. I told him I could prove the time I got back but he just paid no attention – and now I'm locked out of my own house, apparently. And without a car.'

Lilian leant forward and took his hand. 'That's outrageous. You'll come home with us, of course, dear.'

'Of course,' Sinclair echoed. 'And we'll get a complaint in first thing. Pity we don't have a chief constable any more.

340

I knew the last one and he wouldn't have stood for this sort of nonsense.'

'No control at all now, that's the problem,' Ross said. 'Mind you, the girl who arrived just after I did – the PC—'

'Murray,' Lilian supplied. 'What about her?'

'I'm pretty sure she was trying to tell him it wasn't me. And I'm not worried, not really. As long as Gabrielle's all right, she can tell them herself.'

'Always supposing she remembers,' Sinclair cautioned. 'With head injuries, you know . . .'

'She was unconscious when you found her, though? She wasn't able to say anything?' Lilian asked.

Ross shook his head. 'Thought she was dead.' His shoulders sagged. 'How soon can I see her? I have to say, I'm ready to get my head down.'

'Of course you are,' Lilian said. 'Malcolm, can't you hurry them along a bit?'

Sinclair got up. 'See what I can do.'

But just then the door opened, and a nurse appeared. 'Mr Ross? You can see your wife now, but we're keeping her very quiet and she's sedated at the moment. Just a look in – don't talk to her.' Ross followed her out.

Lilian gave a little sigh. 'I'd have liked to see her too. She is my daughter, after all. And I'm just wondering whether the head injury will, well – tip her over. You know how bad it's been. We may have to be braced for that.'

Sinclair put his arm round her. 'No need to assume the worst yet, so let's not worry about it now, my love. You need your rest too. Tomorrow will be a difficult day.'

'It will unless the police manage to get their act together

and arrest that dangerous woman,' she said sharply. 'Gabrielle may have been lucky but poor Niall wasn't. Who's she going to go for next?'

There was a brisk east wind blowing but at least it wasn't raining as DC Murray waited on the helipad at Dounreay for DCI Strang's flight to arrive. She'd been roused at an hour she preferred to approach from the other end and she was shivering; it was hard to believe that only a couple of days ago she'd been wearing short sleeves and still feeling sweaty.

It clattered in just before six-thirty and they were on their way to Thurso ten minutes later.

'It's the only way to travel,' Strang said. 'No in-flight refreshments, though. Is there anywhere that might be open?'

'There's a wee caff in one of the backstreets does breakfast from seven,' Murray said. 'Went there yesterday when I couldn't face the hotel breakfast. I could murder a bacon buttie now.'

'Make that two, and don't hang about.'

'Blues and twos?' she said innocently.

'Don't tempt me! But on the whole, I think waking up the entire town might be a mistake.'

'Do you know how Gabrielle is, boss? That's a wee bit crucial.'

'It certainly is, for all sorts of reasons. I called the hospital this morning and they'll be taking her for a CT scan today. They're fairly satisfied with her, though.'

'When I saw her last night, I reckoned she'd had it, to be honest.'

'Assuming they're right, it's assault not murder. And unless

342

we can link it to Aitchison's murder that's DI Hay's territory.'

'Even if he's got it backside foremost?' Murray was indignant.

He smiled. 'Tact,' he said. 'Wading in with all guns blazing won't help. Oh, is that your caff now? Looks promising.'

The cafe was still quiet, and they had no difficulty in finding a discreet corner table. As their coffee arrived and the tempting smell of frying bacon filled the air, Strang said, 'Right. What have we got?'

Murray waited for him to go on, but it seemed he was waiting for her. She assembled her thoughts. 'Right – we can't get in to the house. It was locked up and DI Hay will have the key. He's planning to send them in for fingerprints first thing but that probably means after nine.'

'You saw it last night so you're my eyes. What would I be looking for, if we could?'

She screwed up her eyes, trying to visualise it. 'Evidence of a struggle. There was a table knocked over – and now I think of it, there was a rug wrinkled up as well. The rest of the room was fine.'

'Any sign of a weapon?'

'Not lying on the floor or anything. Usual stuff in the room that could be used, probably, but nothing looked to have been disturbed and you'd hardly put it back neatly – more likely chuck it away outside.'

'Are you reading it as an assault, then a further spur-of-the-moment attack?'

'Yes. Say it was Morven Gunn, OK?'

'For the sake of argument.'

'She's been bottling everything up. She arrives at

Gabrielle's, loses it completely. Morven goes for her, shoving her over and clawing at her face. Gabrielle falls. Morven's still in a rage, grabs whatever comes to hand then hits her on the head. Gabrielle's unconscious. Morven probably thinks she's dead – I did at first, right enough. She scarpers.'

She looked at Strang for approval. He was studying her, his elbows propped on the arms of his chair and his chin on his hands. He said only, 'So what do we do first?'

'Pay Morven a surprise visit?'

He nodded. 'I'll square it with DI Hay later. Well, I'll do my best. If all else fails, pull rank.'

The bacon rolls arrived and Strang stood up. 'We'll take these with us. Let's go.'

DI Hay had summoned an uncharacteristically early meeting, calling in detectives with crime scene experience from Wick along with PS Lothian and another couple of uniforms. He was definitely twitchy.

'This is one we have to get absolutely spot on, lads,' he said. 'Their fancy SRCS hasn't done much about the murder – let's show them how it's done with a good old-fashioned squad. Maybe that might get them to bring our team back up to strength.

'The woman's going to be all right, fortunately, otherwise we'd have Strang muscling in. Lothian, I want the room searched and fingerprinted first thing – not that I think we'll find anything except Ross's prints, and he'll claim they don't prove anything. Concentrate on what he might have used as a weapon – that constable obviously disturbed him, and he can't have had much time to cover his traces.'

'Sir,' Lothian said, 'should we check his alibi first? He claims—'

'I know what he *claims*, Lothian,' Hay snapped. He harboured dark suspicions about him – far too keen to dance attendance on Strang. 'We're going to do this right.' He turned to one of the detectives. 'I want you waiting at the hospital to interview the woman the minute she's fit. We could have this wrapped up before nightfall.'

Lothian was looking unhappy. 'Isn't there anyone else in the picture, sir?'

Hay glared at him. '*If*, when she comes round, the woman says she and her husband are happy as the little birds in the trees and he didn't touch her – I said "if" – then we'll look further afield. Not that I'd necessarily believe her,' he added darkly. 'When you've had as many years' service as I have you'll know how many wives refuse to admit their husbands laid a finger on them. So, you don't take the first answer. Sometimes not even the second.'

The sergeant subsided. 'So, after we've checked the room—?'

Hay looked taken aback at the question. 'Well – do that first and then we'll take stock. Depends what you find. And if that DC comes whinging around, send her away with a flea in her ear. Same goes for Strang – only make it polite or he'll go and clype to headquarters.'

He looked round the room. 'So, what are you waiting for? Get out there, and I'll be along shortly.'

Francesca Curran woke up with a start, as if something had prodded her into wakefulness. It took a moment but then she remembered: she had gone to bed last night not knowing whether or not Gabrielle would survive the night. Yet she had slept soundly; were the Sinclairs still out at the hospital?

She got up and went to her bedroom window and looked down. Yes, there was Malcolm's car, so she must have slept through them returning. Was that a good sign or a bad sign? She flung on a dressing gown and went out of her flat onto the top landing.

There was the sound of someone walking across the hall below and she looked over the banister. Malcolm had just come from the direction of the kitchen and was going to the surgery door. It must be quite late; she hadn't set her alarm. She shrank back out of sight. He'd been a bit short with her about not going to work but the news about Niall's will would be all over the place by now and she couldn't stand the thought of being there at the desk with everyone looking at her and talking about her behind her back – making fun of her, no doubt. She'd never been popular.

Once the door had shut, Fran went on downstairs in her bare feet. She was feeling almost dizzy with her inner conflict. How would she feel if they told her Gabrielle was dead; Gabrielle, with whom she had warred for so long; Gabrielle, who had thwarted her dearest hopes? Did it make her a bad person that it crossed her mind that David would be a widower? Yes, of course it did. She banished the thought and went across the hall to the kitchen. She could hear the low murmur of voices; someone must be with her mother – David, maybe? No one was, well, crying or anything.

When she opened the door Lilian and David were sitting at the table, heads together in earnest conversation. Lilian jumped. 'Good gracious, Fran, I didn't hear you coming.'

'I haven't got shoes on,' she said. 'I've just got up. How – how is she?'

David turned and smiled at her and she remembered suddenly just how desperately she'd wanted him to choose her, not Gabrielle. But it was obvious that there wasn't going to be another chance; he might look strained and weary, but this wasn't a sorrowing widower.

'It's all right, Fran,' he said. 'I've just phoned and she's going to be fine. She's still a bit woozy and they're doing a scan to check, but it should be OK.'

'That's good,' Fran said, and she meant it, really. Gabrielle was her sister, despite everything. 'I'll get dressed and then maybe I can go along and see her, do you think?'

'That would be good,' Lilian said. 'David's got stuff he needs to sort out and he hasn't even got his car here, so I'll have to be chauffeur. There should be someone there if she's fit for a visitor.'

Fran nodded. 'Are they going to arrest that Gunn woman? If I were Gabrielle I'd want to know that she wasn't going to sneak into the hospital and murder me in my bed.'

'I'll rely on you to protect her, then, Fran,' David said with another of those smiles that cost her another sharp pang.

'Of course,' she said stiffly. 'I'm on my way.'

She padded off in her bare feet. Of course she was relieved and happy that her sister was going to be all right. She'd be a monster if she wasn't.

* * *

There was no answer when they knocked on the door of Morven Gunn's flat. They walked along the pavement to peer in at the windows, one with obscured glass and the other two with net curtains. There was an alleyway down one side but when they walked along they realised that it backed directly onto another flat and that those three windows were all there was. They knocked on all of them but with no response and no sign of movement behind the curtains.

'Across at the cafe, perhaps,' Strang said. 'She may be planning to open as usual if she wants everything to look normal.'

But when they reached the Lemon Tree there was no one in the cafe and the kitchen door was open so they could see right through to the back. It was empty. They looked at each other.

'She's done a runner,' Murray said. 'What do we do now?'

CHAPTER TWENTY-TWO

Gabrielle was drifting between sleep and wakefulness, finding it hard to distinguish between the curious, fleeting dreams and the reality of the cold impersonality of the hospital room. There was a muted throb of pain in her head and when she licked her dry lips her face felt stiff and sore. An Asian man had come to and fro, giving her water and taking her wrist to check her pulse; in the dreaming moments he was a shadowy, robed figure with a great brown pitcher the water poured from; awake, she knew he was a male nurse and tried to thank him.

She knew she had been sedated. She had lived so much herself in that odd, twilit world of late that this state was more familiar to her than full wakefulness. But now her mind was clear enough; with the vividness of a film running before her eyes she could see Morven, her lips drawn back over her teeth in a snarl and her eyes wild, flying at her like a madwoman, her hands like claws aiming for Gabrielle's eyes. She remembered screaming, bringing up her own hands to defend herself, lashing out, losing her balance as she tripped on the rug, feeling the nails raking the side of her face. Then she was stumbling, falling backwards – hearing the crack as her head hit the stone fender. Then blackness coming in as Morven bent over her.

She'd thought she was dying. Death would be the blessed end to the agony she had gone through these past months; death had been wooing her like a lover with that shiny little knife. And yet when it came to it she had fought to try to save her life – and succeeded, though probably only because Morven believed she'd killed her when she left.

The nurse had come back in. He was carrying a mug and when he saw her eyes were open he smiled. 'That's good! Can you sit up, dear? You'll feel better after a drink.' He put it down on the locker and helped her prop herself up on the pillows.

Gabrielle's head swam a little, but the hot milky tea was comforting. 'Is my husband here?' she asked.

'Not at the moment,' the nurse said. 'I heard he and your parents were here till late last night, till they knew you were going to be all right. We'll be taking you down for a scan just as a precaution, so they'll maybe be here after that. You've got a pal, though; there's a constable outside, waiting to speak to you.'

She shrank away. 'No, no,' she cried. 'I don't want to! I'm not well – my head hurts.'

'Now don't you go getting yourself upset. I won't let him near you till you give the OK. Now, they'll be bringing round the trolley in a minute. Cornflakes, roll and butter—?'

Gabrielle's stomach heaved. 'Just more tea,' she said hastily, though her hands were shaking so much that she wasn't sure she could manage to drink the tea she had already, and she set down the mug. If the constable was the woman who had all but directly accused her of murder, she'd probably side with Morven and feel that Gabrielle had got what she deserved. There was a little knot of panic in the pit of her stomach – she couldn't bear the thought of the questions, all the questions. She was tired, too tired. She fell back against her pillows.

When there was a tap on the door, she didn't open her eyes. Even if it wasn't the police, there wasn't anyone she wanted to see. She just wanted to be left alone in this safe place where nothing could happen to her, where by closing her eyes and letting her mind drift she could shut out reality again.

'Gabrielle? Are you awake?' It was Francesca's voice.

Wearily she opened her eyes. Francesca was staring at her, looking shocked.

'God, she made a mess of you! You look like hell. Have you seen yourself?'

She struggled to sit up, but her voice was tart.

'Always the soul of tact, Fanny. No, I think I'd rather not.'

Francesca went round to take a chair on the other side of the bed. 'Oh, well, sorry. I suppose I should have brought you flowers or something, but the shops wouldn't have been open. They say you're going to be all right, anyway.'

'Oh, absolutely fine.' Gabrielle's tone was sarcastic. 'I'm just malingering really – making a fuss about nothing.'

'I didn't mean—oh, never mind. Mum's had to take David back to your house to fetch his car – they took him away last night to answer questions.'

'Questions?' she said sharply. 'What questions?'

'It was him found you last night, after you'd been attacked. Don't know what that was about – he was in a bit of a state when he phoned last night. They'd have been better to go after Morven – he told them it would be her but they didn't pay any attention.' Then she paused. 'It was, wasn't it?'

Gabrielle gave a little grimace. 'Oh yes, it was her all right. She just went berserk. I think she's completely flipped.'

'That's one of the reasons I'm here – to make sure she doesn't creep in and finish you off.'

That hadn't occurred to her. Gabrielle looked at her in horror. Her 'safe place' here could be breached with only a tap on the door. 'You-you don't think she will, do you? Did anyone check who you were?'

'Nope. Just walked in. There was a policeman outside, but he was having a cup of tea and didn't even look at me.'

There was no end to this nightmare. No end, apart from death. Her eyes filled with tears that spilt over. 'I'm-I'm scared, Fran. I'm just so scared.'

Looking at her younger sister's frightened face, so bruised and battered, Francesca felt a lump in her own throat. She leant forward to take her hand. 'Oh, come on love! It'll be all right. We're all looking out for you – me and Mum and David, and Malcolm too, of course, ready to step in for a chat any time you feel the need for sedation. I'll make sure you're not left alone. Can't have my wee sister victimised by anyone except me.' There was a box of tissues there and she took some and leant forward to dab Gabrielle's face gently.

It was surprisingly comforting. Gabrielle managed a

weak smile. 'Thanks, Fran. That's kind. You were good at that when we were small.'

'Do you mean the protection or the victimising?' Francesca said.

They both laughed. When was the last time they had laughed together? Not for years and years.

Francesca went on, 'Now don't you go worrying. The police are probably rounding up Morven even as we speak and then you'll be OK.'

'Mmm,' Gabrielle said. If only it was as simple as that.

'So, what happens now?' DC Murray turned to look at DCI Strang as they stood in front of the empty Lemon Tree cafe.

He said nothing for a moment. Then he said, with more confidence than he really felt, 'Why don't we go and pick her up?'

'Do you know where she is or are you just kidding on?'

'Sticking my neck out, really. I could be wrong. She has to know we'll be looking for her as prime suspect after her outburst at Curran Services. It doesn't sound as if she took any trouble to cover her traces at the Rosses' house. And if she goes on the run – where to? As far as I can tell, she'd got no contacts elsewhere, no understanding of how to disappear.

'I agree with your reading of it, that she may not even have set out to kill Gabrielle and just lost it completely when she saw her. From what we know of Gabrielle, she's unlikely to have made a sweet and soothing response to whatever it was Morven said.'

'Certainly not if she was accusing her of murdering her son.' Murray spoke with feeling, remembering Gabrielle's reaction to her own clumsy question. 'Asking for blood money maybe, now she's got the inheritance from Niall.'

'Exactly. When she calms down she'll realise what she's done – may even believe that she actually killed her. She's in an unbalanced state and my big worry is that she might decide to top herself. So, let's get round there right now.'

'Round where?'

'Her brother's house. The house she feels by rights belongs to her.'

DI Hay strode into the incident centre in the high street and looked round. It was quiet; there were only three uniforms in the place and they were all from his own force. There was no sign of either DCI Strang or the chippy little constable and he went over to the sergeant.

'Have you seen the chief inspector?'

'Not today, sir.'

Hay looked pointedly at his watch. 'You'd think with a murder investigation running into the ground he'd have some sense of urgency, but apparently not. Do you know if there were any developments yesterday?'

'Don't know, sir. I was on the afternoon shift and DC Murray was working here all afternoon, but she didn't say anything. We haven't had any more folk coming in either and the phones have hardly rung.'

Hay gave a little smirk. 'Running out of options now, is he? What was DCI Strang doing yesterday?'

'DC Murray said he was away. Didn't say where.'

'His day off, most likely. Taken the chance to go for a wee look at John o' Groats, maybe buy a couple of postcards.

That's the trouble – they come in like tourists, strut about a bit and then leave us to clear up after. Well, lad, I'm taking you off this assignment. There's nothing happening here so you can come with me along to the house in Forsich where the woman was attacked last night. I'm in charge of that and at least that investigation's moving forward.'

When they arrived at the Rosses' house his squad had already arrived and had assembled in the Rosses' sitting room, ready for their tasks with their rubber gloves on. Hay came in beaming with satisfaction.

'Good to see at least some people are taking police work seriously. I've brought the sergeant along to help – the trail's obviously gone cold in Strang's murder case and we can use him here. Now, how are we getting on?'

A woman detective from Wick had already started dusting for fingerprints while another officer photographed them but the others who were standing by exchanged glances. PS Lothian said, 'We're not sure what we're meant to be doing, sir.'

Hay bristled. 'What do you mean? You're meant to be checking out the scene of the crime. Even though we know it's going to turn out to be the husband in the end, he's claiming it was someone else did it, so we need to be able to show there was no one else here. Right?'

'Who did he say it was?' Lothian asked.

'Oh, some story about bad blood between the victim and some woman in the village. But there's no sign of a break-in, right? And if they were sworn enemies, Mrs Ross wasn't going to invite her in for a cosy chat, was she?'

He strode to the centre of the room and looked round

about. 'We need to reconstruct the scene. He comes home. They have a row. He goes for her. That table's knocked over in the process – see? She's backing away, that rug there wrinkles up and she falls over, bashes her head on the fender. So far, it's an accident. But he's not shocked, is he? He doesn't call an ambulance right then, he bashes her on the head. At that point our helpful little DC trots up and stops him finishing her off and believes him when he tells her, all innocent, it was nothing to do with him. Wonderful the effect of big, innocent blue eyes when it comes to the ladies.'

The female detective looked daggers, but Hay didn't notice. 'Now, what you need to do is find what he used to hit her. Those wooden candlesticks on the mantelpiece there – start with those. And there's that glass vase – you could make quite a dent with that. Look around you, for God's sake. Here am I doing your job for you! Check those out, will you, Wilson?'

'Sir.' She came across with the powder and soft brush and picked up one of the candlesticks. She dusted on the aluminium powder and peered at the result.

'Well?' he barked.

'I'd just be talking about what these look like to the naked eye and that's not evidence – we'd need proper interpretation—'

'Obviously, Wilson. But get on with it – what do you see?'

'Comparing it to the record of Ross's prints it looks very similar—'

'What did I say?' Hay crowed.

'—but, sir, those prints are everywhere. And looking at the base of this,' she turned it up, 'I can't see any sign of blood or tissue.'

'Of course, you can't be sure without a forensic test,' he blustered. 'Try the other one.'

She did that, then shook her head without comment.

'There's a poker there,' PS Lothian said, pointing to the companion set by the fireside.

DC Wilson picked it up, checked, then shook her head. 'Smudges,' she said. 'I can check the vase now if you want.'

Hay was getting irritable. 'And you haven't found any helpful prints?'

'There's another set of marks all over the place that I would guess are Mrs Ross's, sir. There's a full set right on the edge of the fireplace where she probably put down her hand to save herself as she fell. And there's a different set on the arm of that wee chair, over by the window and what look like the same on the side of the door.'

Lothian said, 'Really? That's interesting. Someone sitting there, then touching the door on the way out—'

'Doesn't tell us much,' Hay said dismissively. 'No saying how long ago it was. Must have friends coming and going.'

No one said anything. With a look at the other sergeant, Lothian said, 'What do you want us to do now, sir? Should we maybe search the grounds to see if the weapon was chucked away?'

'What's the point in that? If it was only Murray turning up that stopped him killing her, Ross wouldn't have time to dispose of a weapon, would he?'

Under her breath, Wilson said, 'If.'

Hay heard it but couldn't pinpoint who had spoken. He began to go red. 'I can do without stupid remarks. You've got a job to do. Get on with it.'

The atmosphere in the room was becoming uncomfortable. Everyone looked at everyone else and eventually Lothian said, 'Sorry – what do you want us to actually do?'

Hay went redder than ever, cleared his throat. The pause, as it became obvious that he had no idea at all how to make use of the officers waiting for instruction, was excruciating.

Lothian could bear it no longer. 'Perhaps a couple of us could go and check out the timings for Ross driving from Aberdeen—'

The noise of a car drawing up outside was a welcome distraction. Hay went to the window.

'There's the man now. With a woman,' he said. 'What's he doing here? I told him I'd send for him when we wanted to speak to him again.'

Lothian said, 'He'll be needing his car. And it is his house, sir. Do we have any right to say he can't get back in?'

Hay looked trapped. 'Well, if you lot are sure that you've checked out everything in here, I suppose that's all right. We can clear out – I've no need to speak to him again yet.'

'I've got the keys,' Lothian said. 'I'll go out and give them to him, will I?'

But David Ross and Lilian Sinclair were coming up to the front door. They didn't look happy. Hay said hastily, 'Yes, you go and see them, Sergeant—'

They hadn't paused; they were in the hall, walking purposefully towards the sitting room.

'This is a crime scene!' Hay called out. 'Do not enter!'

They stopped. Ross said, 'Then perhaps you can come out and speak to us here, Inspector. I have further information to give you and now that I know that my wife will recover I'm not in the state of confusion and anxiety I was in last night and I wish to discuss the procedure for making a complaint at the very highest level.'

Hay's complexion took on a greenish tinge. He looked at PS Lothian, as if expecting him to protect him but the sergeant studiously avoided his gaze. The other officers looked as if they had discovered a sudden common interest in their footwear while playing Musical Statues.

At last Hay walked across the room and out into the hall.

'What's this important information you've got for me, then?'

Lilian swept him from head to toe with her scornful gaze. 'Your treatment of my son-in-law has been outrageous. I can vouch for the time he arrived in Forsich because he called in at Westerfield House to see whether my daughter was there. I know the exact time he left because I looked in at my husband's surgery to see how many patients he still had to see, and the receptionist was just locking the door, so it was exactly six-thirty.'

Hay was looking sicker than ever, but he wasn't giving up. 'Very convenient,' he sneered. 'Funny you didn't mention this last night, then. It would have saved us all a lot of trouble.'

'You didn't ask me,' Ross said. 'You asked me what time I left Aberdeen, that was all. Then you started on a series of questions in a manner I can only describe as hectoring. You prevented me from going to the hospital along with my injured wife who, for all I knew, could have died while you were detaining me.'

'Added to that,' Lilian said coldly, 'there has been an

attempt on my daughter's life. How can I be sure that she isn't threatened even now?'

Hay seized on that. 'We have an officer on her ward. And he assures me there has been no problem.'

'With that woman still at large, she can't possibly be safe,' Lilian insisted. 'What steps are you taking to detain Morven Gunn?'

He was stubborn. 'We have no reason to do so, other than a baseless accusation.'

'When you're in a hole, stop digging,' DC Wilson said out of the corner of her mouth to PS Lothian, who had to stifle a smile.

'Let's move on to the procedure for a formal complaint,' Ross said. 'In the first instance, who do I contact?'

Hay had a prominent Adam's apple that bobbed up and down as he gulped. 'PS Lothian will deal with that for you. I've got more important things to do.'

He stalked past them with a signal to the sergeant who had brought him and walked down the path to the car. He looked as if he was having to exert rigid control not to break into a trot.

Morven Gunn had slept for ten hours in the big airy bedroom that had been her mother's, that was still scented by the lavender potpourri on her dressing table. She hadn't slept as long as that in years and she woke disorientated, dry-mouthed. Since Gary's death her nights had been a battleground as she fought for oblivion that would blot out the torturing thoughts of grief, anger, resentment. Such sleep as she achieved on the cheap mattress in the tiny bedroom that was too cold in winter, too hot in summer, came in unsatisfying snatches. For the last few days she had barely slept at all.

Now she stretched, staring at the ceiling, possessed by an unfamiliar feeling of calm. She knew what she'd done. She hadn't set out to kill Gabrielle Ross – at least she didn't think she had – but it had happened that way and now she had delivered for Gary the proper sort of justice he would never have got in any court of law. She had done her duty by him, laid Gabrielle's corpse on the altar of her love for her son. She felt no regret, no remorse, only a savage joy.

They would come after her, no doubt. She wouldn't make it easy for them, though, wouldn't make any sort of pathetic confession. She didn't think she'd left anything that would point in her direction and they couldn't lock her up just because everyone knew how much she'd hated Gabrielle. They'd have to prove it first – and if they did, she wouldn't care. Nothing they could do to her would be worse than the hell she had lived with all these years, seeing that woman alive and prosperous. She wasn't either now. That thought gave her a wonderful sense of freedom.

It was early yet. The birds were singing in the garden. That was a blackbird; there had always been a pair of blackies nesting in the hedge. And she could hear a great tit now too, creaking its *teacher, teacher* song. She'd always loved birds, put out balls of fat for the tits during the winter months. Was there anything left in the house that she could put out for them now?

She eased herself out of bed, a little stiff now after sleeping so long. Morven was still wearing her day clothes and there was a cut on her knuckle that she'd got from breaking the kitchen window to get in. She'd come rushing back here in a tempest of emotions, to the house that wasn't hers but wasn't

Gabrielle's any more either. She had just flung herself onto her mother's bed – and now it was morning and another day.

In the kitchen the fridge stood open and empty but when she looked in the cupboard there were still packets and tins. She wasn't hungry herself, but she picked up a box of muesli and went outside with it. The sun was shining and though the morning air was still chilly she barely noticed it. She tore open the packet and wandered in a wide circle round the old, gnarled apple tree that had the wooden bench below it where she'd liked to sit, sprinkling muesli as she went.

When the packet was empty she sat down and waited. It wasn't very long before the cock blackbird, bouncing across the lawn looking for worms, caught sight of the largesse and studied it, his head cocked to one side. He hopped across and pecked; his hen followed, then a couple of sparrows. Morven watched in tranquil satisfaction as a pigeon swooped down and then another, making comments to each other in low croons. More birds. Then the squawks and squabbles started; a magpie came, and two more. Looking at the live carpet of birds she felt as if she was held in a sort of trance. Morven barely moved when the voices spoke behind her.

'Mrs Gunn? DCI Strang and DC Murray. Could we have a word?'

She didn't turn her head, but as they approached her across the grass she said, 'I always think it's amazing how quickly birds gather when one of them finds a little treat, don't you?'

CHAPTER TWENTY-THREE

'Perhaps we could go inside, Mrs Gunn?' DCI Strang said.

Morven looked up at him. 'Why? I like it here, watching the birds. I always liked birds, you know. When I had my own house I always fed them in the winter.'

'We've got quite a lot to talk about,' he said. 'Don't you find it a bit chilly out here?'

'No.'

Strang glanced at Murray. 'I'm on my way,' she said in a resigned voice as she headed across the grass to the open kitchen door, to reappear a couple of minutes later with a couple of chairs.

Meanwhile he silently studied Morven. She was smiling faintly as yet more birds alighted – a young herring gull now, in its mottled plumage, throwing its weight around and squawking. She had a livid bruise on one cheekbone and when he looked down at her hands, relaxed in her lap, he could see blood across the knuckles and caked under the fingernails. Hard to think anything other than that it was Gabrielle Ross's blood. Any normal person would have washed their hands to remove the traces but looking at her now he could believe that Morven was far from normal. To any competent brief it would be a standout case for diminished responsibility.

He didn't say anything, though, until they sat down, and Murray got out a small tape recorder, speaking the identification in a low voice.

'Morven,' he said, 'are you able to understand what I'm saying?'

The absent look vanished. Morven sat up and snapped, 'What do you mean "understand"? You calling me stupid?'

Taken aback by the transformation, Strang said hastily, 'No, no, of course not. We just want to ask you a few questions.'

'Get on with it, then. I've a cafe to open up and there'll be folk wanting their breakfast.'

Murray said, 'You won't want to go in with hands like that.'

Morven looked down at her hands as if she'd only just noticed them. She shrugged.

The constable went on, 'There's a broken window there. Was that how you got the cut?'

Strang hadn't noticed and glanced across. The back door had glass panes; that must have been how she'd gained access to the house.

'Suppose so,' Morven said.

'Why did you break in?' Strang asked, and she glared at him.

'Because I didn't have the key. Why do you think?'

'Why did you want to get inside?'

She frowned, as if she didn't know the answer. Then she said, 'It's my brother's house,' as if that explained it.

Strang spoke gently. 'You know he's dead, Morven. It doesn't belong to him any more. It belongs to Gabrielle Ross.'

With a triumphant look she said, 'No, it doesn't.'

'Why not?'

Morven pinched her lips together very tightly and said nothing.

Murray looked at him eagerly, but he shook his head slightly. He wasn't ready to ask that question yet. Instead, he asked, 'How did you get that bruise on your cheek?'

She put both hands up to her cheeks as if she didn't know it was there, then probed the soreness on the right-hand side.

'Walked into a door, I expect.' She smirked as she gave the standard excuse for unexplained bruising.

'But you don't remember doing it? No? Morven, was the cafe open yesterday?'

'Yes, it was. Why wouldn't it be? I was perfectly all right yesterday.' She had been looking at Strang; now she turned to Murray. 'You can tell him that. Even when you were asking stupid questions I stayed completely calm.'

'Wouldn't exactly say that,' Murray said unwisely.

Morven gave a sudden scream. 'Liar! She's lying!'

Strang said hastily, 'That's all right. I'll take your word for it. Tell me what happened after the cafe closed. Where did you go?'

She was off balance now. She switched her gaze to the birds; they had almost cleared the crumbs and there were only a few left still pecking hopefully and she pointed at them. 'They all come, the minute there's food around and then when they've eaten it they all go.'

Murray leant forward. 'Like ravens, Morven?' she said eagerly. 'Did you know the ravens would come to the cottage for Niall's body?'

Oh, for God's sake! Ravens and the cottage? Where had that come from? Strang had thought she'd learnt something about not switching the direction of an interview, but no. If Morven suddenly confessed he'd have to forgive her, but otherwise she was going to get a right bollocking. She had glanced at him in triumph; her face changed as she saw his frown.

Morven said, 'My brother's dead. You said that yourself.'

No, she hadn't confessed. Murray visibly subsided as Strang went on, trying to pick up the impetus, 'You closed up the cafe, yes? Now, after that did you go to see Gabrielle Ross yesterday evening?'

'No.'

'I want to go back to something you said. You said that Gabrielle Ross didn't own this house any longer. Why was that?'

'Because—' Morven began, then clamped her lips again, as if realising the implications.

'Were you going to say, because she's dead?'

A cunning look came over her face. 'Is she?'

'No.'

It took a moment to sink in. 'No?' she said, then, her voice rising, 'No?'

'Did you think you'd killed her, Morven?'

She was breathing raggedly. 'Not dead? She killed Gary. I

366

didn't kill her, God did. It was only right.' She began to cry, deep painful sobs.

Strang stood up. 'We're going to take you in to the police station and we'll arrange for a lawyer to be there. I am arresting you on suspicion of attempted murder. You do not have to say anything . . .'

As he finished the caution he took her arm, quite gently, and she stood up without making any resistance, still shaking with convulsive sobs and wiping at her face ineffectually with her hands.

As they led her towards the car Murray said, 'Sorry, boss,' very quietly.

'Yes,' he said. 'We'll talk about that later.'

Ailie Johnston had read the previous day's *Press and Journal* report on Niall Aitchison's murder with considerable interest and picked up the morning edition on her way to work. She was disappointed that there seemed to be nothing new today, apart from an indication that there would be a press statement from the police later. She'd been hoping that they'd be on their way to clearing it up; Bruce Michie had been like a bear with a sore head ever since his interview with DCI Strang had been cancelled. If she had a fiver for every time he'd asked her what she thought that meant and she'd replied that it meant he'd probably been called away, she could take early retirement and never have to speak to the man again.

She heard him come into the office and the buzzer went almost immediately, like a reflex. She groaned, then got up and went through, her face set in 'I've-had-enough-of-this-nonsense' lines.

'What's the matter *this* morning, Bruce?' she said.

He had the *Press and Journal* open on his desk. 'Have you seen this?'

'Saw the headlines. Didn't seem to have anything new to say.'

'Not that. This here.' He was pointing to a brief item on one of the inner pages.

The headline was WOMAN ATTACKED and the article went on, 'A woman was attacked last night in the village of Forsich in Caithness. Mrs Gabrielle Ross was taken to Wick hospital where she is said to be comfortable. In a statement DI Hay confirmed that a man is helping police with their enquiries.'

'Oh no! That's awful! Poor Gabrielle – as if she hasn't had enough to cope with.'

'Yes, yes, but what does it *mean*?'

If he asked her that even once more, she'd be the next to be 'helping police with their enquiries'. She said in the voice she used to her six-year-old grandson, 'It means Gabrielle was attacked and they think they've got whoever did it. All right?' She turned.

'Don't go, Ailie!' he said. 'Listen, do you reckon that's who killed Aitchison?'

'Why should it be? It doesn't say anything about that.'

'I know, but Gabrielle's right in the middle of all this. Wee place like Forsich – you'd not have two murdering maniacs going around, would you?'

Ailie sighed. 'Can't say I've got an opinion on murdering maniacs. Look, Bruce, I can hear my phone's been ringing. Is there any reason why I shouldn't get back to answer it?'

'The thing is,' he said earnestly, 'I'm getting gey worried about all this. Chris Brady phoned yesterday afternoon asking if the inspector mannie'd been here talking to me yet. Wanted to check that I'll – well, say the right things.'

Ailie's eyes narrowed. 'What does that mean?'

She couldn't believe she'd used the phrase herself, but Bruce didn't seem to notice. 'It's all this business stuff. You have to keep quiet about it, or—Anyway, I'm wondering whether I should maybe not bother too much about that. The thing is,' he said again, then stopped, fingering his collar. 'What – what if it's Chris that's attacked Gabrielle?'

'*Chris?*' Ailie said in astonishment. 'Is there some reason why he should?'

'No, no, of course not. It's just, if it was, I could be getting myself implicated in something. Maybe I should just tell the police . . .'

'Tell them what, for heaven's sake?'

He took fright at her horrified expression. 'Oh, nothing really bad. You know me, Ailie – wouldn't hurt anyone. It's just all this is getting me fair puggled, making me think daft things. Of course, Chris wouldn't. It's just I'd like to be sure.'

'Why don't you phone and ask to speak to him? If he's been nicked he'll not be there, will he? But if there's anything at all you know that would help the police you'd damn well better tell them. It's your civic duty,' she said sternly, then added as he didn't look totally convinced, 'and if they find out you didn't, it'll be you getting the jail.'

He was reaching for the phone as she left and before she got back to her office she heard him saying, 'Chris? Oh, just thought I'd touch base with you . . .'

Ailie hadn't thought it was likely that Brady would have gone all the way up to Forsich to attack Gabrielle; it was just evidence of Bruce's paranoid state. But why was he so paranoid, and what did he know? If he wasn't going to go to the police of his own accord, she was going to tell her nice inspector that if he so much as waved the handcuffs at him Bruce would crack.

But it still left the question, who had attacked Gabrielle, and why? Even if the newspaper hadn't made a connection, she rather agreed with Bruce that violent crime wasn't a common feature of life in Forsich. So, what did it—

She stopped herself with a 'Tcha!' of annoyance. He'd got her doing it too, now.

'DI Hay,' DCI Strang said as he and DC Murray escorted Morven Gunn into the police station in Thurso.

The Force Civilian Assistant who was at the desk said, 'He's gone out, sir. He didn't say when he'd be back.'

Murray took Morven over to sit down. She was still crying, but quietly now; she hadn't spoken in the car except to mutter sometimes, 'It's not fair! It's not fair!'

Strang was asking for the duty sergeant but the woman looked flustered. 'He's not here, sir. He was along at the incident room in Forsich.'

'Sergeant Lothian?' he said hopefully.

'No sir. He wasn't scheduled for this morning's shift, but he came in then went out with DI Hay.'

Murray could see Strang was annoyed at this further evidence of police cuts. If you came in with someone under arrest and couldn't charge them, it left you stranded until that could be arranged. She didn't want him to be more annoyed than he already was; she knew she was in the doghouse for having done it again – interfered in an interview. It was just when Morven had said that about the birds gathering, twice over, and it fitted so neatly with her own theory, she'd got excited.

But she hadn't even mentioned it to Strang and now he'd believe she'd been planning one of her solo efforts. She hadn't been; she'd actually been looking forward to discussing it with him when they'd time, but this morning it had all been about practicalities not theories.

'It's not fair,' Morven said again, then, louder, 'It's not *fair*!'

The tears had stopped. She seemed to be working herself up into a state. Strang, who was trying to arrange for a lawyer to attend, shot an anxious glance over his shoulder.

'Tell me what isn't fair, Morven?' Murray said gently. She couldn't help feeling moved by the woman's distress, whatever she'd done.

'My whole life. My whole life! Why should she have everything, everything, and me – nothing. Less than nothing. A hell on earth – and she's the wicked one, the one who should be in hell. Along with my brother. Traitor!'

The words 'Did you kill him, Morven?' were on her lips but she didn't dare utter them. A confession without another witness to corroborate was no confession at all. 'You can tell us all about him later,' she said, and at that moment the entrance door opened, and DI Hay walked in with a uniformed sergeant at his heels.

When he saw Strang, he stopped dead. 'What are you doing here?' he said rudely.

'Good morning, Inspector,' Strang said. He turned to the other man. 'Can you act as duty sergeant? Take this woman down to the charge bar and book her in, please. I've arrested her on suspicion of attempted murder. DC Murray can assist, if necessary.'

'Yes, sir,' he said. 'There's some more officers coming back from the crime scene any minute, so I can get one of them.'

Hay was staring at Morven. 'Who's this?'

'She's under suspicion of attempting to murder Gabrielle Ross. I'll want someone to take swabs from her fingernails, as well as prints, of course. And you have a photographer? I want to make sure we have a shot of the bruise on her cheek.'

A group of officers, including DC Wilson and PS Lothian, had just arrived. DC Wilson came forward to say she could take charge of that and Lothian, who had been looking a bit hangdog, brightened up when he saw Strang, and brightened up further at what he heard.

'That's good news, sir,' he said, and Murray scowled. His reappearance was badly timed for her; would Strang shut her out now after her most recent balls-up?

Hay was gnawing at his lip. 'Go on then, Lothian. And Wilson. You heard what the chief inspector said – what are you waiting for?'

Morven shrank back a little as the two men and the detective advanced on her but made no direct protest as they urged her onto her feet and took her through to the charge bar. She was bewildered now, Murray thought, getting up and going to stand beside Strang.

'I think we'd better have a chat about this, Inspector. Your office?'

'I suppose so,' Hay said. 'You, but not her. She was obstructive to me last night.'

Murray was ready to sit back down again but Strang said smoothly, 'Crossed wires, I think. My constable merely had information that she felt would be helpful and I prefer to have her with me.'

With a face like fizz, Hay stalked ahead of them, Strang having to grab the doors as they swung back in his wake.

It was a small office; Hay took his place behind the desk with Strang taking the chair opposite and Murray perching on a small chair in the further corner, happy enough to be out of the direct line of fire.

'So perhaps you can bring me up to date,' Strang said. 'Has there been any work done at the crime scene?'

Hay took it as a personal insult. 'Well, of course. We've completed our investigation there.'

'Fingerprints?'

'Naturally. They'll have to be compared before we jump to any conclusions.'

'And the husband? I gather you brought him in last night?'

Hay coughed. 'Just helping with enquiries. Voluntarily. As a precaution.'

Yeah, right, Murray thought, but said nothing. She'd get her turn at the inquiry when the guy complained.

'But you were satisfied that he wasn't involved?'

'Absolutely. The man had an alibi.'

'Right. So, he is out of the frame, then.'

'Oh yes. Unless of course his wife tells us something different when she's fit.'

He was still clinging to his theory, Murray thought – one

of these inadequates who could never bear to admit he was wrong. Despite everything, he was still suggesting there was a conspiracy against him that involved David Ross, Murray herself and of course Strang now too. She only hoped the head injury hadn't left Gabrielle with memory loss or Hay would find some other way to prove he was right, even if it meant locking up an innocent man.

'Do we have any indication of when that might be?' Strang asked.

'Having a scan this morning. I have a constable on duty ready to see her whenever he gets the word.'

'Ah. Then could you please get the message through to him now that I will be coming to see her myself later and don't want her spoken to before that?'

'Suppose so,' Hay said grudgingly, but didn't move. Strang pointedly said nothing, only looking at the phone on his desk until Hay picked it up and gave the order.

'Now,' Strang said, 'we have the press statement later. At least we have something positive to tell them.'

Hay looked as if he'd bitten on a lemon. 'I suppose so.'

'I think it would be best if you make the announcement that Morven Gunn is under arrest here in Thurso, then I can go on to talk about the murder investigation and I can highlight our cooperation.'

Murray gave him a surprised look – what cooperation was this? But he knew what he was doing; Hay, who had been looking surly, perked up and said, 'Well, I suppose that would be appropriate, my having informed the press originally. And, of course, my officers have been much involved in supporting your operation.'

'Indeed,' Strang was saying as there was a knock on the door and DC Wilson came in.

'Sorry to interrupt, sir, but I thought you might want to know that I've taken Mrs Gunn's prints. They'll have to go through the proper process of course, but purely on a visual comparison they look very similar to the marks on the chair and door at the Rosses' home.'

'Let me know when you get confirmation,' Strang said. 'And I'll want a full report on the findings from the crime scene – can you manage by this afternoon?'

Wilson drew a deep breath but agreed.

Hay, having been given ownership of the case, was jubilant. 'Excellent, excellent, looks like an open-and-shut case, then.'

Strang said, 'If she's fit to plead. How is she now?'

DC Wilson pulled a face. 'Her brief's arrived and I think he'll be making representations.'

Hay looked, Murray thought, as if someone had stolen his scone. Strang got up. 'I'll leave that in your hands, then, Inspector. We'll meet at two to give the statement.'

Murray held open the door for him and followed him out. 'The hospital?' she said.

'That's right. We can talk on the way.'

She didn't like the sound of that.

The porter had come early to take Gabrielle down for the scan, a big, cheerful red-haired man with a strong Aberdeen accent.

'Dearie me!' he said, looking at her battered face. 'That's nae fine! Still, maybe I should see what you did to the other chiel, eh?'

375

Gabrielle smiled wanly. 'Not really, I'm afraid.'

'Don't you go getting yourself wrochit up, now. I've seen a lot worse on a Saturday night when the Dons have been playing the Rangers – you'll be fine, from the look of you. Now you just get in this chair and I'll give you a hurl down. See if I can maybe get away with a wheelie or two to cheer you up.'

The casual kindness was her undoing. She started to cry, to her new friend's dismay.

'This'll never do! You're not fretting about the scan, are you? Piece of cake!'

As he pushed her down the corridor she found herself saying, 'Not the scan – just what they might find. I-I think I might have Alzheimer's.' It had been haunting her: the evidence might be there, in plain sight on the screen – the tangles and plaques that accumulated ahead of the disease. She would so much rather not know what was going on inside her skull.

'Och, dinnae be daft, quine! You've had a wee dunt on the head, that's all. And from what they were saying, they'll have you back home before you've even time to get your fly cup at eleven.'

That wasn't as cheering as he had obviously meant it to be, but she managed to give a little laugh and when he said, 'I'll tell you what – I'll do you one of the tests they do on the auld yins. Who's the prime minister?' she was actually able to make a joke: 'Well, it was Theresa May yesterday.'

It was greeted with applause. 'There you are! Nothing the matter with you,' he said triumphantly as he handed her over to the nurse.

The scan had been something of an ordeal, though, like being prematurely entombed. Gabrielle had never been claustrophobic but recently she had become uncomfortable in enclosed spaces; they would probably tell her it was a psychological reaction to feeling trapped. It wasn't her friend who took her back either; on the silent journey back to her room she had time to think about what lay ahead.

Francesca was there, with a magazine she must have got from the news-stand. She put it down as Gabrielle came in and was helped back into bed.

'All right? Some people get a bit panicky when they shove you into that thing.'

'No, I was fine.'

'That's good. You know, I was just thinking – surely the police will just go on and arrest Morven now for Niall's murder as well? He told me himself that she hated him, really hated him – he was hurt about it, you know? And I can't imagine anyone else killing him unless they were mad. He was a lovely man.' Her eyes filled with tears.

Gabrielle's did too. 'Yes,' she said softly. 'So kind. And I'm glad she's not still . . . out there, somewhere.'

'Absolutely. Unless she gets bailed, or something.'

Tact had never been Fran's strong point. Gabrielle closed her eyes. 'Do you mind if I have a nap? My head's hurting a bit.'

'Of course not. It'll do you good.' Francesca went back to her magazine.

To Gabrielle's surprise, she did fall asleep and woke up only when she heard David talking to Francesca. Whenever she opened her eyes he came over to her.

'Oh, my sweetheart, what has she done to you?' He kissed her very gently on her uninjured cheek and took her hand as he sat down on the bed.

She shouldn't feel irritated by his solicitude, but somehow, she was. 'Still alive, anyway,' she said.

'Yes, we've all been thanking God for that, at least. I really thought you were dead, you know – I'm still a bit shaky from the shock. And Fran says you still remember exactly what happened – not a nice thing to have in your head.'

'No, it isn't.' Gabrielle sat up. 'Do you know if they've got the results of the scan?'

'I met the doctor on his way in, while you were asleep. He says you're fine, so we can take you home whenever you're ready. So that's great.'

He spoke heartily – too heartily? 'Was that all he said?' she asked sharply.

'He said they were needing the bed, so I guess you'd better make a move. And here's your mother now with clothes for you.'

Her gut was churning. There was something about the way he was speaking – what had the doctor really said? She didn't want to go home, go back to face all her problems again. She just wanted everything to stop.

But it didn't. Lilian was sweeping in, cooing maternal anxiety about the state of her daughter's face, talking, talking. 'And you actually remember that woman coming at you? You know, Malcolm will tell you that you should get psychiatric help now, before flashbacks become a problem.'

'I'll be fine,' Gabrielle said automatically, allowing herself to be helped.

As David drove her home, she tried to think what she could say to him that would ward off questions she didn't want to answer. Something had died in their marriage; a great gulf had opened up between them now.

He spoke first. 'Is it right that Niall left you everything, Gabrielle? It's all over the town that he did.'

Her throat closed over so that she could hardly speak. 'Yes. He was . . . very kind.'

'Have you decided—'

'No,' she said. 'David, I'm feeling very tired. Do you mind if I close my eyes?'

'Of course not, love. You just rest, and you can pop straight into bed when we get there. We'll chat once you're feeling better.'

There was that funny, too hearty note in his voice again. Gabrielle tried not to think too much about it, or about returning to the house where the nightmare that was Morven Gunn had happened. She turned her head away as she walked across the hall and up the stairs to the bedroom. She caught a glimpse of herself in the mirror, her face a horror landscape of red and purple bruising, a black eye, hair sticking up jaggedly above the plaster on the back.

'I won't undress,' she said. 'Just lie down for a bit.'

'Yes, of course,' David said. 'Do you want anything – cup of tea, drink of water . . . ?'

She shook her head.

'Sure? Well, let me know whenever you wake up – your obedient servant!'

He still sounded odd. 'David, what's wrong? I know there's something – what is it?'

He looked at her dumbly for a moment. Then he said with a groan, 'I was going to wait a bit till you were stronger. Are you sure—'

Gabrielle sank onto the bed. 'Yes,' she said, though her head felt so light that it might float off her shoulders at any moment.

David sat down beside her and took her hand. His eyes were moist. 'It's not good news, my darling. They'll want you to go back for a chat soon. There are signs . . .'

Her lips were almost too stiff to move. 'Alzheimer's?'

He bowed his head, nodded. 'But it's at an early stage and they're getting closer to a cure all the time. You mustn't despair – I'm always here for you. We're in this together. For better for worse, remember?'

She couldn't stand the platitudes. 'Please – just leave me.'

'But—'

'Go! Please!'

Her voice had risen, and he got up. 'If that's what you want.'

'*Yes!*'

He went out and left her alone with her death sentence. Her despair was an almost physical presence, some dreadful monster at her shoulder that she would see if she turned her head.

CHAPTER TWENTY-FOUR

Strang had barely fastened his seat belt before Murray began her apology.

'Sir, I'm really, really sorry. I know I did just what you always tell me not to do, but I just forgot. Sorry. I honestly hadn't been trying to work up my own angle on it, it was just when she said about the ravens it fitted in and I got a wee bit carried way, I suppose . . .'

Torn between irritation and amusement, he said, 'Apology noted. Now slow down – where did the ravens come into it?'

'I was going to run this past you when we'd time to talk but this morning you'd other things on your mind. What it was, was – well, you see, we haven't been able to work out why the body should have been moved to the cottage when probably if it had been left in the bog it might never have been found at all.

'Morven really, really hated her brother. She couldn't

hide it yesterday when she was talking to me, even though she was trying to let on she was OK about the will. She's proved she's violent. You can just see her losing the plot and killing him, and then I thought what with her being mental she might have felt that just killing him wasn't enough. Maybe once she'd done that, when it didn't feel as good as she'd thought it would, she wanted to do something else, something worse.

'She could have known about the cottage – like maybe they'd even played there when they were kids. And Fergus Mowat said that whenever there's a dead sheep or something the ravens gather at once – they've got amazing eyesight. She could have got some kind of sick charge out of his body getting torn apart. And she knew about birds – she said that, about them gathering, twice over.

'I just suddenly thought, if we could surprise her into admitting it . . . But I know I shouldn't have jumped in like that. I've really been trying to think before I speak and I'm sorry I screwed up.'

'I can see that,' Strang said. 'But more effort needed, as they used to put on my school reports.'

She looked at him out of the corner of her eye and seemed to sense forgiveness. She said hesitantly, 'But what I said . . . what do you think about it, boss?'

Strang gave a heavy sigh. 'Livvy, I hardly know where to start. You saw her car; it was parked outside the house this morning. It's a Fiat 500. She couldn't take that up across the bog to move the body, could she? And playing in the cottage – when she was a child, the cottage would still have been inhabited. She and Niall were quarrelling too, so it's a bit hard to see how she'd have persuaded him to go with her for a walk in the Flows to give her an opportunity to hit him over the head, and even supposing she'd somehow managed all that I can't come up with a reason for her to leave the cottage door open so that the body would be discovered. And her grudge against Niall – she'd been living with it for years. Even the quarrel over her mother's will was several months ago, and she's a woman who flies into a rage. Why would she wait?'

'Oh,' was all Murray said, but he saw her shoulders slump and then she gave a pitiful sniff. He felt a brute.

'Look, I'm sorry—'

She turned to glower at him. 'Oh, I'm not feeble! Don't think I'm crying because you're mad at me. I'm crying with rage at myself for being so bloody stupid. Why didn't I think that through? No, don't tell me – I know. Fell in love with the idea, didn't I? How dumb can you be?'

'Not necessarily dumb, Livvy, but certainly unthinking. I don't want to stop you coming up with ideas, but for God's sake share them before you put them into operation! Is there anything more bubbling away that I don't know about?'

Murray shook her head.

'Right,' he went on. 'Now, assuming we can speak to Gabrielle, we want to take her through what happened last night, obviously. But I'd like to know more about her movements on the two relevant days, and I'd like to know quite a lot more about the relationship with Aitchison. He was clearly devoted to her and apparently they were allies—'

She looked at him sharply. 'Apparently? Do you think she might have done it, boss?'

He put his hand to his brow, exasperated. 'No, Livvy, I don't "think". I just want to check out where she was when, and whether the devotion between her and Aitchison was mutual. And I want to talk to Ross as well. You've met him – what was your impression?'

'Seemed nice enough – pleasant manner. Few years older than she is but still quite buff, I'd say. Certainly, was very upset about his wife. He was suffering from shock – had to get him hot tea and brandy.'

'The first thing we need to know is his whereabouts at the significant times. He's been a bit elusive, with being offshore. I'll be interested to see him for myself – though the elusive person I'd like most to see is Pat Curran.'

'Gabrielle's father? But—'

'Yes, I know he's dead, but his effect still lingers around here, and he's something different to everybody. To Gabrielle he's the father who was so perfect that when he died she fell apart. To Francesca, he's the father who gave her an inferiority complex that she still hasn't got over, to Lilian Sinclair he was a bad husband, to Morven Gunn he was the villain who destroyed her life, to Niall Aitchison he was a man who commanded his utmost loyalty, to his secretary he was a bit of a chancer but a charismatic man and a good boss. Take your pick.' He gave a wry smile. 'Now that, you see, is the bee in my bonnet. We all have them.'

Murray said, 'See what you mean, though. Oh, that's the sign for the hospital now.'

Just as she turned in at the entrance, Strang's phone rang. He listened to what Ailie Johnston had to tell him, then said, 'I'll put that in hand. Thanks, Ailie. That's been very useful.'

And, certainly, it had been. Apart altogether from the useful information she'd given him, she'd jolted his memory of the other thing that had struck him during the interview with Chris Brady. When he'd asked Brady for the second time if the latecomer had been Niall Aitchison, he hadn't immediately said, 'There wasn't a latecomer', he'd said, 'No, it wasn't,' and then tried to cover up his reaction. He should have picked up on that; it told him that the latecomer was someone else. He'd better check that now.

'I'm just going to make a call,' he said to Murray, and keyed in the number for the helpful DI MacLean in Aberdeen, who proved not only helpful but keen to interview Bruce Michie.

'Anything to get out of the health and safety briefing I'm down for,' he said. 'I'll get back to you as soon as I can.'

Which made up for discovering that Gabrielle Ross had been discharged and they'd had a wasted journey.

Gabrielle didn't cry. She felt hollow, numb – but unsurprised. It felt as if she'd known all along.

In a way, this made everything simpler. She didn't have to agonise any longer over whether she could possibly get well enough and strong enough to get back to running Curran Services. She accepted now that she couldn't, that bit by bit her thoughts would get more confused, more frightening. She wouldn't have to try to work out whether her memory might be getting worse and her behaviour becoming more eccentric; it would be and there was nothing she could do about it.

But it meant she'd have to let Paddy down. He had been so proud of Curran Services, the baby he'd created and

385

grown to successful maturity; once that was gone, he would have no memorial. And nor would she. Their names were writ on water – who was it had said that? Bog water, in their case, sucking them down into the black pools and the smelly mud, forgotten for ever.

Oh Paddy, Paddy! What wouldn't she give now to be able to throw herself into his arms for a bear hug, to hear his Irish voice saying, 'There's nothing so bad that your old da can't fix it!' If only she could find the faith to believe that one day they would be together again, all tears wiped from their eyes, but Paddy had been an irreverent atheist – though, as he always insisted, 'a Catholic atheist'.

Catholics didn't countenance suicide, though. Lucky her atheism was just the ordinary kind.

She hadn't been able to look beyond her own fears and misery but now she must think about David. She owed him so much – everything, really – for his loving protectiveness after she got ill. He'd never reproached her for the house fire or the loss of his baby; he'd always been her rock when the sands were shifting under her feet.

Today he'd said 'We're in this together', and she knew he meant it. Loyalty was his greatest virtue and it would be his downfall. She could picture him in years to come, faithfully tending the vegetable she would have become, like someone cherishing some monstrous prize marrow, while his own life disintegrated. He had been so loyal to Pat too; that was the crucial thing. Niall had been loyal too, at one time.

Death had been stalking her for weeks now and all she'd lacked was resolution. Now there was no doubt at all in her mind about what she should do. Preferably soon, before she had to go through the farce of hospital appointments and doctors trying to sound bright about some treatment that they knew wouldn't do any good. Definitely before she actually started drooling. She just had to make it as easy on David as she could.

It might be a less cruel outcome anyway. If she had just been stressed, if she had eventually got better once the worst had passed, she couldn't see their marriage surviving long term. Somewhere along the line it had died, as she'd realised in the car this morning. She'd have left him, and he might have been more broken by that than by her chosen way out. He could convince himself that it was her love for him that prompted her to set him free from the burden of her infirmities – and from the knowledge that would die with her.

She felt free now too. No more secrets, no more lies, no more obligations. Free, but very tired. She could sleep now and soon, once David left the house again, she'd look for the little silvery knife. If she could remember where she put it.

'How did she take it?'

'Sent me away. Wants to be by herself,' David Ross said.

'Is that a good sign or a bad sign?'

'Damned if I know!' He laughed.

'You'll have to keep up the pressure.'

'I know, I know. But she's tough.'

'I didn't think she'd have gone on as long as this.'

'I didn't either. Tough, like her father, I suppose.'

'Oh, that would figure. So, what next?'

'Trust me. I'll just have to play it by ear.'

'But—'

'That's a car drawing up. Police is my bet. Yup. Bye.'

David Ross opened the front door promptly, saying, 'Oh yes, I've been expecting a visit.' He greeted DC Murray warmly, though the look he gave DCI Strang was cool. 'You'd better come through to my office. The sitting room's an ungodly mess after your lot visited this morning.'

Strang only nodded. Murray walked on with Ross, but she was aware that Strang had hung back; something in the hall seemed to have caught his attention.

At the door to his office Ross paused, looking back, and Strang said, gesturing towards the sitting room, 'Mind if I take a look?'

'Be my guest,' Ross said with an ironic flourish.

Murray looked at Strang uncertainly and he gave her a nod. 'Yes, just carry on. I'll join you in a minute.'

The office was bare of any furnishings apart from a desk, a few chairs and filing cabinets. A trolley held computer equipment and the back wall was shelved, containing box files that looked as if they went back years. Ross sat down on the office chair behind the desk and Murray took one of the seats opposite.

'I do a lot of work from here just at the moment,' Ross said. 'I quite often have to go to Aberdeen, of course, and I get called offshore when there's a problem there.'

'You've been away recently, haven't you?'

'Yes. There's a bug in one of the systems that keeps recurring. Not convinced I've nailed it even now.'

Murray took out her notebook. 'Perhaps you could give

me details of your whereabouts on these two dates.' She quoted them, and Ross frowned in thought.

'On the Thursday I was definitely offshore. I was still there when the news about Niall broke – I contacted DCI Strang from the rig. Saturday 24th – yes, I was away then too. Left on the Friday but they got me back on the Sunday that time. It just depends when there's a place on the chopper – as a humble techno geek I'm a low man on the totem pole when it comes to priority and they just shove me on when there's a seat free.'

She jotted that down, along with the name of the company, just as Strang came back in and took the seat beside her.

'Can I just ask first of all how your wife is?'

Ross grimaced. 'Not great, I'm afraid. Mercifully her injuries are much less serious than we both thought' – this said with a smile at Murray – 'but she's suffering mentally. She's been under a huge amount of stress, first with the shock of her father's sudden death, then the terrible business of the house fire. The loss of our baby was a dreadful blow too, and not unnaturally she's had a few problems with memory and so on. But her grandmother suffered from early onset Alzheimer's and she's convinced that's what she's got. Even when I told her that the scan today showed no signs of it at all she wouldn't believe me.

'To be honest, her mother and I – and Dr Sinclair too – are afraid she's suicidal. It's been markedly worse since Niall's death – that really seems to be preying on her mind, but she won't talk to me about it. We're worried – very worried.'

389

'I see. Does she have any memory of what happened to her last night?'

'All too vivid, I understand from her sister. That won't help her mental stability, but I have to say I'm grateful personally after the treatment I got from your colleague last night.'

Murray shifted uncomfortably as Strang said, 'I can understand your feelings, sir. I'm sorry that DI Hay was insensitive when you were personally distressed, but I think perhaps you aren't aware of how often this excuse is offered when there's a domestic assault. Would you accept our apology? Of course, you are entirely within your rights if you want to make a formal complaint and I can explain the procedure and the investigation that would follow.'

Ross gave a long-suffering sigh. 'Oh, I've enough on my plate without that. Let's pretend that lessons will be learnt, shall we, and I'll let it go.'

'Thank you, Mr Ross. Do you know Chris Brady?'

The question came so unexpectedly that Ross recoiled. 'What – sorry?' he stumbled.

'Chris Brady.'

'Oh – oh, I believe I met him once. Gabrielle's father knew him – he was in the same line of business.'

'And, of course, you know Bruce Michie.'

'Of course.'

Murray was struck by the change in Ross's face. He had been relaxed and pleasant when he was talking to her; now there was a cold steeliness in his expression.

'Are you a keen fisherman?' Strang said.

'No. Not in the least.'

Strang raised his eyebrows. 'The rods in the front hall . . . ?'

'My father-in-law's. Oh, once or twice I went along with him to fish, but it didn't take. I'm just too impatient, I suppose.' He gave a self-deprecating smile directed at Murray, but she didn't respond.

'Where was that?'

Ross's face was calm, but Murray could see that his knuckles had turned white and a little pulse was beating at his temple. 'Oh, just one of the little lochs up on the moor.'

'Has it a name?'

'Not that I know of.' There was a tiny trickle of sweat on his brow, but he went on, 'If for some reason you wanted to see it, Inspector, there's a rough track just on the outskirts of the village you can drive up.'

'Did you ever fish with Niall Aitchison?'

Ross's hands disappeared below the desk but from the tension in his lower arms Murray guessed they were being gripped together, hard. But he said lightly, 'No, I'm afraid not. As I said, it wasn't exactly my thing and he was really Gabrielle's friend, not mine.'

Then he paused. 'Look, I don't want to say this, but I think you perhaps need to know. Gabrielle's big thing is loyalty. Niall held the balance of votes in the company and she told me she suspected that he was scheming with Bruce to take over – sell out, even. And she was obsessive about it – her father's memorial, she called it. I don't know any more than that but,' he bowed his head, 'it's worried me dreadfully. She's not reliable in her present state, you know . . .'

'I see,' Strang said. 'And have you told DC Murray about your movements on the dates we are interested in?'

'Oh yes,' he said with another smile at Murray. 'She'll tell you I'm in the clear – isn't that what you say? A good number of sea miles between me and the scene of the crime – though I'm uncertain as to exactly where that might have been?'

Strang ignored that. 'That's all for the moment, then, Mr Ross. If we could speak to your wife now . . . ?'

'Oh no,' Ross said firmly. 'I'm afraid that won't be possible. She's still suffering badly from the after-effects of concussion and you would have to get consent from Dr Sinclair before you could be allowed to see her.'

For the first time Strang showed his teeth. 'You can stall, Mr Ross, but that interview will have to take place shortly. I will arrange for a doctor to examine her.'

'Of course. I understand that. I have tried to be as helpful as I can.' He gave Murray another of the smiles she had begun to find seriously creepy.

'I appreciate your cooperation.'

As they got back into the car Murray gave a shudder. 'What a scumbag! But we haven't got anything against him, have we?'

'Not a scrap of actual evidence. But trust me – we're going after him. I've to be back for the press statement but the first thing you have to do is check his alibis. Meantime there's something I want to look at.'

'The loch? Back towards the village, then, looking for a track off to the left, yes?'

Strang shook his head. 'That's where he wants us to go.

He was so explicit that I would bet it was meant to mislead us. Drive on towards the old drainage works. I want to see if there's any sign of a shorter way up through the bogs.'

Ross had been sweating. Once they had gone the sweat dried and he felt so cold that his teeth were chattering, and his legs felt shaky as he stood up. There was brandy in the kitchen; he needed it now.

Not too much, though. He needed his head clear and he needed reassurance and advice. He'd have to drive – he didn't dare use his mobile. They were on his trail and they would have a tap on that any minute now. He'd started out that interview so confident and yet somehow without his realising it, a net had been woven to trap him. They'd need hard evidence, though, and he thought frantically back over what they might be able to prove.

Not a lot, he thought. One phone call to Niall, that he could easily say had come from Gabrielle – nothing else. With his trouble-shooting job he was working on his own with no records kept so no one would be able to say exactly when he was offshore – and when he wasn't.

Gabrielle was the weak link. They'd agreed that pressure could be applied gradually; it was getting too late for that now. He scribbled a loving note to leave on the table with an excuse about going to the shop in case she came downstairs and then he left.

It was little more than half a mile to the workings from the Rosses' house. The rain had come on again, heavy, sullen rain that soaked into the ridges and filled up the drains below. The two detectives got out of the car and Murray went round to open the back.

'We'll need gumboots. Will these do for you? They're Taylor's.'

Strang looked ruefully at his shoes – solid enough, but certainly not waterproof. 'I'd better try,' he said, sitting on the edge of the seat and with some difficulty forced his feet in. 'Hope we don't have a long walk to do.'

They went through the gates into the yard. The equipment they had seen before was still there in the mesh cages, the padlocks still in place. Strang walked over to it, looking with particular interest at a small vehicle with caterpillar tracks, not much more than a cabin on wheels.

'I'll get someone down to take a good look at that,' Strang said. 'I think things are beginning to fall into place.'

'She'd be the one with the padlock keys, wouldn't she?' Murray said. 'Maybe Ross wasn't just trying to dump her in it.'

'Yes, maybe.' Strang sounded abstracted as he walked out of the yard area and a little further back down the road. Then he stopped and pointed. 'That's what I was looking for,' he said.

She joined him. There was a small path, just beaten-down earth and barely noticeable, not more than a couple of feet wide, leading directly into the bog and she followed Strang as he set off along it. It was solid enough at first, but after a few yards it degenerated into oozy mud; there were signs of where the track went, but it was a question of picking your way from one hummock to the next and choosing the most solid-looking patches of scrubby grasses in between.

It all looked very different from the way it had been on the hot and sunny day when she had come with Taylor. The insect life was mercifully absent and the stench of rotting plants too, but in this weather the dubh lochs were deepest black, and all colour seemed to have gone from the vegetation. Even the white flags of the bog-cotton were flat and sodden, and the banks of heather looked grey. What a bleak, sinister place this was!

Strang was striding ahead and seemed to have a better sense of balance than she did. Her hands were muddy and sore and red with the cold from saving herself as she slipped and slid, with only sharp reeds and prickly shrubs to grab on to. Little streams ran everywhere, often half-hidden by an overhang that would crumble under her feet. It was the sound that demoralised her when she missed the solid ground, a greedy, gulping sucking noise as if the bog was a living thing, ready to drag her down to her destruction, and she had to fight to quell the feelings of panic. She gave a little scream once, when the mud held her boot so firmly that her foot slipped out and only Strang coming back with a steadying hand stopped her falling over to lie at its mercy.

It seemed to be going on for ever. This place was a hell on earth, but she wasn't going to whinge, no matter how miserable she felt. And at least there was something a bit more like a path now as the ground rose up towards the moor. Strang had gone ahead again and he was standing at the top waiting for her. 'Look!' he said, pointing to the small loch that lay ahead of them.

He didn't seem dispirited by the conditions. His face was alight with satisfaction as he said, 'It's all starting to add up.'

'Is it?' she said bleakly, and he laughed.

'Shall we go back down the track Ross wanted us to take in the first place? It should be quicker and certainly easier.' He was taking out his mobile as he spoke. 'I'm just going to ask the super to send in forensics. We're on our way.'

CHAPTER TWENTY-FIVE

For DCI Strang the toughest part of the press conference in the incident room at Forsich was having to watch DI Hay smirking as he claimed credit for the speedy arrest of Morven Gunn. The rest was routine enough; the more aggressive representatives of the media obviously hadn't fancied the long journey north and the questions asked were anodyne. It had achieved its objective, though, with DI Hay only too eager now to be associated with the murder investigation. JB should be pleased.

PR and spin was such a waste of his time, especially when he thought that at last he had the shape of the case clear in his mind – though he must be on guard against the temptations that presented. He only *thought*, he didn't *know*. Say ten times, 'I could be wrong, I could be wrong.'

His mind was on the interview with Bruce Michie in Aberdeen that might be taking place even now. It had sounded as if Steve MacLean was planning to go straight there so he should hear back before too long. At times during the conference he had looked across, too, at DC Murray, who was busy at a computer terminal; he saw her talking earnestly on the phone, though he couldn't hear what she was saying. As she finished the call she caught his eye and gave him a grin and a thumbs-up. With impressive restraint he waited until DI Hay could be persuaded to abandon the scene of his triumph.

At last he could go across and say, 'Well?'

'Ross's alibi doesn't stack up. They're vague about when he was actually working on the rig, but they have to keep a record of passengers on the choppers. He wasn't offshore at all over the weekend when Aitchison was killed. He was on the rig the night the body was put in the cottage, right enough. But on the Tuesday when he heard it had been found, he told you he couldn't get off the rig until Thursday – that was a lie. He went ashore on the Wednesday morning.'

Strang felt a glow of satisfaction. 'Oh yes,' he said. 'Closing in. Anything else?'

'There's a report in from Wick – DC Wilson. Just gives the details of the search this morning. Nothing much there.'

'Right. According to the super, we should have guys up here later this afternoon. I'll have to show them to the site but then I can leave them to follow the path we went up to look for evidence.'

'Ooh, that'll be a treat for them,' Murray said feelingly.

She was probably unaware that she still had a smear of mud under her chin. Strang grinned. 'And you bear the scars to this day,' he said, indicating.

She felt her chin, took out a tissue and spat on it. She was scrubbing at it when Strang's phone rang. He glanced at the number and nodded to her.

'Steve! Good. How did you get on?'

His responses were mainly confirmatory noises until he said, 'Great! And you'll get a signed statement, yes? Thanks, Steve. I owe you one.'

He was smiling as he turned to Murray. 'Could hardly be better. Bruce Michie will testify that the person who joined his little party at the fishing hotel was David Ross and that he was in favour of selling off Curran Services to Brady. The minute we get the SOCOs sorted we go round there and bring him in for questioning. And this time he's not going to tell me I can't speak to his wife.'

Lilian Sinclair was in the sitting room trying not to chew her immaculately manicured nails when she saw David Ross's car pull up in front of the house. She jumped up and went to greet him.

He was looking pale and agitated. 'Where is he?' he said.

'Out at Rotary. My darling, what's the matter? You look awful!'

'Go through to the kitchen. Is Fran around?'

'Oh, upstairs in her flat, wallowing in self-pity,' she said as they walked across the hall. 'But, David, what's the matter? You're scaring me. My heart's racing.'

'So well it might be.' He slumped into a chair at the kitchen table. 'We're in trouble, sweetheart.'

'What – what sort of trouble?'

'Police. I've just met DCI Strang. There's something

frightening about the man – that scar on his face, the hard eyes. Menacing. And he knows. He asked if I'd gone fishing with Niall. I denied it, of course, but he didn't believe me.'

'He can't do anything, though,' Lilian protested. 'There's no evidence. You weren't seen with Niall that day – no one knows you were even here.'

'Gabrielle does. And he's determined to question her – I'm not going to be able to stall much longer. Do you trust her not to give way once he starts on her?'

'No,' she said slowly. 'No, I wouldn't. She didn't even tell you about moving the body.'

'Still hasn't. She just goes silent when I bring the subject up. I can't think why she did that, unless she's planning to drop me in it. God, I was so unlucky that bloody policewoman came by when she did! She'd be dead by now, with Morven Gunn on a charge of murder.'

Lilian had gone white to the lips. 'So, what are we going to do?'

Ross gave her a long, cool look. 'What do you think we're going to do?'

She put a hand to her throat. 'Oh, David . . .'

'It's not a lot different from driving her to kill herself, is it, and we've been trying to do that ever since we realised what she'd done with the body.' Lilian made a little, dissenting movement and he went on savagely, 'Oh, you just as much as me. If she'd apparently done idiotic things only when I was there she'd have worked it out sooner or later – she's not stupid. And your suggestion about the scan was masterly – I really think if we had time to wait she'd oblige us. But frankly, we don't.'

400

'Oh – this is awful!' Tears came to her eyes and at the sight of them he leant forward to smooth them away with his thumb.

'My love, we've known where this would end. We were neither of us the "all-for-love-and-the-world-well-lost" types. You certainly weren't ready to give up your cushy number with Mogadon Man and Gabrielle was a pretty good meal ticket for me. Once Pat died and she was all that stood between us and our wonderful life together, there was only one solution.'

'Yes, but that was suicide, not—'

'Not murder?' He laughed. 'Sweetie, don't develop scruples now! We're just talking semantics.'

'Can't we just wait a little bit? You said yourself—'

His voice sharpened. 'No! We can't. He's out there, making contacts, asking questions. I've laid the groundwork for saying she killed Niall and if she's killed herself it backs that up.'

Lilian's mouth was dry. 'What – what are you going to do?'

'What she'd do herself – the small knife, you know? But obviously I'll have to dope her first. Have you any more temazepam liquid? I've used up what you gave me.'

'I picked up a bottle last week on the repeat prescription for my "insomnia".'

'Get it, then.'

He watched her hesitate with cold eyes. Would she baulk at delivering up her daughter for execution? The jealousy ran deep – Gabrielle was the usurper who had taken her mother's place in Pat Curran's affections, after all – but she'd taken care before to hold herself apart from the distasteful side of their operations.

Lilian had been standing near the door. Now she came across to him. 'Hold me, David. I need your strength.'

He stood up and took her in his arms. 'And I need yours. We're in this together,' he said, as he had said to Gabrielle only a couple of hours before.

'We're doing this for us,' she said. 'I'll fetch it.'

Ross sat down again, and his mouth twisted in a little, ironic smile. What was that phrase – useful idiot? Did she really think that once he had Gabrielle's money that he would tie himself down with an ageing wife, no matter how accomplished she might be in bed? He just had to make sure that she was fully implicated in this, however reluctant she might be. Her prints would be on the bottle. Along with Gabrielle's, of course.

He took it from her, only touching the cap, and slipped it into his pocket. 'Right. Now don't phone me – they may have it tapped.'

She gave a little cry of fright at the thought. 'Will they know we've—'

'They're not the morality police. They won't tell Malcolm. I'm going now.'

She went with him to the front door. 'I'm scared, David – so scared.'

Ross gave a bright, confident smile. 'Stay strong, sweetheart. It's an awful thing to have to do, I know, but keep thinking about our future, of what we've always dreamt of.' He swept her into a passionate embrace and then he was gone.

Above them, on the top landing, Francesca Curran had just come out of her flat and hearing the voices looked over the banister. She listened then stared in blank astonishment, putting up her hand to cover her gasp of horror, and retreated into the shadows on the upper floor.

Gabrielle Ross heard David's car drive away and got up hastily. She'd no idea where he would be going – the shops, perhaps? – but she suspected he wouldn't be long. He'd been fussing over her like a mother hen and she'd need to take her chance now to track down the knife. The trouble was that it could be anywhere; the last time she'd seen it had been when Lilian brought it out of the downstairs bathroom, that shaming occasion. At the time, she'd slotted it back into the knife box with a nonchalance she didn't feel, but she couldn't be sure it was still there.

In the kitchen she found his note and the knife was indeed where it should be. She picked it up and carried it back to the bedroom and stared at it for a moment, then tested the blade gingerly with her thumb. Bright beads of blood appeared instantly down the tiny slit. It stung, and she sucked at it, screwing up her face at the odd, metallic taste.

It might be easier to do it right now, instead of thinking too much about it. The cuts she'd self-inflicted had been painful yet somehow satisfying: would the much larger cuts she had in mind be as therapeutic? She knew enough to know that the slashes must go down the length of her arm and not across; knew too, that warm water dulls pain. She thought of lying there in the bath, watching as the water turned into a pool of deepening red around her, and without warning she gagged, thought for a moment she was going to vomit. She crumpled onto the bed, feeling dizzy.

But, of course, she couldn't do anything now. For a start, David could come back at any minute and find her and drag her back and it would all be to do again. And she needed to prepare for it properly, with painkillers and alcohol carefully judged so that when the agonising moment arrived she was all but insensible already. And she wanted to leave a note for David, too, explaining that this was a loving, not a cruel decision. And . . .

Coward. The word came to Gabrielle's mind so forcefully that she thought she'd spoken it aloud. She craved oblivion, but she was afraid of the pain, afraid of the fear itself that would strike as she made the irrevocable decision. Yet if she hadn't the courage to do it, she would be condemned to dying by inches, getting more frightened and lost day by day as her rational mind shrank away to nothing.

And what about the glorious freedom she had felt at the certainty of no future – no present, even? The terrible thoughts came crowding back into her mind, their restless fluttering like the beating leather wings of bats pouring out of the hell that was her present life. As if to protect herself, she fell back on the bed, curled up into the foetal position.

'Hello?' That was David's voice, and she heard the front door shut. 'Are you still in bed?' He was coming upstairs.

She sat up abruptly and her eye went to the little knife, lying there on the bedside table. In a swift movement she swept it into the drawer just before the bedroom door opened.

He looked at her lovingly. 'How are you feeling, sweetheart?'

Gabrielle hardly knew what to say. 'As well as can be expected, I suppose,' she managed eventually, with a wry smile. What she didn't want was a long discussion. 'Tired and headachy.'

David nodded sympathetically. 'I'm going to bring you up a cup of tea. And the reason I went in to the village was to fill a prescription they gave me at the hospital – said to give it to you in four hours so it's about that now.'

'Oh, right,' she said listlessly. She couldn't be bothered to ask what it was; another sedative, probably, and at least that would put off thinking for another few hours.

When he came back up with the tray, it was obvious he'd made an effort. It wasn't just a mug with a tea bag; this was a little teapot with a matching cup and saucer she hadn't used for years and a pretty plate with biscuits. Touchingly, he'd even picked a rose from the scrubby bush by the kitchen door and put it in a small vase.

He held up a little glass from the tray, half-full. 'Get that down you and then have some tea and a biscuit to take the taste away,' he said.

Gabrielle sat up and squinted at it. 'That looks quite a lot,' she said.

'Same as a couple of pills, probably. Looks more because it's a liquid. Down the hatch! Well done, sweetie. Can you manage a biscuit?'

To please him, she took one and nibbled at it.

'Now, here's your tea. It's a special one – I had some on the rig and brought a few tea bags home because I liked it. What's it called – redbush or something?'

She sipped it cautiously, then made a face. 'Tastes a bit funny.'

'Full of antioxidants, or something. Terribly good for you.' Then, as she still hesitated he said, 'Oh dear, don't you like it? I thought it would be a nice change.'

'Yes, it's fine,' she said, taking another mouthful. 'Now I've got used to it.'

David smiled at her. 'I'm going to wait till you've finished and then you probably want to shut your eyes again. It's been a helluva day for you one way and another.'

'Yes,' she said. 'Oh yes.'

It was a relief once she finished it and he went out with the tray. She was feeling sleepy; she lay down and snuggled into her pillows. Sleep was her only friend just now.

Francesca sat down with such a plump that the little mushroom-pink button-backed chair almost toppled and she had to save herself from falling to the floor. She hated that chair; it wasn't her choice, it was Lilian's, like everything else in this sickly twee flat with its pale grey walls and rose-pink curtains and cushions. There was nothing of Francesca herself here; she'd let her mother overrule her choices at every stage. She'd allowed Lilian to smother her to the point where she had no life at all, except as an adjunct to her mother.

And this was what had been going on. She'd thought that until Gabrielle came along David was visiting the house because of her, that Gabrielle was to blame for taking him away from her almost as an exercise in spite. So, had it been Lilian all the time; Lilian, whom she'd defended so fiercely against Gabrielle's accusations of betrayal when she'd left their father? And now here she was doing the same to poor deluded Malcolm, who worshipped the ground she walked on.

But she and David hadn't gone off together. Lilian liked her status as the doctor's wife as well as the financial security and David certainly didn't make a lot of money in his job. He owed his lifestyle to Gabrielle, just the way Lilian did to Malcolm.

And Gabrielle had more money now – much more. It still hurt to think about Niall's legacy, but the pain came from wounded pride. She'd known perfectly well that Niall wasn't really interested – known too that she wasn't interested in him as a person, only as a symbol of some kind of validation.

David was different. Her heart had always fluttered when he gave her that special smile and his blue eyes softened. She felt hot shame as she remembered what she'd thought when she still didn't know if her sister was alive or dead. He'd smiled at her then and for a moment she'd let herself dream—

That rotten bastard! How many times had Francesca seen him and Lilian talking intimately together, believing they were talking about Gabrielle's problems? Often – and then there were Lilian's trips to Aberdeen for charity committee meetings too – were they just a cover for trysts with David?

And what was the 'awful thing' he'd been talking about? What would happen now to poor Gabrielle, so lost and broken? Jealousy had become her own default setting where her sister was concerned, but when she'd seen her so pitiful today, frightened and in tears, it had reminded Francesca that they hadn't always been adversaries. Oh, they'd had their spats – what sisters didn't? – but it was the break-up that had forced them to choose sides. If Gabrielle went with

Pat, she had to choose to stay with Lilian. Philip Larkin was right about parents and what they did to you.

So, what was she to do now? Given her strained relations with Gabrielle, going to tell her what was going on might be seen as troublemaking – gloating, even. But she couldn't pretend she hadn't seen that obscene embrace and Gabrielle had a right to know that the 'mothering' that Lilian had done so much of lately was a mockery.

She got up with sudden decision. She didn't know where David had gone – home, perhaps, to look after his sick wife with his usual cossetting? The thought made her feel sick. The back door was never locked; she could slip into the house unseen and wait till she could get her sister alone. Then, if Gabrielle liked, they could confront him together.

With sudden decision she got up and walked out of the flat.

Lilian didn't know what to do with herself. Mercifully Malcolm would be out for the next hour or so because she didn't think she'd be strong enough to put on a convincing act of normality. In fact, she couldn't imagine how she'd do it even in an hour's time. She went into the sitting room and sat down, trying to keep calm when what she really wanted to do was scream and scream. She couldn't even let herself cry; red and swollen eyes would be hard to explain away.

She hadn't thought it would come to this. She had become adept over the years at shutting out of her mind anything that was uncomfortable to think about and she could pretend that the little things she did – the lies about arrangements, the moving around of domestic objects, even the suggestive placing of the knife – were just a kind of practical joke.

Her present torment was all her daughter's fault. She'd been coldly, cruelly angry when Lilian had told her about the divorce. She'd even called her a whore: 'You don't love Malcolm!' she'd cried. 'You're just doing it for his money because Dad's going bust.'

'It's you broke up this marriage!' she'd screamed at her. 'You always had to come first – you had to come between us. Pat talks to you, not me.'

'That's because the only time you talk to him is when you want more money and he hasn't got it just now and you make him feel bad about that. But believe me, he'll succeed. He's clever – he'll move on from this and he'll make far more than Malcolm ever will. You'll regret what you've done.'

And she had, too. It had been intolerable to see Pat prosper, along with the daughter who'd humiliated and rejected her. She'd never, never forgive her for that. Gabrielle had sown the seeds of hatred and it was her own fault that they had grown into this.

Lilian got up to pace around, twisting her hands together. She must stop thinking about the next hour or two, think instead about what would come later, think instead about the dream: the little house in Umbria with an olive grove. She loved Italy; she'd always felt it was her spiritual home. Pat, however wealthy he was, would never have agreed – sophistication wasn't his thing – and Malcolm thought an occasional week's holiday in a good hotel was enough.

But David – he was different. From the moment they'd met they'd known: this was the real thing. They had the same tastes, the same aspirations – yes, even the same faults. They'd both tried poor when they were young and rich was better – much, much better. Now it was within their grasp if they were clever and brave and patient. David's task was the hard one; all she had to do was keep calm and act the way a fond mother should.

She hadn't shut the door and now she saw Francesca coming quickly down the stairs and breathed a sigh of relief that she hadn't decided to come down quarter of an hour ago.

'Hello, Fran,' she called. 'Going out?'

Francesca turned and there was a look on her face that Lilian had never seen before – loathing, contempt. She came quite slowly across the hall and confronted her.

'I saw the two of you. It was obscene. You're a disgusting person.' She drew back her hand and slapped her mother hard across the face. 'That's for Gabrielle. I'm going to tell her now.'

She whirled out of the front door and slammed it behind her. A moment later Lilian heard her car leaving in a scatter of gravel.

Lilian turned white so that Francesca's fingermarks stood out red on her cheek. She could hardly breathe from shock as her world fell apart about her.

There was only one thought in her head – to warn David. She ran through to the kitchen to fetch her phone then remembered – he'd forbidden her to use it. How far would he have got with his plan by now? What if Francesca—

No, that mustn't happen. She must follow her, talk her down, try to persuade her that what she saw had been just a sudden impulse, while she was comforting him about his worries over Gabrielle. Yes, that would do, provided she got there in time.

She found her keys and ran to the car.

CHAPTER TWENTY-SIX

DCI Strang was getting irritated. 'I thought they'd have got here by now. I suppose there must have been some sort of hitch, but it would have been helpful if they'd let me know. I've better things to do.'

'Like bringing in David Ross,' DC Murray said. 'Have we enough to charge him, boss?'

He shook his head. 'Enough to rattle his cage but that's all. Can't see him breaking down and confessing, can you? We have to hope forensics can come up with something from that path through the bog – so far that's only a theory. And now I'm stuck here till we've shown them where to find it.'

'What do you want me to do meantime?'

Strang glanced round. 'There's the tea trolley. See if you can blag me a sandwich and a cup of tea – I think it's marginally better than the coffee.'

'Only marginally,' she said darkly. 'Right, boss.'

As she went to do it he clicked on the computer, hoping

something new might have come in but he was disappointed. The report from DC Wilson about the investigation that morning was there, though. He hadn't read it himself, so he might as well check what they had done.

He was skimming it when something caught his eyes. He stopped, went back and read it again. Was that significant, given what they knew now?

'Livvy, tell me something,' he said as she came back with the tray.

David Ross looked at his watch. How long would it take for the dose to act? Not long, considering how much he'd given her on top of the stuff she'd had last night in the hospital. And he didn't want to leave it too long in case she just vomited it up again – you could never be sure that the system wouldn't rebel. Time was too short to allow for a botched attempt.

He checked what he was taking upstairs for the third time. The temazepam bottle with Lilian's prints on it, that if all went well could be explained by Gabrielle having taken it from her mother's medicine cabinet; the cap wiped, ready to have Gabrielle's fingers clasped round it. The glass that held it, polished clean now, to be left at her bedside with her prints only. The knife—He couldn't find the smallest one – ironic, really, if Gabrielle herself had started moving it about and putting it in odd places. The next size would do: it would have his prints on it but that was reasonable as long as the final grip was Gabrielle's.

Yes, it was all in place. He felt powerful, in control; whatever suspicions the police might have, suspicions weren't proof and once Gabrielle was dead he was safe.

Time to go.

Francesca Curran drove fast down the narrow road. She hadn't a clear plan in her head, except to tell Gabrielle what she needed to know. She didn't want a confrontation with David before that; it would definitely be better to talk to her sister before he realised she was there. She parked the car on the side of the road and walked the hundred yards or so to the back gate. If he was in the sitting room she'd be spotted but there was no sign of him there and she went round to the back of the house.

She pressed herself to the wall as she worked her way round to the kitchen window and peered in; no, he wasn't there either. With infinite caution she turned the handle of the back door and let herself in; so far so good. There was a tray with a teapot and cup – and a vase with a rose in it. She felt furious at the hypocrisy. Gabrielle was presumably upstairs in bed; she'd looked so ill this morning.

Where was he, though? Up at her bedside, pretending to be the devoted husband? Francesca tiptoed out into the hall and listened. There was no sound of voices. He'd obviously brought the tray back down after giving her the tea and the door to the office was shut. That was promising. As silently as she could she went upstairs, keeping to the edge of the treads; she remembered from her childhood that they creaked when you went up the middle.

She tapped on the door and opened it. 'Gabrielle?'

David Ross was standing by the side of the bed, holding Gabrielle's limp wrist. He had a knife in the other hand.

Gabrielle's mouth was open, and she was drooling; there was a thin rim of white showing below her eyelids and her breathing was slow and laboured. Francesca screamed.

The shock made him drop the knife with a stream of obscenities. 'You fool!' he screamed. 'Have you any idea what you've done?'

'Saved my sister's life,' she said with more bravery than she felt. 'And I'm calling the police.' She was groping in her bag for her phone as she ran out of the room, but he moved fast. He was on her; she shrieked as he grabbed her by the hair and pulled her back into the room.

He was beside himself with rage, spittle forming at the corners of his mouth. 'It's bad enough, what I've been forced to do already. But your idiocy—' He looked at the knife on the floor, then from her to Gabrielle.

Francesca didn't really believe it. This couldn't be happening to her. It was too crazy. He was shaking her by the hair so that she couldn't think properly, she could only shudder convulsively and wail in pain. She hadn't known fear like this existed.

A car drew up outside. Ross froze; a moment later the front door was thrown open and Lilian's panicky voice called, 'David! Where are you?'

Francesca yelled, 'Mum! Mum, help me!'

As Lilian's footsteps pounded up the stairs Ross swung her round so that her head came into violent contact with the doorpost. She saw stars, then collapsed.

Lilian burst into the room, then stopped. 'Oh my God, David, what have you done?'

* * *

415

Murray squinted over Strang's shoulder at the screen. 'Seen something, boss?'

'I might have,' he said slowly. 'Livvy, I want you to talk me through exactly what happened after you arrived at Ross's house last night.'

Puzzled, she took him through it again. When she said, 'He was in shock,' he said, 'Stop there. How did you know?'

'He was swaying, shaky on his feet. Said he was cold.' She sounded a little defensive.

'So, you went to make tea. How long did it take?'

She shrugged. 'I had to boil the kettle. And he wanted brandy – took me another minute or two to find that.'

'And when you came back he was sitting beside his wife, at the fireside?'

'Yes, that's right. What do you mean?'

'I may be making too much of this but the thing that leapt out at me from Wilson's report was that she'd found prints on everything she'd tested – apart from the poker beside the fire.'

Comprehension dawned. 'Smudges,' she said. 'It had been wiped.'

'Maybe Hay wasn't so wrong after all – maybe that was what saved Gabrielle's life.'

'You think Morven attacked her, knocked her unconscious, but didn't hit her afterwards? And he saw his opportunity – but why would he want to kill his wife?'

'The same reason that he doesn't want us to speak to her. She knows something. And he knows that I'm going to insist on speaking to her any time now. She could be in serious danger.' He got up. 'Forensics are going to have to wait.'

Lilian Sinclair had begun to shriek, 'What have you done? What have you done?'

She was working herself into hysteria. David Ross, his jaw taut with rage, stepped across and slapped her on the cheek where the marks of Francesca's slap still lingered.

Shocked more than hurt, she stopped with a gasp. Until earlier today she had never been struck in anger and she burst into tears. 'You hit me!'

He was grasping his hands into fists in an effort to control himself. The stupid bitch had ruined everything. It took a superhuman effort of will to sound reassuring as he said, 'Darling, I had to. You were hysterical. It's all right now. Let's calm down and you can listen to me.'

'But look at them, David!' She gestured to Gabrielle, ashen grey and breathing stertorously now; to Francesca, unconscious on the floor. 'We've got to get help—'

'No!' His voice was like a whip crack. Then he softened it. 'My love, we have to be realistic. Yes, we're in a bad mess – this shouldn't have happened.' He put his arms round her and she allowed herself to be escorted to a settle that stood in the window. 'Sit down here beside me. I'll explain what we're going to do, and it will be all right.'

'How can it be?' She sobbed.

'Just listen.' His voice was hard again, and she recoiled but didn't speak. 'Gabrielle is unstable. Everyone knows that. Malcolm will vouch for it, and her head injury tipped her over the edge. She and Francesca have been at daggers drawn for years. Something went wrong – a row over Niall, perhaps? Something like that – we can work out the details of what to suggest later. Gabrielle goes for her with the knife she's been using lately to let out her frustrations – like slashing the towels, OK? – and she kills her, then takes the sedative she's stolen from you and kills herself.

'It would only take minutes and we can be back at Westerfield House before Malcolm even gets back from lunch. Once I've spoken to him I come back here and make the terrible discovery.' It was amazing what you could do when you were under pressure. Not many people would have the brains to come up with a scenario like this on the spot. He went on, 'So you see, my sweetheart, it won't really have changed anything.'

Ross gave Lilian that special smile, the one she had always told him melted her heart. But she wasn't melting this time. She was staring at him, her face a mask of horror.

'I think you must be mad,' she said. 'And I must have been mad too, to go along with any of this. Are you suggesting that I should stand by and watch you massacre both my daughters?'

Fury rose in him. 'You didn't seem to mind when it was one. And I never realised you were so fond of Francesca, either. You've always been scathing about how pathetic she is.'

'But for God's sake, that doesn't mean I wanted to kill her! David, we have to—' She got up, but he pulled her back down.

'Oh no,' he said. 'We don't have to. I'll tell you what – you can choose. Gabrielle killed her sister, or she killed her sister and her mother. It's up to you.'

He jumped to his feet and in two strides was across the room, picking up the knife he had dropped. As Lilian sat, frozen with shock, he came across holding it.

'You – you won't get away with it!' she stammered. 'They'll know you did it.'

Ross paused, looking down at the knife in his hand. 'I suppose they might. But this way, there's a chance they might not. And I was always a risk-taker, wasn't I? All right, Lilian – crunch time. Which way is it going to be?'

DCI Strang reached the narrow road towards the Rosses' house and slammed his foot down. As a trained police driver he was enjoying the exhilaration of the challenge, taking the exact angle into the first corner that would get him round at maximum speed while still setting up the car for whatever might be there beyond. It was only when he heard DC Murray release her breath that he realised she'd been holding it.

He laughed. 'Relax, Livvy – I know what I'm doing.'

'You may know. I don't,' she said tartly, gripping the arm rest, then gasped again as a car appeared, holding the middle of the road. With smooth competence Strang steered the car past with two wheels on the verge and then back onto the road, barely dropping his speed. He caught a glimpse of the terrified face of the other driver; that might teach him to keep to his own side in future.

They were passing Fergus Mowat's farm now. It wasn't a lot further to the house, and Strang suddenly slowed down. There was a Peugeot 108 parked a couple of hundred yards back, and there was an Audi A3 right by the front gate.

'I saw both those cars parked outside Westerfield House,' Murray said.

'Yes. Francesca Curran's and Lilian Sinclair's, I guess. Natural enough that they'd have come to see Gabrielle. That's a relief – I needn't have scared the living daylights out of you after all.'

'Me scared? Nah. I was nearly beginning to enjoy it. Nearly.'

He drew in to park just in front of the Peugeot and they got out. 'If it's possible, I want to see Gabrielle first. If Ross puts up resistance, I slam him with the false alibi while you phone for the police doctor to come and see whether she's fit to be interviewed. Right?'

'Right, boss,' she said as they walked up to the front door. She had just raised her hand to knock when Strang said sharply, 'Wait. Listen. Is that a woman crying?'

She could hear it too, coming from the front room upstairs. Then the voice rose sharply to a scream. 'No! No! David, you can't!'

They were both off and running, Strang in front taking the stairs three at a time. He flung open the door on a scene of horror: a barely conscious woman on the bed, a woman on the floor with her eyes closed, but stirring; a white-faced woman on the settle by the window.

And David Ross, swinging round with a knife in his hand, his face black with rage.

'Put down the knife, Ross,' Strang said coolly.

Murray was calling in backup as she came in and following his lead went very calmly to kneel beside Francesca, who had opened her eyes and was looking bewildered. Gabrielle,

420

though, looked bad, her breathing little more than a rattle in her throat.

Ross grabbed hold of Lilian and yanked her to her feet, holding her to him with his arm across her neck and the knife touching her throat. 'Back off, Strang. Let me go or I use this.'

'Go where? The road has two ends; we've just blocked one end and the other end will be blocked long before you reach it. Harm Mrs Sinclair and they throw away the key.'

Ross had been glaring defiance at Strang; his head dropped for a moment, but then he straightened up, squaring his shoulders. Lilian was standing still in his grasp, barely breathing.

'Oh, I know what this looks like, Inspector,' he said with a weak smile. 'The thing is, I heard a sound upstairs and when I came in Francesca had this knife in her hand, just about to kill her sister. I wrestled it from her and she fell and hit her head. I admit I stupidly panicked when you came in, but Lilian will tell you that was how it was.'

This was a man so overconfident that he still thought he was smart enough to get himself out of this. Should Strang pretend to go along? He didn't believe that would work, with Ross still holding the knife at Lilian's throat. Sap his confidence, then, show him how his so-clever planning had let him down, show how heavily the odds were stacked against him? It was a big decision. He judged Ross had not yet tipped into the unreason that overpowers self-interest, but it was close. He distributed his weight so that if it went wrong he could launch himself instantly, watching with an ex-soldier's eye for the muscle twitch that precedes violent action.

Strang laughed. 'Oh, you're good, David. But your problem is the mistakes you've made already. Shall I tell you what they are? Could be useful in future, once you've put this behind you.'

Ross was listening, anyway. He hadn't moved the knife away but Strang could tell that it was being held in a looser grip. In the background, he was aware that Francesca had sat up and that Murray had her arm round her, quietly shushing her as he went on, 'The alibi, for a start – you thought you could say what you liked about when you were working on the rig because you don't clock in or off, but they do record passengers on the choppers – you should really have thought of that, shouldn't you? The devil is in the detail, you see.'

That went home. Ross blinked, as if confused, and Strang went on, 'You weren't altogether wise, either, to rely on other people keeping their mouths shut about your plans for selling off Curran Services – not once murder was involved. And any time now the forensics team will be checking for evidence on the path that goes from the drainage workings up to the loch. Did you remember to wipe your prints off the priest before you threw it away, I wonder?'

From Ross's reaction, Strang could tell that he hadn't. The man's confidence was ebbing away before their eyes.

'Details again.' Strang shook his head. 'And then, of course, the last time you attempted to kill your wife you made another big mistake. You wiped the poker, didn't you, while my constable was out of the room? What was more natural than that there should be your prints on your own poker? You know, David, if it hadn't been for that you

422

might have done whatever it was you planned to do today before we got here. Bad, bad mistake.'

Ross's head started shifting to and fro, like a trapped animal looking for escape. 'No,' he said. 'It's not like that.' The knife drooped, just a little, in his hand.

And Strang was on him, taking his wrist in an iron grip and twisting his arm up behind him, a bit harder than was strictly necessary so that he gave a yell of pain, just as they heard the siren of the approaching patrol car.

Murray was dialling the emergency number. 'Ambulance,' she said. 'Top priority.' She turned to Strang. 'They'd better step on it. Gabrielle's fading.'

CHAPTER TWENTY-SEVEN

She was swimming in deep, deep water, struggling to force her way to the upper air, up and up, striving to break the surface; at last it splintered, she came through it and Gabrielle was awake.

She opened her eyes, trying to make sense of what she saw. The white walls, the narrow bed – she was in hospital. Still? She put her hand to her aching head, felt the raised scarring on her cheek. But why was her throat raw, as if someone had scraped it with sandpaper? She felt muzzy and confused, nauseous too, and her mouth was parched.

She turned her head. Her sister was there, asleep in a high-backed chair. She looked pale and drawn, with dark circles under her eyes. Gabrielle had no idea what time it was; it was full daylight but just now that could still be the middle of the night. She levered herself up cautiously, giving a small, involuntary groan.

Francesca opened puffy eyes. She looked as if she'd been

crying, Gabrielle thought, in a dreamy, detached sort of way. 'Have you been crying?' she said.

Francesca sat up, rubbing the back of her stiff neck and wincing. 'Thank God you've woken up,' she said, though she sounded weary rather than jubilant. 'They did say you'd be all right but lately I've stopped taking things on trust.'

'Right,' Gabrielle said, but hesitantly. She was coming to, a bit, and things weren't adding up. 'Am I still in hospital? I thought I went home, or did I just dream that? I feel hellish – my throat's absolutely raw,' she croaked.

'I suppose it would be.' Francesca got up and poured her a glass of water from the carafe on the bedside table. 'This may help. Yes, they had to pump your stomach out last night. It was touch and go, quite honestly.'

'Pump—?' As she took that in, a feeling of shame washed over her. 'Oh. Did I take an overdose?'

'Not "take". Were given.'

This was making no sense at all. 'Given? Did the hospital get the dosage wrong, or something?'

Francesca shook her head. 'You were at home. Do you not remember?'

Yes, that was right. Of course she was. She remembered – the tea, the rose on the tray. 'Where's David?' she asked.

For some reason, Francesca seemed uncomfortable. 'Detained,' she said.

It was an odd sort of answer – detained where? – but her thoughts had moved on. She was remembering the scan, the Alzheimer's verdict. It had been touch and go, Fran had said; why had they brought her back? Now it would all be to do over again. Tears of weakness and despair came to her eyes.

But Francesca had started crying again. 'Fran, what on earth's wrong?' Gabrielle said, with a hint of impatience.

'Everything! It's so awful.' She took out a tissue, dabbed at her eyes and blew her nose. 'I don't know if I should tell you when you're still so ill.'

The adrenaline rush of fear seemed to clear her brain. 'Nothing could be worse than trying to imagine what you're talking about,' she said with misplaced confidence. 'Tell me.'

Even so, Francesca hesitated. 'It's . . . it's difficult.'

'Get on with it, for heaven's sake!' Gabrielle tried to arm herself. Danger could come from so many different directions.

It came out in a rush. 'I saw David snogging Mum. I came over to warn you what was going on and when I got there, you were unconscious, and he had a knife, just going to slit your wrist. Then he grabbed me and swung my head against the door and I passed out. When I came round the police were there and he was threatening Mum with the knife against her neck. The inspector got it away from him and then more police arrived, and the ambulance took you to hospital. I thought you were going to die.

'They've taken David away, and Mum as well. She knew about it – knew what he was planning to do. They think he murdered Niall too, because they wanted to sell out Dad's firm and Niall wouldn't agree.'

Every word was like a blow to the head. Punch-drunk, Gabrielle heard her own voice saying, 'No, that's not right. Niall was going to sell us out,' and realised that her sister was staring at her in shock.

'You mean – you *knew* about this? Gabrielle—'

The world was disintegrating round her. There was nowhere to go, and since she was doomed anyway, what did it matter? 'Can you tell the police I want to talk to them? Now?' she said.

Francesca got up. 'I think you'd better. I sat up all night at your bedside, afraid my sister would be lost to me as well as my mother. I've been living with monsters and if I never see any of you again it will be too soon.'

'They've been singing like a wee pair of canaries,' DC Murray said to PS Lothian as they sat at one of the tables in the incident room having a mug of tea. 'They were screaming at each other last night when we were arresting them and now in the gospel according to Lilian Sinclair, David's scheme to drive Gabrielle off her head was nothing to do with her. He'd been daft on Lilian herself for years, wanting her to go off with him but naturally she'd never meant to leave her darling Malcolm. If you listen to David Ross, Lilian's hated her daughter all along and the dementia stuff was her idea for getting the money as well as the man. Their briefs keep telling them to shut it but they're so hell-bent on shifting the blame it's been like Glasgow Fair Saturday for us, just having to choose between the Big Dipper and the dodgems.'

'Charming pair,' Lothian said. 'Has he admitted to the murder?'

Murray shook her head. 'Not him. Flatly denies it, knows nothing, his alibi problems are just a bad memory. We'll have to wait on forensics.'

'They're not enjoying it, I can tell you,' Lothian said,

looking out of the window at the teeming rain. 'Came in last night filthy and sodden wet.'

'The weather here's something else. I'll never complain about the wind in Edinburgh again.'

'But the boss must be feeling pretty chirpy, I suppose?'

Murray shook her head. 'Frustrated. One of these people who can't be happy with pretty good – has to be perfect. They're both swearing blind the cottage was nothing to do with them and he believes them. It has to be Gabrielle, and she's off limits.'

'Still don't get why, anyway,' Lothian said.

'Beyond me. My last bright idea about that got shot down in flames.'

Lothian looked at her with interest. 'What's Strang like as a boss?'

Murray thought for a moment. 'I sort of like him all right now. Well, I like him better than I did. He's lightening up a wee bit – I suppose he was walking wounded last year with his wife getting killed in that accident. That's where he got the scar, you know. I'm sure they could fix it up better, but I reckon he wears it like a black armband, so he's got a way to go yet. And I always feel I'm on trial because I really want to get taken seriously.' Then she paused. 'I've screwed up a few times, right enough.'

Lothian smiled. 'Very fair-minded of you.'

'He's mostly fair,' she admitted. 'But he doesn't see I'm more useful than someone without an idea in their head. Wants everything done his way.'

'Ever met a boss who didn't? Come up with a reason why the body was put in the cottage and maybe that'll impress him.'

She shook her head. 'Looked a right eejit last time I tried. No, he's on his own with this one.'

One of the uniformed constables who had been taking calls got up and walked over to the screened-off area where Strang was working.

'Excuse me, sir,' they heard him saying, 'there's a message from the hospital that Mrs Ross wants to speak to you as soon as possible.'

Murray was on her feet before Strang could say, 'Thank you, Constable. Tell them I'm on my way.'

DCI Strang had a nervous fluttering in his stomach as he walked with DC Murray along the hospital corridor to Gabrielle Ross's room. There was so much hanging on this interview, but he had no idea what sort of state the woman would be in. It was promising that she wanted to speak to him, but what did she want to say?

He had little doubt that with the information he now had he could break down any loyalty she might have towards her husband, but he'd no idea what she knew already, and he'd have to tread delicately, given her current fragile state.

'We'll need to take this one slowly,' he told Murray. 'Let her dictate the pace, no rushing in, trying to surprise the evidence out of her because we're impatient to get this tied up – and that's a warning to me as well as you.'

'She's key, though, isn't she?' Murray said. 'And when she hears what that pair have been up to she'll be ready to join the canary choir.'

'We can always hope. This is the room.' Strang tapped on the door and announced them.

Gabrielle Ross was in a truly pitiable state. The bruises from her previous injuries were turning greenish-purple and the scabs Morven Gunn's scratches had left were puckered with dried blood. Her skin had the greyish-olive, greasy pallor that Strang had seen before in overdose survivors. She was sitting propped up on pillows, though, and seemingly composed, but her nervously twisting fingers suggested that it was only by a considerable effort of will.

'You came quickly. Thanks.' Her voice was hoarse, and it looked as if speaking was a painful effort. 'You'd better sit down.'

Strang took the high-backed chair beside the bed and Murray a metal-framed one beside the door. 'Are you feeling well enough to give a statement, Mrs Ross?' he said.

She gave a short laugh, wincing as it hurt her throat. 'You can probably guess how I'm feeling, looking at me. But I've had to do some hard thinking and I need to get this done now. Can you record it, or something? I don't think my voice will hold up for very long.'

Strang nodded to Murray, who took out a small machine and set it up for recording on the table that straddled the bed, then retreated across the room. He sat back, hands folded, without saying anything and after a heavy sigh Gabrielle began to speak.

'There's something I should tell you first. They gave me a scan after I was attacked, and it showed that I have Alzheimer's disease. By the time any case comes to court, you may not be able to rely on my evidence so it's important that I tell you now.'

Strang and Murray exchanged startled glances. 'Sorry

to interrupt you,' he said, 'but I don't think that's right.'

She gave a small, bitter smile. 'Sadly, I'm afraid it is. The doctor told my husband.'

'Giving evidence to us, your husband said that you had become convinced you had the disease, despite his assurances that the scan was clear.'

Gabrielle gasped, her hand going to her mouth. 'He *couldn't*!' she whispered. But then, with a visible effort she sat up straight and when she spoke again there was a steely edge to the husky voice.

'I suppose after what my sister told me today, I shouldn't be surprised. "You've been taken for a fecking sucker," Paddy, my dad, would have said. He'd be ashamed of me – though David fooled him too.

'Paddy was the most important thing in my life and when he died like that I started losing the place. I managed to set the house on fire, and then I lost our baby—' She choked a little on that, but was preparing to force herself on when Strang said gently, 'How did you set the house on fire?'

She sighed. 'I had these stupid hair straighteners. There was a scarf on my dressing table and I must have put them too close to it and forgotten to turn them off and then the curtains caught. I smelt burning and rushed upstairs and the smoke got to me. A neighbour pulled me out but the baby . . . David was so good about it all, so supportive. I felt so guilty.'

There was a constriction in Strang's throat as he saw her distress. Unborn babies were real children to their grieving parents, and he knew all about guilt too. He said quietly, 'Can you be quite sure it was you who left the straighteners on?'

'I'd been using them. I thought I'd put them off, but I couldn't swear to it.' Then she frowned. 'You don't think – oh God! What more has been going on that I didn't understand?'

'We believe that it was Mr Ross's intention to convince you that you had increasingly serious mental problems. We understand that there was a sort of programme to cause you confusion – objects moved, put in strange places, that sort of thing.'

Her brow furrowed as she thought about it. 'But – often it happened when he was away.'

How did you tell someone that her mother hated her enough to want to drive her crazy? As Strang hesitated, Gabrielle saved him the trouble.

'Oh. My mother,' she said bitterly. 'She was in on this, wasn't she? The towels – the little knife—' She didn't explain, just went on, 'That was a hint, I suppose. I was to use it to kill myself – and I almost did. Stupid, or what?'

'You mustn't blame yourself,' Strang said. 'You were under a lot of stress at the time.'

'Oh yes. I was so confused. I even told a friend how sorry I was when David told me that her mother had died, but it was just a dream—' Then she stopped. Her eyes narrowed. 'Or was it? I was convinced he'd said it, but – was that when it all started? The bastard, the total bastard! And I was so grateful for all his "loving care" that I covered for him. Well, I hope your machine is working and I'll carry on as long as my voice holds out.'

She was, indeed, struggling with it but she was sitting bolt upright now, and her eyes were bright and hard. Instead of the battered, betrayed and humiliated victim, Strang saw

432

the tough, able, chip-off-the-old-block that Ailie Johnston had described.

'I want to tell you exactly what happened. That Saturday, David arranged to go fishing with Niall. He wasn't much of a fisherman but he'd Paddy's old stuff and I saw them set off up the path my dad always took. I was pleased David was getting out because he spent so much time fussing over me and it would be nice for him to have male company for a change. I thought I'd make supper for them, but then when I next looked out Niall's car was gone. David hadn't come back so I thought he must be having some luck with the fish. It was a beautiful afternoon and I thought I could go up to the loch and keep him company.'

She stopped to drink some water and coughed to try to clear her throat. Strang realised he was holding his breath. Murray was on the edge of her seat.

The hoarse, rasping voice went on. 'He was there – Niall. He was face down in the bog, and he was dead. Just – dead. I think I screamed. I was sick, certainly. I couldn't bear to look at him, couldn't bear to think what had happened. I fled down that path, falling in the bog, pulling myself out again, crying. When I got back to the house, David was there.

'When he saw the mess I was in, he knew where I'd been, and he just fell apart. He was in a terrible state; they'd had a row because Niall had turned against me and was going to vote with Michie, who wanted to sell the business – Paddy's business, that meant everything to him. It was betrayal, David said, and he'd just lost his temper. He punched Niall and he fell against a stone. He lifted him

433

up, tried to revive him, but he'd been killed outright. It was an awful, horrible accident and now David would go to prison unless I backed him.'

Strang schooled his features to look impassive but even so she wasn't fooled. 'Oh, I can tell what you're thinking. But abstract justice is your job, not mine. Niall was dead, and what was the point of ruining David's life? The accident had only happened because David was so loyal to my father and me, and I owed him.

'He'd left Niall's car at the information centre; it would look as if he'd gone for a walk in the bogland and got lost. That was the story.'

Again, Gabrielle stopped to drink some water. Her voice was getting thready now and she seemed reluctant to go on. Murray was leaning forward and Strang could almost hear her mentally urging, 'Ask her about the cottage, ask her about the cottage!' and he directed a sharp look that dared her to speak. He murmured, 'But then . . . ?'

Gabrielle's head was bowed. 'I-I couldn't just leave him there, rotting away. Even if he had turned traitor, he was my oldest friend, Paddy's only loyal ally. I couldn't sleep at night for thinking about it, kept seeing him there when I closed my eyes. It was as if he was begging me not to abandon him for the scavengers to find – I couldn't bear the thought.'

She didn't know about the ravens, then. He could feel Murray looking at him but Strang didn't meet her eye.

'So, when David went offshore I got out the Bombi – that little tracked vehicle Paddy never managed to sell – and went up to get him and take him across the moor at the back of the cottage. He was – sort of soft and heavy, very heavy—' She gave a shudder. 'But not – well, disgusting, or anything. I wanted him found, you see, buried properly, and if I propped the door open Fergus Mowat would come to check – we all knew he kept an eye on the place. There was even a rug someone had left there to put him on.'

She choked a little, but Strang wasn't sure whether it was emotion or pain from her exertions. She was pale with exhaustion and he reckoned only willpower was keeping her going.

'I didn't really think there was a risk to David. He was so confident no one would be able to link anything to him. And I never told him what I'd done – just wouldn't answer anything he asked.'

Murray could bear it no longer. 'But why the cottage? Why not beside the road, or something?'

That angered her. 'Like – rubbish, you mean? He wasn't rubbish!' Her voice cracked, and she had to cough again. 'It was fitting, somehow. It was my refuge, the cottage. We'd mucked about there as kids and later when everything was going wrong – Paddy's business failing, my mother cheating on him, the family breaking up, all that stuff – I'd escape there to get away. Niall was a lot older, but he'd still come and sit with me for hours and let me talk and talk. He'd be sheltered there, I thought, though the roof's mostly gone now. I owed him, you see, even if—' She broke off. 'But now, of course, from what Francesca said David lied about that too. Niall was still loyal. I shouldn't have doubted him.'

Her voice was fading to a grating whisper now and she was blinking away tears. 'Sorry. Don't think I can talk any more.

Too sore.' She leant back on her pillows and closed her eyes.

Strang got up. 'You've given us all we need, Mrs Ross. Later when you're feeling better we'll bring you the statement to sign.'

Gabrielle opened her eyes again. 'I've just thought – if I don't really have Alzheimer's after all, what will you do to me?' she whispered.

Strang said carefully, 'I'm not going to give you meaningless promises. It's not up to me and there are serious charges that can be brought against you. But there are powerful mitigating factors and your willing cooperation now will stand you in good stead.'

Murray came to stand beside the bed. 'That's the kind of thing you're supposed to say. But I'd bet my next month's wages you'll not get much more than a slap on the wrist.'

Gabrielle smiled uncertainly, and she was asleep before they were out of the room.

'Shouldn't really have said that, should I? Sorry, boss,' Murray said as she walked back to the car.

'You can't help feeling pity for her when you see her like that, with her life destroyed,' Strang said. 'She's remarkably strong, though. She'll fight back. Now let's return to our Mr Ross. I'm going to enjoy taking a wrecking ball to his life.'

At Westbury House, Malcolm Sinclair was in the sitting room when Francesca Curran got back. He had a phone in his hand, there was a pile of papers on the table in front of him and he was grey with tiredness and stress. His air of comfortable self-assurance had deserted him, and he greeted Francesca with relief.

'Thank goodness. I was wondering when you'd come back, Fran. We need to put our heads together and sort out a strategy. Come and sit down and I'll show you the notes I've taken on what the lawyer's said.'

She didn't sit down. 'Not going to ask how Gabrielle is?'

'Gabrielle? They said she'd be fine. No, the important thing is to make sure we leave no stone unturned in your mother's defence.'

'Defence? When she was in on this too?'

He recoiled, as if she'd slapped him. 'What are you talking about, Fran?'

'She was. I was upstairs when they were talking in the hall. He told her – it was "awful", he said and then they were kissing before he went off to kill Gabrielle.'

For a moment he looked shaken but then, in a voice she'd often heard him use to patients who had the effrontery to question some aspect of their treatment, he said, 'Fran, you actually seem to believe this. I can assure you, you're quite mistaken – picked it up wrongly and jumped to conclusions.

'Your mother was allowed to phone me this morning and has explained to me how it was – David was always a problem to her, harassing her, really, but you can imagine how awkward it was with him being her son-in-law and her not wanting to distress Gabrielle when she was so fragile. She just tried to keep him at arm's length as best she could, but he overstepped the mark last night. She'd decided she really had to talk to him about it and thought with Gabrielle in bed that she'd get the opportunity – and then, of course, she stumbled on that dreadful scene. It's outrageous that the police could even take her in for questioning, when she was a sociopath's victim too, being virtually stalked in her own home.'

Francesca shook her head. 'Oh, she's really got you conned, Malcolm. I feel sorry for you. The reason the police detained her was because I told them what I've just told you, and David told them a lot more at the same time. They've been lovers for years. What sort of woman was she, your precious Lilian, that she could not only betray her daughter but agree to have her killed? You might get some sympathy as an injured party but if you defend her you'll look like a fool.'

Sinclair got up. He was much taller than she was and his was an intimidating presence. 'Say another word against your mother, Francesca, and I will demand that you leave this house.'

'You couldn't make me stay.'

He looked nonplussed by the failure of his threat, hardly seemed to understand what she had been saying. 'But this is going to be a hard time for your mother! She'll need your support. She's always relied on you, Fran.'

'Oh yes, relied on using me in the battle against my father since I was a child,' she said. 'My whole life has been contaminated by the pair of them. I don't know where I'm going – somewhere with normal people, I hope. If you've any sense, you'll clear out too.'

'But the lawyer said you could be a character witness—'

She laughed at that. 'I don't think he'd like what I'd say. I'll give it to you, though – you're loyal. We've always valued loyalty in the Curran family. It's been an obsession, really. But you might want to consider where loyalty got poor Niall. Now I'm going to pack.'

Sinclair sat down, his head in his hands for a moment. This was terrible – how would Lilian feel about her daughter's cruel pig-headedness? For a moment he almost wavered – but no, he wasn't even going to consider what she'd said. He picked up his notes, then the phone, and dialled the lawyer's number for the fourth time that morning.

EPILOGUE

Murray arrived back in Edinburgh ahead of DCI Strang and reported in to Angie Andrews, the administrator for the SRCS.

'Flavour of the week, you two are,' Angie said. 'Want a coffee? Might even stretch to a chocolate Hobnob as a reward. When's Strang going to get back?'

Murray sat down as Angie switched on the kettle on top of her filing cabinet. 'Hard to say. He's supervising the interviews along with the local guy – fully paid-up numpty, by the way. Has to make sure he can't screw everything up when he hands over.'

'Got a lot of good coverage in the media so JB's well chuffed. With the arrest they obviously haven't been able to say much but it sounds as if you had a right lot up there.'

'Got half an hour? We've some pretty sick families down here but they were something else. I'm glad to get out – I was getting feart it was maybe infectious. There was something about that place that was sort of weird – the bogs

and everything. Talking of which, how's my pal "Kevlar"?'
She indicated the quotation marks.

'Ah,' Angie said. 'Bit unfortunate, really. Fully recovered,
but he's been suspended.'

'Suspended? What's he done?' she asked, though she had
a feeling she probably knew.

'He was "Me Too"ed. Couple of the FCAs got together
and went to JB. She pounced on him his first day back and
hasn't let him resign until after the disciplinary panel. Gave
him both barrels – you should have seen him when he came
in here snivelling.'

'Wish I had,' Murray said with feeling and Angie raised
an eyebrow.

'Have problems with him?'

'Nothing I couldn't handle. Pathetic, quite honestly,
but he'd a nasty habit of trying to drop you in it whenever
he could.'

'And did he? How did you get on with Strang this time?
You weren't exactly thrilled when I gave you the allocation.'

Murray paused to think. 'He's a good copper. But he
picks you up on everything – it's a bit exhausting. And I still
don't feel I know him much better than I did. Every so often
you get a wee keek at the person but then he goes back to
being all chief inspectorish. It's like he uses that as – well,
armour or something.'

'Interesting,' Angie said. 'But the big question – if I said
you were going with him on another case, would you be
pleased?'

This time she didn't hesitate. 'Oh aye. I'm getting an
education, you see. I'm not wanting to stay a DC all my life.'

Angie laughed. 'Move over JB?'

'You think you're joking,' Murray said. 'Stick around.'

Detective Chief Superintendent Borthwick greeted DCI Strang like a favourite son.

'This is the first decent coverage we've had in the media for weeks. The chief constable's incredibly pleased. I took the opportunity to put in for a rise in the budget.'

Strang looked suitably grateful. 'It was a quirky case – that's what drew their attention. In essence, the murder was a simple business dispute – Ross just wanted to get his hands on the money from the sale of Curran's firm and, with Gabrielle certifiable or dead, Niall Aitchison was all that stood in his way. It was the psychological warfare round about it that was the hideous thing. There'll be more media fuss when it comes out at the trial.'

'When you told me about it, I thought the worst thing of all was the mother's involvement. How could you be a party to something so cruel – your own daughter?'

'There was real hatred there, I think. She was a solipsist – everything was judged by the way it related to her interests. She saw Gabrielle as her rival because of her close relationship with Pat Curran, and again with David Ross, even though it seems she'd encouraged the marriage. She knew he wanted money and there was always the danger that he'd go off with someone else who had it – this kept it all in the family.'

'Can we nail her?'

Strang grimaced. 'To be honest, I doubt it. She's been careful to distance herself right up until the end. The most solid stuff we've turned up was that he was doping Gabrielle's cereal with temazepam – confusion is one of its side effects – and Lilian Sinclair had it on a repeat prescription, which she collected very regularly, but the connection's tricky. Her prints are on the bottle, but she claims he nicked it from her medicine cabinet.

'The other daughter's testimony about her knowing what Ross planned to do is equivocal – a good lawyer could claim Fran had misunderstood what she heard, and Lilian'll certainly have a good one. The husband, bizarrely, is convinced she's done nothing wrong and is pulling out all the stops. As far as cooperating in Ross's delightful little plans for breaking Gabrielle is concerned, I don't think we have a hope of solid evidence – and if we did she could claim they were just practical jokes – not pretty but hardly criminal.'

'I was afraid of that. Still, at least we've got Ross sewn up.'

'Good and proper, you could say. You'll have seen the forensic reports – prints on the weapon and everything, as well as Gabrielle's testimony.'

'How about her? Any indication of the position over conspiracy and moving the body?'

'Depends on the Crown Office and the Fiscal, of course. With her as their star witness in the Ross prosecution I'll be surprised if it isn't a convenient case of insufficient evidence.'

'She's had a lot of punishment already,' Borthwick said. 'I have to say that her justification of covering for Ross was pretty chilling, though. Of course, by that stage she'd been driven to the verge of a mental breakdown, so she wasn't thinking straight – and it's a point her brief will certainly make. Even so . . .'

'I reckon she'd have seen it like that anyway. She thought David had been acting in defence of her beloved Paddy's firm and even if she didn't know it was murder she felt that excused homicide. It was Pat Curran gave her those distorted views – he was in his way almost as unhealthy a parent as her mother was.

'Morven Gunn was another of his victims, too. I can't think she'll be fit to plead – she's a standout for diminished responsibility.'

Borthwick thought about that. 'I'm sure you're right. But what will happen to Gabrielle now? What state is she in?'

'Not great at the moment. But she won't buckle – she gave us a clear, coherent and utterly damning statement within hours of hearing what her mother and her husband had done. I'd place money on her getting back into the firm looking for revenge on her useless partner.'

Borthwick's phone buzzed. 'Oh, I'm due a phone conference. Anything else, Kelso?'

He got up. 'Just a few loose ends to finish off, ma'am. May have to get back up there a couple of times, but we're nearly there.'

She picked up the phone. 'You've got time off when it's over. Make good use of it. Yes, Borthwick here.'

Kelso drove back to the cottage in Newhaven. He enjoyed the full-on nature of his job and when there was no one to come home to, work-life balance didn't really come into it, but even so the stress wore you down. He savoured the prospect of winding down.

He let himself in and looked around. Everything, of

course, was exactly as he had left it and for a moment he felt a pang of self-pity. Only a moment; life now was what it was and if he couldn't have Alexa, there was nothing he liked better than the peace of this pleasant little house.

First things first. He picked up the mobile he always left behind. As he had guessed there would be, there was a text from his mother, who had worked out that he would be home shortly. He might as well answer it; she'd only keep phoning until he did.

'Oh, it's good to know you're home,' Mary Strang said. 'I worry about what might happen when you're away like that. I saw you on the Scottish news at lunchtime making that statement outside the headquarters today, so I knew you were back – I phoned Fin to tell her to watch but it was only a minute and she missed it.'

'Oh yes. Well, I should be back for a bit now. I'll look at my diary and see when I can get up to see you, OK?'

'That would be lovely, darling. Dad's always so pleased to see you.'

He doubted that but made the appropriate assurances before he switched off. His mind wasn't on his parents; he was thinking about Fin.

He had, a little to his shame, all but forgotten about her problems while he was away. Now he was back, though, he would have to call her and see what he could do but he was going to get his breath back first and work out his programme for the next couple of days. He took out a beer from the fridge, grabbed a packet of nuts and a jar of olives and went to sit down in his favourite seat by the window. There was something about that view that seemed to drain tension and he gave a satisfied sigh as he took the cap off the bottle.

The doorbell rang. He groaned. One of the neighbours, probably, and he'd have to invite them in for a drink when he really didn't feel like company.

But when he opened the door, there was a small figure on the doorstep, bouncing up and down with excitement. Betsy threw herself on him and as he scooped her up in his arms she shrieked, 'We're coming to stay with you, Unkie! Look, I've brought my suitcase!' He looked. There was a roll-along case shaped like a ladybird, and behind it another larger grey case. Finella, tearstained and shaky, was standing beside it.

'Oh God, I'm sorry about this, Kelso. But I've walked out on Mark and I've nowhere else I could bear to go. Do you mind?'

'Of course not,' he said, automatically as he turned to put his niece down in the little hall. He looked over her head, saw the beer waiting on the table, saw the tranquil harbour beyond with its elegant white lighthouse and the little boats bobbing peacefully at their moorings. 'You know I'm always there for you, Fin. Come in and tell me all about it.'